PRAISE FOR D. C. SHAFTOE

"Shaftoe's gift for suspense and willingness to put her characters in real danger ups the stakes, resulting in a vividly realized adventure that one can easily imagine seeing on the big screen. A highly enjoyable thriller with lots of intelligence and heart."

—Kirkus Reviews
on *Assassin's Trap*

"As with all of D. C. Shaftoe's books, she grabs your interest and keeps it throughout the entire book … can't wait for the next one whether it's part of a series or a standalone."

—Customer Review from Amazon.com
on *Lethal Intentions: The Battle for Gideon*

"This is truly a book that all students learning about autism should read."

—Customer Review from Amazon.com
on *Lethal Intentions: The Battle for Gideon*

BOOKS BY D. C. SHAFTOE

Forged in the Jungles of Burma
(Finalist in the 2011 Canadian Christian Writing Awards)

Assassin's Trap
(Winner in the 2013 Word Awards)

Lethal Intentions: The Battle for Gideon
(Finalist in the 2014 Word Awards)

Enemy by Association

Reckless Association

IMPERFECT
THE SECOND CHANCE SERIES

D. C. Shaftoe

IMPERFECT

Copyright © 2014 D. C. Shaftoe.
www.dcshaftoe.com
Previously published as Lethal Intentions: The Battle for Gideon
by Cornerstone Research & Publishing © 2013. All rights reserved.

All rights reserved. No part of this book may be used or reproduced by any means, graphic, electronic, or mechanical, including photocopying, recording, taping or by any information storage retrieval system without the written permission of the publisher except in the case of brief quotations embodied in critical articles and reviews.

This is a work of fiction. All of the characters, names, incidents, organizations, and dialogue in this novel are either the products of the author's imagination or are used fictitiously.

iUniverse books may be ordered through booksellers or by contacting:

iUniverse
1663 Liberty Drive
Bloomington, IN 47403
www.iuniverse.com
1-800-Authors (1-800-288-4677)

Because of the dynamic nature of the Internet, any web addresses or links contained in this book may have changed since publication and may no longer be valid. The views expressed in this work are solely those of the author and do not necessarily reflect the views of the publisher, and the publisher hereby disclaims any responsibility for them.

Any people depicted in stock imagery provided by Thinkstock are models, and such images are being used for illustrative purposes only.
Certain stock imagery © Thinkstock.

Scripture taken from the New King James Version®. Copyright © 1982 by Thomas Nelson, Inc. Used by permission. All rights reserved.

The Holy Bible, New International Version®, NIV® Copyright © 1973, 1978, 1984, 2011, by Biblica, Inc.™ Used by permission. All rights reserved worldwide.

The Gospel of Matthew, Volume 1, Revised Edition, William Barclay.
Publisher: Westminster John Knox Press, Louisville, Kentucky 1975.

Our Daily Bread: Daily Readings from the Popular Devotional.
Grand Rapids: Discovery House Publishers, 2009.

Cameron, Gary, and Gerald R. Adams (editors). Moving toward Positive Systems of Child and Family Welfare: Current Issues and Future Directions. Waterloo, Ontario: Wilfrid Laurier University Press, 2007.

ISBN: 978-1-4917-4996-8 (sc)
ISBN: 978-1-4917-4995-1 (e)

Library of Congress Control Number: 2014920071

Printed in the United States of America.

iUniverse rev. date: 11/19/2014

DEAR READER,

Imperfect, formerly entitled *Lethal Intentions: The Battle for Gideon,* finalist in the 2014 Word Awards, is the fourth of my five novels but the first in the Second Chance series, the story of the Marek brothers.

    The character of Gideon is an amalgamation of many children I've worked with over the past twenty years as a speech-language pathologist. The character Bobby is a tribute to my aunt Carole, who always held a special place in my heart.

    I hope you enjoy this story of second chances, redemption, and the wonderful mystery of autism.

To my children, Nate and Jared, who are perfect.

To all the children with ASD who have graced
my life: you are truly wonderfully made.

Perfect love casts out fear.
—1 John 4:18a

There is no fear in love; but perfect love casts out fear, because fear involves torment.

ACKNOWLEDGMENTS

As always, I want to thank my husband for his everlasting support and guidance. I also want to thank my children for LEGO Assassin's Trap and for names, themes, and plot ideas. In addition, I'm grateful for the help of friends and family who lend their expertise in helping the plotlines work.

I'm grateful to The Word Guild ("Encouraging, Equipping, and Empowering Christian Writers") for awarding the first edition of this book, *Lethal Intentions: The Battle for Gideon*, as a finalist in the 2014 Word Awards. The judges' comments encouraged me to give the book a makeover with a new cover and a new title. Thus was born the revised version forever-after known as *Imperfect*.

PROLOGUE

"Give us your ten-twenty."

"Heading north on the Red Hill to the QEW," Zachary Marek said, applying a burst of speed to the police-issue beige sedan he was driving, passing between a black classic VW bug and a silver Ford pickup. "Suspect in a green, late-model Pontiac G8."

"Ten-four, Inspector. Backup en route," the dispatcher replied.

Zach experienced a surge of satisfaction. After three years of careful investigation and tedious observation, he and his partner with the Ontario Provincial Police, Inspector Carlos Rivera, finally had a break in the case, an opportunity to stem the flow of illegal drugs into the Niagara region. Local drug enforcer, Zander Greave, currently driving the G8 ahead, was a firm link to Albanian mob boss Burim Gjojak, having followed the mafioso from Albania to Niagara. Greave would lead them to Gjojak, and then the drug lord's hold over the Niagara region would end.

"Who is that?" Carlos asked. His flat, round features were set in a quizzical expression.

Zach followed his point to a speed trap: a black-and-white OPP Crown Victoria nestled stealthily into a turnout. *Blast it!*

"Miller from traffic," Zach replied, shoulder-checking before slipping left as the Pontiac G8 shifted right. "If Greave sees him—"

"He will run away and our ..." Carlos paused, searching for the word, "*opportunity* to pursue the man to his meeting with Gjojak will disappear effectively."

"Too late." Zach's eyes widened in dismay as a siren pierced the afternoon air, heralding the demise of any hopes of gaining a face-to-face with the Albanian drug lord. *Blast it again!* Would Gjojak forever remain elusive? The mafioso was ethereal, an inimical phantom leaving behind nothing of his trail but the pungency of addiction and death.

Immediately, the Pontiac shifted to the center lane and accelerated dramatically. Vehicles peeled to the shoulders of the highway. The road belonged to the police and the villains. After tossing the radio transmitter to his partner, gripping the steering wheel in both hands, Zach shifted his vehicle to the right, maintaining a visual on the supercharged Pontiac.

Contacting the dispatcher, Carlos asked, "Where is the backup?"

"Nwosu and Singh, ETA one minute," the dispatcher reported.

Two OPP cruisers screeched onto the QEW from the Centennial Parkway ramp, hurtling past Zach and Carlos on a pursuit trajectory with the green G8.

"Does Greave have Rhan and Shaw with him?" Zach asked, wondering if some good could be salvaged from this curtailed operation. The aging drug dealer, Toby Shaw, had managed to evade arrest during the Clifton Heights bust last November in Niagara Falls.

Shrugging his right shoulder as he tilted his head, Carlos replied, "This is not significant. *Andale!*" A proud Latino, Carlos resorted to his native language when English simply would not do. Gripping the dashboard with his thin fingers, he leaned forward as if that would augment the cruiser's acceleration. "We must get him."

"Greave knows that if he's arrested, he's dead," Zach said grimly. Burim Gjojak had a unique zero-tolerance policy: you failed him; you died. And he got to define failure. "Call dispatch and order Miller to support Nwosu." Carlos relayed Zach's message, pausing each time he interrupted. "Get Nwosu alongside. Tell her to knock the Pontiac on its backside. And tell them to get someone on the westbound lane in case he decides to head for the lake."

Constable Kiera Nwosu's cruiser surged forward until her front bumper ran even with the Pontiac's rear. Applying a hard, sharp right, she sent the Pontiac into a spin, a complete counterclockwise three-sixty. Zander Greave recovered control and continued forward, accelerating.

Miller burst ahead and tried from the right, sending the Pontiac spinning clockwise, but again, somehow, Greave regained control and continued forward.

"*Que Padre!*" Carlos observed, his voice conveying his reluctant awe at Greave's superior driving skills.

"Request ten-ten. I want to speak with Singh," Zach said.

Carlos requested permission to speak with the other unit directly and then passed the radio to Zach.

"Can you do better?" Zach asked Constable Ravi Singh, setting the challenge with his tone of voice.

"Indeed, sahib," Singh replied in his mock Indian accent. A third-generation Canadian, the only accent he had was contrived.

"Then do it."

In a burst of acceleration, Singh peeled ahead of the Pontiac, body-checking the G8 into the fence bordering the highway, skillfully maintaining an inexorable push so that the chain-link fence shredded the G8's front right bumper. The Pontiac ground to a halt.

Braking hard, Zach threw the gearshift into park and charged out of the cruiser, gun out and at the ready. Two bodies with faces cloaked in midnight-black hoodies, likely Keegan Rhan and Toby Shaw, exited the rear of the Pontiac, taking off north across the highway toward Lake Ontario.

"Miller! Nwosu!" Zach yelled, gesturing after the men fleeing the scene. But Zach wanted to question Zander Greave. Surely, three months of stakeouts couldn't be for naught!

As Nwosu skillfully chased the men in her cruiser, never laying a fender on them, more officers joined the pursuit. Trusting his colleagues, Zach put the dealers out of his mind. After closing the distance from the sedan to the Pontiac, he used the bumper as a step onto the trunk as he followed Zander Greave south, up and over the chain-link fence, dropping down the other side to the South Service Road. Two Niagara Regional Police cruisers approached along Fruitland Road, lights flashing and sirens blaring.

The drug enforcer was fast, leaping from the asphalt to the grass, running toward the Lincoln Auto Recycling Plant. He was shorter than Zach's six feet but lanky and in his midtwenties, at least a half a decade younger than Zach. His curly, black hair flowed over his shoulders like an inky mane.

Zach ran full out, Carlos's rapid footsteps reminding him that his partner was guarding his six. Gesturing to the right, Zach sent Carlos to flank Greave as Zach circled left. The move forced Greave away from the parking lot, which was littered with derelict vehicles. No need to provide easy cover.

More cruisers pulled into the parking lot, circling around and essentially containing Greave within their perimeter and out in the open.

"Freeze! Hands in the air!" Zach commanded, coming to a stop, his body set and steady in spite of his pumping lungs.

Carlos moved to a position on the right of Zach and repeated Zach's instructions.

Greave pulled out a knife, shouting, "Come and get me, *mish derri!*" and then spat on the ground.

"Shoot him. I will do it, *amigo.*"

"No," Zach said, crossing his left hand over to gesture for Carlos to stay back. "It's not worth the risk. We need to question him."

"Drop your weapon!" another officer commanded. His voice brooked no argument.

Greave feinted toward the speaking officer. The young officer backed off, maintaining a tactical distance. Another officer, a slender woman with fifteen years of experience on the force, moved in behind. Greave spun and slashed in her direction.

Zach pulled his radio from his belt. "Ten-ten to Singh." Ravi Singh was hands-down the best driver that Zach had ever met. When questioned about his skills, he merely explained that he'd done driver training in Mumbai. No further explanation necessary.

"Singh here."

"Auto Recycling on the South Service Road. Can you get there?"

"Absolutely," Singh replied. "Plan?"

"He's got a knife. We've got a perimeter. I need him alive."

"Just so," Singh said, and before long, Zach spied his cruiser entering the parking lot. Officers moved back to open a space and allow the cruiser through.

"Greave! Give it up, and we'll cut you a deal," Zach called across the parking lot, diverting the man's attention for a moment, long enough for Singh to accelerate and move directly into Greave's space. Leaping at the last moment, Greave twisted, landing on the hood of the cruiser. He grasped the wipers to maintain his position but somehow managed to hold onto the knife as well.

"Shoot him now, Zach. Put him down on the pavement. We are wasting time."

"There's no need. Back off, Carlos." Zach kept his focus on Greave.

Singh, one way or another, managed to propel Greave off the hood of the cruiser and onto his feet.

"Plan B," Singh said through the radio just before he reversed, spun, and accelerated. The cruiser advanced, forcing Greave toward three metal posts marking the entrance to the building. Singh applied a controlled burst of speed, and somehow, faster than lightning, he'd pinned Greave inelegantly between a half-ton police cruiser and a four-foot metal post.

"I need him alive, Singh," Zach complained.

"Just so." Singh backed off an inch. Greave descended to his feet. He immediately dropped his weapon and raised his arms. *Incredible!*

A blast cracked across the crowded space. Greave spun about, a crimson spray arcing, tracing his motion as he collapsed.

"Gun!"

Zach and each officer on the perimeter turned outward to scan the environment.

"Roof, north corner," Carlos's voice rang out.

The officers nearby closed ranks around Greave. Holstering his weapon, Zach dropped to the ground and ripped open Greave's expensive black silk shirt to see a jagged hole in the center of the man's chest, blood pumping out, filling Zach's nostrils with the metallic tang of fear and desperation. Quickly, he searched Greave for weapons, finding none.

"Carlos, take a team and check out the sniper. Singh, get me a first-aid kit," Zach ordered. "Get me a medic!"

"Ambulance is on the way," Singh said, opening a medical kit on the ground across Greave's body from Zach.

As Singh applied a pressure bandage, Zach checked Greave's carotid pulse. *What if they send Christie to the scene?* His stomach knotted in tension. Paramedic or not, Zach did not want his wife anywhere in the vicinity of an uncontrolled sniper.

Gripping Zach's jacket with one bloody hand, Greave slipped his other hand into the front pocket of his black linen trousers. Trapping Greave's wrist there for a moment, Zach nodded to Singh who took control of Greave's hand. Zach reached into Greave's pocket, finding only a small cut-out photo of a young, dark-haired woman and a folded receipt from Moerarty's Winery.

"Vera," Greave said, gasping out the word.

"Your girl?" Zach swallowed before speaking, trying to keep his voice gentle in the face of the man's fear.

Greave shook his head.

"Your mom?" Zach asked, flipping the picture over to read the name *Tammy* printed on the back.

"Vera." Greave was alive but fading fast, his eyes reflecting his terror. Spreading his hands over Singh's, Zach increased pressure on the wound. Greave groaned pathetically.

"The ambulance is on its way. Hold tight, Zander; you're going to be all right." Was it lying to comfort the man that way? Because Zach was pretty sure that Zander's time on this earth was almost at an end. Zach would go home to his wife and son at the end of his shift but Zander Greave? He would likely never go home again.

CHAPTER 1

SIX MONTHS LATER

"Pancakes," Gideon Marek said to Grandpa. Grandpa's name was Bud—not like buddy, just Bud. Grandpa had red and white hair. His belly was big, so big that Gideon couldn't hug him all the way around.

"Pancakes coming up, young fellow," Grandpa said.

"Young fellow," Gideon repeated because he didn't know what it meant.

Grandpa's mouth moved up, and the lines on his cheeks went away, but the lines by his eyes got longer. Gideon didn't know what that meant, but he did know that he wanted pancakes.

"Where does Mommy keep the flour?" Grandpa asked.

Gideon searched through his memory to find a picture of the words that Grandpa was saying. "Flowers. Pretty," Gideon said.

"Flour," Grandpa repeated.

Flowers? Gideon knew that flowers sat in the dirt. They were pink and orange and sometimes white.

"Do you know where the flour is, son?" Grandpa asked.

Gideon was confused, so he started to make a sound. "Eeee." The sound filled his head with noise, and then he couldn't hear the confusing words.

Grandpa started opening and closing cupboard doors. Gideon forgot about his sound and watched the way the shadows changed as the doors opened and then closed again and again.

"Found it," Grandpa said, but then he stopped opening doors.

"More," Gideon said.

"More what, son?" Grandpa said. His voice was calm. Mommy said that Grandpa always used a calm voice.

"Gideon?" Grandpa said.

But Gideon didn't know the words to say, so he said nothing.

"How many pancakes do you want, Gideon?" Grandpa said.

"One, two, three, four, five …" Gideon loved numbers. They always started the same and went the same way. One was always first and then two and then three. Numbers were always the same.

Grandpa laughed a loud laugh that made Gideon's ears hurt.

"Too loud," said Gideon.

"Sorry. How about three pancakes since you turned three years old yesterday?" Grandpa said.

Gideon looked at Grandpa. Grandpa scratched his red beard and then made three circles on the pan with dough.

"Three pancakes for my grandson," said Grandpa.

"No!" Gideon said. "Pancakes Gideon." Gideon wanted the pancakes not *grandson*. He didn't know who that was.

Grandpa put a plate in front of Gideon. "Pancakes for Gideon," Grandpa said, and then he smiled.

Gideon looked at the plate. There was butter on the pancakes. He could see it under the syrup. Gideon gagged. The look of the butter made his stomach feel yucky.

"No. No, no, no!" he said. Gideon tipped his head back so he didn't have to look at the yucky butter on his pancakes.

"What's wrong, son?" Grandpa asked.

"No, no, no!" Gideon cried. "Mommy, Mommy, *Mom-my!*"

"Oh, wait!" Grandpa said. "No butter." Grandpa moved the plate away.

Gideon stopped yelling. "No," he said once more to make sure Grandpa knew.

Grandpa put a new plate in front of Gideon. There was no butter on the pancakes. Grandpa poured syrup on the pancakes and then cut them up. Gideon picked up his fork and ate.

"Pancakes with syrup but no butter," Grandpa said.

Yes.

Christie Marek stood at the door to her kitchen for a moment, watching her father-in-law, Bud Marek, eat breakfast with her son. For such a big man, Bud was a true gentleman, kind and infinitely patient. The first time she'd met him, he'd reminded her of Grizzly Adams, not quite six feet tall, barrel-chested, and tanned. Thick, golden-red hair had framed his kind blue eyes and smiling mouth. Now, seven years later, the red was sprinkled with steel-gray.

A moment later, she felt strong arms around her, lifting her in a super-sized hug.

"Good morning, Seth." She laughed with her brother-in-law, Bud's eldest son, and Zach's adopted brother. In fact, four of the five Marek boys, Seth, Luke, Zach, and Blake, were adopted, a regular United Nations of a family—all except Bobby, who had been born to Bud and the now deceased Grace late in life. The eldest Marek, Seth easily towered over her, not to mention all of his brothers and his father. And unfair as it was, his gleaming black hair was longer than her blonde curls and much easier to tame, held as it was in a feathered, leather hair roach.

"Morning, honey. How's the mommy of the year?" Seth released her to stand. His husky baritone carried just a hint of a western drawl.

"A little less tired than usual, thank you. Gideon was up from three to five, but he actually slept from five to six."

"I don't know how you do it!" Seth exclaimed, and she felt his admiration.

"Autism is not for the faint-hearted," she replied.

"Indeed," Bud said, scratching his beard. "Come in and have some pancakes, you two. Gideon's managed to polish off three."

"TV. TV. TV," Gideon said, speaking right over Bud's words without regard for the fact that he was interrupting.

Ignoring the breach of protocol because, frankly, Grandpas never minded being interrupted by their grandchildren, Bud replied, "Ask your mom."

Christie smiled down at her son, warmth filling her chest. He had her blue eyes and his father's thick, honey-gold hair. The reminder of her absent husband tugged at her heart. "Okay, sweetheart. You can watch television for a little while. Thank you, Grandpa, for the pancakes."

Gideon stared at her.

"Thanks." She simplified her message, adding a gesture, a wave good-bye.

Gideon waved and then ran out of the room.

Bud laughed. "He's a bright lad, Christie. You're doing a wonderful job."

"Thank you," she replied, filling in the unspoken word—*alone*. Alone because her husband, for some inexplicable reason, had accepted a position on an international drugs task force rather than stay home to figure out the rest of their life together. Gideon's diagnosis had devastated him, and he'd run. That was what Christie assumed anyway.

Seth, with his odd clairvoyance, seemed to read her thoughts. "You're coming to the end of it. Zach will be home soon."

"Yeah," she replied noncommittally, dropping her gaze to the floor. What would it be like when Zach finally returned? Everything had changed while he was gone. The entire axis of Christie's world had shifted—speech therapy, occupational therapy, sensory diets, communication facilitation, and so on.

"What's wrong, honey?" Bud asked, resting a gentle hand on her shoulder.

"I imagine that Zach is the problem, Dad," Seth said, interrupting before Christie could respond. "Christie's been on her own now for not just three months, as Zach promised, but six long months. I will never understand why the idiot volunteered for that task force. But you can be sure that I'll ask him as soon as I see him."

"Never mind, Seth," she said, her sorrow heavy in her chest. "We're okay. Gideon's doing great."

"Honey?" Bud asked, exchanging a worried look with Seth. "How are *you* doing?"

"Honestly?" she replied. "I don't really know."

Zach Marek tapped absently at the keyboard on his laptop, scrolling through the latest email from Christie. It consisted of three pages of information on autism spectrum disorders, the only thought on his wife's mind these days. The sight of all those words set a flock of vultures flying in his bowels. Would she expect him to remember all of this when he arrived home tomorrow?

"Zach, *amigo*, it is time to go," Carlos said as he thrust his head through the doorway of the tiny apartment that Zach, Carlos, and Nicholas Raade of the OPP, along with Edwin Bryant and Edrigu Zimmerman of the RCMP, had been sharing for the past six months. A small flat in the west end of Tirana, the capital city of Albania, it comprised a bedroom containing two bunk beds, a small two-piece bathroom, a main sitting room with a pull-out couch, and a small galley kitchen, all painted in an unappetizing eggplant purple.

Relieved at the opportunity to escape the plethora of words on his screen, Zach grabbed his jacket to follow Carlos down the dingy stairwell to the street.

"We meeting at Besian's?" Bryant asked as he, Raade, and Zimmerman joined them.

Zimmerman grunted what was likely a positive response.

Raade hop-skipped ahead to reach the driver's seat first, claiming it. Zach rolled his eyes in irritation at the man. Normally a dour-faced, narrow-eyed man with the charisma of a watermelon, Raade came to life if there was any chance he could be in charge. From his other side, Bryant hollered, "Shotgun!" with great enthusiasm, nearly deafening him. Zach reluctantly joined the crush in the rear seat of the faded-green Mercedes Benz that the Canadian government had purchased for the use of its officers on the task force. Unfortunately, the Mercedes was twenty-three years old and had a floorless trunk and a faulty carburetor, which even German engineering could not overcome consistently.

Ugh! How did he always manage to end up squeezed in beside Zimmerman? The man could not seem to figure out how to use deodorant. *Phew!* Or how to brush his teeth. Zach tried not to breathe for the fifteen-minute ride to a local *kafene*. Taking a great personal risk, the owner, Besian Chocholi, a loyal Albanian who fought in his own quiet way to keep the Albanian mafia from taking complete control of his beloved country, allowed the members of the task force to meet discreetly in his upper story.

"We're here," Raade said, completely unnecessarily. But he was a man who took every opportunity to appear to be in the know.

Bryant, Carlos, and Raade made their way to the rear entrance while Zach, followed by Zimmerman, entered through the front door, hoping to enjoy an authentic Albanian *kafe*. The local brew was made by boiling two-thirds of a cup of water in a small stainless-steel pot with two teaspoons of coffee and sugar. Zach had absolutely become dependent on the strong, sweet flavor.

"*Si jeni*, Besian?" Zach asked. *Besian would have made a good Marek.* He combined the grizzly-bear physique of Zach's adopted father, Bud, with the ebullience of his brother Luke. Zach and Besian had developed a quick if somewhat cautious friendship.

"*Mirë*. Good," Besian replied, smiling broadly. "And you?"

"*Mirë*," Zach replied automatically. Was he good? Not yet, but soon, he hoped, as long as he really was permitted to return home tomorrow and Christie forgave him for leaving. "*I love you, Christie,*" he'd said to her on their last day together.

"*Really? 'Cause this feels like the opposite.*"

"*That's not fair.*"

"*I don't want you to do this,*" she'd whispered, her face hot against his neck as she clung to him.

"*It's not my fault,*" he'd replied, coward that he was. "*I have to go.*"

A thousand times he'd rather face down a drug lord equipped with firearms and muscle than to face up to the terror that his son's developmental issues were somehow his fault. *Maybe we never should have had kids. What do I know about being a father?* His own father, the guy who'd donated his seed, had never acknowledged Zach's existence, leaving him to be raised by Janice Huxley, a spoiled, selfish, drug-addicted woman, until he was six years old when someone had finally intervened. Sure, two years later, he'd been adopted by a wonderful couple, Bud and Grace Marek, but maybe his past was irredeemable.

Besian clapped his meaty paw on Zach's shoulder, shaking him away from the doldrums and back to the present with the force of his greeting. "You miss your *tuaj i dashur*. Why, I wonder, does a man leave his beloved to travel to another man's country?" Besian leaned in close to Zach's ear and spoke in a voice low enough that no others could hear. "Word has come to me that you have an unhealthy interest in the *vera*. Leave now, *miku im*, before you catch the attention of wicked men." Then Besian slapped Zach on the shoulder again and spread his arms wide in a gesture of camaraderie.

"*Kafe*, Mirjata!" he called to his daughter, who stood behind the counter, her long black hair pulled back into a ponytail and her pale complexion flushed with embarrassment. Like most adolescents, she seemed to spend most of her time either embarrassed or angry.

Besian gave Zach a hard look, which he had absolutely no idea how to interpret, before he walked away to greet his other customers.

"What was that about?" Zimmerman asked, sauntering over.

"I have no idea," Zach replied honestly, somewhat dismayed by the cryptic exchange. He paid Mirjata for the coffees, one for himself and one for Damaris Quickle, the indomitable leader of the task force. She rarely remembered to stop and eat during an operation.

Zach led the way outside and around the building to the stairs in the rear.

"Coffee. Excellent," Damaris greeted them in her Texan drawl.

Zach would have called her ageless, but the silver highlights in her coppery hair seemed to indicate that she was at least over forty. She always managed to look self-assured and utterly content, her eyes crinkling in laughter lines when she smiled but equally fierce when she frowned. She was shorter than Christie's five-four by at least two inches but outweighed her by seventy-five pounds or more of solid muscle. As fit as Christie needed to be as a paramedic, Zach was certain that Damaris could take his wife down in a heartbeat.

Damaris removed a coffee from Zach's hand before he could even offer it. Zimmerman frowned at Zach, but he ignored the malodourous officer, instead visually scanning the room to find that, other than silent Mr. Polyester, better known as Damaris's assistant, Anthony Snow, they were alone.

They tried never to have more than a few officers in the same place at the same time. Even though the Albanian State Intelligence Service, the SHISH, had issued the invitation to the Canadian-led task force, there were many Albanians not exactly on the same page as their government. In many regions, the country was so poor that there were ardent supporters of the mafia, individuals and groups who pointed to the economic benefit that the criminals brought to their struggling economies. Not everyone supported the task force's mission to contain and capture Gjojak in order to control the production and trafficking of narcotics through the Albanian mafia.

"We have intelligence that Gjojak will be at his ancestral estate in Memaliaj tonight for a meeting with his lieutenants," Damaris said, getting right down to business. "I want each one of you in there by nightfall. You are to maintain your positions until Gjojak arrives. We're expecting six visitors in total along with two bodyguards per visitor. There are four guards on the estate at all times, one at the gate, one inside the house, and two patrolling the grounds around the main house. You'll need to be cautious because there is a motion detector connected to a floodlight in the swimming area." Damaris finished the hot coffee in one gulp and continued, "Our intelligence indicates that the meeting will occur at midnight and be concluded before dawn. Once the lieutenants leave, Gjojak will remain behind with his mistress, the Russian one, and her two children, who are already in attendance at the estate."

"Are you sure that the children are there?" Zach asked. He wanted to know for certain if there were going to be innocents on the scene.

"We have visual confirmation," Damaris said.

"What's to be done with Gjojak?" Zimmerman continually mispronounced the name as "go-yack" rather than the correct pronunciation of "jaw-jack." "Once the lieutenants leave?" Zimmerman leaned on the table to better view the map of the area.

Damaris shifted back, probably out of nasal range. "You move in and capture Gjojak. I have been given instructions to use lethal force, if necessary. Raade will be in command on the ground."

"You won't be there, ma'am?" Zach asked. A flutter of unease tickled his psyche.

"No, unfortunately. I've been called away to another mission." She offered no more explanation than that. "Now, you two will meet up with Raade at these coordinates." Damaris nodded at the map that Zimmerman was covering entirely with his malodourous shadow.

Damaris stepped toward Zach with a smile twinkling in her eyes. "I understand that you've chosen to rotate home, and I wanted to take this opportunity to thank you for your work." She shook his hand.

"There's one other matter I wanted to discuss with you, ma'am," Zach said, lowering his voice to say, "In private."

"Does it pertain to tonight's mission?"

"Hopefully not," Zach replied. "It's just a suspicion but …"

"Send me an email when you get home," she said, and then her smile was back. "Your assistance has been invaluable. Dismissed." And that was the end of the briefing.

Disappointed by the curtailed discussion, Zach nevertheless followed Zimmerman out to the puce-green Mercedes where he let the man take the wheel. They drove in silence, and Zach used the opportunity to plan for the thousandth time what he was going to say when he finally saw Christie again. He was figuring on some serious groveling. He wanted to make sure that his wife knew just how much he loved her and their son and that he had only left because he'd had to. Mostly. He probably wouldn't add the adverb … or was that an adjective? Zach snorted, inviting a dark look from Zimmerman.

Christie had been so happy when she'd discovered she was pregnant. She'd so badly wanted to be a mother. Zach had been ambivalent. His own early childhood had been less than ideal, and he wasn't certain that he could be a good father. But he loved Christie, and if parenthood was important to her, then it would be to him as well.

Zach remembered when his younger brother, Blake, had come as a newborn to live with the Mareks, but he definitely didn't remember him turning their lives upside down. He didn't remember endless, sleepless nights; the crying; and the unceasing demands on his parents' time and energy. And he hadn't been prepared to become Christie's second love. Zach felt as though his world had faded into sepia. But being away for six months had shown him one absolute, critical truth: Zach loved Christie.

He loved her absolutely. He was prepared to come last in her life if it meant they could remain together as a family.

The Mercedes turned off the asphalt highway and crunched onto a gravel country road just as the sun dipped beyond the horizon in a glow of magenta. Black pines lined the roadway for as far as the eye could see. Soon Zimmerman left the gravel road and turned onto the pine-needle-covered forest floor. The rough trunks of the conifers opened abruptly onto a meadow, across which Zach could see the remnants of the pillow formations of the volcanic rock beneath the grasses and plants. Before long, they turned left again and then onto a trail that was no more than two furrows in the ground surrounded by bushing trees.

From twilight on, Zach—Alpha 5—camouflaged by a small pile of bramble, his black combat suit blending with the darkness, watched in silence. His vantage point looked over the windowed swimming house, which contained the detritus of molding leaves, broken branches, and the odd fast-food wrapper. Beyond it was a plum orchard. Zach had counted twenty-three trees. He couldn't see the individual fruits from this distance.

As the moon waned in the night, Zach heard shuffled movements, the click of automatic weapons. *Time for action.* Quietly, he checked his Beretta 93R machine pistol, ensuring that it was ready to fire. Then he checked his Ka-Bar knife where it was strapped to his leg, and his backup weapon, a Sig Sauer pistol, which was holstered on his hip.

"Alpha five, assist at the car shed."

"Roger."

Slipping stealthily through the pine arbor, which guarded the back door to the house, Zach spied a shadow of movement in the gloom ahead. And then another, as one man, clearly one of Gjojak's guards from his attire and weapon, came up behind a man clad in the same type of armored bodysuit that Zach wore.

Shifting his weight to the balls of his feet, Zach slipped the safety off his weapon, ready to run to the aid of his colleague. But, just before Zach emerged from the trees, his colleague turned and spoke to the guard. Zach couldn't hear what they said, but a moment later, he saw his colleague pointing to positions around the perimeter. Zach froze, disbelief chilling him, as the long, dark arm swept toward the position he had recently abandoned. *A traitor? There was a traitor in their midst. But who?*

As the two men melted into the darkness again, Zach released his body from the stillness he'd attained to camouflage his presence. Whom could he warn when he didn't know who the traitor was? He wished that Damaris was here, because he trusted her implicitly.

Zach selected the channel he needed. "Raade?" he said.

"Busy right now," Raade's irritated voice replied.

"It's important," Zach insisted. He needed to choose someone to trust, and if Damaris had trusted Raade enough to put him in charge of this op, then perhaps Zach could extend him a modicum of the same grace.

Finally, after much muted grumbling, Raade replied, "Hillock. West of the swimming pool."

"Roger."

A barrage of weapons-fire exploded in the night. Transmissions erupted in a flurry of communication.

"Alpha one down."

"Bryant? Report."

"Medic!"

"Officer down!"

Abandoning caution, Zach took off at a sprint around the front of the house and down the side, directly toward the hillock to the west of the swimming pool. He heard a single gunshot in a moment of silence and ran all the faster, his heart in his throat. Doubt and determination blended in a roiling morass in his belly.

Rounding the corner, he almost tripped over a body on the ground, clad in the same black body armor he wore.

"Officer down!" Zach dropped to his knees and turned the individual over. Raade.

"You're going to be fine," Zach reassured him as he continued to check for injuries, holding his pocket flashlight in his teeth. "Where were you hit?"

"Side. Hurts." Raade gasped in pain.

Noting the glint of wetness on Raade's abdomen, Zach sliced the man's bodysuit, stretching the fabric wide to see black blood ooze from Raade's side, just below his ribs on the right side. *Not again.*

In the bodysuit, Zach had no T-shirt, no loose fabric of any kind that he could use to put over the bullet hole to stop the bleeding. So he pressed his hands over the wound.

"Officer down!" Zach called again, raising one hand to toggle the all-communications switch on his headset. "Medic."

Raade groaned, his breathy voice coming in short gasps. "Thought it was you."

"Who?" Zach asked absently, surveying the surroundings for help and threat. Zach checked Raade's carotid pulse. It was definitely weaker than before.

"Didn't. Betray us." Each word was a gasp.

Zach froze as Raade's words filtered through. "What are you saying?"

"Careful." Raade may have had more to say, but he shuddered once and then his eyes rolled into the back of his head.

Ears alert to a shuffle behind him, Zach grabbed Raade's weapon from the ground beside him and spun, ready to defend his life and Raade's, too. His eyes met Carlos Rivera's. The man stood casually, weapon dangling from his hand, his head cocked at an odd angle.

Relieved, Zach lowered his weapon. "Raade's been shot."

"The medic is on the way?"

"Yeah."

Carlos nodded and walked away.

Raade, Bryant, and two agents from CSIS, the Canadian Security Intelligence Service—Zach thought they were named Christof and Juarez—were transported out in choppers to the Albanian Armed Forces base in Tirana for medical care. Zach feared it was too late for Raade. As much as he'd disliked the dour-faced man, Zach didn't wish him dead. And Raade's last words, what was that all about? What was it with cryptic messages today?

Casting off his gory combat suit, Zach pulled on his civvies and met up with Zimmerman for the journey back to the apartment. The front entrance was blocked by *polici*. *What now?* All he wanted was to forget the events of the past twenty-four hours and go home.

Sharing a glance, they silently came to a consensus, slipping around to the back of the building, up the fire escape and through the bedroom window. Lights flashed on throughout the apartment.

"Stop! *Ngrenë armët tuaja.*"

Complying, Zimmerman raised his arms, but Zach merely held his out in front of him in a nonthreatening gesture.

"*Çfarë doni?* What do you want?" Zach asked.

"*Heshtje!*" Silence!

"Which of you is Marek?"

With a sense of foreboding, Zach's attention shifted from the uniformed *polici* holding automatic weapons on him to a pair of men, one tall, thin, rumpled, and wearing a surly sneer on his face. This was the man who had spoken.

"I'm Marek."

The second man, his gray suit neat and tidy, clearly a higher rank than the men with the AK-47s, gestured toward the nearest bed. Zach's duffel bag sat open on the tattered bedspread.

"This is yours?" Neatness asked.

"Yes," Zach replied, nodding. His name was printed clearly on the travel tag.

Neatness nodded, and the uniformed officer dumped the contents of the duffel bag onto the bed. But rather than Zach's shirts and undershorts tumbling out, several sealed paper bags emerged. The bottom fell out of Zach's world. Surly stepped over, flipping open a switchblade as he walked. He sliced three of the bags open, and a fine-grained white powder spilled out.

"You know that this government frowns on *trafikantët e drogës*, drug traffickers," Surly said in heavily accented English.

"I understand, sir—" Zach began, but Surly cut him off.

"Explain this then," Surly demanded, flicking a borderline rude gesture at the paper bags.

"I've never seen those bags before in my life. They don't belong to me.

I'm here on a cooperative task force that's sanctioned by the Albanian government."

"Task force? What is?" Neatness asked, looking confused.

"I'm a police officer working *against* drug traffickers." Zach strained to sound calm and reasonable when what he really felt was an encroaching doom.

"By supplying our criminals with heroin?" Surly asked.

"No, of course not."

"Take him," Surly said and walked away. Neatness crossed his arms and nodded at one of the uniformed officers, who pressed the muzzle of his AK-47 against Zach's chest.

"Zimmerman, get word to Damaris," Zach implored the man. "Please."

Zimmerman was watching him with a pinched, dubious expression, so Zach continued, desperate to escape this doom headed his way. "I didn't do this. Those aren't my drugs."

"Take him," Neatness said, and Zach was spun and thrust against the wall of the bedroom, his weapons removed and his hands confined behind his back in handcuffs. *This can't be happening! I'm supposed to be flying home. Who would set me up as a drug trafficker?* Raade's final message resounded in Zach's head. Betrayal. Was this what Besian was talking about?

How long would it take for Damaris to get him out of this bind?

CHAPTER 2

Gideon was zooming around the living room pretending to be an airplane when Christie heard an actual, real vehicle in the driveway. Maybe Zach had decided to drive straight home rather than calling and asking her to pick him up in Toronto or Buffalo. He'd promised to return home as soon as his term of service was up. However, that day had come and gone a week ago with no word from him.

Christie pulled back the front curtain to see out. An unknown man, fifties or so with flecked gray hair, tall and rather rectangular, sort of like Hank Hill without the paunch, stepped out of the driver's side of a beige Dodge Caliber while a shorter, dark-haired man with flat, round features—it was Carlos!—exited from the passenger side.

Christie flung open the door.

"Neeerneeerneeer!" Gideon flew around her and then back to the kitchen, to the living room, and around the couch.

"Carlos," Christie called, so relieved to see a familiar face. She looked beyond him into the car. "Where's Zach?"

Carlos stepped right up to her and surprised her by hugging her, hard. "I am sorry, Christie," he whispered in her ear.

She froze for a moment and then pulled away, searching his gaze as she processed the possibilities behind his words. Her knees suddenly felt like jelly salad and not the good kind with cottage cheese.

"What? What happened? Where's Zach?" She clutched at Carlos's arms.

The rectangular man took her by the elbow and, stepping over the line of shoes at the front door, guided her to sit on the deacon's bench.

"Outside," Gideon said, coming in for a landing in front of her.

"No, sweetheart. No outside," she replied. Her voice sounded breathless. She cleared it to try to sound more normal, saying, "Not right now."

"Outside later?" Gideon asked.

"No. Maybe. I don't know," Christie said, unable to give a clear response.

Carlos bent down from his place standing beside her, and she realized that he was still touching her, his hand on her shoulder. "Television, Gideon? Want television?" he said, using that unique intonation that people generally reserved for dogs.

Gideon narrowed his eyes at him. "Mommy," he said, frowning more severely at Carlos.

"Perhaps it would be a good idea to let your little boy watch a little television while we talk," said Mr. Rectangle.

"First, tell me if Zach is ..." She gulped, looking at Gideon. "D-E-A-D."

"E-F-G ..." Gideon continued reciting the alphabet.

"No, Mrs. Marek. He is not. I'm Senior Inspector Ian Thomason, and I do have some bad news, but that is not it."

Christie nodded, suddenly weak, but with relief or dread, she wasn't sure. "Gideon," she said. Now her voice was wobbling. She cleared her throat again. "You can watch television."

"TV, TV, TV," he said, running off to the television. After turning it on, he popped in a train DVD and settled in the middle of the couch, his own special spot.

"Okay. Tell me," she said, looking back and forth between the two men.

"I will make you a cup of tea, Christie," Carlos said.

"No. Fine. In the kitchen. You know where." She pushed herself to her feet and led the way. Once there, she filled the kettle and plugged it in. Then she sat heavily on one of the high stools at the counter. "Please tell me what's going on."

Senior Inspector Thomason took the stool kitty-corner to her. "You know that Zachary was in Albania as part of a voluntary task force." Thomason placed his warm hand gently on hers. Christie nodded, and he continued, "Last week, he was arrested by the *polee—poliss*—the Albanian State Police, for possession of illegal drugs. They have produced evidence and plan to put him to trial by the end of the week."

"What? Drugs?" she said in disbelief. "He was there to stop the drug trafficking. How could they think he was involved?"

"They have evidence." Thomason cleared his throat and fidgeted with his collar, clearly uncomfortable with whatever he had to say. "I'll, er, let Rivera speak to this." He flicked a glance at Carlos and then around the room, anywhere but at Christie.

When Carlos didn't immediately speak, Christie prompted him. "What is this all about?"

"Zimmerman ..." Carlos sighed heavily. "Rig Zimmerman was one of the agents working with us on the task force, living with us in our flat. He came to me a short time before Zach was arrested." Carlos stopped and cleared his throat. "He was ... concerned ... about Zach. He said that he was quite certain that Zach had purchased heroin." Carlos took her hands. "He saw that Zach was using ... the heroin, Christie. And when the police investigated, they found Zach's stash in the apartment where we were living, hidden in the floorboards."

"What do you mean, 'Zach's stash'?" Christie asked, using air quotations to emphasize the words.

Carlos rubbed his hand down his face. "I am sorry, Christie. Zach has had a difficult time dealing with Gideon's ... autistic *problema*. He has not been coping well."

Christie dropped onto her feet and pushed back from the counter. "You're telling me that my husband has been doing drugs to cope with the fact that our son has autism?" Her voice was far more level than she would have expected, given that her world had suddenly been switched with someone else's.

Carlos gave her a funny look. "Yes. I am sorry to tell you this. I would have kept it from you but ..." He shrugged one shoulder and tilted his head.

Christie turned her attention to Thomason. "What will happen now? When will you bring him home?"

"I'm sorry, Mrs. Marek, but Zachary broke the laws of a country where we were guests. He will be tried in Albanian courts, and, if he's found guilty, he'll have to deal with the consequences." Thomason truly did sound sorry, even sighing heavily. "And I'm sorry to have to tell you this, but if he's convicted, we'll be required to terminate his employment with the OPP."

Christie felt the blood slowly draining from her face. "Are you sending legal representation?"

"The, er, the Albanian government won't permit it. They have appointed a lawyer," Thomason said.

"I see," Christie said, sounding calm when what she really felt was numb. "What sentence is he facing?"

Thomason glanced at Carlos briefly and then returned to studying his knuckles where they tapped the countertop.

"Ten years," Carlos said.

All the remaining blood drained from Christie's face, and she had to grab the counter to keep from keeling over.

Carlos put his arm around her shoulders. "I am sorry."

"I'd like you to leave now." Each word dropped like lead from her lips. "Thank you for coming to tell me." She walked to the door and opened it, staring back over her shoulder to prompt them to follow her and exit. The men exchanged glances and then rose from the stools and walked toward her. At the door, Thomason turned back and offered her his card.

"Please let me know if there's anything I can do," he said.

"You can send him a lawyer who's experienced in international law."

Thomason shook his head. "I'm sorry. I'm simply not able to do that."

"Have you contacted the embassy on his behalf?" She raised her eyes to meet his gaze directly, heat simmering in her chest, bringing her blood pressure back up. "Have you called our government? Have you done *anything* to help him?"

"I'm sorry, Mrs. Marek, but I've done all I'm able to do. Your husband broke the laws of a country where we were guests," Thomason said and then added, "I'm sorry to hear about your son."

Christie drew back in confusion. "What about my son?"

"You know … what Rivera mentioned. The ADHD."

"He has autism, and I don't really need your sympathy for that," she said, pushing the door behind them.

Carlos grabbed the door just before it closed. "I will speak with you soon. I am sorry you found out." Carlos jogged down the front steps to the Caliber.

Christie checked on Gideon to find that he had exchanged his train movie for a dinosaur movie, probably *Land of the Dinosaurs*, number 62. He was happily bouncing on the couch as he watched.

Christie dialed the kitchen telephone. It rang several times before it was answered with the snap-crack of bubble gum.

"Marek Veterinary Services."

"Dr. Marek, please," Christie said, trying to sound normal to Seth's receptionist. "Tell him it's his sister-in-law."

Soon, she heard Seth's husky drawl. "Hey, Christie, what's up?"

She took a deep breath to keep from bursting into tears and then spoke in a rush. "We need to have a family meeting. Here. ASAP. Someone set Zach up, and if we don't get him out soon, they're going to bury him in an Albanian prison." Christie endeavored to find a toneless, painless place to engage this nightmare that had become her life.

"What are you talking about?" Seth said.

"I've just been told that Zach's been taking drugs to help him deal with Gideon's autism."

There was silence for a moment. "He would never do that. After the way his bio-mom, Janice, abused drugs, he would never touch the stuff. I don't care what was going on in his life." Seth's deep voice was sure and definite.

"Then someone's setting him up." Her breath caught as a sob fought to escape. "Seth, they're going to put him in prison, maybe for ten years." Emotion clogged her throat, and she had to swallow hard to keep it down.

"Hang in there, honey. I'm coming. We're coming," Seth said, and he rang off.

Zach's head snapped back as a fist connected with his cheekbone. His right eye was swollen completely shut, so he couldn't see any of the blows coming from that direction. *Oh, Lord, make it stop.* Seeking escape, Zach pulled against the handcuffs, which secured him to a metal chair, but the effort was futile. Despair pressed down on him. He couldn't move out of the way of the fists directed at his head or the rubber baton that connected with his ribs and shoulders.

Zach heard a groaning sound cut through the noise of fists on flesh. And then he realized that it was his own voice he heard.

Suddenly, where there had been pain, there was coolness and gentleness, and Zach realized that he was dreaming of the past, the recent past, mind you, but the past nonetheless. Relief speared his chest even as fear and confusion tightened his gut.

"Christie." His voice rasped past his dry, sore throat.

A low male chuckle surprised him, and he opened his eye, the left one, which still opened.

"I am sorry. It is only me, Pavel. Christie? She is your wife?"

Pavel? Who was Pavel, and where on earth was he?

The images of the past several days came back in a flood, and Zach felt an overwhelming urge to vomit. Pavel held him gently over the side of the bed as Zach emptied his stomach into a basin on the floor.

"You must go easy, my friend. I suspect your head … It is not well," Pavel said as he helped Zach lie back on the bed. Could you really call this a bed? It felt more like a slab of concrete than any bed, reminiscent of the concrete playground at Zach's primary school where he'd slept several times as a young boy.

"Where am I?" His mouth was swollen and cut—and dry as the Kalahari. Pavel, that sweet man, put a cup to Zach's lips and let him sip cold coffee into his mouth. "Thank you," Zach gasped out.

"Now to your question. You are in Burgu Punës."

"What is that?" Zach levered himself up to his elbow and then paused until his head stopped spinning around the axis of his neck.

"Prison," Pavel replied.

"Prison? But I haven't been to court yet. They arrested me and then beat the snot out of me …"

"This 'snot,' what is this?" Pavel's brows furrowed in confusion.

The humor of the question lightened Zach's aspect. Then he groaned because he started to chuckle and his bruised ribs immediately protested. "They handcuffed me to a chair and beat me," he explained when he could speak again.

"Ah. Yes," Pavel said without blinking, as though this was common practice.

"Why? They didn't ask me any questions."

"No." Pavel shook his head. "They say, 'Judge, sir, this man is too ill to come to court.' The judge meets with the lawyer …"

"I never even saw my lawyer," Zach protested.

"'That is not necessary,' they say. 'He is guilty,' they say. 'We have evidence.'" Pavel spread his arms as if to say, "What else is there to explain?" "Your case has been tried, and you are sentenced. The rumors say that you will be here for ten years."

"Ten years!" Astounded, Zach sat fully upright and then had to grasp the edge of the bed to keep from toppling off. "They can't do this! I have to speak to someone from the Canadian consulate. This isn't legal."

Pavel looked at him with an unexpected pity in his eyes, but before Zach could ask any more questions, an alarm sounded. Zach surveyed his surroundings, trying to deduce the purpose of the noise.

He and Pavel sat on a lower bunk at the westernmost edge of the room, the farthest possible position from what looked like a communal bathroom. The dormitory-sized room was filled with bunks. Some had blankets, some had pillows, and a few even had mattresses. At the moment, it was empty, however, except for Pavel and Zach.

"You must come and work today," Pavel said.

"Work? I can barely move," Zach said, groaning. "I need to try and see the warden—"

Pavel cut him off. "If you do not work, you do not get food."

Zach stared at him. "Are you serious?"

"Yes, I am quite … serious," Pavel said, and he was … quite serious. "Come now. We will help you."

"We?" Zach braced his arm across his bruised ribs and shuffled after Pavel.

"We few brothers in Christ. We work together to help those who are ill or injured." Pavel took Zach by the elbow to steady him.

"If you don't mind my asking, why are you here? In prison?" Zach asked. "What were you accused of?"

"I was accused of stealing twenty-five dollars from my church," Pavel said.

"Did you?" Zach paused, realizing that his question sounded like an accusation. "I mean, I didn't buy those drugs. They weren't mine. So I assume that you may be innocent as well."

"I did not steal this money, but I did speak out against the mafia in my village. They take the young and force them to sell and coerce and kill. It is wrong to corrupt our young. Unfortunately for me, the magistrate who heard my case was the brother-in-law of the local, er, *tregtari i drogës*, er, drug seller, and I was found guilty and sentenced to twelve years at hard labor," Pavel said.

"Twelve years? For twenty-five dollars?" Zach gasped, astounded once again.

"Twelve years for speaking out against the mafia," Pavel said, and Zach could clearly hear the warning in his voice. "Come now."

Zach walked out of the dormitory and into a whole new life.

CHAPTER 3

Gideon put the blue train first and then the coal car and then the tank car and then the passen—The doorbell rang, interrupting his lining up. That was unexpected. Unexpected things were bad. They made Gideon's tummy feel jumpy.

"Mommy!" Gideon called so that she would stop the interruption. Then he put the passenger car after the tank car.

Mommy walked by. Gideon breathed in. Mommy smelled right. Mommy smelled familiar. The familiar smell helped Gideon's tummy stop being so jumpy.

"Hello, Carlos," Mommy said. And then she let the man in.

"Hello, Christie. Have you a moment of time?" Carlos said. "Hello, Gideon."

Gideon put the caboose on at the end of the train and then put the whole train on the straight tracks. He liked to watch the wheels turn.

"Gideon, say 'hi' to Carlos," Mommy said.

No. Gideon was busy with his trains. He didn't want to stop and say "hi" to that guy. That guy came over lots. He drank smelly tea. Mommy called it herbal tea. Yucky!

"Gideon," Mommy said. She got close to him and put her hand on the blue engine. *Hey!* Gideon looked at her face to tell her to stop. "Say, 'hi,'" she said.

"Say hi," he repeated, and then he put his hand on Mommy's and pushed. "Blue train." Mommy moved her hand.

"That's the best you're going to get today, I'm afraid," Mommy said. Gideon wasn't afraid, though.

"I have some news to tell you ... about Zach," Smelly said.

Mommy and Smelly walked away. That was good. Their voices weren't so noisy now.

"There was a riot at the prison where they were holding Zach," Smelly said.

Zach? Zach. Zach is Daddy.

"I'm afraid that Zach was killed," Smelly said.

"No!" Mommy said, and she put her hand on her mouth.

Uncle Seth walked into the room. "What's going on?" Uncle Seth asked in his cowboy voice. Uncle Seth put his arm around Mommy.

"Oh," said Smelly. "I did not realize that you were not alone."

"Tell Seth what you told me," Mommy said.

"Er, there was a riot at the prison. Several of the prisoners were shot in the chaos. Zach did not make it," Smelly said.

Zach is Daddy. Gideon ran over to the table at the big window. Gideon loved the big window. He could see the trucks on the road. Sometimes a fire truck drove by. Every Thursday at 9:35, the garbage truck stopped at the end of the driveway. Garbage trucks were noisy up close, but it wasn't too noisy at the window.

Gideon found the picture of the man with the police officer's uniform and took it to Mommy. He slapped Mommy on the leg.

"Zach Daddy," he said. *Zach is Daddy.*

Mommy got down low and touched the picture. "Yes, sweetheart. That's your daddy." Now Mommy had *sad* on her face.

Gideon gave the picture to Uncle Seth. Gideon liked Uncle Seth. He didn't mind it when Gideon jumped on him. He gave good horsey rides.

"Where's his body?" Uncle Seth asked.

"Rectangle," Gideon said. The head is two big curves. The body is a rectangle. That was what Nora said when Mommy took Gideon to play at The Children's Institute.

"What do you mean?" Smelly said.

"Carlos, what happened to Zach? Where is ... he?" Mommy said.

"They were not very forthcoming with information," Smelly said, bumping his shoulder up and nodding his head in a funny way.

"Wasn't there a fire? I heard on the news about a fire in the prison in Tirana," Uncle Seth asked.

"*Si*. Absolutely. *Desgraciadamente*, it was in Zach's area," Smelly said.

"When will they send his body home?" Uncle Seth asked.

"They do not have it. It was lost in the fire," Smelly said. "I tell you again, Christie, I am very sorry."

Mommy started to talk, but Uncle Seth touched her arm and she stopped talking.

"Zach. Daddy," Gideon said. All those other words were confusing. "Daddy. Albania. Daddy. Home."

Mommy picked Gideon up and gave him a long, hard hug. It felt good. Her face was wet, so Gideon wiped the water off with his shirt.

"Thanks for stopping by, Carlin," Uncle Seth said.

"Carlos," Smelly said, and then he went away out the front door.

"Seth?" Mommy said like it was a question.

"He's not dead, Christie, honey," Uncle Seth said.

"Dead as a doornail," Gideon said because that was where he had heard that word the most.

Uncle Seth picked Gideon up from Mommy's hug and gave him a hug and a kiss. "We need to find a way to get your daddy home."

"Daddy home," Gideon said.

"Why do you think he's ... still okay?" Mommy asked.

"I don't trust that man, Christie. He knows too little and too much at the same time. There was a fire in a prison in Eastern Europe, but it was in Macedonia, not Albania. If there was a riot or a fire, they would still have bodies," Uncle Seth said.

"Carlos is just trying to help," she said.

"Perhaps. It doesn't matter. All that matters is getting Zach home," Seth said. "Don't worry, Christie; I'm calling in the troops."

"Calling in the troops," Gideon repeated. He liked the way those words sounded.

Uncle Seth squeezed him again, good and hard. "You're a Marek, Gideon, so you might as well learn this now; we look after our own."

Zachary Marek looked up into the deep-blue eyes of his wife, a halo of blonde curls framing her sweet face. He knew that it wasn't real, that it couldn't be real, but he prayed for continued sleep because this was, by far, the best dream he'd had since he'd come to Albania.

"You are so beautiful," he told her in his dream. She smiled and warmth bloomed in his chest, seeping gradually through his body.

"I love you," she whispered as she lowered her mouth to his, her weight shifting over her hands, which were pressed to his chest. She kissed him, and he could taste the mint of her toothpaste and smell the rose-scented bodywash she used.

Zach shifted to lighten the weight, which was pressing heavily on his chest, a weight that was much heavier than it should have been. He was shattered by disappointment when Christie's soft features wavered and morphed into Raade's bloody corpse. *No, don't go!* Raade's arm dripped with blood as he pointed at Zach. "Thought it was you, Marek, thought you were a bloodthirsty traitor. Who's the traitor? Better find out. He might know where Christie is. Knows Christie. Christie and Gideon. Watch out!" Raade's voice peaked in a shriek of horror and then dissipated into wobbling waves as his face morphed into Agon's, Zach's principal interrogator. *Christie!* Terror clutched at him.

"Ma-rek," Agon said, pronouncing his name in that peculiar accent he had. "*Thoni.* Tell me. *Dashur.* Wife. Tell me." Agon's voice became persuasive as he paced around Zach where he sat naked on a cold metal chair. "Tell me her *emër*, her name. Anya? Delia?" Clutching his hair, Agon bent Zach's head back perilously as he whispered, "Christine?" Zach jerked, shocked. So close. Too close. "Ha." Agon spit in Zach's face. Bound as he was, he couldn't even wipe the disgusting sputum away. "I will help you. I will visit her for you. Show her the true pleasure of a true man." Releasing Zach's head with a jerk, Agon clutched himself suggestively. "A woman should know her place." Furious, desperate, Zach exploded into motion in his dream just as he had in real life. And they had him. They knew how to hurt him, and the only defense he had was to lock his tender feelings away, to bury them deep beneath his anger.

The dream shifted, and, handcuffed, Zach was prodded down an endless gray concrete corridor, a riot of effluvium violating his senses until the floor disappeared beneath him and he plummeted into a silent, inodorous vacuum permeated with blackness and humiliation and fear. He spun, top to toe in the bottomless pit. Above him stood Christie holding Gideon by the hand. Zach cried out to her, but she narrowed her brows in angry confusion.

"Why, Zach? Why did you leave us? We need you." Her voice faded. Desperately, Zach tried to reach her, but he was bound. Falling. Gone. *Christie!*

Zach jerked awake. A wave of nausea surged through his body. He pressed his fists to his stomach to hold the urge to vomit at bay. He couldn't afford to throw up given that they'd only started feeding him again a week ago, if you could count cabbage soup as food, which he did. It was definitely better than nothing.

Zach pulled the thin wool blanket up around his shoulders, trying to still his shivers because they always triggered a racking cough. He was pretty sure he had pneumonia caused by the waterboarding. Combined with the cracked ribs he'd sustained during the most recent interrogation session, he found himself in a depressing haze of pain and fever most of the time.

What a fool he'd been. He'd played his hand early, and now he was paying for his error. Almost five months ago, shortly after he'd arrived in Burgu Punës, Zach had heard a rumor that a Western Christian group would be visiting the prison. Zach had been desperate, hoping to get word to someone in the Canadian government or to Damaris or, even better, to one of his brothers. Belligerently ignoring Pavel's warnings, Zach had lined up with his fellow prisoners ostensibly to get some aspirin and warm socks but really with the intention of asking for aid.

Zach curled into a tighter ball, trying to pull his bare feet beneath the too-short blanket. Zach had passed a message on a scrap of paper and written with a stub of pencil he'd purloined from a guard who fancied himself the most accomplished crossword puzzle expert. The message had declared, *Canadian, Marek, help.*

The woman with the socks had appraised Zach with widened eyes but hadn't commented. She had sent a fellow back later to inquire why there was a Canadian citizen in an Albanian prison.

Shaken awake in the middle of the night, Zach had been removed from his bunk, beaten unconscious by the guards and transported away under cover of darkness. Zach cursed his own stubbornness. But at least he hadn't betrayed Pavel, revealing nothing about him and the kindhearted men, a band of believers who helped each other and any other who was in need to survive.

Zach spent the next four months in an unnamed prison in solitary confinement, which meant something completely different there in Albania than it did at home. Confined to his twelve-by-ten-foot cinder-block cell, he spoke with no one and no one spoke to him. The quiet had been peaceful at first, but the peace had quickly palled until, in the silence, Zach had heard the quiet voice in his heart: *Be still and know that I am God.* And Zach suddenly understood what Joseph knew as a young child and remembered long after his riven Technicolor dream-coat had been shed: that, even in the midst of terrible circumstances, the Lord was with him.

About three weeks earlier, Zach's isolation had ended with the onset of daily interrogation sessions. His last session had been a week before. He must have passed out during the questioning because he'd woken back in his cell both relieved by the cessation of violence and depressed at his aching loneliness. He had been there ever since.

Where before his incarceration, the beatings had served no point but to dishearten him, this new phase consisted of what the West called "aggressive interrogation" and was punctuated by pointed questions focusing on the task force. Zach was forced again and again back to his six months on the task force, which he had left his little family to be a part of. Good answers were rewarded with rest and food, maybe even strong, sweetened coffee. Uninformative answers? Well, let's just say that Zach hadn't had much of substance to eat in a while.

Zach pulled his little blanket tighter around himself and rolled onto his other side, hoping to give his ribs some relief in a new position. He preferred the beatings to the other more psychological strategies. He knew how to deal with physical pain—and hunger for that matter. He'd spent his early childhood becoming an expert. But since becoming a Marek, he'd lost the ability to be alone.

A clank hailed the arrival of Zach's meal through the slot in the metal door to his cell.

"Dinner is served," he muttered wryly.

Crawling over, he downed the dishwater brew, wiped the bowl clean with a small corner of the crusty roll, and hid the rest near his head, so he could eat later. Soon he drifted back to sleep.

Burim Gjojak was flung sideways, his shoulder connecting solidly with the rear passenger-side door of the metallic-black bulletproof Mercedes SUV currently being driven at speed by Qazim Hoxha. Hoxha was Gjojak's top *vrasës*, an assassin, a cold-blooded killer drummed out of the *Regjimenti Komando* because he enjoyed killing just a bit too much. But he was not a good driver. Gjojak gripped the handle on his armrest just in time to avoid sliding across the rear seat of the SUV and connecting with the opposite door.

"Slow *poshtë*," Gjojak ordered as he swung his head around to gauge the progress of the two army jeeps in pursuit. The specially designed Mercedes definitely had the advantage of speed over the twenty-year-old jeeps, but, on the winding mountain road, that advantage was negligible. Gjojak ordered the injured Kovaç to switch positions with Hoxha. To Hoxha, he gave one simple instruction: eliminate pursuit.

Balanced between the two front seats of the SUV, Hoxha carefully checked his AK-47 before tersely commanding Kovaç to open the sunroof. Gjojak was grinding his teeth to dust as he impatiently tolerated the assassin's fastidious attention to detail. As Hoxha rose to brace the AK-47 on the roof of the SUV, Gjojak turned to watch the entertainment. Two quick pops of the assault rifle and one jeep went careening across the dirt road, spinning top-over-axle down the side of the mountain, a plume of dust tracking its course.

Two more pops quickly followed, and Gjojak almost missed the show as the left front bumper of the second jeep connected with a particularly large rocky outcropping on the mountainside. The jeep rolled, door-over-handle, flinging the soldiers inside in all directions.

Gjojak indulged in a low chuckle. *"Mirë."*

Hoxha nodded once to accept the compliment and then resumed his seat in the front passenger side of the SUV. Gjojak ordered Kovaç to return to Memaliaj. The man needed medical care, but he would not dare to pass out before Gjojak was delivered safe and sound to his estate outside the little town.

Gjojak would take some time to rethink his strategy. Perhaps it had not been the right time to move his drugs operation into Greece. The neoterrorists had certainly seemed displeased with him. He would send Kovaç—no, he did not wish to wait for the man to heal. He would send Thor back to Niagara. With Marek neatly tucked away in prison and the task force scattered, he could resume his North American activities.

CHAPTER 4

Christie came back downstairs.

"Gideon asleep?" Luke Marek asked her, running his fingers through his neatly trimmed afro, his deep-brown eyes a window to his concern for his brother. The more concerned he became, the more evident was the hint of Quebecois in his accent, even now, after spending most of his childhood in Wyoming and his adulthood in Vancouver, British Columbia.

"Yes. I can't guarantee he'll stay that way, but he got a pretty good workout today playing with his uncles," she said with a wan smile, the best she could offer at the moment. "Have you heard from Blake?"

"Not since he contacted me to say that Zach was alive and still in Albania," Seth drawled, setting a cup of coffee on the counter for Christie. "Evidently, Zach made contact with one of the Christian prison organizations. When they made inquiries, the prison officials alerted … some bad guys …" Seth paused, shrugging his broad shoulders as though he wasn't certain who the villains were in this scenario. "Anyway, the bad guys, whoever they are, decided to make Zach disappear. They moved him and, most likely, have held him in solitary confinement, since we haven't been able to glean any information on his whereabouts."

"I used all my contacts and couldn't get any word on Zach," Luke added. He looked so miserable sitting there with his lean body hunched over her kitchen counter. "The only interesting bit of information I discovered is that Zimmerman is dead. He was shot and killed in a drugs' shooting in Toronto a couple of months ago."

"But somehow someone got word about Zach to Blake?" Christie asked. Given that Luke worked for the RCMP and Seth had been a US Army Ranger for four years before setting up his veterinary practice, they should have been able to turn up some news of their brother. How many OPP officers were there incarcerated in Albanian prisons?

"Yeah." Luke chuckled wryly. "Who does that boy work for?"

Seth shrugged in a "beats-me" gesture. "The good guys?"

"So someone told Blake …" Christie paused. This was so confusing.

"The Christian group contacted a government minister who is reputed to be honest on Zach's behalf and then also contacted someone at the Canadian consulate in Tirana. How that information then got to Blake, I do not know," Luke said. "But if it weren't for their persistence, it's unlikely he would have found him."

"Are we going to save him?" Christie asked, subdued. "Zach, I mean."

The familiar cultured tones rang out unexpectedly. "Of course. He's a Marek and …" Blake wasn't allowed to finish his statement as Seth wrapped him in a gigantic embrace.

"You made it," Seth said.

No one bothered to worry about the detail that Blake had just entered an alarmed house that contained an RCMP officer, an ex-Army Ranger, and a cop's wife, without being detected. That was just Blake.

"My turn, Kong," Luke said, elbowing Seth out of the way, and then he hugged Blake in turn.

Christie patiently waited her turn and then hugged him too. "Oh, Blake. Thank you for coming." Tears immediately sprang to her eyes, and she waved her hand as though that would eliminate them. "I'm sorry for blubbering."

Blake set her back from him and produced a handkerchief—an actual light-blue cotton hanky from the front pocket of his khakis. "We look after our own," he said, finishing the family motto.

Christie accepted it, looking gratefully into the deep-brown eyes of her enigmatic brother-in-law. Dwarfed by his brothers, Blake was five-nine on his tiptoes, with broad shoulders and a broad back. A Uyghar from the Xinjiang region of northwest China, Blake carried the olive complexion and the straight black hair of his biological parents. The quiet, unassuming nature, however, was all his own. Short, dark, and shy, Seth used to say.

They gathered around the counter in the kitchen again. "Have you heard anything from Zach or his colleagues?" Blake asked Christie.

"No. I left about a dozen messages on Thomason's voicemail after you sent word that Zach was still alive. I even drove over to speak to him." She well remembered that day.

"What?" Luke asked, likely noting the glint in her otherwise bleary eyes.

"I took Gideon and let him wind himself into a grand ole tizzy," she said.

Luke rapped the table in subdued glee. "Good for you."

"We cleared the office, and I was quickly escorted away with promises of help, but the officer they sent me, a woman named …" Christie thought for a moment. "… Raisa Webster, had never met Zach and didn't know anything about the situation."

"A worthy effort," Blake said, giving her a brief smile and then becoming serious again. "Thomason's out of the country. About a week after your first call, he was seconded to an antidrugs squad in Bolivia."

"What is going on, Blake?" Christie asked, startled by that news. *Thomason is in South America?*

"Damaris Quickle, the agent who was leading the Albanian-Canadian task force, believes that Zach stumbled across a crucial piece of information that put the drugs trade in Albania in jeopardy," Blake said.

"Why didn't they just kill him?" Luke asked.

Seth put his hand on Luke's arm and nodded in Christie's direction. She assumed it had to do with the fact that she probably looked pretty pale with the blood draining from her head.

"Sorry, honey. You okay?" Luke asked.

She nodded, gulping to keep down her coffee. "What else?" she asked, her voice sounding raspy and tight.

"When you contacted Thomason, I think he believed you, and I'm guessing that he made inquiries, which were not well received by someone in the know," Blake said.

Had her careless questions banished the man?

"It's not your fault," Seth said, reading her thoughts.

Relaxing minutely, she nodded bleakly at him, but she wasn't sure that she truly agreed.

"It's true," he said. "Whoever is behind this is responsible."

She nodded again with a little more confidence.

"To answer your question, Luke, Zach has information that they want. They likely set him aside for a rainy day, but word has reached those who took him that people are making inquiries," Blake said.

"Which means that Zach is in imminent danger," Seth said, giving Christie's hand a squeeze of reassurance at the same time.

"They'll interrogate him first," Blake said. "My guess is … aggressively."

"Aggressively?" Christie said. What did that mean?

"We probably have about a two-week window to go in and get him out," Blake said.

"Have you got a plan?" Luke asked.

Nodding, Blake reached into his back pocket and spread out a map of Eastern Europe and blueprints for something called Burgu Punës.

Christie pointed to the unfamiliar words. "What's that?"

"That's the prison where Zach was initially held." Blake flipped that page over to reveal another beneath. "This …" Blake tapped the page. "… is where I think they've got him now."

"We'll need to go into the country as tourists and then extract him by a different route," Seth said.

"Weapons?" Luke asked.

"That's where I've been for the past three days, arranging routes and support," Blake said. "Now, here's what I think we should do."

Once Seth, Luke, and Blake arrived at the ferry dock in Durrës, Albania, Blake transformed from the shy little brother into the agent-in-charge of a potentially lethal operation.

"Weird to be bossed around by the twerp," Luke said, in a stage-whisper, just a hint of a roll to his "r."

"Yeah," Seth agreed. "Ask the expert, right? I suppose if I wanted to know anything about trains, I'd ask Gideon. Makes sense to trust the twerp who knows the most."

"Uh, Blake?" Luke turned toward his younger brother.

"Yup?" Blake replied.

"Would you mind going over the plan once more?" Luke said, running his fingers through his tight curls.

"Of course," Blake said. "We pick up the guns, ammo, and motorcycles, then drive southeast to Lundër and hide the bikes in the wooded area behind the elementary school. We equip ourselves and proceed on foot directly east for one-point-three miles to the southernmost corner of the western wall of the prison. The guard hut is at the entrance to the prison in the narrow north wall surrounding the prison. If we come in directly beneath the southwest tower, we cannot be observed by any of the other guard towers."

"How do we avoid being seen by the guards in that tower?" Seth asked.

"It's arranged. Don't worry." Blake started off into the night.

Luke snorted, muttering, "This is so bizarre, twerp."

Blake paused, turning back. "Having to trust your little brother?" Blake's expression was implacable.

"Nope. It's bizarre that it seems the most natural thing in the world to put my life in the hands of my little brother," Luke said. "What's next?"

Blake's expression relaxed. "Zach's being held in the solitary cells along the south wall of the prison. He's in the third cell from the western wall." Blake hesitated and then spoke again. "He's injured. They've been pretty rough with him."

"And you know this how?" Luke asked.

Blake shrugged. "He's going to be weak and disoriented. Seth, I think it's best if you take him on the bike with you. We're going to need your strength to make sure he doesn't fall off."

"Will do, sir," Seth replied, all joking aside.

"Once we have him, we return to the bikes, drive east through the mountain road to the Mavrovo National Park in Macedonia. We get to the NATO base there, and a military jet will take you home," Blake said.

"What about you, Blake?" Seth asked, immediately picking up on Blake's choice of pronouns.

"I left an operation in the middle to do this. I'll need to fly out in a different direction. But I'll make sure you're safely away first," he said, giving his brothers' shoulders a squeeze of reassurance.

"I'm glad you're on our side," Luke said. "But there's one other thing I need to know." He paused, catching Blake's eye. "Who do you work for?"

Blake smiled. "The good guys."

Luke saluted him again but this time with sincerity.

Rolling onto his back, Zach immediately started coughing. His fever was getting worse, as was the chest-racking cough. After crawling over to the water jug by the door, Zach shakily poured himself a drink of lukewarm liquid rust.

Something faint but out of the normal prison sounds had woken him, and he needed to figure out what it was. Three nights ago, there'd been a jailbreak attempt. The rescuers had been caught just three cells down from him, so close and yet not close enough.

Peering cautiously beneath the flap at the bottom of his cell door, Zach's gaze connected with a pair of black combat boots that rose to the hem of gray combat fatigues. He froze. Someone, not a guard because their uniforms were black, was standing just outside his cell door.

"Marek," a voice whispered, so quietly that it was almost a puff of a breeze.

"Here," Zach replied just as quietly.

"Get back," the barely there voice came floating through the door again.

Zach crawled beneath his cot and huddled into a ball. There was a "pop," not much louder than the sound of an opening soda can, and then the cell door swung silently inward. Whoever had opened it had greased the hinges. Whoever opened it had used just the perfect amount of C-4 explosive to break the lock with a minimum of sound. Incredible! Did he know anyone with that expertise?

"Zach?"

Blake! Hope burst like a fireball in his chest. Zach hauled his body out from under the cot and struggled to his feet. His brother's arms pulled him into a quick embrace, warming his body as the hope he delivered warmed his heart. *Thank you, Lord.* Zach felt Blake place a small device in his ear and around his throat, a whisper mic.

"Can you walk?" Blake asked.

Zach heard the sound as though it was inside his head.

He knew he couldn't speak without risking a coughing fit, so he grabbed Blake's hand, placed it on his clammy face, and nodded.

Blake scouted the corridor and then came back into the cell, propping the cot against the door to hold it closed. Then he removed a glob of gray putty from his pocket and pressed it into the seams between the gray cinderblocks in the back wall. The next thing he knew, Zach was enveloped in his little brother's arms. His head dropped to rest on Blake's shoulder until a "bang" sounded.

That was a miscalculation. Zach looked over to see, through the settling dust, the shocked face of a prison guard peering through a jagged three-foot hole in the rear wall of the cell. First meeting Zach's gaze, the guard blinked twice and then abruptly vanished from sight down the corridor.

Zach and Blake exchanged a meaningful look. And then the sirens sounded.

"No good now. This way." Using his shoulder, Blake shoved the cot out of the way.

"Right." Zach wheezed and then coughed.

"Left," Blake said, pulling Zach in that direction. Zach slipped free and grabbed a fistful of Blake's shirt, forcibly guiding him to the right. Blake hesitated for only an instant, a good thing because Zach didn't think he had the strength to insist. Jogging to the right, Zach stopped suddenly as a voice rang out.

"Help me. Do not leave me."

It was Gerhardt, Zach's neighbor in this forsaken place. Torn by indecision, Zach hesitated a moment before he decided.

"Do you have ..." He coughed. "... more C-4?" he asked Blake.

Blake handed him about a tablespoon's worth. Zach tore off small hunk and rolled it between his thumb and forefinger until it was a smooth ball. Then he pushed it into the lock on Gerhardt's door, and Blake inserted the blasting cap.

"Help the others," Zach said to Gerhardt, tossing the remaining C-4 as well as the rest of the blasting caps through the grate in the door. Zach and Blake were off down the hall before the "pop" sounded.

Two black-clad guards appeared at the end of this corridor, shouting for Zach to *"Ndalu!"* (Stop!) raising their rifles shoulder-high. Blake dropped, dragging Zach down beneath him as bullets punched through the air above their bodies. Relief sharpened the ache in his chest.

"Off," Zach wheezed, unable to draw breath beneath the crush of his brother's body. But Blake was using Zach's head to steady a shot. He fired three bullets from his Glock, nearly deafening Zach but also sending the guards to take cover, giving the brothers Marek time to rise. In three shorts steps, they'd reached Zach's destination, a door to the inner courtyard.

Slipping outside, nestled within the shadow of the wall, Zach surveyed the empty courtyard. Just as he'd hoped, once the alarm sounded, all of the searchlights had been turned outward. Creeping along the wall of the courtyard, they made their way to the left and then left again to the next door—which was locked. *Blast it!* They'd given away the last of their C-4. But Blake wasn't concerned. Pushing Zach behind him, he took aim at the old lock and blasted it away in two shots.

Checking the corridor over Blake's shoulder uneasily, Zach could see that it was swarming with shouting guards. Unease stepped back and let fear take hold. Blake retrieved a Walther P99 from one of the many pockets on his trousers and handed it to Zach. Were they going to try to blast their way past the guards? Zach didn't hold out much hope for success in that particular endeavor.

Puzzled, Zach watched as Blake unzipped his black combat vest and then stripped off his shirt. Turning to Zach, he tugged his prison shirt, a tattered, dirt-brown tunic, over his head and then tossed it behind them.

"I need you *not* to look like a prisoner," Blake said quietly, slipping the neck of his shirt over Zach's head.

Understanding now, Zach took over getting the black shirt on as Blake slipped back into his vest.

"We need to look like them," Blake said, nodding toward the corridor.

Shouting. Clad in black. Waving guns in the air.

"Got it," Zach said, coughing.

Once the coughing had stopped, Blake stepped into the corridor, and Zach followed him. Smoothly, Blake switched into Albanian, shouting, claiming they'd seen prisoners in the courtyard.

"Turn the searchlights inward!" he yelled as he waved the guards through the door from which they'd just exited.

Then Zach and Blake simply jogged down the corridor in the opposite direction, waving their guns and shouting. Well, Blake shouted; Zach was silent, barely having enough breath to keep up.

"*Ndalu!*"

The word chased them down the corridor, but they definitely were *not* stopping. Blake turned a corner to the right with Zach close behind, and there, before them, open and ready, was a large window. An anonymous black-clad individual stood beside it, a rifle at the ready. But this person was dressed more like Blake than the guards. So Zach followed his brother forward. Blake nodded once to the individual, who seemed to disappear into mist.

Tumbling onto the grass through the window, Zach staggered to his feet. Blake grabbed his arm and pulled him forward. Numbly, Zach stumbled along behind him, struggling to suppress his cough and stay upright at the same time. His vision tunneled so he kept his gaze on the ground in front of his bare feet, hoping that would help. One more hole, this time in the prison wall, and then Zach was free, limping along, his fingers grasping the back of Blake's Kevlar vest as they ran across a field to a stand of trees beyond. The wail of alarms pursued them.

Luke wrapped an arm around Zach, pulling him forward. "You're back, *petit frère*. You bin gone so long."

Relief stole his strength. "Luke," Zach gasped, and though his chest felt heavy, his heart felt light. "This time ..." He gasped in a shallow breath. "... *you* came for *me*."

Chuckling, Luke squeezed his shoulders. "Do you think you can hold on behind Seth on a motorcycle?" Luke asked him, taking his full weight and pulling him along to the spot where Blake was rooting through some brush.

"They should be just over here." Seth's voice rumbled from the left.

"Where's Christie?" Zach gasped out the words, his arm banded across his ribs.

"She'll be there when we get you home," Luke said.

Seth started the bike, and Luke helped Zach onto the back. "Just hold on tight to me, *cheéte*, and I'll get you home."

"Anything. Just take me to Christie," Zach replied, his voice breathy and strained.

Seth nodded, and they were off.

The journey was a blur for Zach. He knew they ascended into a mountain pass because he felt the change in temperature, the shivering prompting his cough. Numbly, he held on tight to his brother and tried to stay conscious.

It might have been five minutes or fifty before Zach realized that he was lying supine on the grass rather than clinging tightly to Seth's back on the motorcycle.

"You're back, *petit frère*," Luke said, reaching a hand down to lift him to his feet. "You faded away there for a while."

"Thanks," Zach said, relying on Luke's strength to get up. "Where are we?"

"At the landing strip," Blake said, coming up beside Luke. "I've arranged for the pilot to fly you to Lunéville Base in France, and from there, they'll fly you to the NATO base in Goose Bay."

"Who, Blake?" Luke asked.

Blake grinned. "The good guys."

"Thank you, Little Brother, for saving me." Virtually bursting with gratitude, Zach hugged Blake as firmly as he could without adding to his own pain.

"Maybe you'll return the favor one day," Blake replied.

"Anytime." Zach nodded and turned toward the airplane on the runway, limping closer.

"Zach." Blake put a hand on his arm to stop him. "I think what you're doing is very brave."

"Working on the task force?" Zach asked, puzzled. He couldn't think of any other aspect of his life where he'd shown even the slightest courage.

"No. Being a father," Blake said, and then he was gone, jogging toward an army jeep at the edge of the field.

"Let's go home," Luke said before leading Zach onto the military transport and strapping him in. Relief, hope, fear, all drained from him, leaving him limp. Zach was asleep before they took off. He vaguely remembered switching planes, but the rest of the journey was lost in a fog as Zach relaxed and let the fever take him.

CHAPTER 5

"Zachary!" His mother, Janice, was looking for him.

"Come here, you little piece of toe fungus!" *Ugh.* That was Joey, Janice's new boyfriend.

Zachary squeezed his little body further into the corner of his mother's closet. Why had he chosen to hide there? Foolishly, Zachary had hoped that Janice would help him. *Hah!* She wouldn't help him. Janice never helped him when one of her boyfriends got mad.

"Where is the stupid little maggot?" Joey asked Janice. Zachary heard his heavy steps on the stairs.

"Who cares, Joey? Let's use this stash. Forget about him," Janice said.

Zachary felt a moment of hope because she was using the voice she always used when she wanted one of her boyfriends to do something for her. But Zachary knew that she wasn't trying to help him. She wanted a needle; that was all that she was thinking about. That would be good. If Janice and Joey had a needle, then Zachary could sneak out of the house. He could sleep at the back door of his school. He'd done that before when Janice or one of her boyfriends was mad at him.

He could tell his teacher he was hungry in the morning. Miss Bass always got him something to eat if he was hungry.

Zachary heard a thump in his mother's bedroom. *Oh no!* Joey was getting close. Zachary plugged his nose at the sour smell that meant that Joey and Janice had been drinking the fiery stuff again, the horrible stuff that Janice made Zachary drink when he was sick.

The closet door swung open, and Zachary tried to curl into a smaller ball, but Joey saw him.

"There you are!" he said. He grabbed Zachary's arm and pulled him hard and fast. Zachary fell down hard on his hands and knees. "You touched my stuff, maggot."

"I'm sorry. I'm sorry. I'm sorry," Zachary said. And he was sorry. Joey's stereo had lots of buttons and lights, and all Zachary had wanted was to hear the music on it. But when he twisted the knobs and pushed the buttons while Janice and Joey were out "partying," *boom*! There had been a loud noise, and the lights went out. Smoke started coming out of the big black boxes that Joey called the "sweetest woofers known to man."

Zachary knew there would be trouble when they got home. Oh, why hadn't he slept at the school that night?

Thump. Joey's fist came down hard against Zachary's shoulder. Zachary tried to say sorry again, but Joey was yelling lots of words that Zachary's teacher wouldn't let him say in school. Zachary tried to get Joey to stop hurting him by kicking and yelling and trying to run away. But in the end, he never knew what made Joey stop because finally, thankfully, Zachary fainted dead away.

By the time Zachary woke up the next morning, it was time to go to school. He tried to stand up from the floor of his mother's bedroom to see if Joey was in Janice's bed. But when Zachary moved, pain flashed across his chest and shoulders, and he threw up. *Oh, no.* Janice would be mad that he had made a mess. But he hurt too much to try to clean it.

Zachary went to the bathroom to go pee and wash his mouth, and then he sneaked downstairs. Joey was lying on the couch with an empty bottle in his arms like a teddy bear. Janice was asleep on the floor, still dressed in her clothes. There were needles and candles and a spoon on the coffee table. If Janice and Joey had done the needle, they would sleep for a while.

Zachary slipped his bare feet into his running shoes and walked out the front door. By the time he made it to school, everything looked really blurry and he felt like throwing up again.

The other kids were pointing at him and whispering, but Zachary didn't care. He was there at school until three o'clock. Janice couldn't hurt him while he was at school. Neither could Joey or any of his mother's boyfriends.

He heard Miss Bass's happy voice then. "Good morning, children. I hope you all had a good—" Then she made a gasping sound. "Zachary, what happened this time?" She got down low in front of him. He flinched and made a sound when she touched his sore shoulder.

Miss Bass turned to one of the pretty girls in the class, Darla Cassidy, one of those girls who always made fun of Zachary at school, calling him stupid when he had trouble reading.

"Get Mr. Richmond," Miss Bass said to Darla. "Go fast."

Mr. Richmond was the principal. Zachary started to cry. He was going to get in trouble for touching Joey's stuff. Maybe Janice had called the school last night and told on Zachary.

"What is going on here?" Mr. Richmond said, running up to them.

"I'm sorry," Zachary said, crying harder. "I didn't mean to break it."

"Miss Bass, why don't you take the children into the classroom? I'll deal with this," Mr. Richmond said, and then he got down low in front of Zachary. "You don't need to cry, Zachary. You're not in trouble. Can you walk to my office?"

Zachary sniffed and nodded, wiping his nose with his arm. Mr. Richmond took Zachary's hand, and they walked to his office together. Mr. Richmond gave him a drink of juice and a few cookies. He used a washcloth to clean Zachary's face and talked to him real nice.

After a while, a tall policeman came to the school. His name was Zachary too, Zach Smith. He talked to Zachary and asked him about Joey and Janice, and then he took Zachary to the hospital. He stayed while the doctor looked at Zachary and while he was x-rayed. Then the doctor talked about contusions, a broken collarbone, and a bruised spleen, and then Zach Smith, the OPP officer, took Zachary someplace safe where he could eat as much as he wanted and they gave him clean clothes that smelled nice and promised him that Joey would never hurt him again.

And then Zachary Marek realized that he was dreaming when his memories fast-forwarded, touching briefly on his time with the Barretts, who had been ill-equipped to deal with their foul-mouthed, quick-fisted charge. And then there were the Joneses and the Matthews and the Esmonds.

Zach's dream sped to the day that Rita, Zachary's child protection worker, visited him at the Vandermeers' foster home. Zachary was so excited—he experienced the emotions as though he were back there again—thinking that finally Janice had forgiven him for touching Joey's stuff and that she was going to let Zachary come home. She would stop having boyfriends, and it would just be the two of them.

But Zachary had been very wrong.

"Do you know what it means to be a crown ward, Zachary?" Rita asked.

"My name's Zach," he said.

"It means that your mommy has decided that someone else would do a better job taking care of you," Rita said, and Zach's last hope shriveled into a dried-out pea. "Your great-aunt Mae has just recently returned home from Africa. She's going to take you in on a kinship agreement. Do you know what that means?"

Zach's dream spun forward through his fear and despair to Wyoming and the Cody First Methodist Church where Great-Aunt Mae took him to church for the first time in his life. Zach met Luke Marek in the basement of that church, not actually on his first week with Aunt Mae, but the dream had compressed time again.

"Hey, who're you?" a seven-year-old Luke asked, walking over to Zach.

"None o' yer business. I hate this ..." And then Zach had gone on to use every filthy, foul word he'd ever heard from Janice's boyfriends. Luke had stood, awed by the vocabulary, and then shoved Zach hard.

"Don't talk like that. My dad doesn't like it," Luke said, scowling at him.

"Yeah? See if I care," Zach said, and the next thing he knew, he had pinned Luke to the floor, straddling his chest, his fist reeled back and ready to strike. And then suddenly, he was dangling from a ten-year-old Seth's grip.

"Leave my brother alone, you snot-nosed wazzock," Seth said.

"Thank you, Seth. That will be enough, son." Zach looked up to see a giant bear of a man with a huge chest and enormous hands. The man had a golden-red beard and bright-blue eyes, and he wore a big, shiny belt buckle with a bucking bronco on it. That was Zach's first view of Bud Marek. Bud kept talking to Seth, who still held Zach by the scruff of the neck. "And thank you for not using profanity." The big man lifted Zach out of Seth's grip and got down on one knee to talk to him. "Now, young fellow, what is your name and why were you sitting on my son's chest?"

All the fight went out of Zach, replaced by confusion. "He's an Indian," Zach said, pointing at Seth. "And he's black." Zach pointed at Luke. "But you're white," Zach said, turning to Bud.

"I'm not an Indian, dork-brain. I'm half-Crow, a bona-fide Native American," Seth said proudly.

"I'm a Nigerian-Canadian-American from the Igbo tribe," Luke said from his position leaning back on his elbows on the floor.

"I'm Bud Marek," the cowboy said, shaking Zach's hand as though he were a grown man. "Seth and Luke are both my sons. But I still don't know your name," Bud said.

"Zach. I don't belong here. You guys are just a bunch of dumb cowboys. I'm a big city man from Toronto," Zach said, being sure to put as much acid into his voice as possible. One of his foster parents had said Zach spoke with acid in his voice. Zach had liked that and tried to repeat the effect whenever possible. Zach then added a little profanity, which, to his surprise, Bud just ignored.

"Luke also started his life in Canada. In Montreal. You fellows have a lot in common," Bud said.

"Yeah?" Zach said and then swore to cover up the fact that he was interested.

Luke jumped up from the floor with a huge grin on his face. "I didn't fight back, Daddy. Are you proud of me? He's littler than me, but I still didn't pound him," Luke said.

Bud smiled, clapping his son on the shoulder. "I *am* proud of you, Luke. Thank you, Son."

Luke turned and punched Zach companionably on the shoulder. "Hello, Canuck."

Zach clenched his fists, but then he stopped before he hit back. Luke had such a huge grin on his face and was looking at Zach with such friendly eyes, that he just stopped.

Bud rested a gentle hand on Zach's shoulder. "Thank you, Zach," he said, giving Zach credit for not hitting back. No one had ever done that before. Zach got in trouble, or he was ignored. He knew how to deal with that. But this? This was new.

Bud was talking again. "Well, if we're quite through, then it's time to set up for Sunday school. Luke, you and Zach get the juice and snack. Seth, please finish setting up the chairs."

"Okay, Dad," Luke said, giving Zach's shirt a light tug. He never understood why, but Zach followed him.

That ten-minute interaction started Zach on the journey to being loved and learning to love in return.

Zach's dream shifted, and he was an adult, his first day back at Durham College for his second year in the police foundations program. This was the day he met Christie—Christie who had shown him a future where he could create a family, happily. Christie.

"Christie."

"I'm here, Zach. I'm here." And she was. Forcing open his eyes, he feasted on the sight of her, blonde curls in disarray around her face, her deep-blue eyes dark with worry and lack of sleep.

"Sorry," he mumbled. *Sorry for leaving. Sorry for making you sad and worried. Sorry for everything.*

Stroking the hair back from his forehead in the sweetest of gestures, she told him, "Go back to sleep. You need more rest."

When she shifted in her seat, he grabbed her sleeve, terribly afraid that she would leave. "Stay." His voice was breathy, tinged with just a hint of desperation.

She smiled though her expression looked weary. "Yes. I'll be here when you wake up."

He nodded and drifted off again, this time to a peaceful sleep without dreams.

CHAPTER 6

The next time Zach awoke in the infirmary on the NATO base at Goose Bay; his father was sitting at his side.

"Hi, Dad," Zach said, his throat dry and unused to speaking. Bud pressed a straw between his lips, and Zach drank deeply, nodding when he'd had enough. "Thanks."

"We've been worried about you," Bud said. His red-gold beard was shot-through with gray. The past year had aged his father, Zach realized guiltily.

"How long have I been out?" Zach asked, pushing up on his elbows to try to sit.

Bud leaned in and arranged the pillows for him. "Two days."

Zach searched the room with his eyes. "Where is Christie? And Gideon? I was sure I saw Gideon at one point."

"They're here," Bud assured him. "It's three o'clock in the morning. They're asleep. At least I hope that Gideon is sleeping."

Zach tried to smile, but it quickly fell away. "How am I going to fix this, Dad?"

Bud didn't try to soften the blow; he just met Zach's gaze and let him have it. "Even though your motives were good, you were gone when she needed you. Now you'll have to deal with the consequences of that."

Zach nodded slowly. He knew that.

"Christie asked me to get her if you woke," Bud said. He leaned forward and kissed Zach on the forehead. "I love you, Son," he said and then left the room.

Zach wanted to close his gritty eyes, but he didn't want to fall asleep before Christie arrived. He had a lot to explain.

"Hi." Christie greeted him softly as she came into the room and sat in the chair beside him, looking as though she'd come straight from bed. "How are you feeling?"

He shrugged and then winced; that about summed it up. "Christie, I'm sorry. I'm really sorry."

"We don't need to talk about this right now," Christie said, leaning back from him as though a change in proximity would lessen the hurt.

Hoping to keep her close, he grabbed for her hand. "No, Christie. I need you to know. I don't want a life without you and Gideon," he said, chagrined by the hint of desperation in his voice. "I love you. I know that I haven't done a very good job being a father so far." Glancing briefly at her face to try to find some understanding, he continued, "That's finished, though, if you'll give me another chance. I'm home now. We can go back to the way things were before." He grabbed her other hand and held on tight.

"Is that what you want?" She looked startled, her eyes wide, her voice a bare whisper. And he was feeling frustrated because she seemed to be missing the point.

"Yes, of course … you and me, honey. And Gideon," he said. "I want a life with you and Gid, and I'll do anything to have that. I'll … I'll quit my job—"

"You can't," she said flatly. "They fired you."

"What?" Now Zach let himself fall back onto the pillows. A flurry of emotions warred in his chest.

"When you were convicted of a crime in Albania, they terminated your employment. You don't have a job to quit. Damaris sorted out your passport and all that bureaucracy. She even had you officially exonerated by the Canadian government, but she said she couldn't get you your job back because Thomason, the one who might have believed you, is in Bolivia."

"Bolivia?" He frowned. *What?* "But why would the OPP believe the *polici*? I have a good record. I've had commendations and …"

He watched her larynx bob as she gulped. "An officer named

Zimmerman made a statement that he witnessed you taking drugs to help you cope with Gideon's diagnosis."

Zach had thought he was astonished a moment ago, but now he was completely shocked. "I would never do that." Zach looked up to meet her gaze, a black hole opening in the pit of his stomach. *Zimmerman?* "That's why no one came to help me," Zach said, feeling numb inside. They'd abandoned him, left him to rot in prison because of one man's lies. No one had believed in him, come for him.

"We did," she said, and then she did the most incredible thing; she kissed him sweetly, tenderly, on the mouth. He no longer felt numb as a jet of warmth burst inside him.

"Thank you. For rescuing me. For bringing me here."

"*Are* you here? For good? For real?"

"I'm here," he replied, determined to be. "I want to be with you, need to be with you both."

Studying him, searching his eyes, she finally nodded as though accepting his words. "Gideon needs to get back for—" she began, but he cut her off.

"It can wait." Zach drew her close. Anything could wait now that they were together again. "I want to just take a time-out from life here and sort everything out later. I mean, what can reach us here in Goose Bay?"

"You don't understand. Gideon has speech therapy and occupational therapy appointments."

"Christie. We can discuss the future later—appointments, schedules, all that stuff. For now, it's enough to be here. I've waited a year to be here, to get my life back."

"Zach …" she began and then stopped. She rose, and he couldn't guess the protest tripping from her lips and then didn't let it worry him as she leaned over to kiss his forehead. "Get some more sleep," she said, reaching the door of his room. "Good night."

"Where's Christie?" Zach asked Luke the next morning.

When he'd awakened, Zach had gone searching and, rather than

Christie, had found his father dozing on a bunk in the guest quarters of the NATO base. Seth had taken Bobby home to the Second Chance ranch, but Luke had remained behind and was currently prowling Zach's room.

Turning back from the window, Luke met Zach's gaze. From the expression on his face, he was clearly surprised by Zach's question.

"She went home," Luke said with his brows furrowed in consternation.

"Home? Alone?" Zach asked, astonished.

"With Gideon." Luke frowned, running a hand through his hair. "She said she discussed this with you and that you wanted to stay. I think you're zippo, dude." He spun his finger around his ear in the universal sign of crazy.

"I didn't want her to leave without me. I wanted her and Gideon to stay here. I wanted *us* to stay." Zach made a different kind of circle with his finger. "All three of us. Did she tell you why she left me? Here?" adding the extra word to make it sound less like he'd driven his wife away.

Luke shrugged. "Gideon has appointments."

"Surely it's not the end of the world if he misses a couple of appointments. What difference does speech therapy make when he can already talk?"

"You sure you're ready to enter the great, wide world of autism? Because that's a dumb question," Luke said, and all the humor was erased from his face.

Zach's hands fisted of their own accord. "I don't need you to tell me about my son."

Luke stepped toward him. "Someone needs to, someone who didn't run away at the first sign of trouble."

"Shut it, Luke! I was working on a task force to stop a murdering scumbag terrorist," Zach said. "I was set up and thrown in prison."

"Tell yourself what you want, but don't expect me to believe it. You ran away. You left your pretty, incredible wife to carry the burden alone. And she has. Why shouldn't she assume she needs to continue doing just that?" Luke asked and then added with warning in his voice, "You're going to have to prove you want to be part of that world now."

Zach took a step toward him.

"Boys," Bud said in that soft voice that Zach had learned to honor. How did Bud always know when his boys were set to scrap?

Zach stepped back, and Bud walked across the room and sat in the chair beside the bed. "What seems to be the problem here?" he asked.

Luke gave Zach a hard look and then said, "Nothing," before he started for the door.

"Luke," Zach said, halting his brother's departure. "Thank you …" Zach couldn't maintain Luke's gaze. "Thank you for looking after them … while I was gone."

In two long strides, Luke stepped into Zach's space, hauled off, and punched him in the shoulder, hard enough to hurt—*Ow!*—and then wrapped him in a rib-shattering hug that—yup. *Ow!*—hurt.

"I love you, *petit frère*."

"I love you, too, Luke," Zach stammered, holding his aching ribs.

Luke's normally ever-present smile shone and then quickly vanished. He nodded once, and then he was gone.

Zach wandered back to the bed and slumped down to sit across from Bud, who then stood up and sat down on the bed beside him. Soon, he felt his father's hand warm on his back, that hand that had never been raised in anger against him, the hand that had held him through angry tantrums and night terrors, the hand that had pulled him into the embrace of love and taught him to trust.

"What do I do, Dad?" Sadness didn't even begin to express Zach's emotional state. His head hung low between his shoulders; his hands were clasped between his knees.

Bud was silent for a long time until Zach glanced over his shoulder at him.

"Is this one of those moments when you want me to reassure you of my love, or do you want an answer?" Bud asked.

Zach sincerely thought about that. "An answer. I need to hear the truth."

"When you married Christie, did you mean it?"

Surprised, Zach replied, "Yes."

"Think hard about the words you said, the promises you made."

Zach did. *In sickness and health, till death* … "Yes, Dad, I meant it."

"Until autism do us part?"

Oh, crap! How did Bud do that? How did he see right through his children to their deeper fears and insecurities? "Please don't misunderstand my actions, Dad. I love Gideon. I would give my life for him. If I could give him blood to make him better, I'd let them drain me dry."

"Maybe the way to give your life for him is to give up your idea of who he should be and accept him for who he is," Bud replied.

"I've never thought of it that way," Zach said, humbly considering his father's words.

"You and your brothers, you are all my sons and you each have your own special needs," Bud continued. "Oh, people can see Bobby's differences right away because of his Down syndrome. They see it in his face. They hear it in his speech. It can be tested for and scored. But you, how do we score the pain you experienced the day that Janice gave you over to be a crown ward? I know that now you are grateful she released you and let you escape the pain of her addictions, her neglect and abuse. But it hurt you."

"Yeah. But you and Mom always accepted me for who I am," Zach said.

"Yes. I love you, son, as much as if you'd been born to me," Bud said. "I love you enough to want you to have the best life possible."

"Christie … well, this isn't going to be easy," Zach said.

Bud held Zach's gaze with an eloquent expression on his face. "Did you sign on because you thought creating a family would be easy?"

Zach blushed. "I don't want to lose her."

"And Gideon?" Bud asked softly.

"Yes. I love him more than my own life," Zach said, and he meant it. He loved his son. "What do I do, Dad?"

"Do the hard thing," Bud said as he pulled him into his arms. "And, son, it will be worth it. I promise."

"I'm scared," Zach whispered, leaning his head against his father's shoulder.

"I know," Bud said, pulling back but keeping his arm around Zach's shoulder. "My son, don't you think I was ever scared as a father; taking in four deeply damaged boys who needed so much more than I had to offer?"

"I never thought about it. You and Mom always seemed to know just what I needed."

"Do you remember the day you ran away? Blake had come to live with us about a month previously, and you were very jealous."

"I remember," Zach whispered, overcome again with those feelings of fear and insecurity that resurfaced from that time in his life. "You hadn't asked me to stay yet. Luke told me that when you were ready to adopt one of us, you would ask us if we wanted to stay."

"I told Grace that it was too soon to bring another child into the house. You were still getting into fights at school, stealing food, and disobeying every rule at every opportunity. I was afraid that you would doubt our love for you," Bud said.

"Really?" Zach was surprised. "I thought you were afraid that I would hurt Blake."

"Oh, sweetheart, I knew that you would never hurt the baby. The reason that your great-aunt Mae asked us to take you in was because, beneath the violent, foul-mouthed behavior, there rested a tender heart. No, I was more concerned about that tender heart," Bud said. "Do you remember?"

Zach remembered. He had decided that if he ran away into the Absaroka Mountains, he could live on the edge of the ranch, surviving by hunting with his BB gun and raiding the orchards. He assumed that Luke would bring him supplies if he needed it, like in the winter. That was a thousand times better than having to leave the Second Chance because Bud and Grace preferred baby Blake.

Luke had discovered Zach's plans and refused to let him leave alone. Together, they'd made it across the northwest pasture and up into the foothills before disaster struck. Spooked by a coyote's howl in the midnight darkness, Luke had taken a tumble, coming down hard on his ankle.

Desperate and terrified for his best friend in the whole world, Zach had run the mile back to the ranch house, arriving filthy and desperate. He'd beat a rapid, desperate thumping on the door.

"Daddy! Daddy!" Zach cried, forgetting for the moment that the man before him was "not my dad! I don't have a father!" a phrase that he had yelled at Bud several times in the last six months, usually accompanied by much profanity.

"Zach. Have you decided to come back?" Bud asked, keeping his voice unemotional.

"Please." Zach stopped, looking desperately around the room. His eyes finally lit on a walking stick by the door. He snatched it and ran with it over to Bud, shoving it into his hands. "Quick. Please. Do it quick," he said and then turned his back to Bud and placed his palms on the edge of the kitchen table. When Zach glanced over his shoulder, he saw that Bud was just standing there. What was wrong with him? The sooner he got the beating over with, the sooner they could rescue Luke.

"Hurry. Please," Zach begged him.

A tear in his eye, Bud placed his hand gently on Zach's shoulder. Zach flinched. Maybe a beating wasn't enough for this big man. His hands were massive, which meant that his fists would really hurt. Zach just hoped he could remain conscious so he could tell them how to get to Luke.

"I'm not going to hit you, son, not with this stick," Bud said.

Zach turned to him. "Will you take the buckle off when you use it?" he asked, eyeing the rodeo buckle that Bud always wore.

"I am not going to hit you with my belt or a stick or my fists, son," Bud said.

"Yeah, dork-brain, Mom and Dad don't hit their kids," Seth interrupted, walking into the room with his thumbs hooked in his jeans, a piece of hay between his teeth.

"I'm not their kid," Zach said quietly with a glint of desperation in his eyes.

Bud hugged him, enveloping him in his strong warmth. "While you live in this house, Zach, you are my son. If we decide to part ways ... well, then that is something we will need to discuss."

"Where's Luke?" Grace asked, entering the room with Blake on her shoulder.

Zach began to shake. "He's hurt. He fell. Please, please come and help him. I know you love him. You adopted him. He's yours. Please come. Please." His body shuddered with the sobs that he refused to cry. In his experience, crying never made anything better.

Bud went very still and then rocketed into motion, slipping on his riding boots and his jacket while he spoke. "We *are* going to talk about why you disobeyed the rules tonight, Zachary," Bud said sternly. "But not until after we have your brother safe. Come now and show me where he is. Seth, would you like to come along?"

"Yup," Seth replied, suddenly serious. "I'll get my coat and boots."

Bud clapped Seth on the shoulder. "Good man." Then he moved over to the bewildered Zach and kissed him on the head. "Let's go find your brother."

"Don't forget your coat, Zach," Grace said, holding it out to him.

Zach rode with Seth on his bay mare, Clarice, leading the way to where Luke sat, propped against a tree, eating all the snacks Zach had pilfered for his journey into the wilderness.

"Hey, Daddy. Hey, Seth. I knew Zach would bring you," Luke said, his grin beaming from his face. "Can we adopt him now, Daddy?" he'd asked, and Bud had laughed long and loud as he scooped his second son into his arms and onto the back of his own gelding, Maurice.

CHAPTER 7

Zach stood gazing at the two-story red brick house where he and Christie had lived for their entire married life. They'd chosen Jordan because it was a small town, a village really, with that same small-town air that Zach had grown up in. Nestled in the Niagara region, it afforded beauty, proximity to Toronto, and fresh fruit. They had been happy here ... at one time.

It was three o'clock on Monday afternoon. Their burnt-orange Jeep Wrangler was missing from the driveway, and no one answered the doorbell. *Where are you, Christie?* Feeling a surge of frustration, Zach began a slow circuit of the house. Pausing to peer between the yellow-and-green curtains covering the bay window at the front of the house, Zach surveyed the living room, the muted yellow walls, the patterned green couch and chairs they'd purchased together a month after they'd bought the house. There was a bin overflowing with toys in the corner, a dozen or so toy dinosaurs scattered across the rug in the middle of the hardwood floor, and Gideon's train table, which Zach had constructed in another life. A plastic cup sat tipped on its side on the pine coffee table. It looked like home, though he possessed no proof of that fact. No key. No piece of identification that listed this as his address. No wife to welcome him in.

"Come on, Christie. Where are you?" Zach muttered angrily. There had been no flight out of Goose Bay until this morning, and he'd had to let his father front him the money for the flight from St. John's to Pearson International Airport in Toronto and a car rental from there to Jordan. Other than a temporary Newfoundland driver's license and a few of his father's dollars, he had nothing in his wallet and no key in his pocket. Furious, Zach slammed his palm against the corner of the house, the contact vibrating up his arm and only making him more agitated. Christie had neglected to leave him any way to gain entry to his own home.

Making up his mind, Zach continued his circuit of the house, looking for an open window or some other easy form of entry. Even the spare key was missing from the hook inside the shed door. So he retrieved a metal bucket from the shed and smashed the basement window. Carefully removing the shards he'd created, he surveyed the dimly-lit room to find a bookcase directly below him. Stretching, trying to ease the ache in his chest caused by the too-small seats of the airplane, Zach rotated his shoulders and then crouched low again to peer inside. Turning, he lowered himself into the basement and then looked directly up into the eyes of his wife. She was standing above him with one hand on her hip and one hand holding Gideon's.

"What in the name of Captain Kangaroo's Ping-Pong balls are you doing?" she demanded, her eyes narrowed in consternation.

"You didn't give me a key," he replied, all the frustration of the past several hours coating his words.

"You were in Goose Bay. You didn't need one," she replied, still watching him narrowly.

"Where have you been?" Embarrassment made him angrier. Here he was perched half in and half out of the basement window, feeling like a shoplifter caught with the stolen ice cream oozing down his pant leg.

"You're going to fix that, I hope," she said over her shoulder as she walked away.

Fix it? Yeah, I'll fix it. Hoisting himself back out of the basement, he retrieved the necessary boards and tools to cover the hole before following Christie and Gideon into the house. Entering through the front door now that it was unlocked, he almost knocked Gideon off his feet, earning himself a scowl from Christie.

"TV, TV, TV," Gideon continued chanting despite the near knock on the head, rocking up on his toes and flapping his arms.

"Take your shoes off, and go to the bathroom," Christie said. "Then you can watch television until suppertime."

Gideon dropped onto the deacon's bench by the front door and kicked off his shoes before he ran to the bathroom.

"You didn't answer my question," Zach said, seething with frustration. This homecoming was not at all going as he'd imagined.

"What question?" Christie asked absently as she bent to tidy Gideon's shoes.

"Where were you?" Was she serious?

"Speech therapy." She looked up at him. "You know, one of those appointments that aren't important." She paused on her way to the kitchen, turning back and eyeing him dubiously. "What are you doing here?"

Finally, a question he wanted to answer. "I came back," he said, spreading his arms to emphasize the point.

She snorted. "Obviously." The compassion he'd seen in her eyes in Goose Bay was nowhere to be found today. She eyed him with an assessing look, turning away when the kitchen telephone rang.

"Hello?" She glanced at Zach and then turned her back on him. "No, I don't think I can get away right now." A pause. "No. That babysitter didn't work out at all." A shorter pause. "Look, I appreciate your call, Carlos, but now's not a good time."

Carlos? Carlos gets her time while I get her back?

"Sure, that would be great. Another time. Bye." Christie hung up and walked to the refrigerator without giving Zach more than a brief glance.

Zach opened his mouth to ask her about the call and then stopped. What he really wanted to do was demand she tell him about every moment she'd spent with any other man while he'd been away. Even his imagination—especially his imagination—was green with jealousy at the moment. And red with anger. And blue with sorrow. But the color wheel of emotion was getting him nowhere.

"He's just checking in to see if I'm okay," she said before he could unclench his jaws enough to ask anything.

"Well, everything will be okay now. I'm back."

Crossing her arms, she leaned on the counter facing him as she replied laconically, "So?"

What did she mean, "So?"? He was home. Period. Zach's mind flashed back to Burgu Punës, transposing the frustration and helplessness of those days to today. To right now. *When does my prison sentence end?* Zach remained silent and fuming as Christie extracted sandwich meat, lettuce, tomatoes, and ketchup from the refrigerator.

When she didn't say anything, he did. "I came back. That's what you wanted, isn't it?" Zach did not succeed in keeping the temper from his voice.

"Oh. Of course," she replied with exaggeration. "And what does that mean for us?"

Why was she being so difficult? A wave of wrath rushed over his common sense, and he shouted, "Cut it out!"

"Too loud!" Gideon hollered.

"Sorry, sweetheart," Christie said, calling sweetly in to Gideon. She turned back to Zach, and there was no doubt that the sweetness allotted to Gideon would not transfer to his father. "Don't you dare yell at me again! You've no right," she said curtly, her eyes on fire.

"Well, you had no right to run away with my son," he said, clenching his teeth over his anger.

"I wanted you to return with us, but you wouldn't listen," she said in a terse whisper. "So I dealt with it on my own. I'm used to it."

Zach paled as he recognized Luke's message in her words.

Crimson fury permeated his thoughts. "I am part of this family," he said, tapping the counter with his finger to emphasize his point.

"Are you? *I* have certainly been the one coping with tantrums and eating problems, waiting lists, and therapy appointments."

Before he realized what he was doing, Zach's hand darted out and he grabbed her by the elbow, tightening his grip when she tried to pull away. His brain was telling him to "stop" and "let go," and he was suddenly so angry that he did, abruptly releasing her and stepping back, afraid of the depth of his emotional response.

"Fine." He had to get out of there before he did something really stupid. "I'm going for a drive," he said, reaching for the keys beside the back door.

Christie slammed the ketchup bottle on the counter. "Just like always. Nothing ever changes."

He stopped, still feeling the waves of fury beating at his chest. "What's that supposed to mean?" He gritted out the words.

"You walk away. Things don't go your way, and you exit the establishment. How do I know you're not going to drive away and join some other task force that lets you escape another year of autism?" She glared at him.

He clenched his fists in frustration. "I didn't want to leave." *Blast it!* If you weren't supposed to let the sun go down on your wrath, then you definitely shouldn't go to Albania in the middle of a family crisis. "I had no choice, not if I wanted any hope of a career."

"Well, you have no career now," she retorted, but then immediately he saw regret clearly printed in her eyes. Hauling in a breath, she seemed to be trying to calm down. "Sorry," she said as though the word was an obligation not a genuine response.

Her insincere apology did little to douse his anger. He wanted to punch something. But if he put a hole in the wall, she'd probably make him fix it. He needed to get away from her.

"A shower. Am I allowed to have a shower without being accused of desertion?" he asked harshly.

The sensation of losing control of his life weakened his knees and hollowed out his chest. *I hate this feeling!* Why did he always lose the things that mattered to him?

Feeling his body begin to shake, Zach clenched his muscles to hide it. He wasn't a defenseless child anymore. He wasn't a victim. He was a grown man, and he wasn't going to let anyone make him feel as disempowered as he'd felt as a boy again. But they had. They'd put him in prison, tied him to a chair, and beat him, and he'd been powerless to stop them. They'd stolen him away from his family, from the love of his life. And now?

Christie just stood there watching him with stormy eyes. But he couldn't begin to guess what she saw in *his* eyes. Whatever it was, it seemed to take some of the crimson out of her fury. When she finally moved, he felt he'd lived a lifetime of anticipation in a moment. And then she surprised him once again, reaching out to take his hand.

"I didn't, you know … intend to run away from you. But I needed to get back and you wouldn't come." She wasn't yelling, but there was no tenderness there. "These appointments are important."

"Important enough to—"

"Chocolate milk," Gideon said, appearing as if out of thin air or, perhaps, the mist of his parents' remorse.

Zach watched Christie immediately transform into a calm and patient mother. "It's almost suppertime, Giddy."

"Hmmm," Gideon murmured. "Grilled cheese sandwich and frozen peas."

Her soft smile reached out to the boy. "Chicken sandwiches with lettuce and tomatoes."

"Tomatoes. No," Gideon said.

"I don't like tomatoes," she said, and Zach watched and listened, fascinated by the conversation.

"No tomatoes," Gideon said, rocking up onto the balls of his feet and flapping his elbows.

"I want—" she said, but Gideon cut her off.

"No tomatoes. No tomatoes," he said, his voice rising quickly to approach a scream.

"Okay. No tomatoes," she said, quickly placating him. "You may have a chicken sandwich with just lettuce. Do you want mustard?" she asked and then quickly amended her question to a statement that he could copy, "No mustard."

Zach could see Gideon building up to another shouting session, but then he settled onto his feet and said, "Chicken sandwich. No mustard."

"Okay. Go watch TV, and I'll call you when it's ready," she said.

Gideon narrowed his eyes at her. "At the end."

"Yes, you can come at the end of the show," she said.

Gideon ran back into the other room, and soon Zach heard a repetitive thumping. He looked around the corner to see Gideon jumping on the couch.

"He needs the jumping now to calm down from the tomato question," Christie explained, smiling warmly at their son.

Christie's patience with Gideon shook the anger out of Zach and left him feeling isolated, without any idea of who he was anymore.

Studying him a moment, she asked, "Do you want a sandwich, too?"

"Yes," he said. "Please." At least she was going to feed him.

She scanned his body. "You've lost weight. We'll need to do some shopping."

"I am not spending the first few days of my freedom clothes shopping," Zach snapped at her. *What is wrong with me? There is absolutely nothing to be gained by squaring off against her.*

"Whatever." He could see hurt reflected in her eyes. "There are some clean towels on the dryer in the laundry room." There was no warmth in her voice; no surprise there given the fact that he couldn't seem to keep his emotional responses in line with the reality of the situation. "Do you want a root beer? I bought a case for you ... because I know it's your favorite ... well, used to be." Her voice trailed off to a mutter.

"Thank you." His voice was tight with the strain to sound falsely calm.

"You're welcome," she replied formally.

Zach stopped first at the laundry room to grab a towel, inhaling the fresh, clean scent. Once upstairs, Zach slipped into Gideon's train-adorned bedroom, spying a pink piglet puppet on the floor beside the bed. His brother Bobby had bought that puppet for Gideon on the day he was born. Bringing it to his face, Zach brushed the softness against his cheek and inhaled the odors of baby shampoo and feet. Why would Big Piglet smell like feet?

Zach's next stop was the master bedroom, but he didn't climb onto the bed. He didn't have the courage. He was absolutely uncertain how that part of their marriage was going to play out. She hadn't told him she loved him in what felt like forever, longer even than he'd been gone. He really had been an ostrich, sanding his head, if he hadn't realized that until now.

After stripping off, he stepped into the shower, cranked the hot tap as high as he could bear, and stood beneath the steamy spray. When the water began to cool, Zach turned it off and wrapped himself in the fluffy towel. The softness made him think of Christie and all he'd missed of her in the past year. He was desperate for so many things, sex with his beautiful wife, hugs from his little boy, and liberty. He was actually grateful that the OPP had let him go. Now he didn't have to worry about anything but getting back on his feet, getting his life back under control.

Descending to the kitchen, Zach saw Gideon sitting on a high stool at the counter eating his sandwich. Christie stood across from him. They were telling knock-knock jokes. Gideon would laugh hysterically at his own jokes and used the funniest fake laugh after Christie's.

"Come on over," Christie said to Zach, her voice hesitant but pleasant enough. "Supper's ready."

Zach sat quietly beside Gideon, eating and listening. When Gideon finished eating, he returned to the living room to play with his trains.

"It's so amazing to hear Gideon talking," Zach said.

Christie smiled. It was a fond smile that warmed his heart. "He started talking soon after you left. His first word was *dinosaur*," she said, her eyes soft with nostalgia. "Then he started repeating everything I said, and that's really how he still communicates. He's pretty good at getting his point across, but it certainly makes for unique conversations."

"I've missed so much," he said, and she seemed to cave in on herself. All Zach wanted to do was kiss the life back into her. So he did. He took one big step and hauled her against him, groaning at the feel of her soft body against his. They fit together so perfectly. Lowering his head, Zach kissed the curve of her jaw to the corner of her mouth, burying his fingers in her blonde curls, the warmth of her scalp radiating into his fingertips.

He turned his head to tell her how much he'd missed her, and her mouth was there, her lips parted on a sigh. So he kissed her, deeply, thoroughly, tasting everything he'd missed for the past year. As he pulled back enough to catch a breath, he realized that one of her hands was fisted in his hair, holding his head just so, and the other was spread wide across his backside.

"Baby," he whispered. Then he lifted her to sit on a stool and stepped between her knees. She wrapped her legs around him, her heels digging into the backs of his legs.

"I just want everything to go back to normal again," he said, but then he wished he'd kept his mouth shut because she put her hands on his shoulders and he just knew that she was going to push him away.

"That's not what I want," she whispered. "Not at all."

CHAPTER 8

Stunned, Zach didn't resist when Christie slipped away from him. Her entire manner transformed as she approached Gideon. Speaking to him in a calm, pleasant, and playful voice, she warned him that they were going for a walk at the next commercial. She sat beside him, discussing the show he was watching, some ridiculous cartoon, and at the next commercial, she counted down and then turned the television off.

After sending him to the bathroom first, she then waited patiently as Gideon fussed and fumed about putting his socks and shoes on and pulling on a sweater and hat. Zach moved quickly to catch Christie before she walked out the door, stopping her with a light touch on her arm.

"Where are you going?" he asked, keeping his voice hard and firming his lips so that she wouldn't see them tremble. Was she abandoning him? Already? Without even a chance at redemption? This day just kept going from bad to rat-crap worse, and then worse again.

"We'll walk up the escarpment behind the house to the road there, to the left for about a mile or more and then back the same way," she said, her voice clipped and cold.

So, temporary abandonment only, he realized with some measure of relief. He considered following her but decided that the last thing he wanted was to make her angrier with him, so he stayed behind. He meant to wash the supper dishes but got distracted by the television. It had been a long time since he had been in a position to relax in front of the goggle box. Zach drifted off to sleep. He was still there an hour and a half later when Christie and Gideon returned, waking to find Gideon standing beside his leg and staring at him.

"Hello," Zach said, smiling hopefully.

"TV," Gideon said. There was no expression on his face.

"Do you want to watch television?"

"Watch television? Yes," Gideon replied.

Zach passed him the remote control, but Gideon didn't sit down as Zach expected; he just kept staring at him.

"What's wrong?" Zach asked.

"In your spot?"

"What?" Zach said, confused.

"In your spot?" Gideon asked again, louder this time.

Zach glanced around nervously to see if Christie was watching him, but she was still out of view. So she couldn't see the mess he was making of this conversation.

"Spot, spot, spot!" Gideon shouted, pushing at Zach's leg and shoulder.

"Whoa, honey. Calm down," Zach said, putting up his hands to try to appease his son.

"MommyMommyMommyMommy!" Gideon wailed. Zach panicked, standing to try to get a little height, hoping it would lend him wisdom. Gideon scooted into the spot that Zach had just vacated. Still sniffling, Gideon pointed the remote at the television at the same time that he shoved Zach's leg out of the way.

Zach was stunned. He looked at Gideon, at the television, and then walked away, stopping abruptly when he saw Christie watching him while drying her hands on a towel.

He felt completely defeated. "I … uh … I think I'll turn in. It was a long day," Zach muttered and walked toward the stairs to the second floor. He stopped, realizing he'd forgotten to consider one important factor in his escape. "Uh, where … uh … where should I sleep?"

Christie stopped drying her hands. "Where do you want to sleep?"

Zach stole a glance at her face, but he couldn't read her expression. Feeling needy and embarrassed, he simply dropped his gaze back to the floor.

Sighing, he admitted, "With you," in a whisper. He glanced up when she didn't respond. She nodded, and he chose to take that as permission. Turning, he headed back toward the stairs.

"Zach," Christie said. He stopped walking though he didn't turn toward her. "You don't really know him."

A clot of emotion lodged in Zach's throat. He needed to get upstairs, or he was going to lose control and throw up, not an outcome he desired. Nodding once, he dragged himself upstairs where he lay facedown on the bed. Zach was heartsick.

Slowly and reluctantly Christie climbed the stairs to bed ... where she would find her husband ... who was "back." What did that mean for Christie and Gideon? That was the question plaguing her. Zach was a year late dealing with his inability to accept his son. And that made her angry ... and afraid. Zach seemed to want to skip right over the part where she was allowed to vent her griefs, the feelings of betrayal she carried from the one person on earth that she should have been able to trust without question.

Christie braced herself and opened the bedroom door. The bathroom light was on, painting the room in a soft glow. She could see the shape in the bed that was Zach, turned on his side away from her, and she could hear him breathing deeply in sleep.

A wave of tenderness swept through her as she approached him, reaching out to brush his hair back from his face, to once again feel the thick softness in her fingers. He had the most luxuriously thick honey-gold hair. Tomorrow most likely he would get it cut. He'd never liked his hair long.

As she buried her fingers in the thickness, Zach moved, suddenly, in a blur of motion, grabbing her wrist in an unbreakable hold. He twisted her arm behind her as he fisted the collar of her shirt.

She squealed in surprise. "It's me, Zach," she gasped, her cheek pressed to the wall.

"Turn on the light," he ordered, his voice hard and uncompromising.

Her free hand shaking, her knees weak with trepidation, she reached out and flipped on the bedside lamp. He released her immediately.

"Oh, no!" he gasped. "Christie." When he attempted to turn her body toward him, she resisted, pulling away and backing to the wall. Her eyes followed his every twitch and shudder, flinching away when he took a step toward her. She couldn't miss the misery in his eyes.

"I'm really sorry. I was sleeping, and suddenly, I felt this presence over me. I was—I'm just—sorry."

Christie could feel her entire body shaking. She rubbed her wrist where he'd grabbed her, trying to wipe away the hurt and fright. Who was this man that wore the physical characteristics of her husband but in no way resembled him? Where was her tender sweetheart? He had been missing for so long, much longer than Albania and autism.

"It's okay," she said, unable to control the quiver of her voice. "I'll just get ready for bed." She darted to the dresser, scooped a pair of pajamas out of the drawer, and fled into the bathroom, locking the door behind her. Once inside, she grabbed a towel from the rack and pushed it against her face to muffle her sobs.

After a time, a soft knock sounded on the door. "Christie?" It was Zach. *Duh!* Who else would it be? "Honey, I'm really sorry. You startled me, and I just ... reacted." He was silent for a moment. "Will you please come out? I won't hurt you. I give you my word."

"Just a minute," she managed to say. She washed her face, brushed her hair and teeth, and changed into her pajamas, wishing she'd grabbed the flannel PJs rather than the pink flowered nightie she now wore, so she would feel less vulnerable.

Taking a bracing breath, she opened the door. When she hesitated in the doorway, Zach took a few steps back as though to provide a zone of safety for her.

"That won't happen again, Christie," he said, his expression hidden in the shadow created by the bathroom light. Reaching back, she switched it off, relegating his features to vague angles and lines.

"It's okay," she said. "I ... I shouldn't have touched you."

"It's all right to touch me," he said, and she could hear the frustration in his voice. "I was just sleeping so deeply, and I forgot where I was."

"It's okay," she said in what she hoped was a soothing tone of voice.

His entire body went rigid as he yelled at her, "Stop saying 'It's okay' when it's obviously not 'okay'! You won't let me near you!" Drawing in a terse breath through his clenched jaws, fists pressed to his belly, Zach muttered, "Sorry."

Wrapping herself in a hug, she simply nodded at him because she didn't know what to say. Was he sorry? Yes, she believed that. But had prison changed him in some fundamental way from which he would never recover? He was so angry and aggressive. Was this the new Zach?

It had been anathema to her to consider going back to the way things used to be, to emotional distance and the evasion of reality. But this could be much worse.

"Don't look at me like that!" he insisted and that finished it for her.

Pointing to the door, she yelled, "Enough!"

She kept expecting him to open the door and walk away, but he remained, his shoulders rising and falling with the frication of his respiration. He was the picture of furious misery, and she suspected that this had become his natural state.

Christie wondered if anything would ever be right between them or if it ever had been. Had she really loved this man at one time? Did she ever want to again? Or would he simply break her heart repeatedly until she herself broke into pieces?

His shoulders slumped in defeat. "If that's what you want," he muttered and slammed out the door. Christie heard a second slam down the hall in the spare room.

Fortunately, on the rare occasions when Gideon actually slept, he slept with true devotion and nothing could wake him. Checking on him, she found him asleep in a nest of pillows and blankets with his beloved Big Piglet clutched in his hand. Then she went to bed. Alone.

CHAPTER 9

Zach lay on his back in the too-blue spare room studying the hairline cracks in the ceiling. His mind saw only the cracks in his life. Fear. That had been the expression in Christie's eyes when he'd grabbed her: pure fear. How did he come to be the sort of man who made his wife afraid of him, who prompted a screaming tantrum in his son just by being there?

Groaning aloud his misery, Zach flopped onto his side in the double bed, trying to ease the miasma in his stomach. He had wanted to find his way back into Christie's life and, yes, into her bed. He needed it. He needed the comfort of the physical side of their relationship. Oh, he wasn't asking for sex, not yet. He instinctively knew that she wouldn't give herself to him until she trusted him. And he'd blown that this evening, all day in fact. He just wanted to be loved. *Oh, God, make her see. Make her understand. Make her love me.*

Zach flopped to his other side, his eyes lighting on the Bible on the bedside table. What was it the Bible said about love? *Love is patient.* Yeah, he wasn't going to win any prizes for that. What else? *Love is kind.* He certainly hadn't been very kind to Christie.

An immense bubble of grief welled within, and he jerked up from the bed and launched himself at the bathroom across the hall, losing the contents of his stomach, some weird biological attempt to purge himself of his grief and guilt. His ribs throbbed as the heaving seemed to go on forever.

"Zach?" He heard a soft knock on the door and Christie's voice as the door clicked open. "Are you all right?"

"Fine," he gasped stalwartly. Another spasm seized his gut, and he groaned at the pain from his sore ribs.

Christie touched his back lightly. "I'll be right back." Soon, he heard her footsteps on the stairs.

The spasms eased, and he relaxed his hold on his ribs. First wiping his mouth on some toilet paper, he then flushed the toilet. He slumped against the wall, defeated by the day, the week, the year. Christie returned with a washcloth. After soaking the washcloth at the sink, she crouched beside him and washed his face. The cool cloth felt wonderful on his hot, clammy skin.

Tossing the cloth into the sink, she sat on the floor beside him, but not too close, resting her back against the wall.

"I didn't do it, Christie," Zach said.

Casting him a sidelong glance, she asked, "Didn't do what?"

She didn't sound as though she was being purposely obtuse, but he wasn't sure. Before, he would have said that he knew her inside and out, knew what she was thinking all the time, but now? ... He wasn't sure anymore.

"Buy the drugs. Take the drugs."

"I know," she whispered.

"Then why are you so angry with me?" Shifting sideways, he studied her profile, desperate for an answer.

"I don't want to do this right now," she whispered, rising.

He grasped her arm, tugging to encourage her to sit back down beside him. "Christie," he said, trying to keep the word from sounding like a reprimand. What was her problem anyway?

Now, she was looking him directly in the face. And he was afraid that he was about to hear far more than he'd counted on. "Want to know why I'm angry?" Her features were fierce, and there was fire in her eyes. "You left me. You were so unable to cope with having a son who was imperfect, you walked away. You left me alone to deal with autism." She shoved him in the chest. "And I don't mean Albania. You left me the minute the developmental pediatrician gave Gideon his diagnosis.

Or maybe you really left me on his first birthday when I told you that I thought there was something wrong with our son, that he wasn't going to be the person we thought he would be, and you wouldn't even entertain the idea of having more children. I don't know why it mattered so much because ... because ... he is ..."

Too much. Despair assaulted Zach, and he moved to stand. *Forget love.* "I don't want to hear this." Pushing up off his knees, he made it one step toward the bathroom door and then stopped, unable to walk away.

"Do you remember the last thing you said to me before our life fell apart?"

Slumping down on the closed commode, he said, "No," his voice softer now.

"You said you wished we'd never had kids. You wished our son out of existence. It seemed that, although you were willing to clothe, bathe, and feed your son, you were not willing to face up to the reality of autism; if autism was on the cards, I was on my own to deal with it."

Gulp. "I can't erase the words I said, but believe me, I would if I could. I was grieving. I wanted you to be as sad and angry as I was. But you took it all in stride," he said, accusing her. But of what? Being well adjusted? He shook his head to dispel his confusing thoughts.

"Do you think I didn't grieve? Do you think I didn't imagine our entire future permanently shifted in a new direction? It hurt me, too, Zach." Dragging in a shuddering breath, Christie walked away without a backward glance.

Zach didn't know what to do, primarily because he didn't want to hear any more of her thoughts or opinions. His chest ached. No, his chest throbbed from throwing up. It was his heart that ached.

Love. He loved his little family, and he was willing to do what he needed to in order to keep it. So Zach followed Christie to the doorway of Gideon's room.

"He's perfect," she said belligerently, obviously sensing Zach's approach.

Careful not to touch her, he peered over her shoulder. "Yes," he said. "He has your eyes and your mouth."

"But your honey-gold hair. Water rolls off it like a duck's feathers. And he smiles the same way you do, with that quirky half-grin."

Seeing the corner of her mouth rise toward a smile, he took a risk and moved in close behind her, placing his hands gently on her hips. She stiffened at the contact but didn't pull away.

"It's not autism that's the problem," Zach said, keeping his voice low.

"Then what?" she said, her voice demanding his response.

At the snap in her voice, Zach started to retreat and then stopped. If he walked away now, he might never resolve this with Christie, might never have his life back.

But Christie didn't want their old life back. So what did that leave?

When he didn't immediately respond, she lost patience, pulling away from him. He tightened his grip on her hips.

"I was overwhelmed," he said.

She settled back into place.

"Because of having a special needs child?"

"No." Now it was his turn to sigh. Zach knew that this had become a crucial moment in his future. *Yes.* That was what he wanted, a future—with Christie and Gideon.

"I'm going to just come right out and admit it." He blew out a breath. "I was afraid that you didn't love me anymore. You love Gideon so much more than me, and I was afraid that if we kept having children, there'd be nothing left for me."

As she turned abruptly in his arms, he forced himself not to flinch away, but the anger he expected was absent and in its place was sorrow.

"I never realized..." she began and then just wrapped him in a warm and tender embrace. His arms closed around her. He didn't flinch at the pain in his ribs. He simply held on tight.

CHAPTER 10

The walls were yellow. That was good. There were trains on the wall. That was good. This was his bedroom. He was home from Goose Bay. Gideon pulled Big Piglet to his face and breathed him in. Big Piglet smelled right. Big Piglet smelled like home.

"Mommy," Gideon called.

Something was new. New was bad. When something new happened, Gideon didn't know what would happen next. Sometimes new things were scary. Sometimes new things were loud or smelled bad. You just never knew with new things.

"Mommy!" Gideon called again.

There was a man in the house. It wasn't Grandpa or Uncle Luke or Uncle Seth or Uncle Blake. It wasn't Bobby. Bobby liked trains. Gideon liked trains, especially blue trains. And blue dinosaurs. Haha. That was funny. Dinosaurs were green or brown but not blue.

"Mommy!" Gideon called again. Where was Mommy?

"Good morning, Gideon. How are you?" Finally, Mommy came.

"Six thirty?" Gideon asked.

"Not yet. Want breakfast early today?" Mommy asked.

No, no, no, Gideon thought.

Mommy asked another question, sort of the same but not really. "Giddy, do you want to eat breakfast early?"

Didn't she listen? Maybe if I use the polite words. "No, thank you," he said.

The bed moved, but then Mommy was holding him and it didn't

matter. *Oh, now she's rocking.* Rocking with Mommy was good. Singing. No new songs. Mommy was the best.

Mommy held up her watch to show Gideon. "What time is it?" she asked.

"Six thirty. Time for breakfast. I want pancakes with syrup. No butter," he told her.

"Okay, my sweet. I'll see what I can do. Before we go downstairs, I want you to come see Daddy," Mommy said.

That was new.

"TV. TV. TV." Gideon liked to watch television when new things happened. His favorite shows always made him feel better.

"First, we'll see Daddy and then TV," Mommy said.

"Zach is Daddy. Daddy Albania. Daddy home," Gideon said, replaying all the things he knew about Daddy.

"Yes. Daddy is Zach, and Daddy is home," Mommy said. "Come see Daddy."

"Okay," Gideon agreed, taking her hand and following as she led him to Mommy's room. She opened the door. Purple room. Yuck. Purple was a bad color except on some flowers. Purple was Zurg. Purple was Kang. No one liked purple.

The bed moved, and then suddenly, a man was there, a big shadow across his face. Gideon had seen the man yesterday. The man had sat in Gideon's spot. That was bad.

"Don't even think of jumping on the bed. He's not feeling well," Mommy said.

Grrr. Gideon wanted to jump on the bed, but Mommy said the man wasn't feeling well. Not-feeling-well people didn't like to be jumped on—especially Grandpa.

"Gideon, say hi to Daddy," Mommy said.

But Daddy was the picture of the police officer. He didn't belong there in Mommy's bed. Gideon looked at Mommy, but she looked okay. She said he was Daddy.

"Hi, Daddy," Gideon said. That was what you were supposed to say to people when you met them.

"Hi, Gideon," Daddy said.

Gideon found the shadows in the room and watched them through his fingers. It helped Gideon feel better.

"Do you think I could hug him?" Daddy asked.

Mommy touched Gideon's shoulder. Her touch broke through the warm haze of the shadows, and Gideon blinked once so he could hear better.

"Give Daddy a hug," Mommy said.

Gideon opened his arms and waited for the man—Daddy—to hug him. "Ahhh." It was a great hug, firm and long, and it felt so good. "Good hug."

Daddy laughed a funny laugh. There were lots of words for laugh: *giggle, guffaw, chuckle*. Mommy said they were happy words. She even spelled them for Gideon. C-H-U-C-K-L-E. Seven letters.

"How are you feeling, Zach?" Mommy asked.

"Pretty wiped," Zach replied.

"Wipe your feet," Gideon replied, remembering where that word was usually used.

Daddy laughed again.

"What time is it?" Gideon asked. Daddy moved his head and shoulders, but Gideon didn't know why.

"Six forty," Mommy said.

"Oh, no!" Gideon said. This was terrible. "Six thirty breakfast."

"Come on, Giddy. We'll leave Daddy to get some more sleep," Mommy said.

"I'm okay. I'll have a shower and come help with breakfast," said Daddy.

"That would be nice," Mommy said.

Zach descended the stairs to the kitchen after showering and dressing. Gideon was perched on a high-backed stool at the countertop, still dressed in his blue train pajamas. He played with a couple of plastic dinosaurs while Christie stood at the stove flipping pancakes and singing about David and Goliath.

"Daniel," Gideon said, and Christie seamlessly changed to a new song as she turned to set a plate in front of him.

"Can I help?" Zach asked when she spotted him.

"Chocolate milk," Gideon replied, clearly assuming that Zach was talking to him.

"I'll see what I can do." Relieved to have a simple, positive task to complete, Zach opened the fridge and peered inside.

"I've already got the milk out, Zach. It's here if you want to pour him a glass." Christie pointed with the spatula in her hand.

Ignoring the slight rebuke in her voice, Zach poured the chocolate milk into a glass and put it on the counter in front of Gideon. He reached over, unable to resist the urge to run his fingers lightly through the boy's thick hair. Gideon pushed his hand away with an "unh."

"He doesn't like light touches. He processes firm touches better," Christie said. "Nora, that's the OT, said that's probably why he's always hated getting his hair cut."

"Blue," Gideon said.

"Pardon?" Zach asked, turning back to his son. *Blue what?*

"Blue. Blue, blue, blue!" Gideon quickly escalated to quite upset.

"You don't need the blue cup today, Gideon. Use the glass that Daddy gave you."

"Does he want a blue cup?" Zach asked, confused by the interplay.

"Just because he wants the same cup every day doesn't mean he needs it," Christie said. Now she was annoyed with him. *Yeesh,* he couldn't win.

"Sorry, buddy." He'd be happy to give Gideon a Ming vase to drink from if it would make him smile.

But instead Gideon threw his dinosaurs onto the floor. "My name not Buddy. My name Gideon!"

Zach flinched back from him. *What did I do wrong? Everything was happy not two minutes ago and then I come in and ... whammo!*

"Gideon, pick up those dinosaurs now," Christie said. She was stern as she stood there, the spatula in the hand propped on her hip.

"Pick up those dinosaurs. No," Gideon replied, never meeting her gaze.

Zach moved to intervene.

"No, Zach." Christie's words stopped him.

What is going on here?

"Gideon, look at me," Christie said. "Gideon."

Heaving a loud sigh, which made Zach want to laugh, Gideon looked at his mother.

"Do I look happy?" she asked.

"Happy? No. How are you feeling, Mommy?" Gideon asked, looking confused.

"I'm angry. It is not okay to throw toys when you're mad. Pick up the dinosaurs." The expression on Christie's face was surely exaggerated.

"Don't you think you're overreacting?" Zach said, and then suddenly, the anger was all directed at him. More uncertain than ever, he suggested, "I, uh, can pick up the dinosaurs."

"Don't you dare," she said sternly. "Gideon."

Gideon looked down to the floor and then back to his mother, a look of apprehension crossing his features. "Help me. Down." His eyes flitted to Zach.

Feeling utterly bewildered, Zach glanced over at Christie for some sort of clue. *What am I supposed to do?*

"Help me," Gideon repeated. His hands clutched the sides of the stool.

"Help him, Zach," Christie said, and she sounded disgusted with him.

Hands shaking slightly, Zach reached over and picked Gideon up under the armpits. He set him on the floor. Gideon picked up the dinosaurs, set them on the countertop, and then stood toe-to-toe with Zach, looking up at him.

"Um," Zach began, flicking a glance to Christie and then back to his son.

"Up, please," Christie said, but she was looking at Gideon.

"Up, please," Gideon repeated, and then he lifted up his arms. Zach picked him up and set him back on his stool.

Everything was so happy until I walked in. "I'll, uh, go have a shower." Since he'd showered once already, it was a feeble exit strategy. Fear and anger knotted inside him. Halfway up the stairs, a wave of nausea hit, accompanied by grim understanding. *I don't have a clue how to interact with my own son.*

CHAPTER 11

Zach was feeling disheartened, more so than he'd felt in a good long time. He'd thought interrogation was frustrating, being bound and forced to suffer with no hope of reprieve, but this was worse because this *was* his hope, his love, his future.

He tried sitting back and watching Christie, but none of it made sense to him. Christie played games called Pete's a Pizza and Hot Dog with Gideon, but Zach couldn't see the point. They built castles with blocks, played with a toy farm set, and even engaged in simple board games. All Gideon really wanted to do was line things up, but Christie persisted with this other type of play by sometimes following what Gideon wanted to do and then changing it, by introducing new ideas to the play, and by insisting on being a part of his play. But when Zach tried to join in, he inevitably triggered an angry tantrum or complete sobbing meltdown in his son. Christie was short-tempered and impatient ... with him not his son. With Gideon, she was perfectly calm.

Zach just couldn't sort it out, and his total lack of success forced his terror to the surface, followed closely by anger at Gjojak, the Albanian mafia, Rig Zimmerman, and even Carlos Rivera for passing on Zimmerman's suspicions and ... and ... and Christie. She wasn't doing one thing to make this easier. All she had to offer him was criticism. "When you do that, it makes him feel irritable. When you say it that way, he doesn't know what you mean. Nora says ... Sandi says ... Blah, blah, blah."

And when Christie wasn't criticizing him, she was asking questions about prison. Zach didn't want to talk about prison. He didn't even want to think about the humiliation, degradation, and impotent fury. He simply wanted to forget, bury it deep beneath Janice and foster care.

Week followed week for three quarters of a month. As usual, this Thursday, Christie was already up and gone from bed when Zach awoke at 7:30 a.m. He didn't bother expending the effort to shower. He simply wandered downstairs in his pajamas.

Near the bottom of the stairs, he heard Christie's voice.

"It's all such a mess, Bud. I don't know what to do. He's angry all the time. Everything sets him off." Zach could hear the frustration in her voice.

Is she talking about Gideon?

She paused, obviously listening. "No, he hasn't raised a hand to me or Gideon. He did grab me by the wrist the other night. He was so aggressive."

Oh, crap, she's talking about me.

Christie paused again, and Zach heard her sniffling. "Yes. He was asleep." She paused. "Do you think so?" She paused. "I wish he would tell me what it was like there. But I can see what you're saying. Can you email me the article? I'll try anything." She paused. "I was thinking of asking Luke to come and stay for a few days. They've always been so close. Maybe he could get Zach to talk." She sniffed again. "Thanks, Bud. I love you, too."

Zach heard the water in the kitchen sink and realized that she must be washing her face to cover her tears. Yesterday, he'd accused her of using her tears as a weapon against him. Guilt speared him. He was such a load.

"Okay, Gideon, time to go see Staci. Brush your teeth, and wash your face," she called across the house.

Zach came out of hiding. "Morning," he said, keeping his voice even.

She adopted a deer-in-the-headlights expression, so she had enough awareness of his feelings to feel guilty at sneaking around and talking to his father.

"Good morning. I thought you might sleep a little later," she said as though she wished that he had.

"You going out?" he asked.

She nodded.

A suspicion prompted his next question. "To work?"

"Yes. I have classes all day."

"Classes? Are you in training or something?" he asked, quirking a brow.

"I got a new job. I'm teaching in the paramedic program at Niagara College."

"Oh," was his intelligent response. He hadn't even considered her job. She just came and went from the house, saying that he needed to rest, so she would take Gideon with her. How long had she been back at work? And where did Gideon go while she was working? A brief and disturbing thought occurred to him and then lingered.

"Bathroom all done," Gideon said, hopping into the room. "Ready to go."

"Where are you taking him?" Zach asked.

"Gideon, you can play dinosaurs for a few minutes." He could see that she was building up to something. "I'm taking Gideon to the babysitter's."

"I can—oh, I see." Zach's mood darkened. "I used to be good enough to look after him but not anymore. What? Do you think I'm going—I can't even guess what you're thinking."

"Don't you get all angry with me! If you could go more than fifteen minutes without provoking a tantrum …" She paused and then added in a mutter, "… or having one, then I'd feel more comfortable leaving him with you."

"Fine," he conceded ungallantly. "For the record, I don't appreciate you talking to my father behind my back."

Her mouth was a grim line. "This isn't working."

What did she mean? That was it? She was done with him? No. *I can't lose her. I need more time.* "So, that's it? I get three weeks and then pfft?" He snapped his fingers in her face. She flinched away and then met his gaze again, an unreadable expression on her face.

A dark pit opened at his feet. He was going to lose everything. Who was he kidding? The day of his arrest, he'd lost everything. It had simply taken a year for the illusion to fade, the illusion that he had a life to return to, that there was such a thing as perfect love in the world.

"Fine." The edge of granite pierced his voice. "Why don't you just call a lawyer and get a divorce?" Zach glanced over at Gideon playing with his dinosaurs on the dining room floor. "Take him from me, too." He gestured at his son, plunging on recklessly. "He screams every time I get near him anyway. Leave me with nothing."

Christie watched him for a long time, but he could discern nothing from her expression. Standing tall, he refused to back down. What would be the point? He'd lost everything already.

Finally, she moved, but not to speak, she moved to the phone. He panicked, darting over and covering her hand where it pressed the receiver.

"No. Please. Give me another chance, a little more time." A wave of nausea hit him, and he pressed his abdomen with his free hand to try to settle his stomach. Christie's eyes followed the movement. "I'll try harder. Please, Christie."

"Your dad's been doing some reading on the psychological effects of imprisonment."

Zach's eyes widened in astonishment. That was the dead last thing he'd expected her to say.

"He says that in prison, you have to learn to be alert all the time, even in your sleep. He says that feelings of powerlessness can lead to anger, fear, and, uh, stuff. A-aggressive interrogation can mean a lot of things like pain or humiliation. He says they might have even, uh, you know, beat you and, uh …" He watched sorrow collect in her eyes. "Your father said that was probably why you grabbed me by the wrist that night. Your subconscious just instinctively went into self-protection mode. He said you probably didn't know it was me, that you didn't even wake up until you were on your feet." He could hear the tug of sympathy in her voice. "Is that true?"

"No. I mean yes." Swallowing hard, he continued, "I was at risk. They would tie me up … helpless … couldn't make it stop … could've done anything to me that they wanted to do." That was the most he'd spoken of his prison experience with anyone.

"I wasn't using the phone to call a lawyer, Zach. And I didn't mean to say that we're not working. I meant that this situation isn't working—the situation where you tell me nothing, cover everything you're feeling beneath this anger, which I guess is supposed to protect you. It's not working for me to pretend it doesn't hurt every time you shut me out or every time I see the pain you're in. That's what's not working." She stepped toward him slowly, one step and then two before she touched his arm lightly and then pressed her palm against his chest over his heart. "I know you're hurting."

"Who—" Zach cleared his throat to force his vocal cords into action. "Then who were you going to call?"

"I'm going to cancel my lectures today and tomorrow. And then I'm going to call the counselor that I've been seeing and see if I can get us an appointment today."

"Okay," he whispered in reply. She moved away, and he missed the warmth of her hand immediately.

"Are you ready?" Gideon asked, bouncing over to them.

Christie smiled sweetly at him, pausing in dialing the phone. "Red alert. Red alert," she said, and Zach looked back and forth between them, trying to decipher their secret code. "Change of plans. Change of plans means..." She tucked the phone against her ear and held her hands out, palms up toward Gideon.

"Unexpected things," Gideon said.

Zach could see the tension in his body. Gideon rocked up onto his toes and flapped his elbows. His brow was furrowed, and he was clearly contemplating something. Whether or not to scream was Zach's guess. He braced himself for the auditory explosion.

"No Staci?" Gideon asked.

"No Staci," Christie replied.

"No preschool?" Gideon asked.

She chuckled. "No preschool."

"Stay with Mommy and Daddy," he said, and Zach felt a burst of joy in his chest. He'd called him Daddy.

"Stay with Mommy and Daddy. We will have errands to run, but I don't know what time. We will get some French fries for lunch today," she said.

"Red?" Gideon asked.

"Yes, because you stayed very calm even though we had a change of plans. Come here for a big hug," she said, crouching down and holding out her arms. Gideon ran into her embrace, nearly knocking her over with the force of impact. "Now, I need to make some phone calls. Gideon," she began, waiting until he looked at her face. "Show Daddy your trains."

Gideon frowned. "Don't touch!"

"He won't touch them. You can show them, and he will listen." Christie glanced up at Zach's face as she said those last words. Zach nodded. He well remembered the huge tantrum he'd elicited when he had tried to play with Gideon by hiding one of his trains in his pocket. So the trick was to look and listen. No touching.

Zach crouched down beside Gideon. "Gideon, can I see your trains? I promise no touching unless you tell me it's okay."

Gideon turned to him, his brow furrowed in concentration, and then his face brightened. "See your trains," he said and then raced into the living room.

Zach stood, overwhelmed by emotion for a moment. The sensation felt surprisingly like he remembered happiness used to feel.

"Thank you," he said to Christie. She smiled a little sadly. Zach kissed her on the cheek, unable to resist running his fingers over her soft blonde curls where they framed her face. He swallowed hard. "You've been seeing a counselor?"

"Yes. Since you left. Your dad said it might help."

"Daddy! Trains!" Gideon called from the other room.

"You better go," Christie said. Her voice was a barely audible whisper. And, oh, how he wanted to taste those lips. But it would have to wait. Trains came first.

CHAPTER 12

Chuckling spitefully, Burim Gjojak propped his booted feet on the antique desk in the office of his family's villa on the outskirts of Memaliaj, Albania. He took a great deal of pleasure in defacing the historical works of art that his cleaning staff were fanatical about preserving. This desk was said to have belonged to Ismail Qemali, hero of Albanian independence, founder of the modern Albanian state. Gjojak dug his heels in again, marking the wood. There was to be no independence in Albania if he could help it. And he could.

Stretching back to take in the view from his picture window, Gjojak noted the heavy clouds obscuring the bleak, rocky peaks of the surrounding mountains. *Mut! It is another dreary day in a dry and dusty land.* Albania was such a depressing place to spend time. After three years in the Niagara region in Canada, Gjojak's tolerance for dirt and dull was greatly diminished. However, the benefits of life in Albania, rife as it was with political and economic chaos, were abundant. It was the perfect breeding ground for crime ... and profit. Ah, yes, the perfect place from which to run an empire.

Now that heroin was flowing back into the Niagara region, profits were rising again. The Canadian task force had been so close to scuttling his enterprise without ever realizing how close they'd been. Marek had been the one to uncover Gjojak's process for transportation. Gjojak chuckled to himself. *Tarallak!* These agencies with all their alphabet of acronyms could not hope to defeat his genius. Now that he had Thomason where he wanted him, it was only a matter of the right word in the right guerrilla's ear and one more problem would cease to exist. *What a pleasant thought that is*, he mused, savoring the idea. Gjojak's grin grew.

Christie sat in the reception area of the counselor's office drawing trains for Gideon. She drew the train, and he added the face. The occupational therapist, Nora, had told her that pencil and paper didn't have to be tedious and academic to be useful. Anything that got Gideon to put a writing utensil on a flat surface was therapy. The speech therapist, Sandi, had told her to use Gideon's interests to teach him new skills. Well, he loved trains. Period. And, recently, dinosaurs, though less so.

Christie glanced at her watch. Zach had been in with Mildred Baines, PhD, for fifty-seven minutes. And it was her turn next. Christie had been able to speak with Dr. Baines on the phone when she'd called to get the appointment. She'd laid out her main concerns at that time, but Dr. Baines still wanted to meet with her in person.

"Caroline, Mommy," Gideon said.

"Hmm?" She brought her attention back to the task at hand. "I don't know her. What kind of engine is she?"

"Not an engine," Gideon said, and then he adopted a particular voice and intonation pattern, which Christie realized mimicked the narrator on one of their British train videos. "Caroline is a vintage automobile. She enjoys a leisurely drive with her friends along the country roads."

Christie laughed. When they had told her that kids with autism were gestalt learners, Christie had had no idea what they were talking about. But now she got it. He focused on the entirety of a situation, the whole. Gideon didn't just learn about Caroline from the video. He memorized the name, the words, the accent, and the pictures on the screen. If someone with a different voice tried to give him the same information, he'd never tolerate it because changing one piece of the whole changed it all for him. Just like the time she'd had her hair straightened. Gideon had yelled at her in blank grief, "I hate your hair!" and had spent the next month trying to curl it around his fingers, to make her back into "Mommy."

The door to the office opened, intruding on her thoughts.

"Here's my card, Mr. Marek. Please feel free to contact the office at any time. There is always a counselor on call," Dr. Baines said.

Zach nodded, pocketing the card. He looked different, not happy or sad, just perhaps a little relieved.

"I'd like to speak with you now, Mrs. Marek," Dr. Baines said.

Christie nodded and then began to root around in the bag of goodies she'd brought to amuse Gideon. But she couldn't find the gaming system she thought she'd packed so that Gideon could watch a video while she was in with the counselor. Panic clutched her. *I can't talk about Zach with Gideon in the room with me. And I don't want to put Zach through another tantrum.* Zach had made it through the morning without agitating his son, but he was such an autism newbie in so many ways. Her thoughts trailed off. Christie looked up to find both Dr. Baines and Zach eyeing her curiously.

"I forgot a video for Gideon," she explained.

Zach's brow furrowed. Dr. Baines looked interested.

"There's a doughnut shop downstairs," Dr. Baines said.

Christie blushed. Of course, she should have thought of that. She could have better spent her time getting a snack and chocolate milk for Gideon than coloring trains.

"I ... do you mind waiting a few minutes while I get him a snack?" Christie asked.

"His father can take him," Dr. Baines said and then turned to face Zach. "Feel free to bring the food and drinks here to consume. I'll ask the receptionist to find a children's program for your return." She nodded over her shoulder at the flat-screen television in the corner of the room, which had been broadcasting news for the past hour. "Please come with me, Mrs. Marek." Dr. Baines gestured into the room behind her.

Christie felt trapped until she looked up into Zach's pleading gaze, and then she felt hopelessly out of control. If she refused, Zach would be hurt, publicly embarrassed, and Gideon had been patient for so long. If she took him down herself, it would add at least fifteen minutes to the already long afternoon.

Christie touched Gideon's chin lightly. "Giddy, I'm going to go into that room with Dr. Baines." His gaze flicked in the general direction of the office door and then back to the picture of Caroline he was scribbling over.

"No needles," he said, his intonation flat.

"No. No needles," Christie reassured him. "Daddy will take you for a doughnut and a drink. Stay with Daddy. Be a good boy for Daddy."

"Chocolate milk?" Gideon asked, turning to look at Zach.

Zach crouched down to meet his gaze. "Let's go find out," he said, holding out his hand.

Gideon dropped his crayon on the coffee table and walked over to Zach. "Have to hold hands."

Zach smiled at him and took his hand, nodding once at Christie before he walked Gideon out and away.

"Christie? Shall we talk?" Dr. Baines's words pulled Christie back to the present and away from imagining every little thing that could go wrong with this scenario.

Brushing away her reluctance, Christie followed the psychologist into her office.

"That was difficult for you," Dr. Baines said.

"Yes. But not for the reason you suspect," Christie said, feeling defensive and subverted.

"And what do I suspect?" she asked.

"It's not that I don't trust Zach. He just doesn't know how to deal with Gideon, and he won't ask for help when he needs it." Christie pulled her gaze from her lap to Dr. Baines's face. "It's been such a disaster. I gave Zach all sorts of reading to do while he was away … you know, before he went to prison … while he was on the task force … but he didn't bother. He seems to do everything possible to upset Gideon. He won't ask for help." Christie stopped when she realized that she was babbling, a pathetic, defensive verbalalia.

"I understand," Dr. Baines said.

"You do?" Christie asked before she thought better of it.

"Yes. You are a wonderful mother, Christie. I see it. My receptionist sees it, and your husband definitely sees it. You sacrifice a great deal of yourself to give your son his best chance at a rich and happy life. Your husband is very proud of you ... and of your son."

Christie bowed her head in sadness. "But I make him feel inadequate."

"Why do you think that he didn't read the information that you sent him?" Dr. Baines asked.

"Uh, I don't know," Christie replied.

"But you must have a theory," she said.

"I suppose ... I guess ... I figured he just wasn't interested," Christie said. "He didn't cope well with Gideon's diagnosis."

"Why is that, do you think?"

"He told me ... well, he said that I loved Gideon more than him. I didn't know that before. He just recently told me ... I ..." Christie said, her eyes flitting to the pictures on the wall. "But I have to put Gideon first. Everything I read, every article and blog says that early intervention is the key to treatment for autism. I have to get this right, now, while he's young or ..."

"Or?" Dr. Baines asked. "Will he die?"

Astonished, Christie met Dr. Baines's gaze. "No, of course not," she replied with disdain in her voice.

"What then?" Dr. Baines asked. "I've read many of those articles as well. But the real key seems to me to be your goal. What do you want for Gideon?"

"I want him to be happy, to do as well as possible. I want him to have friends and a job and a wife and children." Christie felt a wry smile on her face. "I'd really like him to sleep through the night. Every night." Glancing up, she met Dr. Baines's friendly smile.

"So you have some short-term goals and some long-term goals," Dr. Baines said.

"Yes. I guess so," Christie said.

"Do you think that life was better when Zach was away?" Dr. Baines asked.

That was really the question, wasn't it? Was life better without Zach? "Sometimes," Christie replied. "But not always."

"Explain, please," Dr. Baines replied.

"No," Christie said and then amended her response. "I mean, no, life wasn't better without Zach. I mean, sure, there were times when he irritated me and times when he was less than helpful. But there were also the times he bought me flowers just out of the blue, or offered to play with Gideon so I could make supper. Even now, he'll do a load of laundry or some other little chore just to help me. Without him … no help." No help. No hugs and kisses, well, not grown-up ones. No anger, it was true. But no making up.

"Christie?" Dr. Baines said her name softly.

Christie met her gaze bleakly. "Why is he so angry all the time? Things were not going well before he left but he wasn't angry, just distant. I simply don't know what to do?"

"Have you done any reading on the psychology of imprisonment?" Dr. Baines asked.

"No. I, uh, guess he told you about my call to his father," Christie said, blushing. "Frankly, I've spent all my time reading about autism. I don't have time to deal with a post-traumatic husband."

"Why?" Dr. Baines asked.

Incredulous, Christie replied, "Why? I'm only one person. I can't do everything!"

"No, of course not. But I'm fairly certain that there are two of you to share the load. And what about the promise? 'Come to me all you who labor and are heavy laden and I will give you rest.' Are you in this alone?" Dr. Baines asked.

"No," Christie said, and a small ray of warmth settled in her heart. "I'm not alone."

"Is your husband worth the effort?" Dr. Baines asked.

Zach. Was he worth a little effort on her part? Could she try to understand where he was coming from and the effects of his suffering? Was he worth it? Wasn't every person worth a little effort?

"You asked me where the anger is coming from," Dr. Baines said. "Look, from his perspective, on what he lost when he joined that task force in Albania. He has no job, no career, and he has lost his place in his family. You and Gideon have become a unit without him. Simply put, your husband is hurt and terrified, and I think his terror has colored every word and action he's taken since being rescued, and, I suspect, even before that."

Feeling as though all the air had been sucked from the room, Christie sat silently digesting those words, but Dr. Baines wasn't finished yet.

"Correct me if I'm mistaken, but are you waiting for your husband to prove himself trustworthy, maybe even simply worthy, so that you will know how far to trust him, how far to involve him in your life?" she asked.

"Yes," Christie said, breathing out the word. *What else am I meant to do?*

"I would suggest trying it the other way 'round. Offer him little bits of trust and expect him to succeed; let him know that failure isn't terminal to your relationship. Try that over the next three days and see what happens," Dr. Baines said.

"All right," Christie agreed, her mind spinning around the ideas in her head as she tried to fit them together into a recognizable pattern. "What, uh, what do you think we should do about … never mind."

"Sex?" Dr. Baines asked, and Christie blushed. "That, of course, is up to the two of you."

"I can't really tell if he still wants me," Christie admitted, her voice barely above a whisper, her head tilted down to hide her embarrassment. Okay. That was a lie. She hadn't meant to lie, but who was she kidding? She didn't need Dr. Baines's *Are you crazy?* expression to realize that Zach wanted her. Of course he did. He was her husband. She was his wife. But she was so confused about her feelings for him.

She knew he desired her, could read it in his eyes. What did she want? Him, but with a few improvements, like no more anger, and patience with Gideon, and … But she didn't fully understand the mix of anger, disappointment, joy, and love she felt now that he was home. Was it fair, though, to force him to be celibate because she was confused? They were married. *Oh, Father, I'm beginning to fear that I don't know anything about love.*

"I don't know what to do," Christie murmured. "He never initiates anything. He always seems to be watching and waiting for me to tell him what to do. It's frustrating and confusing."

"In this matter, Christie, you are definitely in the driver's seat.

Your husband is very afraid of losing you. Remember that terror that I mentioned?" Dr. Baines said.

"Yes."

"I think you'll find that everything flows from his fear of losing you," Dr. Baines said.

"What, uh, what do you think love really is?" Christie asked thoughtfully.

"First Corinthians thirteen," Dr. Baines asked.

"Love is patient, kind, not rude, doesn't seek its own way," Christie paraphrased. "Can you really live that way?"

"Try it and see what happens. I would like to see the two of you again on Monday. That gives you three full days to try it and see."

"I can do that," Christie said. *Okay, Father. Love. Love me so I can figure out what to do with my husband. Please.*

Christie rose and shook Dr. Baines's hand.

"Don't be afraid to ask for help, Christie. I don't want you ever to feel that you're in this alone."

"Thank you. We'll be back on Monday," she said and then walked out of the office to find Gideon and Zach huddled together over the coffee table.

What on earth? "What are you two up to?" Christie asked.

"Mommy!" Gideon launched himself into his mother's arms, and she no longer cared what they'd been doing.

Zach placed a half-eaten doughnut from the table into a paper bag and then stood to go.

"Get your chocolate milk, Gid," Zach said.

Gideon wiggled down, picked up his bottle of chocolate milk, and then moved quickly toward the door.

"Wait, Gideon," Christie said, moving quickly toward him before he started down the hall. She called back over her shoulder. "Zach, could you please make Monday's appointment?" *Little bits of trust.*

"Sure," he replied. He sounded surprised or uncertain; she wasn't sure which.

Once Christie caught up to Gideon, she took his hand and waited. When Zach caught up, he said, "I got a two o'clock again. Is that okay?"

"Yes. That's perfect. Thank you," she said, and then she took her husband's hand.

Zach froze, and his eyes widened for a moment. And then he intertwined their fingers and held on tight.

CHAPTER 13

Christie found Zach sitting hunched forward on one of the wicker chairs on the back deck of their house. She leaned against the door frame and watched him for a moment, while he was oblivious to her presence.

"You going to sit down?" he asked.

Or so she thought. Christie pushed off the doorframe and sat in the chair beside him.

"You okay?" she asked.

"As compared to what?" he said, releasing a huff of humorless air. "I've been in a holding pattern for so long that I don't even know what 'okay' feels like. How about you?" He looked over at her.

"Same," she replied. "Did, uh, did you find that helpful today?"

"That's what I've been thinking about. I came out here because I hoped the fresh air would center my thoughts."

"Maybe if you tell me what you're thinking, I can help," she suggested. *Tell me even one little thing. Please.*

"Dr. Baines said that I need to explain my *feelings* to you, 'to open the door to two-way communication'." He sat back in the chair, slumping down in the seat. "But it's so hard." He covered his face with his hands.

When he didn't go on, Christie said, "To be honest, I'm afraid to hear what you have to say. If what you tell me about prison and … stuff … doesn't justify all your anger, then what do I do? And if it does, how can I bear it?"

Resting her hand on his thigh, Christie turned partway in her chair so she could study him. Her pulse accelerated with a leap. He was still so attractive—just over six feet tall with gorgeous hazel eyes, broad shoulders, and a long, lean body. As long as she'd known him, he'd carried a perpetual golden tan ... until now. Now his skin was a sickly shade of gray as though the walls of the prison had leeched into his skin.

"It makes me angry that, when I finally have you back, have your help, you're so bound up in your own issues that you can't help me," she said.

"Jeez, Christie, don't hold back," he said, his voice soaked through with wryness. "Tell me what you really think."

In spite of his sarcasm, she continued, "I guess I wanted you to flip some switch that would shift all your negative experiences—Janice, foster care, Albania—into a deep, dark corner where they wouldn't bother us anymore. Stupid, eh?" she said. *And if that didn't work, I thought that Dr. Baines would do it for me.*

"Not stupid. I tried. Believe me, I did, but they just won't stay hidden."

"Is that why you're having nightmares?" she asked.

Zach blew out a breath. "Yeah. Being in prison brought them back. Feelings of helplessness, I guess," he muttered. "I think it might help to visit my father, to be back on the Second Chance. I've been thinking we could fly—"

Christie blanched, whispering, "We can't afford that." Zach frowned. "Your income stopped when they fired you," she explained. "The rescue was expensive. We're only just barely making it financially."

"Great," Zach muttered sarcastically. "It's very humbling for a man to realize that he can't provide for his family." Abruptly, he stood and began pacing the deck. "We'll drive then." He seemed to be considering the matter, and then his face brightened. "Yeah. We can drive. A road trip. A time to grow closer as a family. My parents took us on a road trip every summer. It was a riot, all four of us, five once Bobby was born, crammed into a camper van, sleeping in tents, building fires, visiting historic sites. It would be a great opportunity to grow closer ..." His voice faded, and she realized that he was seeing the stricken expression she hadn't managed to hide from him. "What?" he said, snapping out the word.

"Oh, Zach," she said miserably.

"Oh, Zach," he began, mocking her voice and misery, continuing in what she assumed was supposed to be her voice, "There is no way on earth that I am going to agree to this proposal, and I blame you for making me miserable by even bringing it up."

"Maybe Seth would help pay for the tickets," she suggested, but that was obviously the wrong thing to say because Zach scowled fiercely at her.

"I don't need my big brother to pay for my family's vacation," he said. She could see the anger within him building by degrees; she could see it in his flushed cheeks and his clenched fists, which were pressed to his stomach.

"It would mean days in the car. And Gideon …" She stopped. Gideon was okay in the car for a few hours. Actually, he managed traveling in the car very well, but what he didn't manage well was a disruption to his routine. And sleep. Oh, sleep could be such a problem when they travelled. And—

"Well?" Zach interrupted her thoughts. She watched his jaw clenching repetitively for a moment. "Christie, can't you let me contribute something useful to this family? I'm supposed to be the husband and father. But whatever I try to do, you just make me feel like a failure."

What? "I didn't … I don't … I do not!" she said, shooting to her feet in indignation. *How dare he?* She stormed into the house, through the kitchen, directly to the laundry room. How could he accuse her of that? It wasn't her fault that he didn't know what he was doing. She was just trying to tell him what to do…all the time—as though he needed to do everything exactly the same way she did it. *Oh, gosh.*

"Christie."

Her hands paused in the act of shoving dirty clothes into the washer. She felt his warmth as he moved in behind her.

"I shouldn't have told you that," he murmured in her ear. His hands rested on her hips, but she held herself stiffly away from him, laughing without humor.

"Why? Because it might cause a fight?" she said. That hadn't stopped him in the past.

"I don't want to fight," he said, gently drawing her back against him. "It feels like we've done nothing but argue since I got home."

"Yeah," she mumbled and then sighed. "I never meant to make you feel like a failure," she said, sinking against him as he offered her comfort with his body, warm around her. After turning her, he embraced her, stroking her back and her hair.

Heaving a breathy sigh, he said, "You're so soft."

Chuckling weakly at the strange compliment, she slipped her hands beneath the hem of his T-shirt, moving in a slow caress up and down his back. He was too thin still, his spine too easy to trace.

"What, uh, what … did … uh …" he began, but then he seemed to lose his focus of concentration, prompting her to laugh.

"What exactly are you trying to say?" she said, teasing him.

"Could you, uh … oh, right there," he said. She'd clearly found just the perfect spot to scratch his back. "Ahh! Thanks."

"Okay, Zach," she said, simply letting her fear go for a moment to deal with at a later time. "We'll drive, if it means so much to you."

"It does," he said.

Nodding, she pulled out of his arms and added detergent to the washing machine before turning it on. "We'll need to wait until my term is finished. That'll be a few more weeks," she said, warning in her voice.

"Fine," he said. "I, uh, won't ask anything else of you."

"Really?" She actually squeaked as she said that because she'd been planning to talk to him about their relationship and maybe moving it on to the next step. "Do you … uh … want anything … else from … our … you know, physical relationship?" She groaned inwardly at her pathetic attempt.

Zach just looked confused. "Everything." And then contritely, he added, "But I don't want to push you. I know I frightened you that night. I can wait until you're ready …" Zach said, his voice trailing off.

She turned toward him more fully. "Do you want me, Zach?"

He lunged for her hands and held them firmly in his. "Yes, Christie, every moment of every day."

Now she welcomed the blush that spread across her face. "Oh. I thought …" She shook her head. "It doesn't matter what I thought."

Releasing her hands, Zach traced a tingling path down the column of her neck and along her shoulder. His other hand cupped the nape of her neck and pulled her gently closer, and then his lips were warm and soft against hers. He pulled back too soon.

"I need you, baby. I love you," he said, his deep voice sweet and perfect. "When does Gideon go to bed?"

Chuckling, she replied, "That's actually why I came to find you. It's time for his bath, and I wondered if you'd like to either bathe him or read him stories."

"I'd love to do either … or both." Zach's eyes dropped. "But I don't want to mess with his head."

"What if we did the whole sequence together for a few nights?" she asked. "And then you'd know the routine."

Zach's eyes deepened with emotion. "I'd love to do that."

When she moved to go, he pulled her gently back toward him. "Christie, sweetheart, I will find my way back to you and Gideon."

"Not back, Zach. I don't want what we had before," she said. "I want something new."

"I'll do my best," he replied earnestly, kissing her once before following her upstairs.

Gideon absolutely loved having both his parents' attention at the same time. They played fishing and drew pictures with colored soap in the bathtub. The rule was anything but trains in the tub. Dinosaurs were allowed but only if they were water dinosaurs.

"Where does he learn the names of these things?" Zach asked Christie as she dried Gideon after his bath.

"I do. Not. Know," she replied, emphasizing each word. "I mean, I know the books he gets them from because I read them to him, but for him to remember *plesiosaurus* and not be able to ask for a banana when he's hungry?" She shook her head. "Someone once told me that if you want to understand autism, you need to take everything you know and turn it upside down. I feel like my world's been upside down for three and a half years."

Zach stood up from emptying the tub and gazed at her, his brows furrowed. She couldn't read the emotions in his eyes except to tell that he wasn't angry.

"What?" she asked, suddenly feeling exposed.

"I've been feeling like my life is divided in two, pre-Albania and post. It's nice to look at life in a different way."

She watched him for a time because she didn't know how to respond. And then she simply helped Gideon into his pajamas before setting him up with his plain blue toothbrush. For some reason, blue was the only color he wanted to use to brush his teeth. And since brushing teeth was important for good health, Christie was happy to go with the flow.

Once Gideon was finished, Christie crouched in the hallway like a sprinter readying for a race. Gideon lined up beside her as they'd done ever since he'd seen the sneaker ad on television. "On your marks. Get set. Go," she said, and he took off like a shot. Soon, she heard him bouncing on his bed, singing at the top of his lungs.

Zach laughed. "I've never seen him move so fast."

"It's the most expedient way to get him into his room at night. He's not a big fan of bedtime."

She started down the hall, but Zach stopped her with a hand on the arm. "I did try to read those articles you sent me. Reading is so hard for me. It all just got so muddled in my mind, and, frankly, some of them were depressing. I'm sorry I didn't make more of an effort. Do you still have some I could read now?"

He looked so contrite and meek that she flung herself into his arms, kissing him soundly on the mouth.

"I'm sorry," she said. "I should have handled that so differently. I have a fantastic book, just one book that will pretty much tell you what you need to know. It's kind of thick, but it's full of examples and cartoons and it's a really easy read. Maybe ... well, it's been a year since I read it. We could read it together if you want. I could even read it to you."

"I'd like that. I haven't touched a book in six months so I'm definitely out of practice."

Her heart melted within her, and her breath caught in her chest. "I'm so sorry I—"

Zach pressed his fingertips against her lips. "Whatever you were going to say, I don't want to hear it. You're amazing, Christie. I never would have survived without you. You believed in me when my colleagues threw me away. You rescued me. Seth told me how you called him and how you insisted they come after me."

"I couldn't let them leave you there, Zach."

"I couldn't have asked for a better wife, a better friend than you. I need to thank you for all of that."

"Mommy-Daddy, Mommy-Daddy, Dinosaur Train. Ha ha hahaha. Stories!" Gideon called down the hall, each syllable punctuated by a thump as gravity pulled his feet back into contact with his mattress, causing the bedframe to bump against the wall.

"Coming, Giddy," Christie said, but Zach swept her into his arms.

"If you're still interested in a little mattress hockey ourselves, I'll read to that boy of ours and meet you in the bedroom once he's asleep," Zach suggested.

"Okay." There was that darn blushing heat again. "Three stories," she reminded him.

"Got it," Zach said as he disappeared into Gideon's room.

Zach swallowed a throat-clogging lump of trepidation as he opened their bedroom door, scanning the familiar space. The bed was empty and neatly made, the bedside lamp the only illumination. Scanning to the right, he encountered Christie's shy gaze. She looked so beautiful with her blonde curls still messy from the day, her face flushed, and her eyes wide and dark and that deep, deep blue.

"Hi," he said. He knew it was a lame greeting, but he was so nervous that he couldn't seem to do any better. "Are you okay?" He shut the door firmly behind him.

"Why do I feel so flustered?" she said. "It's not like we haven't done this before."

He thought about that for a moment. "Because we're creating something new." And that was the perfect response because she beamed him an expression of joy and moved across the room and into his arms.

"I love you," he said, leaning down to kiss her, releasing the passion he'd held in check since returning home. When he pulled back, Christie looked a little dazed.

"Wow," she said in a whisper, her eyes fixed on his mouth. And then she raised her eyes to his. "My turn." Fisting his shirt, she pulled him so close not even a breeze could pass between them and kissed him back. His mind exploded in a cascade of sensation, familiar and yet new in its rawness and hunger. And, oh, she was hungry for him. He could feel it. See it. Taste it. And he loved her.

CHAPTER 14

Burim Gjojak gestured to his driver, the faithful Thor, to unlock the rear doors of the metallic black Mercedes Benz so that his own personal *zyrtari Kanadez*, his informant, could slip inside.

"Thank you for meeting with me," the informant said, adding, "sir" when Gjojak raised an arrogant brow, adopting a daunting expression. This man was so simple to intimidate.

"What progress have you made with Marek's woman?" Gjojak asked.

"It will not be a long wait. She will tell me what I need to know," the informant said and then amended his comment, "what *you want* to know." The man fidgeted for a time, clearly gathering what little courage he had. "Er, um, Thomason?"

"You have no need to trouble yourself with him. It is arranged," Gjojak replied, snapping his fingers to end the discussion. It took the informant a moment to recognize the fact, but at Thor's ugly expression, the sallow, self-important twit finally jerked into motion, exiting the vehicle. Really, with a face like Thor's, it was a wonder that his presence alone didn't send the officer running. Gjojak chuckled at his own private humor, eliciting an expression of confusion on the informant's stupid face.

"Um, sir, the, uh, money?" the informant asked.

Gjojak snapped his fingers again, and the beady-eyed Thor shoved his massive hand into his jacket pocket to retrieve a small manila envelope. He shoved it at the informant's chest and then returned to the vehicle. He accelerated away before Gjojak was submitted to the tedious gratitude of his little Canadian mole.

Christie gathered the breakfast dishes into the sink and filled it with hot, soapy water.

"Chocolate milk," Gideon said, and Christie sighed wearily. It was finally the day to depart for Wyoming and the Second Chance ranch. The Jeep was packed, the maps were marked, and their passports were ready. Christie had insisted they finish out Gideon's block of therapy, which accounted for the fact that it was now mid-July. Gideon could sense the upcoming trip and had been cranky for days.

"Sometimes it's okay to have white milk," she said. They had finished the chocolate milk last night, clearing out the fridge.

"White milk okay. No! Chocolate milk, chocolate milk!" he cried. A keening sound erupted from his chest.

Christie sighed again. *What I wouldn't give for a chocolate cow to follow me wherever I go.*

"Gideon likes chocolate milk," he said, his voice thick with emotion.

"I like chocolate milk," she paraphrased, trying to help the boy learn his pronouns. Why not? At least then something could be gained from this miserable morning. "Yes, you certainly do. But we only have white milk today. Remember, today we go—"

"Chocolate milk! Chocolate milk!"

All the preparations for the trip had created too much upset in too short a period of time. "Sweetheart, I simply don't have chocolate milk."

"Daddy has chocolate milk," Gideon said, his little face upturned and hopeful.

Good try, sweetheart. "Let's go watch TV," she suggested.

The boy calmed enough to reply in hiccupping sobs, "TV. TV. TV."

"TV and then get dressed," she said. "Today, we drive to Detroit."

Hiding her weariness behind a smile, she picked Gideon up and gave him a hug. When she tried to put him down again, he lifted his legs into the air, clinging to her neck like a monkey, so she carried him to the living room. She found a program that seemed somewhat calm—at least there weren't several geometrically shaped cartoon characters screaming at each other—and set him up there. Then she returned to the kitchen and finished cleaning up for the trip.

It was nearly time to depart for Wyoming and the Second Chance ranch. First checking that his Sig Sauer and permit-to-carry were secured in the lock box beneath the driver's seat of the Jeep, Zach then returned to the kitchen, filled the last thermos with water, packed the last sandwich in the cooler, and then loaded them into the Jeep as well. He was determined to make this trip perfect. Christie was convinced that it would all go horribly wrong, but he knew that he could make it work. He'd plotted out the entire trip to include activities Gideon loved.

Zach just needed to call his father and let him know they were leaving.

"Hello?" Zach heard the slow, lispy speech of his youngest brother on the phone.

"Hi, Bobby. It's Zach."

"Hi, Zach. You been gone so long! Did you go to any beaches?" Bobby said and laughed. Bud had chosen not to fill his youngest son in completely on Zach's situation. Bobby was a young man who saw the world through the eyes of innocence. Bobby knew that bad people went to prison, and he knew that he loved his brother, Zach. Bud had decided to keep things in that order.

Zach indulged his brother's humor. "Not this time. Have you been to any beaches?"

"Noooo. I only seen horses for the rest o' my life," Bobby replied, bemoaning the fact.

"Bobby, is Dad around?" Zach was very nervous, and he didn't have the patience to spend on pleasantries.

"I get him," Bobby said.

"Okay. Thanks."

Zach heard Bobby in the background. "Dad, it's Zach. He says he needza talk t' you."

Zach heard a mumbled response, and he pictured his father pushing himself out of his heavy, wooden rocking chair. He would take a moment to straighten his protesting joints and then limp across the great room of the ranch house to the telephone where it sat on the counter in the country kitchen.

"Zach, son. How are you?" Bud asked.

"I'm fine, Dad. How are you?"

"We're doing well here. I've heard from Seth and Luke. They'll plan to stop by as soon as they know you're here. Blake's gone under so I don't think we'll see him."

"Thanks, Dad. I just wanted to let you know that we're going to leave in about an hour. We'll stay in Detroit tonight. I want to pamper Christie for a night at the Marriott and take Gideon to the GM showroom at the Renaissance Center. He's going to love all those cars."

"How is Christie holding up?" Bud asked.

"Honestly? She seems to think this is going to be some sort of disaster. But I'm determined to prove her wrong. I tried to tell her about all the amazing car trips you and Mom took us on when we were kids."

He heard his father sigh. "Son, something that you wouldn't remember is that, although the trips were wonderful for you boys and even an adventure of a different sort for me, your mother bore the brunt of the work. She did it because she loved us, not because she enjoyed it."

Impatiently, Zach brushed away the thinly veiled warning. "I'll keep that in mind, Dad, but I'm determined to make this fun for her. I won't make her do all the work."

"Have a safe trip, Zach. I love you," Bud said. "Bobby's very excited about seeing Gideon again. They've become very good friends this past year."

"We'll see you in about a week. I love you, too."

Zach hung up. No one had any confidence in him. It was just a simple road trip. What was the big deal?

CHAPTER 15

Two hours waiting in line to cross the bridge from Windsor to Detroit was tolerable because Gideon was entranced by an audiobook on his mp3 player. It was the four hours at the Canada-US border that put the frown on his wife's face. They were pulled over, checked, and searched, and then Zach was removed to be strip-searched and interrogated.

"You deny that you were arrested and convicted in Albania?" officer number one asked, the smelly one with gorilla-sized hands who'd performed the cavity search.

"No," Zach replied, again, sighing deeply. More questions. But at least they'd finally let him put his clothes back on. "The charges were a setup."

"You were convicted?" officer number two asked, the tall, skinny guy with bad acne and a squeaky voice.

"Yes, but not in a legal trial. I've been exonerated by the Canadian government," Zach replied.

"And yet the Ontario Provincial Police terminated your employment." This was the third officer, an ageless woman with unusually light-gray eyes and stern hair. Zach couldn't think of any other way to describe it. It was tightly rolled into a bun on the back of her neck, but Zach couldn't see any means of containing it. He figured it was probably too afraid of her to budge an inch. She reminded him of the Trunchbull from the Roald Dahl book, *Matilda*.

"Yes. But they really had no other choice at the time," Zach said.

"And I haven't pursued the matter. I'm just grateful to be home with my family."

"The United States does not allow foreign convicts to cross the border," said Gorilla-fingers, fanning himself with Zach's American passport.

"I am not a convict, and I am not a foreigner," replied Zach.

"Yet you live and work in Canada."

"I have dual citizenship," Zach replied.

"How did you manage that?" the Trunchbull asked him, the implication being that Zach had somehow managed to circumvent national security to obtain it.

Working to camouflage his growing irritation, Zach replied evenly, "I was born in Toronto. When I was six, I was apprehended by the Children's Aid Society. I spent a year in foster care. Then my great-aunt agreed to take me in on a kinship agreement. Because I'd had a rather difficult time finding a place that would keep me, the US government agreed to let me move to Wyoming."

"This great-aunt. She would be Marek?" Gorilla-fingers asked.

"No. Things didn't work out very well there either, but her friends Bud and Grace Marek took me in and when they adopted me, I was granted dual citizenship," Zach said.

"Three-time loser, huh, Marek? No wonder you wound up in prison. You know what they say, *blood will tell*," the Trunchbull said to him.

Yeesh, I hope not, Zach barely kept from muttering. He'd heard similar slurs his entire life from foster parents, police officers, and teachers. These customs officers were trying to provoke him into a response, which would entitle them to deny him entry to the United States, and he was determined not to give them the opportunity. Sitting taller in his chair, he lifted his chin defiantly.

By the time Zach was led to the waiting area, Christie looked like she'd survived a cyclone—just barely. Gideon was rocking in her arms, a shrill cry emanating from him. Everyone in the room, including the staff, had clearly had a crash-course in autism.

"Uh, hi," Zach said to Christie. Scowling darkly at him, she shoved Gideon into his arms, turned her back on him, and walked away. Add guilt to the mounting pile of humiliation he was suffering.

"Mommy! Mommy! Mommy!" Gideon shouted, rocking back and forth in Zach's arms as he reached for the retreating figure of his mother. Zach followed, holding Gideon tightly around the waist to keep him from launching himself into orbit.

Once they were buckled into the Jeep again, Zach pulled out and took the exit for Renaissance Drive.

"Only a few more minutes now," Zach said, determined to cast off the misery of the past few hours and then repeated himself a little louder to be heard over Gideon's keening cry. Christie just stared out the passenger-side window.

In spite of heavy traffic, they made it to the Renaissance Marriott in just under fifteen minutes. Zach shifted the Jeep right and prepared to pull into the driveway.

"What are we doing here?" Christie asked, turning toward him, confusion printed across her features.

"This is my surprise for you. We're staying here tonight. It houses the General Motors showroom, and I thought Gideon would enjoy seeing the cars," Zach said proudly.

"No cars! No cars! TV, TV, TV!" Gideon interrupted and then returned to the single vowel he seemed to be favoring today.

"Just a little longer, Gideon," Christie said and then turned to Zach. "We can't afford this, Zach. It must cost a fortune!"

"I got a good deal. The showroom's great, Christie. I wanted to pamper you, a little luxury to thank you for the past few months. It will be worth it," Zach said, using his most persuasive voice.

Horns bleated behind them. "Look I need to pull in here," Zach said and then parked in a space for registering patrons.

"Zach, find someplace cheaper," Christie said, beseeching him.

"No! No, no, no!" Gideon yelled. "Mommy, Mommy, Mommy!"

"We're here now. Let me just get us registered and into a room." Zach didn't wait for a response. Instead, he slipped out of the Jeep and took his place in line at the reception desk. There were three individuals in the slow-moving line between him and the young Asian woman stationed at the desk, but he couldn't change that and maybe the wait would be beneficial. The echo of Gideon's "Eeee" rang through Zach's head, and he almost missed his cue to move forward in line because of the ringing in his ears.

"May I help you, sir?" the attendant said. Her nametag read Elaine.

"Yes … please. I have a reservation for Marek." Zach spelled the name.

"Yes, we have you here. A concierge room with two double beds," Elaine said as she pushed a lock of her long, silky hair behind her ear. "How will you be paying?"

"American Express," Zach said, retrieving the card from his wallet, except it wasn't there. He'd forgotten to borrow Christie's. It was taking longer than he'd expected to replace all of his identification. "Um, if you could make up the bill, I'll just need to ask my wife to sign for it." Zach could feel the heat of his embarrassment rising up his neck. "If you could give me two minutes."

"Sir, there are several people waiting," Elaine said with her longsuffering expression.

"Just … can you just give me the key and she can come down to sign later?" he asked.

"No. I'm sorry, sir. Do you have another card?" The smile slipped from Elaine's mouth.

Zach searched through his wallet. He had three hundred dollars American and fifty-seven Canadian in his wallet. "Cash. I'll pay with cash. How much?"

"Two hundred and eighteen, fifty-two, sir," Elaine said.

"Thanks." Zach counted out the bills. The first thing tomorrow, they'd have to take the time to get more cash. Christie was right. This was a lot of money to spend on one night's sleep, but he wanted to do something special for her, pamper her a bit. She'd certainly had little pampering for the past couple of years, probably more like three and a half.

"Here are your key-cards, sir. Enjoy your stay." Elaine's smile was plastered on her face again, but her attention was on the next patron in line.

"Thank you. Uh, parking? Where do I park?" Zach asked.

"For twenty dollars, I can give you a pass to the hotel parking lot. It's good for twenty-four hours." Elaine glanced at Zach briefly.

"Yes. Great." *Not.* Zach passed over another bill and accepted the parking pass.

By the time Zach returned to the Jeep, Christie's voice was hoarse from singing to Gideon whose keening wail had settled into a whimper.

"Sorry it took so long," Zach said. Passing the key-cards over to Christie, he pulled out and into the line to the parking garage. They were three levels up before Zach could locate a parking spot. He backed into the tight space and then turned off the ignition.

"Okay, let's get up to our room. Television, Gideon? Want to watch television?" Zach asked, trying to coax a positive response from his son.

"TV," Gideon whimpered in a pitiful tone.

"Okay. We need to get our bags, and then we can relax," Zach said. "If you can get Gideon, Christie, I'll grab the bags."

Nodding first, she gathered up their son and then waited at the elevators while Zach grabbed the suitcase, Gideon's backpack full of toys and books, and his duffel bag and followed her into the elevator and up to their room. The room was luxurious, absolutely the fanciest room he'd ever stayed in in his life.

Christie turned on the television, scanned for a channel, and then put Gideon on the foot of the bed closest to it.

"Next commercial, go pee, Giddy," Christie said, but Gideon just curled his arms around his knees and rocked on the foot of the bed.

"Christie—" Zach began.

"I just want to get him into the bathroom before he wets his pants," she said.

"Okay. Why don't I find someplace to get food?" Zach asked. "Should I bring it here?"

"Yes. But I need you to wait. Once he pees, then I need to go to the bathroom, and I don't want to leave him in the room alone when he's so upset," she said.

"Okay. I'll wait," he replied.

Finally, the show went to commercial, and Christie managed to convince Gideon to go to the toilet where the boy relieved the equivalent of Niagara Falls.

"Good job, sweetheart," Christie said, praising him and giving him a big hug, which he pushed out of.

"TV, Mommy," Gideon whispered as though he'd used up his voice at the border.

"Yes, sweetheart. TV," she said. Christie pulled off Gideon's socks and shoes. She got a wet cloth and washed his face and then retrieved his little thermos, rinsed it out, and filled it with water. She then stood over him until he drank from it.

"I need to use the bathroom," Christie said. "Can you please watch Gideon? If he finishes the water, fill it again." Walking into the bathroom, she shut and locked the door without ever looking him in the eye.

Soon Zach heard the shower running and over the thrum of water in the tub, he heard the sounds of muffled vocalizations, the sort of noises a person would make if she were holding a towel to her mouth to muffle cries of frustration.

"Christie?" he called while he knocked on the bathroom door.

"Leave me alone, Zach," she said. And he heard more muffled vocalizations.

One day in and he'd made a huge mess of things. The least he could do was watch Gideon as she'd asked him to. Zach sat beside him on the bed. Gideon continued rocking, so Zach curled his body up and started rocking as well.

"That feels pretty good, sweetheart. I can see why you like to do this." After a while, Zach felt Gideon leaning toward him until his body was pushed up against his side. Reaching over, he slowly drew his son onto his lap and held him close. "I love you," he murmured and kissed Gideon on the head.

After a while, Christie came out of the bathroom. Her bangs were damp, and her eyes were red. She'd clearly tried to wash away the evidence of her frustration.

"If you take little man here, I'll go get us some supper," Zach said, hoping that an offer of help would be well received.

Making a sound halfway between a grunt and a snort, Christie picked Gideon up and resettled on the foot of the bed with him on her lap.

"Big Piglet," Gideon said, releasing a huge, jaw-popping yawn.

Christie paled. "Oh, no." She looked up at Zach. "Did you put Big Piglet into Gideon's backpack when I asked you to?"

Zach gulped. "Er, I'll check," he said, but he knew he'd forgotten. What he did remember was the moment when he had decided that the little puppet was less important than something else, something he couldn't even remember now, but something which had led to something else again until he'd forgotten. Perhaps ... maybe ... could there be ... by some miracle did that little pink pig end up in Gideon's backpack? Zach searched through every bag. He found a plastic dinosaur, which he offered Gideon. The boy took it, clutching it tightly in his fist.

"Big Piglet," Gideon repeated.

"I don't see it," Zach said, adopting an optimistic tone. This wasn't an irredeemable situation. Of course it wasn't. "We'll just buy him a new one. There must be a mall around here somewhere."

Christie didn't respond.

"I'm hungry, and Gid needs to eat," Zach continued. "Why don't we get supper and a piglet at the same time?"

She gave him that grunt-snort sound again, which he interpreted as an affirmative since she put Gideon's shoes and socks back on.

After finding a local department store, they bought some sandwich meat, buns, and lettuce for supper along with some chocolate milk.

"Christie, you okay?" Zach asked, concerned by her pallor and silence. He'd convinced Gideon to sit in the shopping cart and had been playing an "I Spy" game with him while Christie wandered through the store finding the food they needed.

"I'm tired," she replied. "And we still need a P-I-G."

"Well, then, pick one out and buy it," he said, trying to stay calm. Christie wandered off, returning soon after with two stuffed pigs, which looked similar to Gideon's. Holding them up in front of Gideon, she asked, "Which one for sleeping, Gideon?"

"Big Piglet," he replied without glancing up.

"We need a new Big Piglet, honey. Which one?" Christie persisted.

"New Big Piglet. No." Gideon looked up, narrowing his eyes. "Not time for bed."

She sighed heavily. "No, it's not time for bed. Pick one."

"Christie, just pick one. He'll get used to it," Zach said.

"You have no idea," she replied acerbically, glaring at him. Suddenly, there was color in her cheeks again. *Gulp.*

"Fine," Zach said, trying again to sound calm and reasonable. If he could just get her to see the bright side of the situation, all would be well. "Get them both then."

She clenched her fists around the pigs and stiffened her body as though she was trying to contain her emotions tightly. "This isn't going to work," she said. "You just have no idea how difficult this is going to be. Taking a kid who needs routine and throwing his world into chaos?"

"We can do this. Just get one for him, and let's go," Zach said, clenching his teeth to guard his reaction. She was simply determined to see only the negatives.

"It doesn't work that way," she insisted through gritted teeth. "You—"

"Big Piglet?" Gideon asked. He still had a death grip on the plastic dinosaur that Zach had given him earlier.

"We need a new piglet, buddy." Zach retrieved the two piglets and held them up. "Which one?"

Gideon looked back and forth between the stuffed animals and then took one. Christie turned and walked away. "Time to go?" the boy asked, his eyes trailing his mother.

"In a minute. We need to wait for Mommy and then pay," Zach said.

"Wait for Mommy. No. Just get one for him and let's go," he said, repeating the exact words and intonation Zach had used earlier.

Zach chuckled wryly. "We'll pay now, but we still need to wait for Mommy."

Christie joined them at the cashier. "Let's go."

Zach loaded their things into the trunk while Christie snapped Gideon into the booster seat for the return trip to the Marriott.

Christie made the sandwiches while Zach played with Gideon. She didn't even care what they played. Nearly blind with fatigue, she was so emotionally wrung out that she could barely think.

Laying out a quilt from one of the beds, she made a little picnic for them. Then it was past time for Gideon's bath and bed. She hoped the emotion of the day would make him tired rather than wind him up further, but she knew it could go either way.

"Okay, sweetheart, say your prayers and then to sleep," Christie said.

Half asleep already, Gideon said his prayers and then curled onto his side. "Big Piglet," he said.

"Remember, we had to buy a new Big Piglet," she said, searching around in the shopping bags until she found it. She pulled off the tags and held it out to him. "Here it is."

"Big Piglet," he said, but he wasn't labeling the item, it was a simple request for his favorite stuffed animal.

Christie sighed heavily. *I knew this would happen.* "Everything okay?" Zach mouthed to her, and when she shrugged, he went into the bathroom.

"The old one is at home, honey. We have a new one for the trip," she said, keeping her voice calm and reasonable.

"Old one at home, honey. No. *No!*" Gideon rocked up onto his toes and then flung himself backward onto the bed. His head collided with the wall, and he screamed.

Christie scrambled over to pull him onto her lap, but he flailed and hit at her. "Don't hit me! Don't hit me!"

Virtually leaping over the bed, Zach rushed to their side. "What on earth is going on in here?"

"He hit his head," Christie explained tersely, trying to contain Gideon's flailing arms and rub his head to dull the pain at the same time.

Somehow, Gideon had managed to hold on to the plastic dinosaur through the entire episode, and he swung it now at Christie. She dodged, but the tiny plastic claws scratched three tiny grooves along her cheek.

"You're bleeding!" Zach cried. He reached down and grabbed Gideon by the upper arm, pulling him back from Christie. "Stop it!" he ordered.

Gideon paused briefly in shock and then screeched, rocking and pulling back, right out of Zach's grasp, landing on the back of his head on the floor. His screech morphed into a wail of torment that lasted and lasted.

"Stop it! Stop it! Stop it! Daddy, *no*!" Gideon wailed.

"You're just making it worse, Zach. Get out!" Christie shouted, falling to her knees beside the traumatized child.

A knocking sounded on the hotel room door. "Excuse me, sir." They heard a muffled voice from the hallway. The knocking continued as Gideon continued to wail in her arms, flinging his body against her.

Zach stormed across the room and flung open the door. "Yes?"

"I'm sorry to bother you, but we've had a complaint that there's a child crying in here," said the assistant manager, "Tell-me-how-I-can-help-you" Toby.

"Well, Toby," Zach began, his voice dripping with sarcasm, "as you can see, there *is* a crying child in here. Now, if you'll excuse me, I need to go find him something to help him calm down."

"Sir. The noise is disturbing to the other guests. I'm going to have to ask you to quiet the boy," Toby said in his high and snooty voice.

After moving Gideon into the center of the room, away from anything that could hurt him—not easy in the crowded hotel room—Christie walked over to the door and elbowed Zach out of the way.

"He has autism," she said. "He's had a very long, very traumatic day, and now he's having a tantrum because we forgot his favorite bedtime toy. Do you have any suggestions?" she asked Toby. Dim little twit. He had no idea what poor Gideon had been through today. She turned to her husband. "Were you going somewhere?"

Zach's face darkened thunderously, and he pushed past Toby without a word. *Zipperhead.*

Toby seemed to watch Zach go and then turned his attention to Gideon, gesturing at him with a sort of long-armed flick of the hand. "Will, er, he be okay?" Toby asked, adding a nod toward Gideon, who was slamming his fists and heels against the floor as he wailed.

"Eventually. I'll turn the television up so it doesn't disturb our neighbors. I am sorry, but he did have a horrible day," she said.

"Er, it looks like you have everything under control here," Toby said, sniffing contemptuously. "Just call the front desk if there's anything you need."

"Just some Xanax," she murmured.

Clearly dubious, Toby paused briefly before he retreated. After closing the door behind him, Christie sat down on the bed and waited. *What a misery!*

Eventually, Gideon's tantrum lost force, and he began to simply cry.

"Big Piglet," he whimpered.

"Come here, sweetheart," Christie said, opening her arms to him. He walked into her embrace and curled into a ball on her lap, where he sat running the back of his head against her cheek and mouth.

"Kiss it better. Kiss it better," he said, his words full of whimpers and sobs.

She kissed his head several times and gently rubbed around the small bump she found there. "You're going to be okay, sweetheart."

"Be okay, sweetheart. Be okay," he repeated.

She held him and rocked him as he calmed and eventually fell asleep. With Gideon asleep, Christie showered and went to bed herself, but in spite of her exhaustion, she couldn't sleep, not with Zach somewhere roaming the city.

Feeling lower than a first step, Zach returned to the Marriott. He shouldn't have grabbed Gideon. He shouldn't have shouted at him either. Poor Christie. She was fierce as a lion when it came to protecting their son.

After slipping quietly back into the room, Zach stripped down in the bathroom. He was encouraged to see that Gideon was asleep even though the new piglet had been cast onto the floor. The little boy's eyes looked puffy and bruised, and his hair was a chaos of cowlicks. Zach kissed his clammy forehead. *Poor kid.*

Sitting on the other bed, he realized that Christie was awake. He knew that because she welcomed him home by punching him in the chest, not hard but certainly not playfully.

"Ouch! Hey!" he said, astonished by her greeting.

"Where have you been for so long?" she said, her voice a whisper in loudness but the equivalent of a shout in intention.

Grasping her wrist firmly before she could swing again, he asked, "What was that all about?"

Sitting up against the headboard, she apologized with just a hint of actual remorse. "I'm sorry, but where have you been?"

"I went to find something to make the situation better," he said, his chest tight and his belly roiling. *Besides you told me to get out.*

"What did you find?" she asked, clearly challenging him to come up with something spectacular. But he had nothing to offer her, so he told her so.

"I have no idea how to fix this situation. I would say we should just go home, but I definitely don't want to cross the border again tomorrow." Releasing her, he shut his eyes, completely defeated by the situation.

Christie was silent for a long time, and Zach remained still, not at all eager to provoke any sort of response from her.

After drawing in a deep breath, she asked, "What if something happened to you and I didn't know where you were? What would I do? I don't want to lose another year with you."

His eyes widened in shock, and he met her gaze. *Really?* "Oh, baby, I'm sorry," he said, and she finally wrapped her arms around him, resting her head on his shoulder, and he felt like he could breathe again. "You … uh, you do remember that you told me to leave," he said, taking the chance that she was ready to be reasonable.

Glancing at him through her eyelashes, she nestled against his chest. "Maybe," she murmured.

Pulling back, he raised his eyebrows in disbelief. "Maybe?" he asked, questioning her sanity.

She pulled him close again. "Yeah. Sorry."

"Because?" he prompted her.

"I didn't really want you to go," she said.

That wasn't the answer he'd been expecting, but it was a great one nonetheless, more than he'd hoped for.

Reaching out, he gently stroked her cheek just below the tiny dinosaur wound.

"I would like to take care of this," he said, waiting for her nod before retrieving the first-aid kit. He cleaned the wound and applied some antibiotic ointment.

"If you had the choice, would you really go back and unmake him?" she asked him, and it took a minute for him to understand the segue. But he didn't respond quickly enough, so she clarified her meaning. "Do you really wish that we hadn't had children together?"

Wiping the ointment from his hands, he used the excuse of putting away the first-aid kit to avoid meeting her gaze as he composed his answer. "When Gideon came along, it was terrifying. And hard. There were plenty of times when I could only think about sleep. And, on days like today, I wish I could conjure happiness out of thin air, perhaps little pink piglets, as well," he said, and Christie smiled at him. "But I love Gideon and I want him." *I just don't have a clue how to be his father.*

Reaching up, she graced him with a peck on the cheek, and he leaned down for more, accidentally knocking her on the chin with his forehead when Gideon jumped on his back.

"Ouch," she said, rubbing the red mark.

"Hi, Daddy," Gideon said, his little chin poking Zach in the shoulder, his little voice cheery and very awake.

"You're supposed to be asleep, little man," Zach said, laughing in surprise.

"Asleep. No," Gideon said. "TV."

"No TV. Sleep. Come on," Zach said, lifting Gideon up and lying down with him on the other bed, sending one last look of longing to Christie as she snuggled under the covers.

Zach sang to Gideon all the songs that Grace had sung to him when he was a boy. By the time Gideon fell asleep, Christie was sound asleep as well. *Oh, well.* Tomorrow, they'd do the GM showroom in the Renaissance Centre, and then they'd drive to Gary, Indiana, a trip of just over four hours. Tomorrow would be better.

CHAPTER 16

"R-E-N-A-I-S-S—" Words with two S's were good words. Except the one that Mommy didn't like. Gideon didn't understand why she wouldn't let him say it.

S's were like hugs; they curved around you. That's why snakes were nice; they curved around you and hugged you tight. E's were poky. C's were okay, but not as nice as S's.

"Have a look at this map," Daddy said.

"No," Gideon replied, but he did anyway. There were numbers. Zero-zero numbers. "One hundred, two hundred, three hundred, four hundred, five hundred, six hundred. One hundred is green—"

"The vintage cars seem to be beneath Tower 400. Can you get your bearings from this map?" Daddy asked.

"No," Gideon replied. "Two hundred is red …"

"No, I don't think so, but if we stay together, it'll be fine," Mommy said.

"Let's go," Daddy said.

"No," Gideon said. Three hundred is blue … Daddy pulled on his arm. "No! Not all done," Gideon said.

"We need to go now, Gideon," Daddy said. "You can see the numbers later."

"Later? Don't say that unless you mean it, Zach. You can't just fob him off because he's three. Set a limit, and give him a warning," Mommy said. "Gideon. One more number, and then we have to go. Which one do you want for the last one?"

Last one? But there were lots of nice numbers and colors there. Adults were so annoying! "No."

"No is not an acceptable answer to Mommy's question, Gid. Choose, or I will choose for you," Daddy said.

Gideon wanted to growl, but Daddy didn't like it when he growled at Mommy. "Two purple," he replied instead. There were two towers with purple on the map.

"Mommy said one only," Daddy said.

This time he did growl.

"If you growl at me, Gideon, then that means we're finished. Growling at people is rude. You can say, 'I don't want to go,'" Daddy said.

No! "No! No, no, no!" Gideon pulled against Daddy's hand, reaching back for the map. "Two purple, two purple!" he yelled.

"Just let him look once more," Mommy said. "We need to get going, but making a scene isn't going to help anyone."

Daddy pulled Gideon close and got down with his face very close. Gideon saw that Daddy had a grumpy face on. *Uh-oh.* Grumpy-Daddy-face meant trouble. Gideon stopped pulling on Daddy's arm.

"Let it go, Zach. It's not like he didn't have a rotten day yesterday. Do we really have to ruin today?" Mommy said.

"It doesn't make sense to give in to bad behavior," Daddy said, looking up at Mommy.

"He can't help that he likes numbers and colors. It's just the way he's wired," Mommy said. She sounded a little bit mad.

"This is not about preferences. This is about behavior," Daddy said. "He's three, almost four."

How old are you? Three. Numbers were great.

"Yeah. So, you know how old your son is," Mommy said. She lifted her hands high in the air and then slapped them on her legs. Gideon copied her, but she didn't clap or say "good job."

"What I mean is that he's young and small. What happens when he's fourteen and he's as big as me?" Daddy said. "We have to get his behavior under control now before he's bigger and stronger than we are."

"Fine," Mommy said. She walked away.

"Mommy go?" Gideon asked, and Mommy stopped walking.

"If it's not one thing, Christie, it will just be another. Let's go see the cars. You know he'll like the cars," Daddy said.

"Cars?" Gideon said. "Yellow cars?"

Daddy's grumpy face was gone. *Good.* Now he was moving his mouth to ... a smile. Smile was good. Smile meant happy.

"I'm sure there will be some yellow cars," Daddy said.

"Yellow cars. Mommy, four hundred is yellow," Gideon said.

"Is it?" she said.

Gideon walked with Mommy. He remembered all the colors and numbers, turning the pages in his mind like a picture book. And then they entered the big, big room, and Gideon froze. There were people everywhere moving around. And the smell! *Ugh!*

Someone brushed past him, setting his senses alight. Gideon rocked up onto his toes while he flapped his arms. The movement gave him something to think about besides the touch, which had sent electric shocks through his skin.

"Up. Up. Up," Gideon repeated, pulling hard on Mommy's shirt.

She picked him up, and the first thing he did was bury his face against her neck and breathe in. Mommy's smell was familiar. Mommy's smell was nice. The electric shocks started to go away. Mommy squeezed him hard, and his body stopped feeling so floaty.

Gideon looked around now and saw cars between the people.

Daddy took Gideon's hand and said, "Yellow car."

Gideon looked at Mommy. Then he looked at Daddy. Daddy touched Gideon's chin and stretched his arm out. Gideon looked down Daddy's arm and saw it. "Yellow car," he repeated, and his body began to feel calmer. "Yellow." Yellow was good. Yellow cars weren't as noisy as red cars. Red cars were loud and scary and made his ears hurt. Yellow cars were quiet. Blue cars were quiet, too. Of course, Mommy said that color wasn't important for cars; some cars were noisy, and some weren't. He could never understand why she said things like that. That red car at the grocery store had made a very loud sound just as he and Mommy were walking to the front door. You just never knew when a red car might be very noisy. But yellow cars never did that.

CHAPTER 17

Zach pulled off the I-94 into a rest area, a simple brown building with a chalet-peaked roof housing bathrooms and vending machines. He needed to stretch his legs, and Christie had warned him that it was too risky to go more than two hours without stopping for Gideon to use the toilet.

Reaching over, Zach shook Christie awake gently. "We're stopping. Gideon's awake, listening to a story."

She yawned and stretched. "Okay, Gideon, we're going to stop and pee, and then we'll get back in the Jeep and drive some more. Shoes on, please."

"No," Gideon replied, holding his hands over his headphones and scowling.

"Pause it. Five-second warning," Christie replied in a bright and optimistic voice. And then she slowly counted down to zero before reaching back over the seat to pause the mp3 player. Gideon scowled again but didn't argue. *Hmmm, interesting.*

After climbing out of the Jeep, Christie unbelted Gideon and started walking with him toward the ladies' room.

"I'll take Gideon to the bathroom with me," Zach offered. *Today needs to be a better day for my wife.* Maybe if he pitched in and helped more, Christie could relax and enjoy the journey.

"I don't—" Christie began as she turned to face him.

"It's no big deal," Zach said when she didn't continue. "It's just the bathroom." Moving beyond a desire to help, Zach felt like this simple act, taking his son to the bathroom, had become a critical phase in his relationship with his little family.

"You have to watch him carefully," she said.

"I will. I've been paying attention," he said, trying to convey confidence and wisdom in his voice and then whispered, "Trust me," applying just a little twist of guilt.

Nodding slowly, Christie passed Gideon's hand over to Zach. She pointed to the spot directly in front of the soda-pop machine in the foyer of the building. "I'll meet you right here."

Feeling her eyes on the back of his neck, Zach led Gideon into the men's bathroom. Zach knew that he was supposed to keep close to Gideon, and since Gideon didn't object, he stayed by his side as the little boy used the toilet with practiced ease. Gideon hopped off, and Zach reached back to flush, very proud of himself. How difficult was it supposed to be to take a three-and-a-half-year-old to the bathroom?

Gideon screeched, flattening himself against the door of the stall. "Too loud! Too loud!"

Suddenly, Zach heard the roar of the toilet flushing, something he'd never noticed before. Public bathrooms were a great deal louder than those at home.

Thump-smack! "Too loud!" Gideon's screeches increased in volume as he rocked his body, bumping his bottom against the stall door, rolling backward and then smacking the back of his head against the door. Reaching for him, Zach tried to pull him away from the door so they could get out of the room, but the boy kicked and slapped.

"Zach?" He heard Christie's voice calling in. *Ah, crap.*

Wrestling, trying to get a grip on the flailing child, Zach finally lost his patience and shouted, "Stop it!"

Gideon shrieked once, slamming the back of his head against the door one final time and then slid to the floor and slipped under the door. Zach heard his terrified footsteps running away, and by the time he opened the door and stepped out, Gideon was nowhere to be seen. Following the sound of his gasps and shuddering sobs, Zach jogged out of the men's room to see Gideon clinging to his mother as though his life depended on it.

Furious with himself, Zach followed them to the Jeep and unlocked the doors before going back to the building to purchase a candy bar and a root beer, hoping to bribe his way back into grace. Approaching the Jeep, he found Christie rocking Gideon in her arms in the backseat.

"I, uh, brought some treats," he said as he held them out.

"Do you want to wear them?" she asked, clearly at the end of her rope. She whipped her head up to meet his gaze, and he subconsciously stepped back from the red flare of anger directed at him. "He'll just scream and fling them away. Just—" She waved him away brusquely.

Wandering away, Zach circled the building, wondering whether he should just eat the candy bar himself. But his stomach had seized, and all he really wanted was to be away from them; well, not really, he just wanted to be away from his embarrassment and self-recrimination. Wow, he was learning a lot about himself today ... and yesterday. *Oh, joy,* he thought bitterly.

Public bathrooms were noisy. His son was bothered by loud noises. It wasn't exactly rocket science, but, yeesh, a little warning would have been nice.

Finding a bench at the front of the building so he could keep an eye on his family from a "safe" distance, Zach spent the next twenty minutes slumped there.

Finally, he heard Christie's stilted voice. "Zach. We're ready to go."

Stuffing his fists into his pockets, he strode over and peeked into the backseat to see that Gideon was asleep. Christie was belted into the passenger seat.

After keying the ignition, he belted himself in and then reversed out of the spot and back onto the highway, careful not to meet her gaze. It took no skill, as she kept her face turned to the countryside.

"I think we cross into Indiana soon. I thought I'd stop and get a state map in case there are any detours or anything." His voice trailed off when she gave him no response of any kind. Sighing deeply, he turned his eyes back to the road and the traffic around them. Not his finest hour. Or day. Or lifetime. *Blast it!* At least his son knew who his father was. So he could console himself that he was doing better than Janice's one-time lover.

Resting his elbow on the armrest, his fingers sunk deep in his hair, Zach spent the next thirty minutes parboiling in silence. He had promised Christie that he would make this trip wonderful, a special time together as a family. He loved his little family—enough to survive prison, enough to take the hard road and … enough to apologize.

Zach blew out a breath. "I messed up."

"You realize that it's going to take days to undo this trauma," she said, and he swallowed a defensive retort that was best left unsaid.

"I don't know what else to say. I'm sorry," he said instead, working hard to keep his voice even, so that he sounded reasonable. "I never noticed how loud flushes can be." He cleared his throat, slanting a few glances her way. "What will happen now?"

"We start ten steps back." Wearily, she sighed. "He'll scream and refuse to go. You see, we have to convince him it's safe again. It's a multistep process, and in the meantime, we can expect wet pants because he's not even four yet and since we're on a cross-country road trip, there's no *home* in the offing."

Blast it! Why did the consequences of his mistakes always have to be so severe? "So how did you get him to go in public bathrooms in the first place," he said, hoping to move quickly past the need for recriminations and on to comprehension and cooperation—or at least to keep his wife talking to him.

"It took six months of visiting public bathrooms before I could get him to go pee away from home. It was a very gradual process. Can you picture it? 'Come on, son; let's just go stand in the stall in the ladies' room. No, we won't sit down. We'll just stand here, and then we'll get an ice cream.' I'm pretty sure that the mall staff was sizing me up for a straitjacket. The day I brought the camera with me was the day that me and the security guard are not likely to forget. Fortunately, Gideon had a huge tantrum when the guard let slip that the ice cream store was closed, and after fifteen minutes of a screaming, kicking meltdown, the guard was just glad to see the back of us." Christie shook her head with a slight grin on her face. "Finally, we worked out a system where I would wait until Gideon was finished and standing just outside the cubicle before flushing. And I always warn him so he can put his hands over his ears."

"So you knew that the flushing could freak him out?" Zach asked carefully. He felt that familiar angry rush of heat. "You couldn't have warned me, maybe, like, 'Guess what, Zach; Gideon freaks out when he hears the sound of public toilets flushing.'"

Christie's cheeks burned with embarrassment, but her response was interrupted by a newly wakened Gideon.

"Chocolate milk," he said as he kicked the seat in front of him.

"Gid, ask politely," Zach said, swallowing hard to keep the anger from spilling over onto his son. "You can say, 'I want chocolate milk, please.'"

"Chocolate milk. Chocolate milk," Gideon repeated, gaining momentum even over the ringing of Christie's cell phone.

"Hello," she greeted the caller. Her voice sounded tight, but he wasn't sure if it was a result of his own barely camouflaged accusation or Gideon's noisy demands.

"Carlos?" Christie said, surprise in her voice.

"Carlos?" Zach mouthed, frowning at her. She nodded. "Put it on speakerphone," he whispered. She shrugged and complied.

After pulling off the highway onto Mississippi Road in Hobart, Indiana, Zach stopped in the parking lot of the Comfort Inn. He could still feel a red simmer heating his blood.

"Chocolate milk," Gideon said again, kicking the seat. Zach reached over the seat and intercepted his foot as Christie held up her hand in a nonverbal request for "quiet."

"I returned from my journey, and you were gone," Carlos said.

"Where did you go this time?" she asked.

"To bind up the loose ends for the task force. Where are you, babe?" Carlos asked, the endearment sounding odd in his accented voice. "*Que onda?*"

The task force? Hadn't it been disbanded after Zach was arrested? Why would Carlos be traveling to Eastern Europe? Confusion cooled his anger, and Zach could feel a frown creasing his forehead. What was this all about?

"Just headed to the ranch for a few days," Christie replied.

Carlos made a sound that Christie seemed to interpret as regret at her absence. "I have wanted to take you to that new restaurant in

Vineland," Carlos said. "You are not getting away from the house enough now that you are on your own."

"What do you mean?" she asked, clearly confused.

"Now that Zach is gone …" Carlos's voice trailed off.

Why was Carlos dating Christie? Was she encouraging this relationship? Did she feel like he, Zach, was "gone"? Zach's heart squeezed.

Christie's frown deepened, and some instinct within Zach sent her a warning look. "Don't," he mouthed.

Cocking her head at Zach, she replied noncommittally to Carlos, "Maybe next time."

"Be certain to call me when you return. You will call me, babe?" Carlos asked, his voice taking on the intonation that best accompanied his persuasive weasel words.

"Yeah," she said, but Zach thought she sounded insincere. Didn't she?

"See you," she said and rang off.

"How long has he been calling you 'babe'?" Zach asked in a chilly voice.

Christie turned in her seat to look at him directly. "Are you serious?" she asked him.

CHAPTER 18

Things are going well. Don't rock the boat. Babe, it's only one four-letter word. The red flare of anger morphed into bright green and began pounding closed the door to Zach's good sense. "Is there something I should know about—" he began, but he had no idea how he sounded to his wife. Certainly not calm and level because Christie slammed out of the Jeep.

"Christie!" Zach called angrily after her, lowering his window to track her progress.

"I have been completely faithful to you, Zach, through everything. I don't deserve this," she said, and he had no difficulty reading her mood—indignant and angry.

After flinging open the back door, she unclipped Gideon and helped him out. "Gideon, honey, let's go find some chocolate milk," she said and then just walked away.

"Christie?" Zach said, launching the single word that was her name on an intercept course.

In the past twenty minutes, Zach had gone from calm to angry to confused to furiously, neon-green jealous. His head spun with the vertigo of his abruptly shifting emotions, and he fought to discover what was a true and appropriate reaction to this situation and what was a post-traumatic mirage. *Emotional lability.* That was what Dr. Baines had called Zach's rapidly shifting, unstable emotional responses; it was a clear post-traumatic stress reaction.

Zach needed to calm down and think rationally. So Carlos had called

Christie. What did that mean? Most likely, Carlos hadn't heard that Zach was back in Canada—well, in the States at the moment.

Throwing away his plans for the night, he took control of the situation and decided that tonight, they would stay here. After opening the Jeep's hatch, he gathered up the bags and then slammed them back onto the floor. Control? Hah! As if he had any control over the careening missile of his life.

Breathing deeply, he tried to focus. *Lord, help me get this straight.* Okay. What did it all mean? Carlos. Christie. No way! Christie had risked everything to rescue him. Not Carlos. Him. And she had not believed Zimmerman's report. The heat of Zach's jealousy chilled to warm. If Christie was on his side, then what was the problem?

Zach slammed the hatch shut, locked the Jeep, and took off down the street, scanning the empty parking lot and then following the most likely path that Christie had taken.

"Christie! Gideon," he called. *Restaurant, fast food, corner store. Where are they?* He jogged toward the corner store, the most likely source of chocolate milk.

As Zach reached the entrance to the store, he spotted Christie and Gideon coming around the corner from the restroom. He knew the exact moment she spotted him because her smile that was meant for Gideon turned flat on her mouth and her deep-blue eyes grew glacial.

"Christie," Zach said on a breath.

"Hi, Daddy," said Gideon, oblivious to his father's emotional pendulum.

Zach smiled; he couldn't help it. "Hi, Gideon. Did you get chocolate milk?"

"Pee first then chocolate milk," he replied.

"That was a good idea," Zach said, falling into step beside them.

"Gideon likes chocolate milk," he said.

"*I* like chocolate milk," Christie amended his comment. Gideon repeated her words.

"I like chocolate milk, too," said Zach.

Christie launched an arrow of heat at him. It was not the good kind of heat that implied passion and attraction, just the irritated kind. "Can we please talk about this?" Zach asked, taking her by the elbow.

"Chocolate milk first then talk," said Gideon as he tugged on his mother's hand.

And Gideon won the day. They picked out a small bottle of chocolate milk and a straw and then sat out on the curb so he could drink it.

"Christie, I want to say, I'm sorry. I approached that in completely the wrong way. I'm pretty sure that my reactions are still out of whack. Did you read that article that Dad sent about disempowerment in victims of incarceration? Well, it—" he said.

Placing her fingers over his lips, she chuckled in surprise at him and the ice in her eyes melted away. "Yes, in fact, I did read that article. I'm surprised that you did, though."

"Why? Because I have trouble reading?" he asked, feeling defensive. She'd never seemed to be bothered by his learning disability in the past.

"Of course not. I'm surprised because I happen to know that it was holding my place in the middle of a ladies' magazine," she said and grinned at him. "Were you checking out fashion tips?"

Breathing deeper as the vise of anger loosened from his chest, he smiled in chagrin. "Very funny," he said wryly. "There was an article on autism in that magazine, and then when I found the article on prison, I read it, too." He cleared his throat. "I've noticed that my reactions swing pretty quickly from one extreme to the other and that they don't always match the situation. I even talked to Dr. Baines about it."

Her eyes got all soft and misty. "I'm glad ...that you talked to her ... and told me. I, uh, I may have overreacted in the Jeep. Come on, Giddy; let's go back."

"Not finished yet," Gideon answered flatly.

"So, uh, Carlos ..." Zach said, forcing himself to approach the subject cautiously in case his jealousy took over again.

"I know that he's your best friend, but I'm really not comfortable with him," she said, speaking haltingly. "I just can't get past the fact that if he hadn't reported Zimmerman's suspicions, then maybe Thomason would have sent help. Are you upset with Carlos?"

"I guess not. Well, not entirely. I was surprised that he didn't stand up for me, but I guess all that proves is that I thought he was a better friend than he actually was. It happens. Not his fault. Uh, so you didn't …" He let his voice trail off. *Go to dinner with him?* Slowly, slowly.

"No," she replied. "I've never betrayed you, Zach."

"You know, I'm pretty sure that *you* are my best friend. You believed in me. You came for me," he said, willing her to accept that he believed this to be true.

"I'm hungry," Gideon said before Christie could respond. "Burgers, French fries, pizza, these are all foods."

Christie laughed fondly. "That's from a speech test he took a few weeks ago."

"You ready for supper?" Zach asked Gideon.

"Are you ready?" Gideon asked. "I'm ready."

"We passed a restaurant just off the interchange, Cactus Dan's," Zach said. "We can walk there from here."

Gideon took up a position between them, swinging from their arms.

"You know, uh, it was Blake who told me I should maintain a relationship with Carlos. He said that Carlos had information and maybe it was best to keep an open line of communication with him, that perhaps it would help us find you," she said, surprising him.

"That makes sense," he said cautiously.

"It was not because I like him. Gideon doesn't like Carlos at all. He calls him 'Smelly,'" Christie said. Smiling, she leaned in to kiss Zach on the mouth. "Are we okay?"

Gideon pushed them apart so he could return to his swinging.

"Yeah, I, uh, the *babe* thing, I don't like it," he said, surreptitiously judging her reaction.

"Me neither," Christie said, her response sure and definite.

"Hey, sir, ma'am," the waiter at Cactus Dan's met them at the door, gesturing toward the nearest of four empty tables in the restaurant. He was a barely adult male in tight black jeans and a T-shirt, which read "Cactus Dan's Best Foods Eatery" and had a picture of an angry bull across the chest. "We got ribs, any sauce, with rings and sides for $12.99

and the fish sandwich with fries for $9.99. The rest is on the menu board at the front. You want anythin' to drink?"

"Just water, please," Zach replied.

"Chocolate milk," Gideon said.

"Do you have chocolate milk?" Zach asked.

"Nah. Cola?" the waiter replied hopefully.

"Just water, thanks," Zach said and then turned to Gideon. "We'll get some chocolate milk later, okay, buddy?"

"Okay, buddy," Gideon replied. "Do you want to see the pictures?"

"What pictures?" Zach asked. When he looked around the small restaurant, he saw a line of black-and-white photographs on the near wall which seemed to record the efforts of locals to consume copious quantities of highly spiced barbecued ribs. "Okay."

Christie is awfully quiet. He glanced over at her tense profile.

"The only vegetables or fruits on this menu seem to be apple crumble and cornbread," Christie said, clearly disgusted. *So, not mad at me then. Good.*

"Daddy," Gideon said. "Daddy, how are you feeling?"

Zach rose slowly to join Gideon. "Pardon me?"

Gideon glanced over at Zach and then back at the picture he was studying. "How is he feeling?"

Zach followed Gideon's line of sight and saw a photograph of a large man, face covered in barbecue sauce, an empty plate before him, and a case of serious indigestion. "Sick, I would say. He ate too much, and it made him sick."

When the food arrived, Zach led Gideon back to the table.

"This looks horrible!" Gideon exclaimed.

"Lower your voice," Zach said, but Gideon stubbornly stuck to his estimation of the food and refused to eat any of it.

"Why don't we just go?" Christie said. "He's building up to a volcanic meltdown."

"Red. Red. Red. No ketchup," Gideon demanded, and Zach didn't have a clue what he was talking about. He still hadn't figured out the color codes. Red. Blue. Yellow. Christie and Gideon seemed to share some mysterious language unknown to Zach.

"Christie, could you help me out a little here? What is he talking about?" Zach said.

"He wants large fries," she replied.

"There are French fries on his plate," Zach said, pointing to the obvious evidence.

"They're not the right fries. It all looks very different from what he's used to. Let's just go, Zach."

"Christie," he began and then stopped. Why was she always so afraid of public tantrums?

Her eyes betrayed the fact that she'd read his thoughts. "Okay, you're right. In fact, you've been right about that all along. Could we start tomorrow? Maybe problem-solve a few strategies first?" she asked, and so that peace should reign …

"All right," Zach conceded the argument. He got the food to-go so that, he, at least, could eat it later.

"I'm pretty sure I saw a large yellow sign for the place that sells the fries he likes a few blocks over," Christie said. "Come on, Gid. You can have fries."

"Red?" Gideon asked cautiously.

"Yes," she said.

"Chocolate milk?" he asked. His little voice was so full of hope that Zach just shook his head in dismay, a reward for publicly and quite rudely rejecting a meal?

"Sure," she said.

Gideon felt very jumpy and yucky after looking at that horrible food, so he began to recite the names of his favorite dinosaurs: "*Apatosaurus … Tyrannosaurus rex … Stegosaurus …*"

"Carnivores eat meat. Herbivores eat plants, like Vegisaurus but Vegisaurus isn't a real dinosaur, it's just a joke. Gideon likes French fries. Gideon's a Fryosaurus." He used what Mommy called his "fake laugh."

"Mommy?" Gideon said.

"Why do you think that Carlos reported Zimmerman's suspicions?" Mommy asked.

Mommy wasn't listening to Gideon, so he spoke louder. "Mommy! Mommy, Mommy, Mommy."

"Yes, Gideon?" Mommy finally said.

"What kind of dinosaur is Mommy?" he asked, knowing the correct answer already: *a Boyasaurus because I love to eat little boys*. Asking questions that he already knew the answer to was fun, and it felt good. After that horrible supper, he needed to feel good again. His stomach hurt. He felt like he had the throw-ups. The dinosaurs were helping, but Gideon still felt jumpy and grumpy.

"A Mommysaurus," she replied, but her voice didn't sound right, sort of like she wasn't listening.

"I suppose Carlos thought he was doing the right thing," Daddy said.

"What did Zimmerman see that made him think that you were doing D-R-U-G-S?" Mommy said.

"D is for dinosaur. What kind of dinosaur is Mommy?" Gideon demanded to know. *Mommy said it wrong*. What was wrong with her? He needed to hear the right answer. He couldn't wait any longer. The words were building up inside him until he felt like he would explode. *Boyasaurus. Boyasaurus. Boyasaurus!*

"*Boyasaurus!*" Gideon yelled, stomping his feet and grabbing at Mommy's arm. "Say it! Say it!"

"For Pete's sake, Gideon. Settle down," Daddy said, reaching out to hold his arm.

"Say it! Say it! Say it!" Gideon slipped out of Daddy's grip, flopping onto the sidewalk.

"Would you just say the right words, Christie?" Daddy said. His voice sounded angry or frustrated or some other mad feeling.

"Zach," Mommy said.

"Zach, Zach, Zach. Zachary Clyde Marek. Say it, Mommy!" Gideon demanded. The jumpy feeling was getting worse and worse.

"A Boyasaurus because I love to eat little boys," she said ... finally!

Mommy knelt down and gave Gideon a big hug, hard and long. It felt so good. It made the jumpy feeling calm down a little. *Thank you, Mommy.*

"Sorry, Christie," Daddy said. "Just ... please ... don't be upset, baby."

Upset? Sometimes *upset* meant mad. Mommy's face didn't look mad. Sometimes *upset* meant sad. Did Mommy look sad? Was Mommy going to cry? "Don't cry, baby," Gideon said. "Have some French fries. You like French fries. No ketchup. Red," Gideon said, trying to make Mommy feel better. He didn't want Mommy to cry. Sometimes Mommy patted him on the back when he was sad, so Gideon patted her on the bum. "French fries and chocolate milk."

Mommy and Daddy laughed. *Good.* Laughing was happy.

"Let's go get you some large fries, sweetheart," Mommy said, taking his hand and walking again. "Do you want fries with your *Apatosaurus* burger?"

"That's silly," Gideon said.

CHAPTER 19

Paralyzed in the blackened pitch of his nighttime prison cell, Zach struggled helplessly as, with rising dread, the mysterious rhythm repeated, matching the beat of his heart. "Dead. Buried. Gone." Another scoop of earth was dumped on his face, obscuring his vision and making it hard to breathe.

"Zach."

Zach lurched up in bed, banging his head into the headboard. *Headboard?* Where was he?

"Zach, you're dreaming," Christie said.

Zach visually searched the room, rubbing the emerging bruise on his forehead. Christie was sitting propped against the headboard of the second bed. Of course. While prison bunks did not have headboards, motel beds did. Beside Christie, Gideon was jumping on the mattress, flapping his arms like he was trying to take off and fly into the flickering lights of the muted television, thus explaining the repetitive thumping woven into Zach's nightmares.

"Time is it?" he gasped, his chest still pumping in reaction to his nightmare. *Safe. You're safe,* he reminded himself.

"Almost six," she said. "You okay?"

Okay? Yes? No. Maybe. Avoiding the question, Zach said, "You look like you haven't had much sleep."

"Hmmm," she replied, sounding weary.

She waved him over, and Zach gratefully accepted the comfort she offered. He crawled up along her body, hooking one arm beneath her knee and wrapping the other around her waist. Resting his head on her leg, he sighed in absolute contentment as she ran her fingers through his hair, massaging his scalp.

"What did you dream about?"

"Prison."

"Is that happening a lot?" she asked, and he could hear the concern in her voice.

"No. Well, a bit, but it's no big deal. I can handle it." He rolled abruptly out of bed and grabbed his jeans and a T-shirt before she could sense the doubt in his statement. He wasn't certain of his mental state. However, he refused to let anything interfere with their holiday.

In the bathroom, he splashed cold water on his face, combed his fingers through his hair and got dressed. What he really wanted was a brisk shower to wash away the cold prickle of fear. More than that, he wanted to get outside, to breathe a little fresh air and see the sky. How he'd missed the broad, blue skies of Wyoming when he'd been in prison. His solitary cell at the unnamed prison had been fitted with a single, six-by-six-inch window, which saw the sun only briefly just before noon.

Zach stepped back into the main room and rifled through Gideon's duffel bag. He retrieved a set of clothes for the boy and said, "Okay, Gideon. Get dressed." He needed to get outside. If he took Gideon with him, he wouldn't look like he was running away. He would not make that mistake again.

"Dressed, dressed, dressed. Time to get dressed. Mister Dressup. Dressed, dressed, dressed," Gideon chanted, obviously at the point of full-blown dysregulation. Zach was very proud to know that word. He'd read it in one of the articles that Christie had given him.

Striding to the bed, he caught Gideon midbounce, pulling him close and tickling him. "Hey, monkey-boy, put your clothes on, we're going out."

"Out?" Christie asked.

"Yeah," Zach said. "We'll bring something back for breakfast."

Gideon was still chiming away his "dressup" tune but stilled immediately upon hearing the reference to food.

"French fries," Gideon said. "Red."

"No way. Not for breakfast," Christie told him.

"Okay, okay. White paper. White, white, white," Gideon said.

"Not a chance," Christie said. "Breakfast food."

Gideon rocked up onto the balls of his feet, elbows flapping.

"Get dressed," Zach reminded him, hoping to stave off the impending tantrum at least until he could get outside. If he could figure out what "red" and "white paper" had to do with breakfast, he'd be miles ahead.

Gideon wiggled out of Zach's arms and pushed his pajama pants down.

"Go pee first," Christie called to him.

Gideon paused in the act of undressing and then hopped into the bathroom with his pajama pants down around his knees. Zach chuckled.

Turning back, he caught Christie's amused grin and stopped, breathless at the beauteous joy in her eyes. "You're so beautiful," he said, and his panic receded.

Sitting on the edge of the bed beside her, he reached for her and she came into his arms. He had chosen right when he'd fallen in love with her. She'd given him an amazing son, and she'd given him steadfast fidelity. Beyond all that, she'd given him hope, hope that one day they could create something wonderful together.

Zach reached out to brush a lock of hair from her forehead, and then because he didn't want to stop touching her, he caressed her face with his fingertips. Leaning in, he kissed her, lightly resting his mouth against hers. A bolt of desire shot through his body when her tongue came out in a little exploratory lick against his lips. He wanted to pull back and see the expression on her face, but he was reluctant to end the kiss. So instead, he opened his mouth and kissed her deeply. He tasted her, exploring her lips, her teeth, and her tongue, sensation buzzing through his system. When he pulled back, she looked so very serious.

"I love you, both of you, more than life itself," he said, sure and definite.

"Still?" she replied. "In spite of everything?"

"Always."

Zach kissed Christie once more and then rose from the bed because he knew that if he didn't move soon, he was going to curl up in her arms and stay there forever. As much as it sounded like a good way to go, Gideon needed breakfast.

"Come on, Gideon. Let's go," Zach said.

Gideon bounced back into the bedroom. "Go, go. The train goes fast. Time to go."

"Say bye to Mommy," Zach said.

"Bye to Mommy," said Gideon.

Christie laughed. "Be good for Daddy."

Zach took Gideon on a walking tour of the vicinity, finally finding a park and then a restaurant that served an acceptable breakfast food: pancakes with syrup but no butter. They took it to-go.

On the way back to the motel, Zach practiced the little verse that Sandi the SLP had taught him to help Gideon learn new phrases. He practiced as often as possible, whenever he and Gideon were alone together, especially the one phrase he'd kept secret from Christie. Zach had learned a lot attending those few speech and OT sessions.

"Okay, Gideon, let's get Mommy and get in the Jeep. Today we drive to Des Moines, Iowa," Zach said.

"Ohio. High in the middle and round on both ends. Yuk. Yuk. Yuk," Gideon said. Zach recognized the voice from his own childhood cartoon-watching days. In spite of the hilarious laugh that accompanied the joke, Gideon was speaking much more slowly after their long walk rather than the hyper-speed rate he'd been using when Zach had awakened.

"Iowa not Ohio, son," Zach said. He opened the door to the hotel room. Gideon broke free and jumped directly on Christie, who was sitting on the edge of the bed fastening her sandals.

"Gid!" Zach said as he ran forward toward the bed trying to intercept the little boy. "Sorry, Christie."

"It's okay," she said as she pulled Gideon close for a firm hug. "I love you," she said to Gideon and then kissed the boy on the forehead.

"I love you, Mommy," Gideon replied, echoing her words.

"Zach! Did you hear that? He's never said that before," she said, her voice raised in wonder.

"I've been working on it with him," Zach said proudly. "I asked his speech therapist for advice. You're a great mom, Christie, and I wanted you to know that."

She shone him that happy smile that he'd been longing to see directed at him. "Thank you," she said to Zach and then turned her attention to Gideon. "You may watch television for a few minutes."

"TV," Gideon said, always assuming that everyone was talking directly to him anyway, and then happily jumped up, landing on his bottom on the end of the bed nearest the television.

Tiptoeing up, Christie kissed Zach on the mouth and then backtracked, with her eyes locked on his. She stretched out against the headboard while giving him her best come-hither expression. Zach prowled up along her body, maintaining eye contact the entire way, Christie's smile fell away to be replaced by heat. Rolling, Zach pulled her over until she was lying against him with her head on his chest.

"You know," he said, "this is what I missed the most when I was in prison, just having someone to comfort me."

She kneaded the muscles in his arm and shoulder. "I missed..." She hesitated. He lifted his head to see her. "The fun. The horseplay."

"Like this?" He started to tickle her, and she broke into giggles, wiggling to escape. She grabbed a pillow from the other bed and swung it at him. Finally, he got the pillow from her and tackled her onto the bed. She shrieked with laughter.

"Too loud!" Gideon said, glancing over at them with a reprimand in his eyes as well as on his lips.

"Too bad," Zach replied. "First pillow fight then be quiet."

"Pillow fight?" Gideon said, stepping closer to his father, confusion in his eyes.

"Yep," Zach replied and then hit Gideon softly with the pillow.

Gideon looked at him like he'd lost his mind. Thwump. Christie hit Zach with a pillow forcefully. Laughing, Zach handed a pillow to Gideon and showed him how to hold it and swing it at Mommy. They played around, laughing together until Gideon finally called a halt.

"What time is it?" Gideon asked.

"Nine o'clock," Zach replied after checking his watch.

"Oh no! Go to Des Moines, Iowa," Gideon said and groaned pathetically, shaking his hands vigorously at his sides.

Zach laughed. "Well, let's get this show on the road!"

"On the road!" Gideon replied, giggling, jumping up and down, and chanting loudly.

"Uh-oh. It's not going to be easy to get him into the car now," Christie said. "That was fun, but it was definitely not the right kind of activity just before a long day's journey."

"The right kind of activity?" Zach said.

"Yeah. Some movements are calming for him and some just rev him up," she said. "That's why he's not sleeping. He's just too revved up."

"So we need to avoid excitement?" he asked, disappointed at the thought of that. Gideon was excited, well, manic, at the moment but his smile would eclipse the sun.

"No. That wouldn't be fair. It's okay to have exciting things, but he needs the calming stuff, too. Stimulation, like seeing new things and being out in different situations seems to help him sleep too. We just have to watch out not to overdo it or he gets overstimulated and then he can't sleep."

"I think I'm starting to get it. You know how revved up he was this morning? Dysregulated?" Zach asked.

"Oh, yeah," she said, and then she looked startled. "Dysregulated?"

"Yeah, it's like when a child's sensory system gets out of balance and they're at too high a level or too low a level," he replied. She looked amused. "What?" he said, suddenly feeling defensive.

"You read that in one of the articles I gave you," she said, allowing her smile to escape.

"Yeah. So?" he said.

"Very impressive," she said and smiled at him.

Relaxing a little, he said, "It gets better. I noticed that after we walked all around the neighborhood, he was talking much more slowly."

"I guess walks help him calm down," she said, still smiling.

"Help him regulate," he said, feeling rather smug now. "We don't really have time for another long walk now, so …" Zach searched through his memory for another idea. "The right kind of activity," he murmured, very pleased when Christie smiled her encouragement. "We could play hot dog."

"Hot dog," Gideon repeated. "What do you want on your hot dog, sir?"

"You got it, buddy," Zach said, and then he smiled at the boy. His heart clenched in that feeling of warmth again.

Zach grabbed a quilt and spread it out on the floor, encouraging Gideon to lie in the middle. Christie sat on the other bed, her back resting against the headboard, watching them with a smile in her eyes.

"Ready?" Zach asked.

"Are you ready?" Gideon corrected him.

"Are you ready?" Zach repeated, using the proper words.

"I'm ready," Gideon said, as though they were the words that should be said.

Zach rolled him up in the blanket with his head and shoulders free. "What do you want on your hot dog, sir?"

"Ketchup," Gideon said.

Zach firmly rubbed his hands down Gideon's sides just as he'd seen Christie do.

"What else, sir?"

"Mustard," Gideon replied.

Zach repeated the process.

"Relish?"

"No, sir. No relish," Gideon replied. It was incredible how, when he repeated another person's words, he also repeated their intonation.

"Hot dog's ready," said Zach. He took hold of the edges of the blanket and unrolled Gideon.

Then Zach took his turn, and Gideon rolled him up. It was all going well until Gideon knelt on him in his enthusiasm. Christie smothered a laugh.

"Oomph. A little lower buddy and you'd never have a brother or sister," Zach muttered, groaning. *If I can't keep things good between your mom and me, there won't be no brothers nohow.*

Gideon unrolled Zach with his help. "Big hug," Gideon said, holding his arms up like a little toddler. Lifting him into his embrace, Zach gave him a firm hug. Gideon melted into his body, beginning to relax.

"Nice job," Christie said, kissing Zach on the shoulder.

Score one for Daddy.

CHAPTER 20

"Where are we staying tonight?" Christie asked from the passenger seat of the Jeep.

"I was planning to make it to Des Moines," he said. "Why?"

"Gideon's getting restless. Is there anywhere closer to stop?"

"There's not much until Iowa City," Zach said. "Hey, look, Gid, the Mississippi River." Paddleboats chugged along the riverbank near a series of waterfront condos.

Gideon's voice rang out from the backseat, perfectly familiar though absolutely not his own. "The mighty Mississippi is the largest river in North America, rising in Minnesota and meandering southward to the Gulf of Mexico."

"National Geographic," Christie said.

Zach laughed aloud. His boy was one of a kind.

"Look, Zach, there's a fast-food place across the river. Oh, and, look, they have dollar drinks. Why don't we stop so Gideon can pee? And I would love an iced coffee."

"That sounds good. I wonder if they have iced tea," said Zach. "Er, I think you should probably take Gideon to the bathroom. I'll get the drinks."

"Okay, Giddy, time to go pee. Shoes on," Christie said as Zach parked the Jeep.

"Go pee. No. No pee! No pee! Too loud!" Gideon struggled against the restraints on his booster seat.

Christie stepped out of the vehicle and raced around to his door. "It's okay, Giddy. It's the flushing that's too loud. We won't flush this time. Okay?"

"No pee. No pee!" he said, his voice rising in blatant distress.

She struggled to get him out of the seat as Zach stood back, scanning the parking lot to see a curious crowd of people staring at the commotion.

"Come on, sweetheart. We won't flush. It'll be okay," Christie said. She sounded so calm, but Zach was feeling anything but calm. He felt embarrassed, and he could feel himself getting angry. The temptation to turn Gideon over his knee and make him stop fussing was growing. He needed to step away. He wanted to get Gideon's behavior under control, but the bathroom issue was clearly so distressing for the boy. Anxiety and discipline didn't mix. Zach knew that only too well from his own childhood.

Zach tapped Christie on the back. "Is there anything I can do to help?"

"No," she replied, tersely, clearly just wanting to deal with it, not give a dissertation on the subject.

"I'll go get the drinks," he said, feeling incredibly guilty for the relief he felt that he was free to walk away. But he knew that getting angry at a three-and-a-half-year-old for being traumatized, whether or not he understood the trauma, was pretty pathetic.

Once inside, Zach used the toilet and then lined up for drinks.

"Did you see that kid?" Zach heard a couple of older women talking beside him. "Parents these days don't know anything about discipline…"

Off to his right, he could hear a young family chatting as they ate their burgers. "What was wrong with that boy, Mommy?" the little girl asked.

In front of him, a young couple stood hand in hand. "If that were my kid, I'd turn him over my knee. That mother doesn't have a clue."

Zach could feel his embarrassment quickly giving way to indignation. These people didn't have any idea how hard Christie worked to give Gideon the tools he needed to function in this neurotypical world.

"He has autism," Zach said.

"What?" The man in front turned toward him.

"The boy has autism. And he's my son."

"Sorry, man," the fellow replied. The woman blushed at being caught in her criticism.

"If you're the dad, then why aren't you helping?" she asked, innocently enough.

Because I'm the reason he's freaking out. "If I can get him some chocolate milk, it might help him calm down." *Christie's right. Autism is not for the fainthearted.*

"Go ahead of us, man. If it'll help your kid," the man said and the woman beside him nodded.

More embarrassed now, Zach tried to backpedal. "No, that's not necessary."

"I'm serious, man. Go ahead." They stepped out of the way.

"Thank you," Zach mumbled. He stepped forward, placing his order and moving away. *I've entered a whole new life here, Lord, haven't I?*

Carrying the drinks out to the Jeep, he found Christie putting a new pair of trousers on Gideon while he gazed over her head, watching the shadows through his fingers.

"Hi," Zach said.

"I couldn't get him in time," she said.

"I'm sorry."

She looked up to meet his gaze. "It's okay. It's not the first time. At least I didn't have to go in there and see all the disdainful looks of the other customers. He saved me from that anyway."

Zach was so proud of her because he knew exactly what she was talking about now. He'd experienced it. People were always quick to judge and slow to understand. "I love you, Christie."

She looked up in surprise. "What made you say that?"

"I just continually realize how amazing you are." She kept watching him until he couldn't bear the scrutiny any longer. He looked away, setting the drinks on top of the Jeep. "I got you an iced coffee and got a chocolate milk for Gideon."

"Chocolate milk. Chocolate milk," Gideon replied, dropping his hands to look up at Zach as though he'd just realized he was standing there. "Hi, Daddy."

Zach smiled. "Hi, sweetheart. Finish getting dressed, and you can have your milk."

Gideon lifted his feet dutifully as Christie pulled on his socks.

"Why don't I take him for a walk while you use the facilities?" Zach said.

"Okay. His running shoes are soaked. I don't know why I had him put them on when I knew this would most likely happen. But if you're careful, you can probably walk around without them."

"I'll be careful," Zach replied, meaning so much more than he could have.

She stopped and looked him directly in the eyes. "Zach? I'm sorry that I didn't warn you about toilets. I wasn't purposely trying to sabotage you. It's just really hard to remember everything."

His chest expanded. Maybe, just maybe, he wasn't to blame for everything that went wrong in his little family. "I know. It's okay."

She graced him with a smile and then returned to business, finishing dressing Gideon. "The clothes smell pretty strong. Do we have a plastic bag to put them in? We'll have to wash them out tonight and maybe pick up an extra pair of shoes for him."

"I'll find something," Zach assured her.

"Chocolate milk. Are you thirsty? Yes," Gideon said.

"Walk first, then chocolate milk," Christie said. She passed his hand over to Zach and walked to the restaurant.

"Let's put these drinks inside, and then we'll go for a little walk," Zach suggested.

"No shoes, Daddy," Gideon said, looking down at his feet. "Ewww. They're wet," he said, in Christie's voice.

Zach chuckled. "Usually, we wear shoes when we go for a walk, but right now, it's okay to walk without them."

"Okay to walk without them." Gideon looked up and held out his hand to Zach. "Hold hands."

Zach took his hand and warmth enveloped him.

CHAPTER 21

It was proving to be a long day, longer than the day before. Zach clenched his teeth together as a barrier to prevent his temper from escaping as Christie flipped from station to station on the radio. "Could you please choose one?" he asked, trying to sound reasonable and not snap at her as he so badly wanted to do.

"I don't like any of this music. We need to get some CDs or something," she said.

"Mommy, Mommy, Mommy," Gideon said.

"Yes," Christie replied.

"All done," he said.

"What's all done?" she asked.

"All done. All done," Gideon repeated.

"What's all done, sweetie?" she asked again, and Zach could see her fraying a little at the edges though her voice was perfectly calm. *Maybe she gets her mad out at me so she can stay calm for Gid.*

Gideon whipped the earphones off his head. "Fix it," he ordered, holding them out to his mother.

"Fix the story, please, Mommy," Zach said and Gideon repeated his words. *A few manners could take you a long way in life.*

Christie fiddled with the mp3 player for a little while and then turned to Zach. "There are only two more stories on here. If we use them up today, he's going to have nothing tomorrow."

"Maybe we could stop at a bookstore and buy a couple more," Zach said.

"Audiobooks are very expensive. I should have brought more from the library," Christie said.

"Mommy, Mommy, Mommy. Fix it," Gideon said. He began to kick the back of Zach's seat. Thump. Thump. Thump.

"Gideon, please don't kick my seat," Zach said. Gideon kept right on kicking.

"Maybe we should stop and let him run around for a little while," Christie suggested.

"It hasn't even been an hour since we got back on the road. We need to put some distance behind us," Zach replied. The thumping in his back became increasingly irritating. "Can't you find a way to amuse him?"

"What am I supposed to do? He's great in the car for a day but …" She left the sentence hanging as she did a whoop-de-doo gesture for him.

Great! Zach gritted his teeth again. "Could you please do something so he will stop kicking my seat? Please." He used perhaps a tad more emphasis on the last word than necessary.

Sighing dramatically, she released her seat belt and climbed into the back and belted in beside Gideon. The first thing she did was to remove his shoes and set them on the floor. Why? Zach didn't know.

"Okay, sweetie," she said. "Let's play *Name that Dinosaur*. My turn. He's large, bigger than a house, with a long neck and a long tail."

"Is he a herbivore?" Gideon asked. He always sounded so different when he said things that he'd rehearsed many times.

"Yes."

"Is he *Apatosaurus*?" he asked.

"Yes. Good job. Whose turn is it?" she said.

"My turn. He has big teeth. He has a big head and little arms," Gideon said, waving his arms gleefully.

Christie laughed. "That's from a movie, isn't it?" she asked. "Is he *Tyrannosaurus rex*?"

"Yes," Gideon replied, smiling.

They continued the game for long enough that it became irritating to listen to, and Zach wondered how Christie could stand it.

"Zach?" she asked, tapping him on the shoulder. "I think he needs to pee. Can you find us a place to stop, please?"

"Sure. Is it urgent?" Zach asked.

"From the look on his face, I'd say it's urgent," she replied.

"Will do. Beresford's straight ahead. ETA five minutes." Zach accelerated. "Let me know if his status changes."

"Will do," she replied, and he could hear a hint of humor in her voice.

They almost made it. Two steps toward the gas station bathroom and Gideon created a yellow puddle between his feet.

"I'm sorry, Christie. I tried," Zach said, taking the blame for Gideon's wet pants.

"It's okay," she said and then sighed. "He won't admit when he needs to pee because he's afraid of the flushing. Can you please get me a change of clothes and the wipes, and I'll take him into the bathroom to change him?"

"No flushing," Gideon said. His eyes were wide in that deer-in-the-headlights expression that spoke of shock and awe.

"No flushing," Christie agreed.

Zach handed over the items to her. "I'll see if I can find something to amuse him inside."

She nodded and led Gideon away.

Zach found a couple of comic books, some candies in a hard-to-open container, which he thought might keep Gideon busy for a while, and some dinosaur stickers. He gassed up the Jeep and then used the facilities. He met Christie while she was belting Gideon in.

"Would you like to drive for a while, and I'll take a turn amusing him?"

She looked surprised. "Okay." She pointed to the objects on the seat beside Gideon. "Did you buy those?"

"Yep. That okay?" he asked, suddenly uncertain.

"Yes. Definitely." She kissed him on the cheek. *Whoa!* How desperate was he when he felt like he'd do anything just to earn another one of those?

She took the keys and seemed very pleased to be in the driver's seat. Zach belted himself in beside Gideon. He read the comics to Gideon using different voices for the characters and then played a game that he didn't truly understand but resulted in his face and body being covered in stickers. He repeated the game and stuck the stickers all over Gideon's legs so he could look at them. Then he gave the candies to Gideon and leaned his head against the back of the seat. *This is far more exhausting than driving.*

"Zach, look at that sign," Christie interrupted his musings. The sign said "Dick's 24 HR Toe Service."

Climbing back into the front, he chuckled. "Is that like an all-day podiatrist?"

"Boy, spelling really does count in life!" She laughed.

Leaning forward over the seat, he pulled out the tour guide for the area. "Want a detour round Falls Park in Sioux Falls?" he asked when her laughter died down.

"Sure. Can we actually get out for a few minutes?" she asked, channeling her finest coquette.

Huffing in mock disdain, Zach replied, "Always wants to get out of the Jeep. Never satisfied."

Finding just the right spot beneath his arm, Christie gave him just a little pinch.

"Hey, lady. Keep your hands to yourself," he said, reprimanding her playfully.

"Hands to yourself," Gideon chimed in from the backseat.

At first glance, Sioux Falls gave the appearance of an industrial city with its various quarries and agricultural industries, not unlike Hamilton, Ontario, just west of Jordan Harbor, with its factories and steel mills. The juxtaposition of railway tracks across the waterfall put the lambent beauty of the geology in direct contrast to the harsh reality of industrialization. Unless you were Gideon. Then the trains just made it all perfect, in spite of the roaring thunder of the falls, dumping 7,400 gallons of water one hundred feet each second.

Ten minutes in Falls Park became a half hour as they fell captive to the beauty of the falls of the Big Sioux River, following as it dropped step by step through the park.

Zach took over the driving again after they picked up dollar drinks. Gideon actually made it to the toilet in time, earning himself much praise from Christie. While they were in the bathroom, Zach bought Gideon large fries in a red cardboard packet as a reward. *Hah!* It finally made sense. "Red" meant large French fries from McDonald's. The small and medium sizes came in white paper packets. *Finally!*

"That's a great idea," Christie said when he presented the fries to Gideon, and then she kissed Zach on the mouth. *Woo-hoo!*

Gideon fell asleep as they passed Salem, South Dakota.

"That's the worst thing about car rides," Christie said.

"What's that?" Zach asked.

"He's really great in the car, but if he decides to fall asleep, there's no way to keep him awake."

"How is sleep bad?"

"Naps are very bad. Even if he only sleeps for an hour, a nap means he's awake all night. And I'm so tired."

"Do you want me to take a turn tonight?"

She smiled at him. "Yeah, I'd really like that." *Three points for Zachary.*

Once they pulled into the Thunderbird Motel, Gideon was awake and raring to go again.

"TV, TV, TV," Gideon said, jumping between the two beds in the room.

Christie groaned as she flopped spread-eagled on the mattress, her body lurching every second bounce. "We need to eat first," she said.

"No eat! TV, TV, TV," Gideon repeated. Christie must have given in because as Zach returned to the Jeep for the last load of items, he heard the unmistakable drone of the news in the background.

"No, Mommy," Gideon said. "Cartoon rabbit."

"Just a minute, Giddy, I want to hear the news," Christie replied.

"News. No," Gideon said, his displeasure clear and definite.

Zach dropped the last bag on the bed nearest the window.

"Zach, come look at this," Christie said, and Zach turned to see a picture of Senior Inspector Thomason.

The news reporter continued. "... Americans Cirillo and Domenico, along with Ian Thomason of the Ontario Provincial Police, were taken by kidnappers. The three visiting law enforcement consultants were traveling from Copacabana to La Paz when their transport was stopped by gunmen. Their driver, local Mauricio Larralde-Gomez, was shot and killed. Thomason, who was seconded to the South American country of Bolivia, is connected to convicted felon, former OPP officer Zachary Marek. Marek was convicted of dealing heroin while taking part in an international antidrugs task force in the country of Albania. Marek is currently serving a ten-year sentence in a federal prison in Albania. Thomason's whereabouts are unknown, though the guerrilla faction *Libertad Ejército* is thought to be responsible." The newscaster paused and shuffled some papers, a smile now plastered across his face. "In local news …"

"Zachary Marek is Daddy," Gideon said, looking up at his mother for confirmation.

Christie flipped the channels until she found a familiar cartoon. "Yes, sweetheart, Zach is your Daddy," Christie replied, her voice soft and sad.

"That's why they gave me such a hard time at the border," Zach said, his mind dull but rapidly booting. "I'll get some ice."

"Zach," Christie said, giving him pause. "We all know you didn't do it."

Turning, he reluctantly met her gaze. "Who knows?"

"Everyone who matters," she replied. Her eyes were soft and sad just like her voice.

"I'll, uh … thanks," he said and stood there stupidly.

"It looks like we have a choice of Chef Louis' giant bull diner or the Pizza Ranch," Christie said, changing the subject, something for which he was extremely grateful.

"Pizza, pizza, pizza," Gideon interjected, his voice cheerful in its exuberance.

Zach couldn't do anything about the past, but he could make his son happy for a few hours. And one thing he'd discovered recently, if Gideon was happy, Christie was happy, too. "Well, pizza it is then," Zach said.

The Pizza Ranch was a pizza buffet.

"At home, you don't have to pay before you eat. Do people really eat and then skip out?" Christie said.

Zach shrugged. "Different country. Different customs."

She looked around the room. "Where's the salad bar?"

"This is it," Zach said, nodding at the table in front of them.

Her jaw dropped. "You're kidding. I see pudding, mousse, jelly salad. I don't see anything green at all."

"The jelly salad is green," Zach said, tongue-in-cheek.

She gave him a horrified glance, which he found hilarious.

"So no veggies tonight?" he asked and then laughed again at the quelling glare she shot him.

"Not unless you count mashed potatoes," she said, and she didn't sound impressed.

"No detatoes," said Gideon, frowning, clearly not impressed either.

CHAPTER 22

Christie got three entire hours of sleep that night before Gideon woke her. She kept hoping that Zach would wake up and take over, but he slept peacefully in the other bed. She found herself actually hoping that he'd have another nightmare just so she'd have an excuse to wake him.

Flipping on the bedside light, she insisted Gideon sit with her, and she read him every book in his backpack.

"Ready for beddy?" she asked, feeling a foolish hope.

"Not time for bed. TV," he replied as he bounced up to his feet and dropped to his bottom on the foot of the bed and then the floor on his feet. He climbed back on the bed and started again.

"No TV. Let's go have a bath," Christie said. She glanced over at Zach, but he continued to sleep. *Hmph. So much for taking a turn.* Christie's mood swirled down the drain of parental sleeplessness, down there beside walking pneumonia and right next door to committee meetings.

After retrieving a few dinosaurs, Christie filled the bathtub with warm water and emptied the contents of one of the miniscule motel shampoo bottles to make some bubbles.

"Okay, sweetie, undress and you can have a bath," she said, smiling at him.

"Bath, bath. Time for a bath," he replied, undressing. He took Christie's hand as she helped him into the tub.

By dawn, Christie was curled on the end of the bed, building towers out of all the minimarshmallows she had extracted from the packets of hot chocolate they'd brought along. Gideon would look to her to say, "Ready! Set! Go!" and then he would take a run at them and kick them over, after which he begged her to pick them up so he didn't have to touch them with his hands. And then the game started again. It was perhaps not the best use for food, but she'd gladly let him play with the last steak and broccoli on earth if he would just let her sleep.

CHAPTER 23

Snowflakes were falling through the window and into Zach's prison cell. The beauty of the crystalline structures, stark against the dull gray of the walls, carried Zach away from the cold and hunger to a time before prison, before Christie had fallen out of love with him—if only he could deduce when that had happened. The first Christmas after they'd married, Zach had built a snow shelter in the lee of Beartooth Mountain and lined it with tarps and a sleeping bag. He'd supplied it with sparkling grape juice, caviar, and candles. And then he'd lured Christie out. As they'd ridden his horse, Clyde, across the pasture, the snow had fallen in large flakes, coating their eyelashes—beauty and love, deeper than the glacial snows.

Except these snowflakes seemed to be marshmallows.

"More marshymellys, Mommy," Gideon said, his voice reaching into Zach's dream.

"Ready, set, go," Christie said. Her voice was heavy and thick with exhaustion.

Surfacing from his dream to awareness, Zach asked, "How long you been awake?" seeing her slumped onto the floor at the end of Gideon's bed while Gideon kicked the snot out of marshmallows. Why was she letting him do that to food?

"A while," she replied. She'd been awake a lot longer than a while from the looks of her. Her pale face was sporting dark circles under the eyes.

Rolling out of bed, he grabbed his shorts and a T-shirt. "Time to get dressed, Gid," Zach said before he turned back to her. "Why don't you hang out here, and Gid and I will get breakfast and then pack the car?"

"I'm having a shower," Christie said.

Christie bumped her lip with the spoon while scooping granola into her mouth.

"I thought maybe we could stop at the Corn Palace after breakfast. What do you think?" Zach asked.

"Yeah," she said, not really caring as long as it meant she didn't have to entertain Gideon in the car for part of the day.

Parking behind a small building, which could have been a restaurant or a pub or a derelict building from the looks of it, Zach led them across a boardwalk lined with shops that sold Corn Palace T-shirts, Corn Palace hoodies, Corn Palace blankets, Corn Palace salt and pepper shakers, and even Corn Palace corn cobs. Of course, none of them were open yet because it was still so early.

"Hey, look, Gideon! A giant corn," Zach said, pointing to a statue.

"Giant cornelius," Gideon said.

Zach chuckled. "Christie, come over. I'll take a picture of you and Gideon with the giant corn," Zach said.

Christie took Gideon's hand and obediently stood by the statue of the giant corn. She felt like scowling at the camera but tried to find a semblance of a smile.

"Okay," Zach said. "Let's go see that Corn Palace."

"Cornelius Place," Gideon repeated.

Christie kept one hand firmly on Gideon's wrist as they crossed the street. The so-called Corn Palace was a large building with turrets and onion domes. The walls were covered in mosaics made of ... what else? Corn.

"Sounds like they create new mosaics every year," Zach said as he led them down the hallway toward a large auditorium. The upper walls were covered in over a dozen mosaics: plains natives, a cowboy on a bucking bronco, the Last Supper, and many more.

"This is more impressive than I expected," Christie murmured.

Gideon pulled her toward the enormous gift shop in the middle of the auditorium. "Mommy, giant corn."

"Yes, honey, there's lots of corn here," she said, but he continued to pull on her. Finally, she gave in and followed him. He grabbed a stuffed corn-on-the-cob from a shelf.

"Giant corn," he said. "Little corn. Cornelius."

"Okay, sweetie. You can have that. We need to buy it first, though." Christie reached out to take the little stuffed corn person from Gideon.

He pulled it back. "No, no. Mine."

Christie crouched down. "Yes, you can have it, but we have to pay for it first." She released the stuffed corn and took Gideon's wrist firmly in hers so he couldn't bolt. "Come with me, and we'll pay."

"Mine?" he asked, looking up at her with shimmering eyes.

"Pay first, then you can have it," she said.

Once the little corn was well and truly Gideon's, Christie went in search of Zach, finding him beneath the Native American mosaic. It depicted three riders on horseback, dressed for battle, riding off toward the sunset.

"We're ready to go," she said. She knew she sounded snappish, but she was tired and fed up.

"Okay," Zach said, meeting her gaze. He shifted his gaze to Gideon. "Hey, what's that you've got?"

"Cornelius," he said.

"Wow. That's cool, Gid. You ready to go?" Zach asked, stroking a finger across the hairy top of Cornelius's head.

"I'm ready," said Gideon.

"Where to today?" Christie asked as they settled into the Jeep.

"Rapid City. It should be about five hours or so."

Christie actually groaned.

CHAPTER 24

That night, Zach stayed awake until Gideon fell asleep at midnight. Christie stayed up as well, and they read stories and had another pillow fight. It was good to be together. But in the morning, they were back to grumpy Christie.

"Get ready," Christie grumbled.

"What's wrong with Mommy, huh?" Zach asked Gideon quietly.

"Six thirty breakfast," Gideon said.

"I don't think that's it," he said, chuckling wryly. It was generally best not to take Gideon's words at face value. "Do you want a hug?"

"Do you want a hug? Yes," replied Gideon.

"Could you hurry up, please?" Christie said impatiently. "I've been up since 4:00 a.m. I'm hungry."

"Ah, our first clue," Zach said to Gideon.

"A clue! A clue!" Gideon mimicked.

"Is that from a TV show? Christie, do you want me to shower later?" Zach asked.

"Yes. Hurry up," she said, clearly annoyed.

"Come on, Mister Clue. You can go pee while I get dressed," Zach said. He took the boy's hand and led him into the bathroom. Gideon balked at the door.

"No pee. No flushing," Gideon yelled, pulling on Zach's arm.

"Oh for goodness' sake! Can't you help me at all?" Christie said.

Her words caused a clenching in his gut, but he ignored it to focus on Gideon, trying to remember the words Christie used to help Gideon.

"No flushing. Go pee, and then you can put your hands on your ears and I'll flush."

"No flushing?" Gideon asked, quieter now.

"No flushing," Zach confirmed.

"Okay," Gideon said.

Hey, got it right for once. Proudly, Zach spared a glance at Christie's face, hoping to see approval but she'd turned her back on him. Feeling disheartened, he stepped into the bathroom and closed the door. Gideon relieved himself and then brushed his teeth as Zach got dressed.

"Okay, buddy. You step outside the bathroom, and I'll flush. Tell me when you're ready," Zach said.

Gideon quick-stepped out of the bathroom and covered his ears with his hands.

"Are you ready?" Zach asked.

"Are you ready?" Gideon repeated. "I'm ready."

Zach smiled, flushing the toilet.

"Okay. Your men are ready. I shall treat you to a complimentary continental breakfast, my darling. If you will accompany me?" Zach said, gesturing grandly for her to precede him out the door.

She made a sound suspiciously like harrumph. *What on earth is wrong with her?*

"This is the worst continental breakfast I've ever seen. Stale muffins and cornflakes. Not even brand name, it's generic," she said.

"Maybe it's the best they can provide. There's toast here as well," said Zach, keeping his manner positive.

There was that harrumph again.

Zach prepared some toast for Gideon. "What shape, buddy?"

"Triangles. Jam, no butter," he said.

"It looks like they have white milk only. No chocolate milk," Zach said.

"No chocolate milk. Okay," said Gideon.

"Good boy," Zach praised him, kissing him on the cheek.

Christie approached with her banana muffin. Zach shifted over on the bench, gesturing to the seat beside him. "There's a spot here next to us, Mommy."

She eyed him skeptically and moved to another booth. "I'll sit over here."

I cannot for the life of me figure out what is going on with her. Maybe she's got her monthly or something. We certainly haven't spent enough time intimately for me to know.

"Would you like me to stop at a drugstore today?" Zach asked.

She looked at him like he was crazy. "No. Why would you ask me that?"

"Well, I thought maybe there was something you needed to pick up ... at a drugstore ... ladies' things," he said, feeling a blush rise up his neck.

"Are you trying to ask me if I have my period?" she asked indignantly.

"No. Well, yes. But not if it will make you angrier," he said, retreating verbally from her.

"Angrier? I'm not angry." She propped her hands on her hips and glared at him some more.

Gideon looked up. "How are you feeling, Mommy? Angry."

Christie calmed her voice. "Well, sorry. I've had about three hours sleep in the last three days. I'm a little tired."

"Is that what's wrong with you?" Zach asked, relieved to finally have the answer.

"As if I don't have enough to deal with on this trip," she muttered as though she didn't know whether to cry or break something, hopefully not him.

"It's not just you," he replied, keeping a firm grip on his emotions.

She mumbled something dark and angry.

"Pardon me?" he said.

"I said it feels like it's just me," she said, her voice quiet, but not soft enough to camouflage the barbs in her words.

"Where exactly does that leave me?" he asked.

"I don't know," she replied in a mumble.

His spirit groaned within him. He'd never understood what that meant before, "groanings which cannot be uttered".

"Christie," he protested.

She looked up at him. "I'm really tired, Zach. After I spend the entire day entertaining Gideon, you just go to bed and go to sleep and … well, I don't."

"Oh," he said, finally realizing that once again, he was the cause of the conflict. "I didn't realize … Why do you think he woke last night?"

"Believe me, Zach, if it had just been last night, I would have been fine. He hasn't slept through the night since we left home."

Zach pulled back as though she'd pinched him. "What do you mean? You've been going without sleep for days?" A sudden anger surged in his chest. He breathed deeply to push it back down to his gut where he could add it to the morass of anxiety, fear, and anger constantly bubbling there these days. "Why would you do that? Why didn't you just tell me, ask me to help?"

She braced her shoulders for a fight, and he could see the sweetness drain from her expression. "Maybe if you paid the slightest bit of attention to something other than your own selfish focus on this stupid trip, you would have noticed."

"Christie," he said indignantly. *Why is she making this so hard? Help me, Lord. Please.* "Christie," he said again, taking her by the arm, insisting she pay attention to him. "I'm not clairvoyant. I cannot possibly know if you need help unless you tell me. Tell me what you need, and I'll shift heaven and earth to give it to you." He took her by the shoulders. "Okay?" When she didn't immediately answer, he released her with a sigh of regret. "The Air Force and Space Museum, do you still want to go?"

"Why not?" she mumbled, sounding about as enthusiastic as if he'd announced that after breakfast they'd be dipping their toenails in acid and then bathing in tomato sauce.

CHAPTER 25

Airplanes. *Wow!* Gideon felt like he was floating until he bumped into something.

"Hey, buddy. Are you trying to walk through my legs?" Daddy asked.

"Airplanes. Look, I see airplanes," Gideon said, waving his arms at the objects of his affection.

"That's a B-29," Daddy said.

"B-29." Gideon reached behind him, waving to get Mommy's attention. "Mommy. Mommy, Mommy, Mommy." He turned his head when Mommy didn't respond. She was looking into her purse. "Mommy," he said. When she still didn't respond, he walked over and grabbed her purse away. "B-29."

"Gideon, don't do that," she said, and her voice sounded ... Gideon's thoughts drifted off before he decided. "Two B-29."

"You weren't listening to him," Daddy said. "What was he supposed to do?"

"I'm trying to find some acetaminophen. I have a headache. So excuse me for living," Mommy said.

Gideon reached over and grabbed her hand, pulling her forward. He needed to get past the two B-29s. There was a different plane behind them. He pulled harder to speed her up.

"I'm coming already," she said, finally speeding up.

This one was a giant plane. Gideon dropped Mommy's hand and hopped over to Daddy. He pulled down on Daddy's hand. "Daddy. What's that?"

"A B-52."

"Not the same," Gideon said.

"No, they're different. They were used for different jobs," Daddy said.

Gideon looked him in the eye. *This is good.* Gideon had never seen such large airplanes before. He had a few toy airplanes, but he didn't play with them. They didn't have as many wheels as the trains, and they didn't drive on tracks so you never knew where they could go.

"Different," Gideon said. *I want to know what's different.* Gideon tugged on Daddy's hand again. "Different." *Tell me what I want to know.*

"Christie, what is he asking me?" Daddy said.

"Different," Gideon repeated louder. Maybe if he yelled the word, then Daddy would tell him the difference between the two planes.

"He probably wants to know what's different about them," Mommy said.

Daddy's head was bobbing … like … a nod … a nod was "yes." Gideon said, "Yes."

"The B-29 is a propeller-driven heavy bomber. It was used during World War II, and I think it was used during the Korean conflict," Daddy said.

Gideon was nodding. This was good. This was what he wanted to know.

Daddy talked some more. "The B-52 is a long-range strategic bomber, and it's jet-propelled."

"World War …" Gideon began.

"No, not during the wars. It's been in use since the fifties. The US Air Force still uses them today," Daddy said.

"Still today," Gideon repeated. "Fifty. Sixty. Seventy."

"No, son. The fifties means during the year 1950. I think its maiden voyage was in 1952, if I remember correctly," Daddy said.

"Made in China," Gideon said.

"What? China?" Daddy asked.

"He's trying to work out what maiden voyage means," said Mommy.

"Not 'made in' … maiden voyage … M-A-I-D-E-N… It means the first trip," Daddy said.

"First trip to the hospital," Gideon said, desperately trying to find a picture in his mind to match the idea.

"Maybe. The first trip to the hospital could be your maiden voyage to the hospital. The very first time a new airplane flies in the air is called its maiden voyage. The very first time a boat sails in the water is its maiden voyage," Daddy said.

"Maiden voyage. First trip," Gideon said, looking up to Daddy's face to see if he could find a clue as to whether he'd guessed right. Daddy nodded. Gideon built up a picture in his mind of a B-52 with a great big number one on it and labeled it "maiden voyage" in his mind.

Gideon's body stopped feeling floaty as he ran from plane to plane. Daddy kept giving him information. It felt like his mind was all about airplanes today. His worries, the jumpy feeling of having people walk too close, nothing mattered except airplanes.

After they'd seen every single airplane outside three times, Mommy said it was time to go inside. Gideon's eyes opened wide as they stepped into a paradise of airplanes. There were airplane pictures on the walls, T-shirts, sweatshirts, and hoodies. There were airplanes on pens and on T-shirts and on stuffed animals. There was even a stuffed bear wearing a red hoodie with a B-52 on it.

Gideon walked slowly up to it. "Mine," he said, pointing to it. "Mine."

"Yes, sweetheart. We have to pay first, then you can have it," Mommy said.

"Pay first. Then mine."

"Look, Christie," Daddy said. "Here's the matching hoodie. It looks a little large, but he'll grow into it."

"Mhmm," Mommy said.

And then Gideon sat in the Jeep feeling calm and content. He had lots of pictures of airplanes in his head, and he reviewed them again and again in his mind. In his arms was a stuffed bear wearing a B-52, and he himself was warmly snuggled inside a B-52 hoodie. He pulled the hood up to keep the noise out. It was cozy with the hood up. Today was a very good day.

CHAPTER 26

Zach was pulled reluctantly from sleep by the shaking of his shoulder. Through bleary eyes, he saw Christie, tousled and pale, looming above him.

"Zach. Zach, could you please take a turn with Gideon?"

Rolling onto his back, he brushed the sleep from his eyes. "Sure."

Lifting the covers, he held them as she slipped in beside him and then immediately closed her eyes and curled onto her side. Brushing his fingers along her face, he kissed her forehead. Her eyes slowly opened, watching him.

"I'm sorry. For some reason, I thought … thanks for taking a turn," she said, and she looked utterly adorable. Rolling over her and out of the bed, he pulled the covers up to her ears and kissed her on the cheek. She sighed, one long expression of relief, and he kissed her again.

Gideon was jumping on the other bed with his new B-52 bear tightly gripped in his fist. "Hi, sweetheart."

"Hi, Daddy," said Gideon.

"Now, what could we do to calm you down for sleep?" Zach asked aloud. Gideon didn't respond. He just kept jumping. It was a good thing they'd gotten a room on the ground floor.

"Gid, jump into my arms." Gideon ignored him. Zach reached out and grabbed him midbounce. Gideon wiggled in his arms like he was being tickled. Zach braced one arm across the boy's shoulders and one across his waist and held him snugly against him. He felt Gideon begin to settle in his arms.

"Jump, Daddy," he said.

"Okay. Three jumps and then a big hug," replied Zach, the sensation of surety growing within him. He set Gideon back on the bed. He jumped, and they counted quietly, and then Gideon flew into Zach's arms. He caught him in a firm hug, held him, and then slid him down his side to provide a firm squeeze the whole way. They continued this for a while. And then Zach shifted activities when he felt like he was nearly sleeping on his feet.

Zach retrieved one of Gideon's books from his backpack—not a book about numbers or dinosaurs, which would be very exciting, but a book that was familiar. He had Gideon lie on his tummy on the floor, and then he tented his own body over the boy's, giving him deep pressure through his legs and a cozy, closed-in feeling. At least that was what he was trying to do.

Zach read for a while until Gideon laid his head down on his arms and yawned. Zach kissed him on the side of the head and then carried him to his bed where he lay beside him. Gideon was soon asleep.

"It only took two hours aside from the time Mommy already spent with you." Zach brushed the boy's hair once with his hand. "You are exhausting, child."

Zach rose, feeling more than ready to return to bed. He stood over Christie for a moment just watching her sleep in sweet anticipation. And then when he couldn't resist any longer, he crawled in beside her and pulled her close.

Zach awoke the next morning to a glorious sensation. Christie was kissing him, tracing a line from the corner of his eye to his ear, nipping his earlobe, making him shudder in response to the delicious tickle.

Tugging gently, Zach drew her hand to his mouth and kissed her fingertips and then the sensitive skin of her wrist. "Morning," he murmured, and when he opened his eyes, he could see the deep, dark blue of intense emotion in hers.

"I'm sorry for being so grumpy yesterday. I think I was just tired.

That sleep last night really helped and … anyway, thank you. And I'm sorry."

"I—" he began, but Gideon bounced over, hopping once more and landing in Zach's arms.

"Hi, Daddy," Gideon greeted cheerfully.

"Do you want to go swimming, Gid?" Zach asked.

"Swim, swim, swim. Daddy, Daddy, Daddy," Gideon said, wrapping his arms around Zach's neck and kissing him on the cheek.

Zach carried Gideon to the bathroom to find the swimsuits.

"I thought maybe we could have a slow day today. We could spend some time in the pool. There's a diner up the hill we could go to for supper. How does that sound?" Zach asked.

"Great," said Christie, and he could read the relief in her eyes.

CHAPTER 27

Sitting in Big Al's, a 1950s-style diner, Christie awaited Zach and Gideon's return from the bathroom. Given the silence emanating from the men's room, it sounded like Zach had finally managed to take Gideon to the bathroom without provoking a smoking, flaming tantrum.

"You from outta town?" the waitress asked as she set their supper orders on the table.

Christie returned a friendly smile, shifting her focus from the treeless, vermillion hills to their server, dressed in her black-and-red Laverne-and-Shirley wear complete with a monogramed A.

What had she asked? *Outta town?* "Yes," Christie replied.

"Canadian?" she asked in her broad accent.

"Yes. From … near Niagara Falls," Christie said. No one had ever heard of Jordan Harbor, but most people had heard of Niagara Falls.

"I seen Niagara Falls. My stepdad took us when we was kids," the waitress said. "Well, youse guys have a good visit." She whirled away, her taffeta rustling in the vortex of her brisk movements.

"Thank you," Christie murmured to her vapor trail.

Zach and Gideon hadn't yet returned, so Christie prepared Gideon's plate, removing the pickle and the celery, leaving the finger-thick carrot stick beside the fish sticks but removing the matchstick carrots, onions, and tomatoes from the salad. If the plate was clear, they had a greater chance of remaining tantrum free. She then opened the straw and placed it in Gideon's cup of water.

Zach and Gideon returned halfway through the process.

"No flushing," Gideon said, smiling brightly.

Christie glanced up into Zach's face, expecting to see his proud smile, but instead, he looked annoyed. "What's wrong?" she mouthed at him.

"Why do you do that?" he asked. "Why do you sanitize his plate for him?"

She narrowed her expression, shooting flames of irritation from her eyes, or at least she wished she could. The day had been going so nicely. "He doesn't eat those things. It's not bad behavior, Zach."

"I understand that," he replied, quickly revising, "Well, I don't really understand it, but I accept it because you tell me so."

What is this all about?

"But why does he need his own personal butler to cull all the *dislikes*," Zach said. "You are creating more stress and work for yourself. We need to teach him how to deal with the things he doesn't like in an appropriate way." As Christie reached over to Gideon's plate, Zach placed his hand on top of hers, stilling it before she could remove the last pickle. "Please don't."

Why does he have to interfere in everything? Struggling with herself, she debated whether to shake off his hand and cause a scene or indulge his ideas and deal with him later.

"Gideon, do you like pickles?" Gideon asked, beginning to rock in his booth, swinging his legs forward to bump against the seat between Zach and Christie.

"I don't like pickles," Christie automatically paraphrased, a little surprised when Zach reprimanded her. *Excuse me?* She felt her fists clench in consternation.

"I don't like pickles," Gideon repeated.

Zach turned his attention to Gideon. "If you don't like pickles, Gid, you don't have to eat them."

"Don't have to eat them," Gideon repeated as the swing of his legs increased in intensity.

"Take the pickle off your plate," Zach instructed gently.

"Take the pickle off, Daddy." Gideon's eyes flitted to Zach's.

"Watch this," Zach said, and Gideon slowed the momentum of his legs, watching carefully as Zach took his fork, speared the offending vegetable and put it on the edge of the plate. But then Zach replaced it in its former position beside the fish sticks.

Thump! The momentum increased again. "Take the pickle off. All the way off!" Gideon demanded, his voice rising in volume and pitch.

Christie slipped her hand onto Zach's leg with a message to stop, glancing around the nearly full diner. Zach continued his lesson regardless.

"You do it, Gideon," Zach said, his voice calm and reasonable. *Thump!* "Pick up your fork." *Thump.* "You can do it." Thump. Gideon reached for his fork and picked it up between his thumb and forefinger, studying it a moment before fisting it and jabbing it at the pickle.

Looking directly at Zach's eyes, he requested, "Help me, Daddy. Pickle off."

Astonished, Christie watched the interchange as Zach reached over and placed his large fist over Gideon's, helping him spear the pickle and move it to the edge of the plate.

"All the way off." Gideon was clearly distressed. "Off. Off. All the way off!"

"Gideon!" Zach spoke sharply and then quickly softened his manner. "You don't have to eat the pickle."

"Off, Daddy. Please. Mommy. Off. Please." His distress grew with each word.

Torn by her son's distress, Christie intervened, "Zach, he thinks he has to eat it if it's on his plate."

"I understand." His eyes never leaving his son, he corrected the situation, dumping his coleslaw onto his own plate and pushing the empty bowl over to Gideon. "Put it in here." Gideon, eyes damp with distress, looked back and forth between the bowl, the pickle, and his daddy's face.

"Help me," Gideon begged, and Zach reached over, engulfing the little hand in his. Together, they speared the pickle again, dropped it into the bowl, and then tucked the bowl behind the menu stand where it was out of view. "Squish," Gideon requested, holding his hands out toward Christie. She squeezed each in turn between her palms, and Gideon began to calm visibly.

Suddenly engulfed by emotion, Christie pushed on Zach's leg. "Let me out, please."

"No," he replied, sitting back from her and returning to his meal, lifting a forkful of coleslaw to his mouth.

Gaping, her eyes wide in surprise, she punched his leg, saying, "What?" and then narrowed in suspicion, "Why?"

"You're going to go into the bathroom and cry because you're not perfect. I won't let you do it," he replied, setting his fork down and placing his arm around her shoulders. She stiffened at the contact. When she finally gave in and slumped down in the booth, he drew her closer. "Why do you think you have to be perfect, sweetheart? You're an amazing mother. Gideon is incredible because of how you work with him and love him, not in spite of it. And I don't know what I'd do without you either."

Shrugging, she dismissed his words. Clearly, she was not doing as well as she sometimes thought if she had missed something so important to Gideon's independence.

Sighing deeply, Zach kissed her on the temple, murmuring, "What am I going to do with you, my darling?" Lifting one shoulder, she shrugged morosely. Sighing again, he continued, "Am I a contributing member of this family?"

"Yes, of course," she replied, his question taking her by surprise.

"Well, then—" He left the thought unfinished and returned to his meal.

"I suppose you're right," she conceded. "I'm only one person. I can't really be expected to do everything."

"No, baby, you can't. You set the bar at perfection, and it's simply not fair to you or to me." Surprised, she watched his face as he chewed and then continued speaking, "I'm proud of you, Christie. Please stop trying to be perfect. I simply can't keep up!"

She leaned in to kiss his cheek, and he tilted his head to receive it, murmuring quietly, "Thank you."

"Now, may I go to the bathroom?" she asked peevishly.

"Of course."

"No flushing," Gideon intoned, happily eating his fish sticks. Zach laughed.

After a long walk and another swim in the motel pool, Zach returned to the room with Gideon. Slipping off the bed, Christie greeted them with a smile. "I'll fill the tub for your bath, Giddy."

"Bath, PJs, and three stories," he said.

"How about four stories today, Gid," Zach asked. He felt so happy and proud of himself. He had actually had a good idea at supper and carried it off. He had taken Gideon to the bathroom without causing a tantrum, and he had returned a sleepy boy to their motel room. Also, Zach thought, congratulating himself again, he had supplied time for Christie to rest. His chest felt full and warm. He was the best!

Gideon furrowed his brow at Zach, and so did Christie. Then she shrugged and walked away into the bathroom. Doubt flickered across Zach's mind.

"Three stories," Gideon insisted.

Back down now … quickly or blaze the trail full steam ahead. "Fifty-six," Zach teased, tickling Gideon's ribs.

Still serious, Gideon pushed Zach's hands away. "Three stories."

"One thousand, nine hundred and eleven," Zach said.

Gideon watched him for a long time, his eyes flitting from Zach's hands to his forehead and finally to his mouth and then his eyes. Zach maintained his position and facial expression even though his cheeks were aching. Slowly, Zach watched a smile spread across Gideon's face. "That's silly."

"Yes," Zach announced proudly, grabbing Gideon close and tickling him, alternately slower and then faster, and then he stopped, letting the boy have a break. He sat back, hands at the ready until Gideon moved back toward him to let Zach know that he wanted more of the game.

"Bath time," Christie announced. Zach looked up into the adoring eyes of his wife, and he felt as weightless as a dust mote.

"I'll go get some ice," Zach offered, starting toward the door and then pausing for a moment, retracing his steps and giving Christie a kiss on the corner of her mouth. "Enjoy your bath and sixty-seven stories, Gid." Gideon bounced gleefully in Christie's arms.

"Daddy's silly, Mommy," he said.

"Perhaps," she replied thoughtfully. "Silly and sweet."

Zach stopped at the door, turning back to face her. "I'm really glad you asked me for help last night," he said. "I've been so focused on the journey that I haven't paid enough attention to the daily struggles caused by it. I'd like to talk about a plan so that I can help."

"There's no need," she replied, ducking her head.

"I beg to differ; there has got to be a way to make things better for you and for Gideon. I think—"

She cut him off. "I expected you to just know, I guess. I was so sure that you weren't willing to help," Christie said, her eyes studying the carpet and then his shirt buttons.

Zach stepped toward her. "I'm sorry that I didn't realize you weren't getting sleep, and I'm sorry for accusing you of doing something wrong by not waking me. It would be easier for me if you could please tell me when you need my help. I would do anything for you and Gideon, Christie. Just ask me, and the world is yours."

"Now would be a really good time to kiss me," she said. Her voice was husky and warm, inviting him closer. But he moved just a little too slowly, and so was interrupted by the cell phone.

Grabbing the phone, Christie tossed it to Zach and then carried Gideon into the bathroom.

"Thanks," Zach said, trying to keep the disappointment from his voice. "Hello?"

"Hello, Son. How is your trip going?" Bud asked.

Zach's heart lightened. "Hi, Dad. Well, I would say that we've learned a lot about each other," Zach replied.

His father released a loud guffaw. "Not exactly the experience you were hoping for?"

Zach blushed. "Definitely not, but things are going better."

"Well, if Christie hasn't murdered you yet, you must be doing all right," his dad said.

"Gee, thanks," Zach said wryly.

"I did try to warn you, Son," said Bud.

"Yeah, thanks a lot," Zach replied dryly.

"Where are you tonight?" Bud asked.

"South Dakota," Zach said. "I want to take Christie and Gideon to Bear Country USA tomorrow, and then we'll drive to the ranch the next day."

"Bobby has been after me to hasten your arrival, and I wondered if you'd like to meet at Shell Falls. Then perhaps Gideon could travel to the ranch with Bobby and me, and you and Christie could have a few hours alone," Bud suggested.

"That would be terrific, Dad. I don't know why I thought that this trip was going to be in any way positive for our relationship, but I would dearly love to pull something good from it. Thanks."

"Zach, your mother always said you were our space walker, 'never give up, never surrender.' I'm glad that prison hasn't stolen that from you. I'm proud of you, son," Bud said.

Zach felt the warmth of emotion in his chest. "You don't know how much that means to me, Dad. I just wish that I could make Christie proud of me, too."

"You will, Son. Just keep loving her," he said.

"I do … love her … very much," Zach said.

"See you soon."

"Good-bye."

CHAPTER 28

The next day, midmorning, Zach pulled into the line at the entrance to Bear Country USA.

"Gideon's not going to be able to see anything from his booster seat," Zach said.

"He's safest in there, though," Christie replied.

Zach turned off the air conditioner and rolled down his window.

Christie tapped his hand where it rested on the steering wheel. "We just passed a sign that said to keep the windows up."

Zach gestured around them at the road, the cars and trucks, and the fields of nothing. "What exactly would be the point?"

He got himself "humphed" with that comment. Once the car ahead moved on, Zach inched the Jeep forward, handed his money over to the park staff, and drove into the park.

"Oh, look at that," Christie said, and there was awe in her voice. "Look, Gideon. There's an elk. It says they are also called *wapiti*, a Cree word for 'white.' Awesome."

"One, two, three, four, five ..." said Gideon, his gaze fixed on his fingers as they made patterns in the air. Zach watched him in the rearview mirror.

"Can't we bring him up here, Christie? He can't see anything," Zach said and then pressed his point. "The speed limit is fifteen miles per hour. And look ahead. The cars are stopping all along the way."

She followed his line of sight, and he could read the concern in her gaze. But, come on, for goodness' sake.

"Okay," she replied reluctantly.

Yes! Score one for Papa. "Hey, Gid," Zach began. "Take off your seat belt and come sit with me."

"Seat belts in the car," Gideon said.

Zach sighed. Nothing was ever easy. "Most of the time, we wear seat belts in the car, but sometimes, when we're in Bear Country USA, we take off our seat belts and sit on Daddy's lap."

"Daddy's lap?" Gideon said. "Mommy?"

"Yes, sweetheart. You can sit on Daddy's lap while we're in Bear Country USA," Christie said.

Gideon whipped off his seat belt and launched himself from his booster seat and into the front. Zach laughed at the boy's enthusiasm.

They drove ahead to the reindeer enclosure. "Hey, look. It's Santa's reindeer," Zach said.

Gideon stood in rapt attention, his feet planted on the driver's seat between Zach's legs and his fingers gripping the edge of the window, which was lowered just enough to allow for his grip.

"Santa's reindeer," Gideon repeated. His head swiveled to and fro. "What's that?"

"Um, the reindeer's antlers?" Zach said, uncertain what Gideon was referring to. "They look different than in a storybook, don't they, son?"

"Different. B-52. What's that?" Gideon asked.

Zach craned his head to try to see what Gideon was asking about. "Show me what you're looking at. Point," Zach said.

Gideon laid his palm flat against the window. Zach shaped Gideon's little hand, pointed toward the arctic wolf ahead, and then labeled it. "You need to point so I know what you're talking about," he said.

"Wolf," Gideon repeated and then, "Bighorn sheep, Dall sheep, Rocky Mountain goats," and then finally, "Bear." Gideon gaped in awe.

"Put up the window, Zach," Christie said urgently.

At that moment, Zach noticed a scruffy-looking brown bear pacing along the front of each car and then down the side and across behind the rear fender. A second bear had set up a patrol across the cattle guard, which marked the entrance to the bear enclosure. Sergeant Bear paced across, blocking the forward progress of a van, and then turned and paced back the other way. Zach laughed aloud. Only one vehicle was allowed access at a time.

"Look at how the bear guards the way, Gideon," Zach said, pulling Gideon away far enough to raise the window so that Christie's frown didn't deepen any further. "Christie, did you see that?"

"Yes," she said and then laughed as well. "I wonder what he's paid for that duty."

"A couple sheep maybe?" Zach suggested.

Christie playfully smacked his arm. "Very funny," she said, and, at last, he saw her relax.

Finally, it was their turn, and Sergeant Bear let them into the enclosure. Brown bears roamed the area, sat on rocks, wrestled in the grass. Some ignored the tourists, some observed, and others even performed. There were brown, blond, and auburn bears, large, medium, and small bears.

Zach applied the brake as three bears wandered in front of the Jeep and squared off against each other.

"Are they going to fight?" Christie asked, clearly disturbed by the prospect.

"Fight, fight, fight," Gideon said, lurching forward. His hand connected with the horn to release a startling beep. The three antagonists scurried off.

"Thanks," Christie mumbled.

Zach laughed again. It was so good to be together as a family.

Out of the bear enclosure and on a little ways, Zach spotted only one timber wolf before the Jeep was surrounded by bison.

"B-U-F-F-A-L-O," Gideon spelled.

"Bison," Christie said. "That word spells buffalo, but they are really bison. I don't know why they insist on calling bison buffalo here."

Zach chuckled. "Different country, different customs?"

She humphed, but this time, it wasn't directed at him.

They returned to the Thunderbird, went for a very long swim, and then put a sleepy boy to bed.

"You tired?" Zach asked Christie.

"Yeah. You?" she replied, continuing to tidy Gideon's toys and clothes.

Watching her looking so happy and relaxed brought simmering warmth to his belly, and, for once, it wasn't the heat of anger in his gut but the swell of passion.

"Um, what are you thinking?" she asked.

"I'm thinking about you. I'm thinking that it's been days since we've been alone," he said.

"Um, yeah. I had noticed that," she said, still sounding uncertain. But there in her expression, he could see an answering desire darkening her eyes to the color of the Pacific.

Fixing his gaze on her, he moved to the motel room door, locked it, and engaged the deadbolt. Then he pushed a chair in front of it.

"Would you say that will keep Gideon inside?" he asked.

Her brows furrowed. "Yes."

"Come here, please," he said, holding out his hand to her. She took it and followed when he tugged her toward the bathroom. "Not exactly a suite at the Hilton, but it does afford some privacy." He turned on the red-glow heat lamp for "ambience" and pulled her close.

Warmth suffused his body when she relaxed against him, resting her cheek on his chest and releasing her breath on a long, happy sigh. Zach stroked his fingers through her hair, cupped her cheek, and tilted her face up for a searing kiss.

"I love you," he murmured against her lips and then again against her cheeks and then her eyes. With each kiss, he felt the dark doubt and fear of prison, which had torn him from the people he loved most in the world and dragged him back to a time of impuissance, dissipate.

Her breathing deepened, and she pressed against him, murmuring, "I love you, too."

Zach froze. *What?* Pulling back, he tenderly cupped her cheeks in his hands, searching her face. "Really?" he asked with tears burning the backs of his eyes.

"Yes," she said dreamily, and she looked happier than he'd seen her look in years. "I love you, my darling husband."

She loved him. She really did love him. "Say it again," he begged her.

"I love you." Hooking her hands in his waistband, she levered herself up to meet his lips and then settled on her feet to lay her lips against his chest and then his chin. "I love you, Zachary Clyde Marek."

He chuckled breathily. She hadn't called him that in the longest time. "My middle name is not Clyde. Clyde's my horse."

"Nuh-uh. Clyde is the super steed of the desert ... and more than just a little stubborn." She smiled as she kissed him again.

Shaking his head, he admitted, "I don't know why you call me that."

"The song? By Ray Stevens? You know," she replied. "Remember that time we argued about where to go for supper? And that song came on the radio?"

"Clyde is super faithful, not stubborn, as I recall the song," he said, narrowing his brows at her.

"Well," she said, and her voice was soft and sweet. "That works, too." She kissed him, long and deep, and he totally lost himself in her warmth.

CHAPTER 29

Getting an early start the next morning—not much choice when Gideon was in control of sleeping and waking—Zach drove as Christie navigated, from Sheridan, Wyoming, west along the I-90 to Highway 14 toward the mountains. The cultivated flatland rose to tree-topped foothills as the farms gave way to ranches.

"Cowboy," Gideon said, pointing out his window to the mounted ranch hands persuading a small herd of cattle back through a broken fence.

"Yes, son. Real American cowboys," Zach said. Finally, home. *There is nowhere on earth like Wyoming.* Lowering the window, he drew in a deep draft of air. He always felt like he could breathe freer here than anywhere else on earth.

As they passed through Ranchester, Zach heard Christie gasp, and he followed her line of sight.

"Look at those mountains! It's like they suddenly appeared," she said. "I've never driven this route before. We've always flown to visit the ranch. This is so beautiful."

"Yeah. That's the Bighorn Mountain Range," Zach said. "It's about four thousand feet above sea level here. We'll travel up through the pass to eight thousand feet at Shell Falls and then back down to four thousand before we reach Cody."

She peeked shyly at him through her eyelashes. "I, uh, I guess I can see why you would want to drive through such a beautiful landscape. It's breathtaking," she said. "Thank you for bringing us here."

Zach grinned, gloriously pleased by her comment. "Ranchester's the last stop before we drive up into the pass. There is absolutely no way to stop once we're on that road," he said.

"It's okay, you know, if you want to be a bit smug for a while," she said.

He laughed loudly enough to be told off by Gideon. "Thanks for the offer, but I'm good," he said. "Do you want to stop?"

Nodding, she pointed to a log building at the side of the road that looked like it was still using the gas pumps from the Depression era. "It looks like there's a little variety store in there."

Zach parked alongside a pickup truck loaded with leather Western saddles. Christie took Gideon to the bathroom while Zach got them each a cappuccino from the machines in the store, noting the handwritten sign above the coffee and soda bar. "Fountain drinks can be purchased with food stamps." *Whoa!* What comment did that make about the economy of this area?

Christie returned with Gideon just as an Amish family took up their place in line, six blond boys and girls, stepped down in age from about eight to a babe on his mother's hip, dressed in identifiable, conservative attire.

Back on the road again, they climbed along the pass, past the blasted rock-face, which was dotted with caves. The pinkish hue of the rock was covered in swathes of conifers, and the rolling hills were topped by a ziggurat of craggy granite.

"Babe the big, blue ox," Gideon said.

"Mhmm," Christie said, and Gideon repeated himself, clearly not satisfied with her response.

"Poo," Gideon said as though that clarified his message.

"Yes," she said, though she was clearly confounded by the boy's reference. "Do you see what he's talking about, Zach?" she asked, searching diligently from the passenger seat.

"Point, Gid," Zach said. This was what Gideon needed to learn to do. Just pretending you understood everything he said didn't help him learn to get his message across when he was misunderstood.

"Poo," Gideon repeated, pointing at massive rock formations, which did indeed resemble gigantic oxen droppings. Zach bellowed with laughter.

"Too loud," Gideon complained.

"Sorry, Son," Zach said, containing his glee. "Ox poo. Of course, why didn't I see it?"

Christie joined in, chuckling lightly, before exclaiming, "Oh, look, Zach! Cyclists. I cannot imagine biking up these mountain roads. They must have the strength of Goliath in their legs or a mighty optimistic outlook on life."

Zach chuckled. "There are bicycle clubs that do this route several times a summer."

"Phew. I can't imagine," she said.

"Horse," Gideon said. "I ride Clyde."

A line of trail riders, a tourist expedition from the looks of the majority of the individuals on horseback, crossed ahead of the Jeep, joining a trail on the near side of the mountain.

"Yes, horses," Christie said. "Maybe you can ride Clyde tomorrow."

They reached Shell Falls around midmorning, and Bobby and Bud were there to meet them.

"You go on," Bud told Christie. "See the falls. I'll stay here with Bobby and Gideon." He nudged Zach's shoulder. "Take Christie to see the falls."

"Thanks, Dad," Zach replied, slapping his father lightly on the shoulder.

"Zach?" Christie questioned him quietly, but rather than respond, he took her elbow and led her away, slipping his hand down to take hers.

Leading her down the steps to view the falls, he couldn't resist sliding his fingers up the nape of her neck and into her blonde curls, enjoying the silky soft feel of her hair.

"That *is* lovely." She commented on the brisk narrow falls as she leaned into him. But he could feel the tension in her body in spite of her feigned nonchalance.

"*You* are lovely," he said and then playfully reprimanded her. "Stop worrying. Dad can look after Gideon for a few minutes."

She laughed breathily. "Busted! Bud's stayed with him before, but I always worry in a place like this. If Gideon suddenly decided to check something out, the fence wouldn't be much of a barrier."

"It's okay to enjoy a few minutes to ourselves—"

Shriek!

"Gideon?" Christie asked, but Zach had already taken off at a run.

Honing in instinctively to the sound of his son, Zach raced to his side. "What happened?" Zach shouted at his father.

"Motorcycle," Bud replied.

"Too loud! Too loud!" Gideon shrieked, his body quivering in terror.

Placing his hands over Gideon's where they covered his ears, Zach repeated, "The noise is gone. The noise is gone."

Very slowly, Gideon opened his eyes, looking over Zach's shoulder to see the offending motorcycle directly in front of him.

Shriek! "Too loud! *Too loud!*"

Zach reacted without thinking. Using Gideon's elbow to spin him about, Zach scooped the boy into his arms and tight against his chest, keeping his knees bent and an arm firmly across his chest so he couldn't squirm out of his grip. Charging up the steps, Zach found a clear space near the gift shop under a shady bush. It was safely out of sight of the motorcycle.

Forcing his mouth past Gideon's elbow and as close to Gideon's ear as possible, Zach spoke in a firm but calm voice. "Gideon! The motorcycle's gone." He repeated the same words several times until he felt the tension slowly ease from the boy's body and Gideon's hands dropped from his ears.

It was only then that Zach felt Christie's hand on his back and noticed that she was standing there beside him.

"Motorcycle gone," Gideon repeated, his breath shuddering in his chest.

Zach felt Gideon lurch forward in his arms, and he realized that his son wanted his mother. She scooped him up, and he clung to her. Expecting Christie to take Gideon and walk away, Zach was surprised when she pressed her palm to his chest, leaning up to him. Zach tilted his head down, not certain what would come next.

"You are amazing and absolutely perfect," she whispered to him and then kissed him on the mouth.

She thinks I'm perfect. Stunned, a slow smile spread across his face, which he quickly subdued as a small crowd gathered around him.

"Hey man, what's wrong with your kid?" one fellow asked from his position astride a Harley Davidson. He was tall and broad, heavily tattooed and wearing a black leather bandanna emblazoned with a red skull. His sleeveless jacket bore a patch for *Sturgis*, home of the Annual Motorcycle Rally.

Wrong? "There's nothing wrong with him," Zach replied. "He has autism."

A second man approached; he was about six and a half feet tall—as tall as Seth—but still, with his sleeveless T-shirt pulled tight across his barrel chest and his massive, tree-trunk arms, he looked much larger. The only hint of softness in the man was a rim of snow-white hair, pulled back into a ponytail.

"I'm sorry, man. The older boy wanted to hear the Hog," Ponytail said.

"Sorry, Zach. Is's my fault," Bobby said, sorrow in his eyes. "I did'n wanna scare Gideon."

"Why'd he scream that way, dude?" Skull bandanna said.

"He can't handle loud noises, especially if they're unexpected," Zach explained.

"Sorry, man," Ponytail apologized, and Zach shook his hand, nodding in a genial manner.

Realizing the rest of the crowd had dissipated except Bud and Bobby, Zach canted his body against the railing, hoping to adopt a casual pose and hide the shaking in his hands. When he'd heard that shriek, he'd been so afraid for Gideon's safety.

"I sorry, Zach," Bobby apologized. "Gideon gonna be okay?"

Zach could see the signs of trauma in his brother's eyes. "He's okay, Bobby. Gideon just doesn't like loud noises. They really scare him."

"Not good t'talk t'the bike guy," Bobby said, woefully shaking his head.

Bud placed an arm around Bobby's shoulder, and Zach reached out to squeeze Bobby's arm reassuringly. "It wasn't your fault, Bobby. Gideon just sees the world differently, and it's not always easy to know how he's going to react. Don't worry, Bob; he'll be okay. You'll see," Bud said.

"Okay," Bobby replied, looking less distressed.

"Gideon's feeling much calmer now," Christie said to Bobby, reappearing at their side.

"I was planning to offer to take Gideon back to the ranch with Bobby," Bud said.

"Ranch with Bobby," Gideon repeated, hope in his voice. "Play trains?"

Bud smiled. "Yes. If you drive with me, you and Bobby can play trains."

"Play trains. Mommy, play trains," Gideon said and then turned to Zach. "Daddy, play trains."

"You still scared?" Bobby asked Gideon.

"Scared? No. Trains," Gideon replied.

"He's still going to be irritable, Bud. He could go off pretty easily," Christie said, clearly considering changing her mind about the arrangements.

"Dad can handle it, Christie," Zach said, hoping to maintain his plans. "We could stop for supper; have a couple of hours ... alone." Zach's voice trailed off.

"We'll be fine, honey," Bud said as he pulled her into a hug and kissed her on the cheek. Gideon pushed him off with a grunt.

"Trains," Gideon said.

"You need to use the bathroom before you go," Christie said to Gideon.

"No. No flushing," Gideon said. He began to rock in Christie's arms.

"Pee first, then trains," Zach said. "No flushing. Come with Daddy."

"I want trains," Gideon insisted.

"Then come with me," Zach said, holding out his arms.

"Come with me," Gideon repeated as though he were considering the offer. Then he began to wiggle in Christie's arms. "Down."

Christie set him on his feet. Gideon hopped over and took Zach's hand. "Okay," Zach said, smiling down at his son. "Let's go."

Christie watched Gideon and Zach walk into the men's room.

"This trip has been good for the three of you," Bud said.

"Oh, Bud. This trip has been so difficult," she replied.

"Did you miss the significance of what just happened here?" Bud asked, and Christie could hear the reproach in his words. *What have I done to deserve that?*

Bud placed a hand on her shoulder to turn her, and she felt like he was demanding a response she didn't want to supply.

"Christie?"

"Yes. I mean no. It's great, but—" she began and then stopped.

"Honey, you have unrealistic expectations of Zach. He spent six months in prison for a crime he didn't commit, forced to endure a variety of torments and completely powerless to help himself. Expend a little grace. If you hold everyone to the ideal of perfection ... well, no one can achieve it," Bud said.

Christie flushed in annoyance. "Zach said almost exactly the same thing to me. Are you guys comparing notes?"

"Listen to me for a moment, Christie. You know that I have taken great pains not to interfere in your relationship with Zach. But I have to tell you that the man I see today is a man who has found hope restored, a man who can see a future where happiness exists as a possibility, rather than the defeated man who was terrified that he'd lost everything good in his life through one minor misstep," Bud said, and then he straightened, clearly telling her by his voice and manner that the conversation was at an end. "Please bring Gideon and his booster seat to the truck when he's ready." And then he walked away with Bobby.

I always thought Bud was on my side. That hurts! How much more was she expected to sacrifice for her husband? She'd stood by his side while the world called him a liar and a scumbag. She'd given up friends and any hope of a social life to look after their son alone while Zach was gone. She'd taken Zach back, and together they were rebuilding a happy life. How could Bud say those things to her?

"Where's Dad?" Zach asked, pulling her back to the present.

"He said to bring Gideon and his seat to the truck," Christie said. She knew her voice sounded funny, but she couldn't get her emotions under control.

Crouching down in front of Gideon, she hugged and kissed him and admonished him to behave for Grandpa.

"You okay, sweetheart?" Zach asked, looking concerned.

"Can you take him for me, please?" Christie said.

"Sure," he replied, but she could see him watching her closely.

Zach returned to the Jeep before long. "You ready to go?" he asked.

"Yeah," she replied, but Zach didn't start the vehicle. Soon she felt his hand on her thigh.

"What's wrong?" he asked.

She shrugged and kept her face turned to the window.

"Are you upset with me?" he said.

She didn't answer because she wasn't sure. Was she angry with Zach? With Bud? With herself?

"Christie?" he asked. And she could feel his confusion. She felt mean. He had run to Gideon's rescue and handled the boy expertly. Maybe that was what was bothering her. Maybe she was jealous. But she didn't feel jealous.

She turned to him. "I'm okay. Let's just get to the ranch."

"Well, I think Dad's idea was to take a little time alone together. We're only an hour from Cody, and it's only another half hour to the ranch. There's plenty of time. I thought we could go to a restaurant for supper, and maybe we could drive out to Bighorn Lake and walk there or along the Shoshone River. What do you think?" he asked.

Dad's idea? Blaah! "Let's just get to the ranch," she said and turned away from him again.

CHAPTER 30

They drove in silence for a time. Christie tried to enjoy the journey down the twisty mountain road. The view was spectacular with the red rock mountains rising and falling beside them.

Back down to four thousand feet above sea level, the road widened, and Zach pulled off sharply at the first turnout.

"Listen," he said, turning to her. "If you're mad at me, then tell me what I did. Scold me, whatever." She kept her face to the window. "You haven't had any trouble telling me when I've messed up in the past weeks. Why start now?"

"You haven't," she said, looking over at him.

"Blast it! I can't figure you out," he said, slamming out of the Jeep and over to the waist-high stone wall guarding the stop-off. He leaned on his clenched fists, his shoulders visibly bunching beneath his cotton shirt.

Christie watched his visible torment. *What am I doing? Torturing him* for *my confusion?* After slipping out of the Jeep, she joined Zach, sitting on the wall beside him.

"Is it terrible to feel like this trip has been difficult?" she asked.

As he met her gaze, she could read the astonishment in his eyes. "No," he said. "I like to think about all the good stuff, like the fact that we figured out how to take turns with Gideon at night, that I learned what 'red' means, that Gideon told you he loves you for the first time ever. But I can see that it's been pretty rough ... from your perspective."

"From my perspective? How nice! But from yours, it's been wonderful?" she asked, snapping at him.

He slapped his hands on the wall. "What is this all about? Why are you angry with me?"

She sought to gather her resources to attack and then wisely thought about it one more time. "I'm not." And she wasn't. She was hurt. "Your dad said something that you also said to me, and I just don't think it's fair. This trip has been rough. I don't understand why it makes me an awful person to feel that way."

Stepping in front of her, Zach cradled her face in his hands, gently tipping her chin so that she could see the kindness in his eyes. "I certainly don't think you're an awful person. I apologize for whatever Dad said because I think you're wonderful. It has been a rough trip, but I'm grateful that you stuck it out with me."

"Really?" she asked. She studied his face pensively, looking for the truth, saying, "Do you think I'm too hard on you?"

"Sure," he replied quickly. Then he must have seen the hurt in her eyes because he revised his response. "Well, not really. I wish I could get away with more, but I think you're actually very sweet to me. You always give me a second chance. You never give up on me, and you always drag us back to 'happy.' I'm grateful," Zach said, and then he leaned in to kiss her once. "What did Dad say to you?"

"He said that I have 'unrealistic expectations' of you," she replied, mimicking Bud's deep voice. "But that's not true. I don't think I expect too much of you. But maybe I do and the reason everything's been so difficult … I'm afraid that … well, could it all be my fault?" she said, winding down.

"You are very generous with me, baby. I guess you do hold me to a pretty high standard, but I know that you also hold yourself to the same or a higher standard." Zach pulled her close. "I don't care what my father or anyone else says; to me, you are perfect."

Perfect. She huffed ungraciously. "I'm not perfect."

Suddenly excited, Zach said, "I read this article about a month ago—I think it was by a guy named Barclay—that talked about the concept of perfection." His entire body conveyed his enthusiasm. "You know that verse that says, '… be perfect, just as your Father in heaven is perfect'?" He continued without awaiting her response. "The western concept of 'perfect' is closer to the meaning of 'blameless,' but, in fact, the true meaning of the word as it's used in that verse is more like 'exactly fitting the need in a certain situation or for a certain purpose.' Like a Phillips head screwdriver perfectly fits the needs of a Phillips head screw but is definitely not perfect for a slotted head." Throwing his arms wide, he grinned broadly. "See?"

"Screwdriver?" she asked, quirking a brow comically.

He laughed aloud. "You get the idea, right?"

She nodded slowly and then shook her head.

"You're perfect," he said as though it was self-evident. "You're an amazing mother. You work so hard to help Gideon learn the skills he needs to have a happy, successful life. You're determined for the three of us to be happy, and you work hard to get us there and keep us there. I love you, and I think you're perfect for me and for Gideon and for any other Mareks we can make together."

Perfect. I don't have to be faultless ... and neither does Zach. Her smile expanded, and he reached out to trace it with his finger.

"Are you ready to make more Mareks?" she asked softly.

His face fell. "I'm afraid," he replied, his voice barely above a whisper. "I've been afraid so long, afraid of being a bad father, afraid of losing you."

"Do you believe that God loves you, Zach? In spite of the fact that your mother was a drug addict and you barely escaped juvenile hall as an adolescent? In spite of who you are now and the mistakes you've made?"

"Yes. I believe that Jesus is Lord and that God raised him from the dead. And through that, He's saved me and given me everlasting life," Zach replied.

"If you believe that God loves you, Zach, then you can safely assume that He was acting in love toward you when He gave you Gideon," she said. "Right?"

A slow smile spread across Zach's face. "Yes."

"And so you're perfect, too," she said. "Assigned as his father."

He huffed out a laugh. "As long you think I'm, uh, perfect, that's more than I could ever hope for."

Wrapping her arms around him, Christie kissed him.

Pulling back, he took her hands in his. "Are you ready to go? Shall we find a cozy restaurant with a table for two?" His voice was soft and tender, making her heart melt.

"Hmm. You say we have a few hours of freedom?" He nodded. "Then how about a picnic in that little meadow we found along the Shoshone?" she asked and waited. She knew the exact moment when he remembered because his hazel eyes deepened to the blue of the sea.

"I remember," he said, silkily. "Maybe we'll have the same luck we did that day."

"Are you sure you're ready for that?"

"Indubitably. The Shoshone brought us one amazing, perfect child, maybe it could bring us another," he said.

"I'd like that." Christie kissed him, this man, the love of her life. "In fact, I think it would be perfect."

CHAPTER 31

Gjojak admitted to himself that he'd had a lapse in judgment today. Attending his bimonthly meeting with the personal assistant of the undersecretary to the Albanian Minister of Foreign Affairs, Gjojak had learned that a man answering to the name of Marek had crossed the international border from Canada to the United States exactly one week ago. Losing control at the news, Gjojak had ordered Hoxha to shoot the man, forgetting to first remind the assassin to wound only, not to kill.

Now he stood side by side with Hoxha, looking down at the dead minister, who lay in an expanding pool of blood. It was unfortunate, but government ministers were simple to corrupt. Gjojak would find another source of information.

"The prison you delivered Marek to?" Gjojak said, aware of Hoxha immediately coming to attention. Hoxha would remember. He never forgot a detail of a job. "Kill the warden."

"Marek escaped," Hoxha said, a statement not a question.

"Indeed. I do not care how, only that the individual responsible is eliminated. Understood?" Gjojak said.

"*Po*," Hoxha replied.

Several glorious hours later and with his heart accelerating in anticipation, Zach turned down the familiar drive of his childhood home—well, the portion of his childhood he cared to remember. This was, by far, the greatest place on earth.

Fifty meters down the gravel drive, they found the wooden gateposts heralding the edge of the Marek homestead, Secundo Forte, the Second Chance ranch.

In the dark, Zach couldn't see the horses in the pastures bordering the laneway, and he supposed that they would be sleeping closer to the barn at this time of night. But he could picture them, grazing in the sun-drenched pastures. He could hear their happy nickering in his memory as he and his brothers fixed a fence or practiced their roping skills. Or maybe he and Luke were sneaking off for a little fishing in Sunshine Creek.

Zach eagerly anticipated the morning when he would see the sun glint off the Absaroka and Beartooth Mountains, which bounded the western edge of the property. The massive Bearslide Hill dwarfed the ranch house, a sprawling log bungalow.

The house was really two connected buildings, one the original log home, containing a massive multipurpose great room, which served as living room, coat room, kitchen, and dining room. Doors on either side of the massive stone fireplace led to the second house. Originally one bathroom and a master bedroom, after a series of renovations, it became four bedrooms, two bathrooms, and one very special train room in the loft. There was an extra half-bath, which Bud had added early on just off the front porch for the boys to wash off the dirt of the ranch before tromping across Grace's clean hardwood floors. Zach's chest expanded, and his spirit soared. This place was home.

"Well, he's wearing PJs, but that's as far as I've gotten," Bud said by way of greeting as they stepped inside. "Bobby conked out and went to bed half an hour ago."

Zach looked past his father to see Gideon jumping on the couch and singing at the top of his lungs.

"Elephants go to sleep. Giraffes go to sleep. Pillows go to sleep. Hahaha. That's silly …"

Zach chuckled, warmth bubbling up within his chest.

"I, er, tried to convince him that it was time to go to sleep, that even the horses were sleeping. The idea got a little away from me," Bud said sheepishly.

"I'll get him," Christie said with amusement sparkling in her eyes.

"Okay. I'll join you soon," Zach said.

Christie smiled brightly and his heart warmed in his chest.

Once Christie moved away, Zach turned to his father. "Dad, I want you to stop criticizing Christie. You hurt her feelings, and she doesn't deserve it." He turned fully to face his father, very uncertain of the expression he'd find there. Bud's face was serious, closed. "She's amazing. She stood by me when most women would have divorced me and run for the hills. Even when she thought I was losing it, she gave me a chance to prove myself. She's a wonderful mom and wife, and I love her." Zach braced himself for his father's reaction.

Bud studied him for a long moment. "I'll apologize," he said, a simple response but one which meant the world to Zach. Bud turned away and then back to squeeze Zach's shoulder affectionately. "I'm proud of you, son. I seem to recall having a similar conversation with my own mother after we adopted Seth." And then Bud walked away, and Zach released the breath he'd been holding.

Now to find Christie. "Hey, Beautiful," Zach said, coming up behind Christie in the doorway to Seth's childhood bedroom where Gideon was currently sleeping. "That was quick."

Christie leaned back into him. "I think he was just waiting for us to come home," she said. "I played a game of hot dog with him just like you taught me and he calmed right away."

"I taught you?" *Cool! Score one for Daddy.* "Are you tired?"

"Yeah. But I'm not quite ready for bed yet." She turned in his arms and hugged him. "Do you have an idea?"

He kissed her right beside her eye where he was certain he'd seen a twinkle.

"Would you like to saddle up Clyde and ride out to the south pasture? We could take a blanket and watch the stars," he suggested.

"Mhmm. That would be nice," she said dreamily.

He pulled back. "You sure you're not sleepy?" She sounded sleepy.

She kissed him languidly on the mouth. "Are you sleepy? No," she said in a perfect imitation of Gideon.

Zach laughed. "Okay, then," he said. He was not going to miss this opportunity, not with that expression on her face. "I'll see if Dad will listen for Gid; then I'll grab a blanket and meet you at the stable."

"Sure," she said, stopping for another kiss.

Oh, yeah! This was going to be awesome!

Zach found his father watching the news. "Hey, Dad. Gideon's asleep, but I wondered if you'd listen for him. I want to take Christie out to the south pasture. It's such a clear night," Zach said, tucking the blanket he'd retrieved beneath his arm.

"I'd be happy to," Bud replied with a knowing smile.

Zach refused to blush.

"You love this ranch, don't you, son?" Bud asked.

"Yeah. I feel like I can breathe here," Zach replied, smiling wistfully.

"For a city-born boy, you have the countryside in your heart. Before long, we need to have a conversation," Bud said.

Zach went still. *What now?*

"About the Second Chance," Bud clarified.

The ranch? What about the ranch? Was his father planning to sell it? What did that mean for Zach?

"I turned seventy-two on my last birthday, and I'm feeling the need to retire. I'd like to pass the ranch on to someone who loves it as much as your mom and I," Bud said.

Zach's brow furrowed. "Seth. I assumed that Seth would take over the ranch."

"Seth would ... but out of a sense of duty. He has his veterinary practice and his own small holding. Luke, well, you couldn't pay Luke enough to move back to Wyoming. And Blake. He's rarely in-country. But you and Gideon, you love this ranch, Zach, like none of the others," Bud said.

"Yeah, but I can't really—I'm not really free to—" Zach stuttered through his thoughts.

"I'm not asking you to make a decision today. Pray about it. Talk to Christie. Talk to Seth," Bud said. "Think about what's best for your family. Are you free to do that?" Bud's voice was gentle.

"Yeah. Of course."

"You're a lucky man, Zach, a good man. You have certainly survived some devastating circumstances, but, still, through it all, that fine and good man remains. I'm very proud of you, son. You have a good life, a wonderful wife and son," Bud said.

"Dad." Zach's voice caught. "I made her fall out of love with me." The memories of those hard, guilty days swelled within him.

"I know, Son. But you won the heart of a wonderful woman. She stayed around long enough to fall in love with you again. And I know that Gideon is a challenge, but have you stopped to consider the possibility that God has entrusted you with a precious gift? There is a reason that Gideon needed to exist on this earth, and you and Christie are the perfect parents for him," Bud said.

"Perfect," Zach mused.

CHAPTER 32

The following day, Bud dusted off the barbecue and was serving up a steady stream of steaks, hot dogs, and affection.

"Here's your hot dog, Gideon," Seth said, handing him the ketchup-enhanced version.

Gideon took a swipe at Seth's arm. "That's horrible!"

Christie started to intervene but stopped when Zach immediately stepped over. "That's rude, Gid. You can tell Uncle Seth, 'I don't like it.'"

"No, Daddy. No ketchup. No ketchup." Gideon's upset was escalating quickly.

"Tell Uncle Seth, 'No, thank you. I don't like ketchup,'" Zach said, relieving his brother of the offending hot dog. "No, thank you," Zach repeated.

"No, no, no!" Gideon stomped his feet in anger.

Changing strategies, Zach crouched down beside his son and took a gigantic bite out of the hot dog. "Mmmm," he said as though he'd just sipped the finest ambrosia. "Dinosaur tails and slug sauce." He made more sounds of gustatory satisfaction.

Gideon stopped. "Dinosaur tails?" he asked.

Zach took another bite. "Mmmm. Dinosaur tails and slug sauce." He looked back and forth between the dog and the boy. "Want a bite?"

"Bite," Gideon replied.

Zach held the hot dog carefully so that none of the ketchup touched Gideon's cheeks. Soon Bobby, Bud, and Luke joined them.

"More," Gideon said, past the tiny bite he'd taken.

"Please," Christie added, elbowing her brothers-in-law out of the way to stand beside Zach, so pleased and, frankly, surprised, by what she'd just witnessed.

"Please, more," Gideon said, looking up at his daddy. "Dinosaur tails with slug sauce," he said, taking another huge bite. Not at all concerned when some of the ketchup got on his cheek, he simply wiped it on his sleeve.

"Zach, you are amazing," she said, sinking her fingers into Zach's thick honey-gold hair and smiling at him when he looked up to meet her gaze, a sincere smile of love and devotion.

"A step forward?" Seth asked.

"Yep. Do you know that he has never eaten a hot dog or anything else with any kind of sauce? This is a red-letter day, a ketchup-red-letter day," she said.

Zach stood, wrapped an arm around her shoulders, and pulled her close. "I love you," he whispered against her ear.

"I love you, too," she replied.

"I love you, Mommy," Gideon said around a mouthful of ketchupy hot dog.

Christie chuckled happily. "I love you, too, eater of dinosaurs tails with slimy sauce."

"Dinosaur tails with slug sauce," Gideon corrected her.

Zach kissed her again on the side of the head. She turned into him, finding his mouth with her own.

"Mmm. Hot dog," she murmured against his lips in her best Homer imitation.

He pulled back to smile at her. "It was the only way to convince him."

"I hate to break up this love fest," Luke began. "But, *mon petit frère*, do you not have a question to ask your sweet wife?" When Zach didn't immediately respond, Luke continued, "Yellowstone? *Mano y mano?*"

"You're mixing your languages again, Luke," Seth said in mock derision.

Luke made an exaggerated bow. "Well, if the linguist were home, he could tell me how to say it in Mandarin ... or Korean ... or Marathi ... or Italian. But since he's gone deep, you'll just have to cope, King Kong." Luke turned back to Zach. "Well?"

"Shut it, Luke," Seth said, punching his brother on the shoulder. Luke fixed him with a dirty look as he rubbed his shoulder. Bobby laughed aloud at the play, punching Luke on the shoulder, too.

"Hey, no fair guys," Luke complained.

Christie scanned the group of Mareks. Was this a conspiracy to back her into a corner where she couldn't say no? What were they asking? To take Gideon?

"Le's getta 'nother hot dog," Bobby said to Gideon.

"Hot dog dinosaur tails," Gideon said, hopping along beside Bobby. Bud followed to help.

"Zach?"

"I, uh, was going to ask you later." Zach slanted a quelling glare at his two brothers.

"Ask me what?" she said, feeling trepidation at Zach's hesitation.

Luke poked Zach in the shoulder. "Not afraid, are you, *petit garçon?*"

Christie took a minute to really study the brothers standing shoulder to shoulder. Luke looked smug. Seth looked ready to smile, a very unusual state for him. Zach looked … sheepish, or was that fear she was seeing? Was he afraid of her response to him? He shouldn't be. All at once, Christie felt indignant on his behalf. He shouldn't be the brunt of his brothers' humor.

Stepping into Zach, she locked her gaze with his. Then, stroking her palms slowly up his chest, she linked her arms behind his neck. Slowly, very slowly, she tiptoed up to kiss him languidly on the mouth. Tightening her arms, she pulled him closer and he sank into the kiss, deepening it. She felt his palms on her lower back sliding lower and pulling her closer.

"Ah-hem," Luke cleared his throat loudly. "Excuse me a moment." Then he stuck his finger in his mouth and mock-gagged.

Seth followed suit and then laughed outright. "We get it, you two."

Christie chuckled, and Zach pulled back. "Eat your hearts out," he said and then turned back to her. "Christie, do you mind if we three take off for a few days of backwoods camping?"

"Seth's already got the back-country permits," Luke added, unable to keep out of the very smack-dab middle of the discussion.

Christie couldn't help but laugh. "I think that's a great idea," she said, shoving Luke good-naturedly at the same time.

Luke scowled playfully back at Christie and then shoved both Zach and Seth in exchange.

"Let's get this little trip planned," Luke said, grasping Zach's shirt and pulling him toward the house.

The maps came out, produced as if from thin air. Seth propped Bobby's laptop open on the dinner table and the negotiations began.

"We should definitely hike our way into Cascade Corner," Luke suggested.

"What are you smokin' these days, twerp," Seth replied. "That area's full of swamps and sloughs. The bugs will be horrific. Think vampire mosquitoes." He spread his hands to indicate the size.

"Yes. But it also has the most beautiful waterfalls in the park: Union Falls, Terraced Falls, and Colonnade Falls. And it's been a dry summer. It'll be fine," Luke said.

"Exactly how *far* are you planning to hike?" Seth said, clearly questioning Luke's sanity.

Luke flipped the map of Yellowstone around. "All right, Kong. If it will preserve your dainty little sensibilities, we could go here." Luke pointed to the southwest corner of the map. "We could drive to Cave Falls and then hike into Bechler Falls."

"You want to go to Yellowstone via eastern Idaho?" Seth said incredulously.

"It's not that big a deal," Luke said. "Read this." Luke flipped through the guide book until he found the page he wanted. "… 'From Cave Falls you can get a view of both the upper and lower cascades'…" He shoved the book into his older brother's face, pointing so there could be no doubt about what he was saying. "… 'Cave Falls, at only twenty feet in height, is one of the widest falls in Yellowstone' …" Luke pulled back. "Then we could hike on to Bechler Falls and into one of these backcountry sites here." Luke pointed at three different spots on the map.

Luke lowered his voice. "Look, if we want to give our *petit frère* maximum chance to see wildlife …" His voice faded out.

"You don't need to make a special journey just for me," Zach said.

"Moose, beaver, elk, coyote, black bear, grizzly bear, osprey. Come on, Zach. Are you telling me that after six months in prison, you don't want to be in the wild? At least these animals will smell better than your fellow prisoners," Luke said.

"Yeah," Zach said, and then he laughed. "You're right about one thing, hygiene and prison don't seem to have much in common."

Luke slapped him on the back. "Good. Great. We're set."

"Grab your gear," Seth said to both of them. "It's all in Dad's shed. Shall we do bivy sacks or hammocks?"

"Can't guarantee convenient trees in that area," Luke said.

"I'm going to bring my bivy sack. I could handle the feeling of being completely out in the open, no walls at all," Zach said, smiling at the feeling of oncoming freedom.

"We'd better bring a water filter, too, unless you want to haul in enough water for three days," Seth said, ever the cautious and overprepared one.

CHAPTER 33

Parking Seth's beaten and abused Chevy Avalanche in the public lot, a smoothed area bounded by long pine logs, Zach saw his second waterfall of the summer, an unnamed falls that stretched across the Fall River. The little waterfall was only about eight to ten feet in height, but Zach paused to enjoy the sparkling dance of the sunlight off the cold waters.

"There've been a few bear sightings over the past two weeks, so be cautious," the ranger said, a Yogi Bear–shaped fellow named Chad. "We've had a few sightings of osprey, a blue-gray gnatcatcher, and a squadron of pelicans who stopped by briefly yesterday. Remember to bring out what you take in ... and enjoy. It's been a dry season, so the bugs aren't too bad."

Luke looked very smug after that comment.

Map in hand and pack on his back, Seth led the way, silent and thoughtful as he followed the trail. Zach encouraged Luke to take the middle ground as the trail narrowed along the Bechler River, quaking aspens on the right and tall, lodge-pole pines on the left. At the rear of the single file, he could keep half his attention on Luke's ongoing conversation, which generally only required the occasional grunt in response, and the rest on the incredible feeling of freedom burgeoning in his chest. With each inhalation, Zach drew in a clarifying draft, reminding him of the richness of his life and then expelled the bitter rot of prison, reminding himself, *I am not powerless. I am not worthless. I am loved. I am protected.*

The roar of the waterfall reached his ears long before the falls came into view. Even though the cave for which the falls had been named was hidden beneath a pile of rubble, Zach recognized Cave Falls from Luke's tourist-guide description. Not a high waterfall by Niagara Falls standards, quite puny in fact, still the sheer volume of water cascading down the rocks was immense. It was moments like this—the scintillating effect of the deep-blue waters as they rushed over the wide expanse and others, the laughter of his son, the sweet love of his wife, and the protection of his family—these were the moments, the reminders, that he lived a rich life.

As they forded the Bechler River, thigh-deep in the strong, bracing currents, Zach was glad for every inch of his six-foot height. *Blake will be glad he missed this adventure.* At five-nine, the next youngest Marek would have found the crossing rather more exhilarating than any man could enjoy. Zach laughed at the thought, and then he just couldn't stop laughing. Both Seth and Luke stopped to stare.

"You all right, *cheéte?*" Seth asked.

Zach wiped the laughter from his eyes. "Yeah. Yeah. Just ... thanks." He moved off and around his brothers. *Thank you, Lord.* He imagined that Seth and Luke shared a meaningful glance behind his back, but he didn't mind.

"So tell me, *petit frère*," Luke began, slapping Zach on the back as they reached the bank. "Who set you up in Albania?"

"Give him some time," Seth said, sending Luke a quelling glare.

"It's all right," Zach said. "It would be great to have some help figuring it out. I spent six months thinking about it, and I still have no answers."

"Christie called me after Karl and your senior inspector arrived to say that you'd been arrested and were going to be fired," Seth said.

"Carlos Rivera. Yeah, Christie told me. She said that Zimmerman reported me for doing heroin," Zach said.

"Pah! Like you'd ever be so dim," Luke said.

"I can't figure out why he did that. We weren't exactly friends, but we weren't enemies either. At first, I thought it was him who planted the drugs ..." Zach shook his head. "Except he was with me for hours before we returned to the apartment."

"I was there the day that Carlos Rivera showed up and told Christie that you were dead," Seth added quietly. "She put up a tough front, but the light disappeared from her eyes. She was devastated."

"Thanks for being there for my family," Zach said, including both of his brothers in his gratitude. "How did Blake find out?"

Luke shrugged. "He was in deep cover in some unknown corner of the world. But somehow, once Damaris Quickle—what kind of a name is that anyway?—found out, Blake appeared."

"Blake was sure that the Albanians had kept you alive because you had useful information," Seth said.

"Yeah. They asked a lot of questions about the task force—Who was on it? Who were our local contacts? What did we discover?" Zach said.

"What *did* you discover?" Luke asked.

"Well, the task force followed up a few leads and shut down a warehouse or two, interrupted the local networks, and arranged the arrest of some low-level dealers and enforcers. Not much, really, in the grand scheme of things," Zach said.

"Was there any information that you had that no one else did?" Seth asked slowly.

Zach juggled that idea around in his mind for a while. "I found a nebulous connection between a winery in Albania, the Vera Pliny, and a Niagara winery, Moerarty's," Zach said. "A pretty flimsy connection."

The trail narrowed, ending the conversation for the moment. Luke took point, leading the way, the scree of the mountain on one side and the river on the other. Before long, the trail took them east up the mountain and then down into a valley. This path was little traveled compared to many trails in Yellowstone, and Zach had the sense of unspoiled beauty.

"You know, there was a national park in Albania, Parku Kombëtar i Lurës, on Lura Mountain. It was covered in pine forests—black pine, red pine, white pine. It was very near the town of Peshkopi where we located one of Gjojak's drugs warehouses. That bust was bloody, a waste of human life. But I went back to the mountain with a friend of mine, Besian Chocholi, a café owner. We hiked up the eastern side to one of the glacial lakes. There was a herd of roe deer grazing in a meadow." Zach trailed off, remembering the feeling of the beauty transposed over the death from the previous day. Yes, they'd found the warehouse. And Gjojak's men had defended it. Even the men lifting and carrying crates had risen in arms and dug in to defend the drug lord's empire.

"You're home now," Seth said in his calm and confident baritone.

They traveled on in silence for a time. Stopping for a break at one of the pit toilets at the side of the trail, they relieved themselves and then moved several feet away to stop for a snack of GORP—good old raisins and peanuts. Zach lay back on the ground feeling totally at peace—until he heard a snuff and a grunt from the woods behind them.

"Bear," Seth said, speaking low. "Over Luke's shoulder."

Zach followed Seth's gaze. Yep, one black bear sighted. As quietly as possible, Zach fastened his bag full of snack and slipped it into his pack. He knew not to run. One of his first lessons on the ranch after coming there as a boy was, if you encounter a bear, do not run. Running may trigger an attack.

Zach could still remember the day he rode out with Bud to check the stock in the far pasture. They'd been tacking up a broken line of fence when out of the trees lumbered a massive grizzly. Bud had clamped his hand on Zach's thin shoulder, holding him firmly in place as he recited the rules of a bear encounter. Fortunately, the beast had remained upwind and it had soon wandered off. But ever after, Zach listened when Bud gave lessons on wild animals.

This, however, was a black bear, a much lesser danger and yet more likely to cause a nuisance. Moving slowly, Zach and his brothers shouldered their packs and walked carefully back down the trail, keeping an eye on the small bear but never making direct eye contact.

The bear reared up on its hind legs, clearly curious, testing the air across its tongue. They obviously smelled boring, just bug spray and perspiration. Soon, the bear huffed once and scampered away looking for something more interesting to do.

Cautiously, they hiked back down the trail and continued their journey.

CHAPTER 34

Christie was here. He could smell her, taste her. He could feel the silky softness of her hair as it ran through his fingers. He pulled her against him, thrilling at the weight of her in his hands. Suddenly, the weight of darkness descended, and her aroma was blotted out by the stench of male sweat and hopelessness. Zach was back in the unnamed prison in Albania. He was tied down on his back, and there above him were the leering faces of his interrogators. They were furious, their lethal intent transparent as they held Christie between them. "She's next!"

A wave of helplessness crashed over Zach. "No!" He reached above him, his knuckles sliding against something soft and yielding.

"Get him out. Quickly." Voices filtered through the darkness burying him. He struck out, punching and kicking. He needed out. He needed air.

Punching again, he finally connected.

"Hey, little brother, calm down."

Zach froze. "Seth?" How did his brother get into his prison cell?

"Zach, you're safe. It was just a dream," Luke said.

Zach opened his eyes and looked around him. He was half in and half out of his bivy sack with his sleeping bag tangled around his legs. Seth's and Luke's heads were just above him.

"Sorry," Zach murmured. He was still shaking from his experience, and his throat felt dry and sore from yelling. "What time is it?"

"Four thirty in the a.m.," Luke said after checking his watch.

Zach nodded. "Who'd I hit?"

"Me," Seth said, rubbing his jaw dramatically. "You okay now?"

"Yeah." *No. Will I ever feel okay again?*

"What were you dreaming about?" Seth asked in a subdued voice.

"Prison." Zach sighed heavily. "What else?" He shoved the sleeping bag off his legs. "Get back. I'm standing up."

"Move on back," Seth said, pushing Luke back by the shoulder.

"You going back to sleep?" Luke asked.

"No. I'm up. I'm for a walk and maybe a swim," Zach said. There was no way he would be able to sleep after that.

"Sounds good to me. You weren't thinking of skinny-dipping, were you?" Luke raised an eyebrow in question, a look of mock-disgust on his face.

Zach huffed out a laugh that almost contained a little humor. "Not likely with all these mosquitoes about."

Seth eyed Zach carefully and then seemed to come to a decision. "Midnight swim sounds fun to me." Seth stopped for a moment. "Why don't you give Christie a call first?"

"It's the middle of the night. She could use a little break from my trauma, I'm sure," Zach said and then wished he hadn't revealed quite so much.

Luke shoved Seth. "We don't need no girls to deal with a little ole nightmare. Last one in the river cooks breakfast!" Luke grabbed his flashlight from the ground and took off. Seth and Zach exchanged a look, and with a grin, Zach shoved Seth, which was a pretty useless way to move a mountain.

There was enough moonlight that Zach could see his brothers as they broke the surface of the water. They wrestled and splashed until Zach's muscles were tired, and he felt like maybe he could sleep again.

"I'm hungry," Luke said, hauling himself out of the water.

"Let's make a fire and break out the oatmeal and coffee," Seth suggested.

Zach followed them out, wrapping his towel around his shoulders. There was enough of a breeze that he felt chilled from the swim.

"So if it wasn't Zimmerman," Luke began. "Then who else had an ax to grind with you?"

Zach smiled in the dark. He was home with his brothers, a band of misfits and castaways that had been fashioned into a family by two amazing people. Zach had his posse around him again, and together, they would solve the mystery. If they managed that, maybe they could clear his name as well and get his job back.

"There must have been a leak on the task force, someone in Gjojak's employ," Zach replied.

"This tenuous connection you discovered must have had truth to it if you scared them enough to try to get rid of you. Had you told anyone of your suspicions?" Seth asked.

"I was going to speak to Damaris about it after the takedown at Gjojak's villa, but I never got the chance," Zach said.

Seth froze. "What about your partner? He would be one of the few people who knew enough about your history, foster care, Janice's drug addiction, and so on to choose drug-trafficking as a plausible lie."

"Yeah, but he was my friend," Zach protested.

"Who knew about Gideon's diagnosis?" Luke asked. Zach frowned at the nonsequitur. "That was the supposed excuse for you to take drugs," he explained.

Zach felt a blush rising up his neck. "No one else. I, uh, didn't really talk about it. But, I guess, anyone who had access to my computer would be able to see the emails from Christie and check my search history..." His voice trailed off.

"Well, now, isn't that interesting," Luke said, and then he was actually quiet for a time.

CHAPTER 35

"Pool," Luke said two days later. He sat in the diminutive backseat of the Avalanche, his knees bent almost to his chin.

"You want to go swimming?" Seth asked, glancing askance at his brother in the rearview mirror.

"Snooker, billiards, pool, doofus," Luke replied. "We're about four blocks from Woody's Pub and Grub."

All Zach wanted to do was see Christie again, but he didn't want to be a buzzkill. "Sounds good."

"The Pub and Grub it is then," said Seth, taking the next left turn.

"Get us some pool cues, Luke, and I'll get the drinks," Zach said once they were inside. Pool with his brothers, camping, late-night discussions over marshmallows and hot cocoa, life was returning to normal. Normal was good. From now on, adventures would have to be limited to situations that didn't sacrifice his family.

"What'll ya have?" the barkeep asked.

"Coffee, four sugars; a ginger ale; and a root beer," Zach said, pulling out his wallet to pay for the drinks.

Luke was racking the balls when Zach found his brothers. "Coffee, Seth. You have to add your own sugar," he said and handed out the drinks.

"Seth, you break," Luke said.

After the third game of pool, Zach noticed it was getting noisier in the bar with some commotion ongoing across the room. In time, the buzz of noise drew closer. *Time to go.*

Without warning, a cold, sticky ooze slid down the back of Zach's shirt. He turned to see the source of the pungent liquid, and stars exploded behind his eyes. Zach ducked to avoid the next punch, coming up from a crouch to shove the leather-clad pugilist away. The heavyset man landed against a pool table and came back up swinging in a new direction. *As if the world needed more proof that inebriation lowers the IQ.*

"Seth, let's go," Zach said, reaching out to grasp his brother's arm.

"Where's Luke?" Seth asked, searching the room with his eyes.

"Here." Luke popped up from behind a pool table with a man in each fist. "What gives?" he asked as he tossed one man away from him and decked the other.

"We're leaving," Seth replied, nodding over his shoulder at Zach, before exclaiming, "Duck!"

Luke heeded Seth's warning, crouching low to miss the bottle flying toward the spot where his head used to be. "Thanks, Kong," he called out from the floor behind an upended wooden chair.

Shoving Seth forward, Zach followed and Luke soon joined them. Zach was eager to get out and back to Christie. The smell of the spilled beer was making him feel ill, and the sticky ooze glued his shirt to his back.

Abruptly, Seth changed direction as the morass of confusion shifted, heading instead for the side exit and then halting without warning. Zach plowed into his brother's granite shoulders. "Seth?"

Seth stepped aside to reveal Sheriff Matthew Alexander Reeves III. *Groan! Not Matty Reeves.* From the first day of high school, Zach and Matty Reeves had gone head to head more times than Zach could count.

"Well, well, well, look what we have here. Three of the Marek brothers in the middle of a barroom brawl." Matty circled the three brothers. "Seth, Luke ... but this can't be Zachary, can it?" Matty hooked his thumbs in the front pockets of his dark-brown uniform trousers. "Zachary Marek of the Ontario Police? Except, wait, you're no longer a police officer with any police force. You're the lowest of the low, a thieving drug dealer, or so the paper said, the scum of the earth—"

Luke grabbed a fistful of Matty's shirt. "He's not a thief or a drug dealer."

Placing a restraining hand on Matty's arm, Zach reached over to rest a hand on Luke's shoulder. "Let it go," he murmured to Luke, stiffening his spine as he stiffened his resolve to ignore his rival's jibes. "It's not helping."

Matty shook him off, hatred contorting his features. "He's resisting, Walsh!" Matty hollered.

Deputy Walsh, a young freckle-faced redhead, jogged over.

"Everything okay, Sheriff?" Walsh asked.

"He's resisting. Cuff him," Matty said and then spat onto the floor beside Zach's hiking boots.

Shooting a baleful expression at Matty, Luke put his hands out in front of him in a placating gesture. Walsh stepped toward him.

"Not him," Matty said. His expression shifting from hatred to malice, he nodded at Zach. "Him."

"Why?" Luke asked in dismay.

Ignoring Luke, Matty spoke to Deputy Walsh. "Now you be sure and pat him down first." He turned his gaze to Zach. "Assume the position."

Zach buried his emotions behind a mask of blankness and did as he was instructed, placing his open palms against the wall and spreading his legs.

"Be thorough," Matty instructed the young deputy who followed his orders to the letter.

His forehead pressed to the wall, Zach blanked his mind so that he could barely feel the deputy's hands on him. He could tell, however, when Matty took over by yanking his arms behind his back and slapping on the cuffs just a little too tightly. Immediately, Zach felt the blood begin to pool in his fingertips.

"They sent you to prison, didn't they? Where were you, Afghanistan?" Matty asked, bringing his face close to Zach's profile.

"Albania," Luke muttered.

Zach could smell tobacco and peppermint and the sour odor of whiskey. "I can't believe they let you go already; must not have much of a crime law in them backward Asian countries."

"Albania is in southeastern Europe," Luke interjected, but Matty ignored him.

"I've been exonerated by the Canadian government," Zach said. The feeling of being bound was raising his blood pressure, making his head pound.

Matty spun him around and drew him close, his hands fisted in Zach's shirt. At this proximity, Zach looked down on the pale roots in Matty's bad dye job.

"Ex-cons don't got no call to cross into our country," Matty said, stepping back when Zach maintained his gaze.

"I'm not an ex-con," Zach said through clenched teeth. Grinding his molars into dust was preferable to pounding a sheriff into the same dust. Christie would not be best pleased if he wound up in jail, for real this time.

"Then what are y'all doin' here?" Matty sniped, gesturing around him.

"I'm visiting my father," Zach said.

"Perhaps you're here, in my county, for your own renarious schemes," Matty said.

"The word is *nefarious*," Luke said.

Matty cursed in reply but was interrupted by another young deputy, her coppery hair pulled back into a ponytail. "What d'ya want, Sheila?" he asked, clearly irritated by the intrusion.

"We've rounded most of them up, Sheriff. What would you like done with them?" she asked.

"Start transportin' 'em to the jail. You can take them two along with you," Matty said, indicating Luke and Seth.

"No, not without Zach," Luke protested. Matty grinned with malicious splendor, his little piggy eyes practically gleaming with sadistic pleasure.

"What are you going to do with him, Matty?" Seth asked quietly.

"We're goin' t' take a little ride out to 'the ranch.'" Matty made air quotations as he mocked the term. "So I can collaborate his story."

"I'm not sure you're using that word properly," Luke said, mocking the self-important twit.

"We'll see what Daddy thinks of a drunken brawl. Hmmm." Matty broke off. "On second thought, Deputy Per-sodd, you can transport them *three*." Deputy Sheila Persaud took hold of Zach's elbow. "Keep them cuffs on, Sheila." Matty leaned in and gave a sniff. "You done smell like beer, Zachary. We might have t' file charges of public drunkenness. Wouldn't be the first time, would it, Zachary?"

"That was you, Matty," Zach muttered, referring to the more distant past, and then added, "I was drinking root beer. Give me a breathalyzer."

Matty spread his arms wide to indicate the entire barroom. "We're a little busy." He turned to Sheila, his voice hardening to granite. "Get 'em out o' here now or find another job."

Zach watched her visage tighten, but she nodded brusquely.

"Walsh. Juarez." Matty hollered across the room, and two deputies approached, one the young redhead who was accompanied by an older man with flecks of gray in his black hair. He had the paunch of an over-forty, but the bleary, bloodshot eyes of a drinker ... or, possibly, the father of a sleepless child.

"Wrap this up. I got some calls to make," Matty said, interrupting Zach's thoughts.

"When did you become sheriff?" Luke asked, his irritation slipping into his voice. Matty stopped and turned back to him.

"Eight months ago. The old sheriff, my granddaddy, done had a heart attack. People was most comfortable with another Reeves in the seat. They was used to following the orders of those born to lead," Matty said proudly.

"I thought you were studying business. Didn't you open a store over in Sheridan?" Luke asked.

"My talents was wasted there. This here is much more my thang," Matty said.

Yeah, I bet. It sounded like Matty had again failed at whatever he did and, once again, been rescued by his wealthy family.

Zach could feel the numbness of confinement encroaching throughout the ride in the rear of the sheriff's car until the cell door clanged shut, when it took over completely. Zach found his corner and claimed it, gesturing his brothers over. Shoulder to shoulder, they stood, but Zach felt suddenly alone.

CHAPTER 36

"Yes?"

Christie heard her father-in-law's voice as he answered the telephone. Maybe it was Zach. It was nearly midnight, and Zach and the others still had not returned. She was beginning to worry.

One look at Bud's face told her that something had gone terribly wrong. "What is it?" she asked urgently when he hung up the phone. "Is it Blake? Is it the others?

"That was Seth," Bud replied slowly, and the look of compassion in his eyes frightened her. *What's happening?*

"Apparently the boys stopped at the Pub and Grub—that's a bar in Cody—to play a little pool. There was a fight of some sort, and when the sheriff arrived, they were arrested. Zach was cuffed for resisting," Bud said.

"No," she whispered.

"They're in the county lockup. Young Matty Reeves, that's the sheriff, is refusing to release Zach until someone comes to pick him up, claims he's been drinking. Evidently, Reeves doesn't feel any of the boys should be driving themselves," Bud said.

"What? That makes no sense," she said. She found it hard to believe that all three Marek brothers were so inebriated that they couldn't drive home. "Do you have a lawyer we can call?" Christie gulped as she saw the next year of her life dissolve like a snowflake on a toddler's tongue.

"Yes. Floyd Blackhawk. He's been my lawyer through all five boys'

235

adolescences. This will be a piece of cake for him." Bud gave her a hug. "Shall I go pick up our boys?"

"No. I think I'd better go. It's going to be difficult enough for Zach as it is. Can you please keep an ear out for Gideon?"

"Sure, honey," he said. "I'll draw you a map and ask Floyd to meet you there."

"Thanks." Christie's heart filled with a desperate sadness.

"It'll be okay," Bud said, patting her on the shoulder. "Seth seemed to feel that young Matty was overreacting."

"But why would he do that? Why would he arrest Zach unless he'd committed a crime?" she asked, desperate for some reason to feel optimism in this situation.

"Because he's a pompous little troublemaker," Bud replied bitterly. "Zach and Luke came up against that boy more often than I can recall. Some things never change."

Christie just nodded and then got dressed and drove to the jail.

"Hello, I'm Christie Marek," she said to the first uniformed officer she met, a young red-haired man dressed in dark-brown trousers and a light-brown uniform shirt labeled, Walsh. "I'm here for Zach, Seth, and Luke Marek."

"Marek," Walsh replied, repeating the name. "Sheriff Reeves will wanna talk to you." He waited for her nod and then left to knock on the pine door marked "Sheriff," before disappearing inside. When he returned, he was blushing to the tips of his ears. "The sheriff is ready to see you," he said, gesturing for her to go in.

Christie did, doing her best to steel her nerves. "Hello, I'm Christie Marek, Zach's wife," she said, holding out her hand in greeting.

Rising from his seat, Matty Reeves walked around his desk to sit on the corner, gracing Christie with an expression of disdain. She decided to dislike him on the spot.

"Have a seat," he said in a pleasant voice, which lost its conciliatory effect because of the languid up-and-down he gave her, his gaze lingering where it should not. Christie urgently felt the need to bathe in order to wipe off his disgusting appraisal. And he smelled bad, too.

"I'll stand, thank you. Mr. Reeves—" she said.

Matty's face lost all attempt at conciliation. "Sheriff."

"Sheriff," she repeated, even managing to keep a matching sneer from her voice. "I'm here to pick up my husband and my brothers-in-law."

"Soon ... perhaps." Matty surveyed her body once again. He looked up at her face, finally, and she felt another burst of anger at this little man. "You're not from around here, huh?"

"No, I'm not. I met Zach at Durham College in Toronto," she said.

"Hmm. My second wife did a summer in Toronto before we was married," he said.

"That's, uh, nice," she said. "When can I see Zach?"

"I'll have him brung in," Matty replied. Christie jumped when he hollered out into the hall. "Walsh! Get Zachary Marek."

"You got some kind of special needs kid, huh?" Matty asked.

Christie's eyes flew open in astonishment and then narrowed in annoyance.

"Our son has autism, if that's what you mean?" she said. Yes, she had definitely decided not to like this man.

"Tough luck," he replied, clearly not sympathetic at all. Not that Christie needed sympathy, only sleep.

Soon, Zach was led into the room, his hands cuffed behind his back. She recognized this man, but she hadn't seen him in weeks. This was the man who was soaked in anger smoothed over with the bitterness of betrayal and coated in an unhealthy dose of disempowerment. She felt the familiar tug of fear at the memory of all she'd lost because of Zach's grief. But that was superseded by pity as she saw behind his steely gaze to the horror and humiliation that her lover and best friend was experiencing.

"Hi," she greeted Zach, her voice soft as she tried to transmit some sweetness to him. He nodded once in her direction, but when she stepped toward him, he shook his head and frowned. She desperately wanted to fold her husband in her arms, but she understood he was telling her that he couldn't maintain his resolve if she showed him pity.

"Why was my husband arrested?" she asked, shifting her gaze back to Sheriff Matty little-piece-of-rat-crap Reeves.

"Disturbing the peace. And public drunkenness," Matty said.

"You were drinking?" Christie asked, surprised, her eyebrows springing up in question. Shifting closer, she sniffed Zach's shirt, making a sound of disapproval. She wasn't convinced, however, even with the evidence before her. Zach had never been much of a drinker. None of the Marek boys were. They each had their own tale of the woes of substance abuse.

"No. The beer's not mine. Someone spilled it on me," Zach said softly, keeping his eyes on her.

"Fighting," Matty added.

"You got into a fight?" she asked, softer now.

"No," Zach replied, though she could clearly see the red indentation of knuckles on his cheek. Some things you had to take on faith.

Arms crossed, brow furrowed, Christie turned to Matty. "Then what's the problem? If he wasn't drinking and he wasn't fighting—"

A knock interrupted them. Before Matty could reply, the door opened and a lean man walked in. He had the blackest hair she'd ever seen—even darker than Seth's, so dark that it was almost blue—pulled back from his narrow face into a ponytail, which was held in a woven leather thong hung with white feathers. His lean body was clothed in what even Christie could tell was a very expensive suit.

"Floyd Blackhawk, attorney-at-law." The man introduced himself. "Hello, Zach."

"Hello, Floyd. Dad give you the late-night call again?" Zach replied, relaxing minutely.

Floyd released a small smirk. "I thought you boys had finally outgrown your need for me."

"Why are you here?" Matty interrupted, quite rudely, Christie thought.

"I am the Messieurs Mareks' lawyer," Floyd said. "I would like to see my clients."

"Well, you can see one right here. I'm not sure if you're aware that this one is a crooked cop, a convicted felon in Armenia." Matty was clearly enjoying himself.

"I'm aware. Albania, though, wasn't it? You need to ensure you have your facts straight, Sheriff, particularly if you intend to take this matter any further." Floyd shifted his gaze to Zach, taking in the situation in a glance. "You should have called me, Zach," Floyd said, reprimanding him, though whether for the present trouble or the past, Christie wasn't certain.

"Can't afford you," Zach replied, but there was a look of deep regret in his eyes.

"My clients, Sheriff?" Floyd said, reminding Matty that there were two brothers still absent.

"Walsh! Bring them other two Mareks," Matty hollered.

Soon, Seth and Luke arrived. They were not in handcuffs, another point on Christie's list of "reasons why I don't like Sheriff Matty kumquat."

"Them two're free to go," Matty said, waving them away.

"And Zach?" Floyd asked.

"I'll be holding him overnight," Matty said.

"Why?" Zach asked.

Christie could feel his anger rising.

"I need t' check into your story about why you're out o' prison. Tch. Tch." Matty shook his head, barely concealing a smirk of derision.

"Matty, don't—" Zach began.

All the blood had drained from his face, and Christie was very concerned about what that meant. But she didn't have long to wonder as Matty lurched to his feet, anger coming off him in waves.

"Don't tell me what I can and can't do," Matty said viciously.

Floyd stepped into Matty's space. Luke and Seth moved closer to flank Zach.

"Drunk," Matty said, spitting out the word, clearly trying to defend his indefensible position. "He was drunk. And fighting."

Zach stepped toward the sheriff, but Seth laid a hand on his shoulder, restraining him, and he subsided.

"Have you conducted a breathalyzer?" Floyd asked, not backing down an inch, not even a millimeter.

"Uh, well, no," Matty said, deflating instantly. "There weren't no time or opportunity."

Floyd turned to Seth. "Were you or your brothers drinking alcohol?"

"No. I was drinking coffee, Luke had ginger ale, and Zach had a root beer," Seth said.

"He reeks of beer," Matty said, sounding defensive.

Floyd stepped in and gave Zach's shirt a sniff. "Your beer?" he asked him.

"No. Someone spilled it on me," Zach said.

Floyd studied him intently for a long minute. "A blood test should clear this up."

"Blood test?" Matty squeaked and then seemed to gather himself together. Before long, a cunning expression crossed his face but then slipped away as it had nothing to hold onto. "And a urine sample ... observed." Matty narrowed his eyes.

"You want to watch?" Zach muttered, but Floyd sent him a quelling look. Unfortunately, Matty had heard Zach's words and his ears reddened in embarrassment, which morphed naturally into anger.

"Persaud!" Matty hollered. "Escort Zachary here to the medical room and take a blood and urine sample to test for alcohol levels. Tell Juarez that he can do the honors."

"Handcuffs?" Christie said. "How can he pee if he's handcuffed?"

"Remove the cuffs," Matty said, and then he turned to Floyd with a look meant to say that he was the most cooperative sheriff in the whole, entire world.

"If you'll wait here, Mrs. Marek," Floyd said. "I'll accompany your husband."

Christie nodded. Soon, she was surrounded by her brothers-in-law, their arms warm around her shoulders.

"He didn't do it, honey," Seth said, kissing her on the side of the head.

"I got important work to do. Wait out there," Matty said, pointing toward the foyer.

"Oh, thank you so much," Luke replied sarcastically. Matty's ears reddened again.

"Luke," Seth admonished him firmly as he led Christie to the waiting area. Luke told her everything that had happened.

"It was strange, Christie," Luke said. "The minute they snapped the cuffs on Zach, he altered, morphed. It was like he erected this huge wall to hide behind and then emerged a different person. It was weird."

"I've worked long and hard to get him back from behind that wall.

What will happen now?" she asked. Luke shrugged, and Seth shook his head sadly.

"I'm sorry, Christie," Luke said. "I never meant for this to happen. I just wanted to play pool."

It took over half an hour for Zach to return and then another forty-five minutes for the results to be processed from the urine test. The blood sample was sent off to the labs.

"Negative, sheriff," Persaud announced.

"He was still involved in a drunken brawl," Matty protested.

"Look at his hands," Floyd insisted. "Zach put your hands out, palms down." Zach complied. There were a few scratches that looked like they'd been made by raspberry bushes and a healing blister on his left thumb. Christie loved those hands. They could be so strong and yet so gentle.

"This man has not been in a fight this evening," Floyd said. "Wouldn't you agree, Sheriff? I think one of your deputies was perhaps a little too enthusiastic in making assumptions."

Someone else? Christie was sure from what Luke had said that it was Matty who had overreacted and she hated the idea that someone else would take the blame for this pathetic man's cruelty. The little worm could not even think up his own ways to blame others for his vengeful ineptitude. An excuse had to be provided for him. But when she went to rise in protest, Seth put his arm around her shoulder and pushed her down ever so gently. She cast him a sidelong glance, but he just patted her shoulder.

"Yeah, ah, I guess so. I'll look into it," Matty said.

"Are my clients free to go?" Floyd asked.

"Yeah." Matty rose and turned his back on them. "They can g—"

A shrieking cry splintered the air. Deputies came running. Bud walked in barely holding onto a shrieking, flailing Gideon.

"Daddy!" Gideon wailed, jerking about in Bud's arms.

"I'm here, sweetheart," Zach said, stepping over and pulling Gideon into his arms.

"Daddy," Gideon whimpered, locking his legs and arms around his father.

Matty stared open-mouthed. "What is that?"

"Who is that, you mean?" Seth said. His quiet voice was loaded with barely concealed anger.

"This is my son," Zach said proudly, kissing Gideon on the head.

"What is wrong with him?" Matty asked.

"Nothing," replied Bud, Christie, Seth, Luke, and Zach as one.

"Evidently, his mother told him that when he woke up, his daddy would be home," Bud explained. "I'm sorry, son, but he was inconsolable to find you absent when he got up."

Christie watched Zach bury his face against his son's neck, and she was sure he was hiding a pleased grin.

"Well," Luke said in the silence that followed. "Let's hit the road."

"Hit the road," Gideon repeated in a hiccupping voice. "Daddy, hit the road."

"It's a saying," Zach said, pulling back to look into Gideon's eyes.

"Don't really hit the road. It means time to go," Gideon said.

"Yes, sweetheart. You remembered," Zach said, giving Gideon a hug.

Gideon's smile fell away. "Time to go with Daddy?" he asked.

"Yes, son," Zach said.

Gideon melted against him. "Daddy!" He sighed happily.

CHAPTER 37

After holding Gideon's hand in the Jeep on the way to the ranch, Zach put him to bed. Christie got ready for bed and then curled up in the covers to wait for Zach. This bedtime story, she definitely wanted to hear.

When Zach joined her sometime later, after a shower, he slipped into bed and rolled onto his side, facing away from her. She had been half asleep, but she was pretty sure that Zach could tell the difference between that and full sleep.

Well, avoidance wasn't going to work. Shifting closer, she cuddled against him, kissing him on the neck. "It'll be okay," she said and kissed him again, trying to coax him to relax the muscles in his jaw. He was wound tight and ready to snap.

"We'll go home," he said evenly.

"What?" she asked. Why would he suddenly want to leave the ranch after they'd been through such trouble to get here?

"I just … I think it's best if we go home," he said and then rolled forward an inch, just enough to pull away from her.

"Why?" she asked again, demanding an explanation.

"No stops on the way back. That should be easier for everyone to deal with," he said as though she hadn't spoken.

"But that means …" It certainly hadn't been her choice of a vacation, but neither did she want to pack up and head home immediately into another five-day journey.

"Exactly. It means we get in the Jeep and drive straight home," he said, and now his voice sounded hard.

Her instinct was to move away from his anger, but instead, she moved closer, propping her knee on his hip and placing her hand on his chest. His heart was beating rapidly and his breathing was erratic though he was clearly working hard to control it. She held him close, massaging his neck, shoulder, and arm rather than trying to reason with him since she knew he really wasn't listening to her anyway.

After a time, when he seemed to be relaxing minutely, she said, "Hey, Clyde. How are you?"

"I thought that traveling together and being here on the Second Chance would help me … and it started to … but some things don't change … and Reeves won't let this go now that he has some real power over me," he said.

"Why does Matty hate you so much?" she asked.

Zach blew out a breath and said, "A girl. Raelynn Jones."

"Hmmm. Do I want to hear this story?" she asked, quirking a brow.

Rolling over to face her, he replied, "Up to you."

Tapping her finger on the corner of her mouth, she pretended to consider the matter. "Yup. Spill it, Clyde."

He took her hand and played with her fingers as he spoke. "Freshman year in high school, grade nine, they took us on an adventure hike in the Absaroka Mountains. It was meant to be a team-building exercise to help us bond. What a joke!" he said, bitterly. "We were divided into groups of eight, four guys and four girls, matched to one teacher. Unfortunately, my group was assigned to Mr. Radcliffe, the English teacher. I hated English. It took so long for me to read a book and then reading took such effort that it was hard to pull out the meaningful information."

Giving a morose shake of his head, Zach continued, "You know, my accomplishments never mattered, the awards I'd won for marksmanship, and kick-boxing, the roping competitions. It never mattered that I had to work twice as hard as Luke to get significantly lower marks in school; teachers were always disappointed in me. I was always just that foster kid," he said. He adopted a snotty tone of voice. "'*Blood will tell, Zachary.*'"

"Whose blood?" Christie said.

Furrowing his brow, Zach asked, "What do you mean?"

"Whose blood matters? Yours? Janice's? Bud's? Gideon's?" she said. He cocked his head at her as she spoke. "Nothing but the blood of Jesus." A slow smile crossed his face as she continued, "The Bible says that if we walk in the light as God is in the light, then we have fellowship with one another and ..." She paused dramatically, drawing a chuckle from his lips. "The blood of Jesus, His Son, purifies us from all sin. So whose blood matters, Zach?"

"Nothing but ... the blood of Jesus," he said, and she quoted along with him.

"God doesn't measure you by your history or genealogy but by His Son's sacrifice," she said, holding his face tenderly in her hands.

Turning his face, he kissed her palm. "Thank you," he said. His voice was husky and warm.

"Please tell me more about this adventure hike," she said.

After a long moment of studying her with wonder in his eyes, Zach nodded slowly, pulling back to rest on his elbow. "Luke and I were assigned to separate groups. I was paired with Robin Snake-eyes, Zapf Manning, Raelynn Jones, Matty Reeves—a baby-faced tot who looked barely old enough to cross the street without his mommy—Tiffany ... something, and two other girls. I can't remember their names. Everything was going fine. The day was overcast but a perfect temperature for hiking," he said, and she could see the memories in his eyes.

"It's rugged terrain up the volcanic peaks, but if you can get high enough to see down into the valleys ... covered in lodge-pole pines and willow trees ... it's really beautiful." He met her gaze, a smile on his lips. "We followed just a portion of the Beaten Path trail.

"Matty spent the entire time hitting on all the girls, especially Raelynn. She was the daughter of the mayor of Cody. I didn't know that until later. But Matty did, and he was becoming really obnoxious. So Raelynn dropped back to walk with me. She asked if I minded since Matty was getting on her nerves, and I said, 'Sure,'" Zach said.

"Not anything to do with the fact that she was pretty?" Christie asked with a knowing look in her eyes paired with a small, mischievous grin.

Zach's eyebrows rose innocently. "She may have been pretty, but certainly not the most beautiful woman *I've* ever met." He slid his hand up along her hip and beneath the hem of her shirt, stroking his fingers gently across her stomach.

Christie graced him with an appreciative smile and no attempt to halt his caress. She prompted him. "So you and Raelynn?"

"We talked. Her grandmother was a Canadian, and that launched a conversation." Zach shrugged with one shoulder. "She was easy to talk to. But I could see that Matty was fuming, glaring back at me, offering gestures, which, frankly, I'd seen plenty of times but had given up the use of after my mom caught me giving the finger to the ranch manager, Garvin Black Eagle."

"What did she do?" Christie asked, imagining the possibilities.

"She called Garvin over, and—you've seen him now, but he was more massive then, as tall, at least, as Seth is now, but with massive shoulders and hands. I was quaking in my cowboy boots. Mom made me tell Garvin what I'd done and what it meant. And then she turned and walked away. I was terrified."

"What did he do to you?" she asked with her eyes wide in speculation.

"He picked me up—I couldn't have broken his hold if I'd wanted to and believe me, I tried—and balanced me on the corral fence so we were eye to eye, and he proceeded to give me a lecture on respect. When he was finished, he lifted me down and ordered me to report to my mom immediately. He swatted me on the behind because I guess he didn't think I was moving quickly enough." Zach stopped. "You know, that's the only time anyone ever laid a hand of discipline on me at the ranch."

"I'm glad." Christie stroked his hair back from his face and then slipped her hand beneath his shirt to run her fingers through his chest hair. "What did your mom do?"

"She asked me if I had a good chat with Garvin, asked me if I was okay, and then hugged me and told me she loved me and was very proud of me for standing toe-to-toe with a man like Garvin. Then she kept me indoors for the rest of the day cleaning the house. Blaah! But I've never felt the need to flip people off since then."

Grinning, Christie kissed him. "I wish I had met your mom."

"You would have loved her, and she would have loved you," he said, moving in for another kiss, but before he could deepen it, she pulled back, giving him a "continue" gesture. Sighing in disappointment, Zach continued his story, his speech rate accelerating. "Okay. So it starts to rain. We get to the part of the trail that's a mite precarious, and Matty starts freaking out because he 'don't like them high places so much.' So Radcliffe takes him and two of the girls ahead. Robin cuts off and disappears over the mountain. And that left two guys and two girls."

"Was Raelynn your girlfriend?" Christie asked with just the right lilt of teasing in her voice.

"Hmmm," he replied dubiously. "We were friends and that drove Matty crazy, that and the fact that Luke and I took great pleasure in keeping the little twit from bullying the entire freshman class year after year. The end. Now can I kiss you?"

Smiling, she moved in close to him, aligning their bodies. "I love you, and I would love to kiss you. You make me very happy."

Frowning, he pulled back to meet her gaze. "Happy? When you say *happy*, what do you mean? Because I know that you've been plenty unhappy with me these past few weeks. I wish I could believe it but ... How do I know what happy means?"

"Happy," she replied simply. "I'm not talking about laugh-out-loud funny all the time." Pulling him back against her, Christie ran her fingers through his thick honey-gold hair, enjoying the softness. "I don't mean normal-all-the-time or the way things used to be. It's more like knowing that no matter what happens, everything will be okay ... because we're together."

"Happy," he repeated with wonder in his voice.

She had more to say. "I'm sorry I didn't take the time to understand how you were feeling about Gideon and autism. I think maybe if I'd listened early on, you wouldn't have felt like I could survive without you. Because I couldn't. I can't. I need you. And Gideon needs you. You really are the perfect husband and father."

"Is this to make me feel better?" he asked, his brows furrowed in skepticism.

Pressing her fingers to his lips, she replied, "It's the truth. It just took me a little Albania and a small dose of road trip to realize it. Forgive me?"

Pulling her tightly to him, he kissed her, hard and long, and then he softened the kiss, exploring her mouth as he rolled her beneath him.

"Forgive me?" she repeated, her voice still breathy from his kiss.

"Nothing to forgive, love." He kissed her on the neck, one loud smooch. "We'll stay," he said as though submitting to her desires.

Laughing, she kissed him again. "Well, good then."

He pulled his T-shirt off and tossed it across the room. "I love you and Gideon more than any other," he said, and she laughed at the happy expression on his face.

"We love you, too," she replied.

He went still for a moment, and she realized that his mind was heavy with thoughts and responsibilities. "I think that Carlos may have been the one who betrayed me?" he said, surprising her.

Carlos? Another betrayal? Poor Zach. But Carlos? Running her fingertips up his side, she tickled him. "Well, I never liked him anyway. Gideon calls him Smelly."

Laughing outright, Zach rolled so that she was on top of him. "I don't like him either." He ran his hands up her body. "But I really like you."

Beaming him a bright smile, she leaned down to kiss him. "I really like … oh, do that again."

Chuckling happily, Zach complied.

CHAPTER 38

Carlos Rivera was terrified. Zachary Marek had been rescued from prison and not only rescued but reunited with his wife. *Christie.* Carlos's desire for her thrummed through his body. She had accepted his friendship. But that was all. No matter how he tried, how conciliatorily he behaved, she would allow him no closer. He had even spent time playing with her brat of a child to no avail. He remained merely some sort of neutered arm's-length companion.

It was nearly a quarter to two in the morning there in Toronto where Carlos paced the confines of a deserted office. He was due to contact Gjojak in fifteen minutes, which would be eight o'clock in Tirana. Carlos frowned. He had been ordered to locate Zach. But Christie had not even told him that Zach had returned. Carlos had failed, and Gjojak did not tolerate failure. Zander Greave was a constant reminder of that, which had likely been Gjojak's purpose in arranging the hit.

Carlos slumped into the wheeled vinyl desk chair in the office. There was simply no avoiding it. He was going to have to admit to Gjojak that he had no idea where Zach was.

A knock sounded on the office door before it opened to reveal Constable Brenda Clock.

"There's a call for Thomason on line 2. Everyone upstairs has gone home for the night. Can you handle it?" she asked.

He started to refuse her and then changed his mind. If Gjojak was connected to Thomason, then it might be wise for Carlos to deal with this. A bit of information about Gjojak's misdeeds might give Carlos a little leverage. But that was a dangerous idea.

"I will handle it," Carlos said.

Constable Clock thanked him and departed.

"Inspector Rivera," Carlos answered the call.

"Yeah, well, this here is Sheriff Matthew Reeves of Park County, Wyoming. I've got me here one o' your guys," the sheriff said. "If he still works for you."

"Who?" Carlos asked.

"Zachary Marek. He was supposed to be in prison from what I heard, but he's here at his father's ranch. If he's escaped, I'd be happy to haul him in for you," the sheriff offered with an optimistic tone in his voice.

Relief flashed like a shockwave through Carlos's chest. "What would be very useful is if you would keep your eyes on him. It would be worth your while …" Carlos smiled. Another enemy for Zachary. Perfect.

The telephone rang, interrupting Gjojak's careful calculations.

"*Flas*," he said. "Speak."

"Sir, it is Rivera," Carlos said by way of introduction.

"Yes," Gjojak prompted impatiently.

"I received a call from a Sheriff Reeves in Wyoming that Zachary Marek has been arrested on a charge of drunk and disorderly," Rivera said.

"*Kështu që çfarë?*" Gjojak replied, allowing his voice to drip with boredom. "Of what significance is this?" Gjojak had long ago read the personnel file of Inspector Zachary Marek. He knew that Marek had been in lots of trouble as a youth. Many children in foster care had that problem. Not news.

"Uh, no, sir. I am not talking about the past. This happened three days ago," Rivera said.

"*Mut!* What are you saying?" Gjojak's boots dropped to the floor with a thunk. "Explain to me why you are so tardy in contacting me." He pressed his fingers to the bridge of his nose. "Never mind. Details."

"The sheriff called for Senior Inspector Thomason to discover whether Marek was still working for the OPP. With Thomason out of the country, I took it upon myself to handle the call," Rivera said.

Tarallak! Rivera, his little Canadian informant, was not shaping up to be the brilliant operative which Gjojak had predicted. He was tarallak, a simpleton. And yet had the nerve to sound proud.

"I told him that Inspector Marek had been fired after he was arrested and convicted of possessing illegal drugs," Rivera said. "Reeves tells me that he detained Marek in the middle of a barroom brawl."

Gjojak could feel the expectation of praise in the other man, so he let him stew for a time before he replied blandly, "Well done, Rivera. You can expect a little bonus in your next pay packet … *if* you get to this Wy-o-ming and confirm events. Find out whether Marek is truly in this place."

"Yes, sir," Rivera said. "And, sir, this Reeves expressed a willingness to keep his eyes on Marek … for a price."

"This 'keep his eyes on,' what does this mean?" Gjojak said.

"Observation. Surveillance."

"At what cost?" Gjojak asked.

"Two thousand American dollars," Rivera said.

Gjojak chuckled. *Such an inexpensive price for a man's life.* "Contact him and make the arrangements. Five hundred now and the rest if he gives us any useful information."

"Yes, s—"

Gjojak hung up in the midst of the officer's gratitude. Rivera had been surprisingly easy to corrupt four years ago with his gambling debts and penchant for drinking hard and womanizing while off-duty. Legalized casinos were absolutely an organized crime wet dream. And if the rumors were true about Rivera's penchant for rough treatment of the women he spent time with, well …

Gjojak pressed the buzzer on his intercom.

"*Po, zoti,*" Marthe replied. Good little secretary, so respectful.

"*Sjell mua të dhëna për* Zachary Marek. *Polici Kanadez,*" Gjojak ordered her. If he could discover something in Marek's past that would make him vulnerable, then they could more easily capture him and discover what he had learned during his time on the so-called task force and how he managed to escape his cell. Rivera had implied that Marek knew which Canadian winery Gjojak's empire was connected to. If so, it would be necessary to take lethal action, to eliminate him as a threat. But Gjojak wanted to be certain. That was the secret of his success: be thorough and never rush in too quickly.

Marthe knocked softly, waiting for his permission before entering. Gjojak's mouth began to water. *Ah, this is beauty, no emaciated stick; Marthe with her curves and flesh blessedly distributed.*

She placed the file folder on his desk without a word, pausing but not flinching when he touched her, caressed her.

"*Shumë e mire.* Very good," he said, releasing her, watching her sway out of the room. She was married to a local peasant, but Gjojak had never found that to be a hindrance to him in his pursuit of what was his.

"Get Qazim Hoxha on the line. Now," Gjojak ordered through the open door.

"*Po, zoti,*" Marthe replied.

Opening the file, which had been supplied by Rivera several years before, Gjojak perused the contents before going back for a more thorough examination.

"Hoxha on line one, *zoti,*" Marthe said moments later.

"Are you alone?" Gjojak asked his assassin.

"*Po. Çfarë doni?*" Hoxha replied, revealing his audacity in daring to question Gjojak's right to his employee's undivided attention.

As punishment for his nerve, Gjojak made him wait, picturing the way the assassin's pale dead eyes would stare fixedly at the wall as he refused to fidget in his impatience.

"Travel to the …" Gjojak flipped through Marek's file. "*Shans të Dytëk, Secundo Forte.* This is a ranch in Wy-o-ming of the United States. Contact me from Wy-o—*Mite! Vetëm thirrje mua.* I will arrange to have your usual equipment in place and ready for you as well as backup," Gjojak finished. "Once you have Marek, I will come. And Hoxha?"

"*Po?*"

"Do not be seen. No one must know you are again in the United States," Gjojak said.

Hoxha was a consummate assassin partly because he looked so ordinary—average height, medium build, not particularly attractive or stand-out-in-a-crowd ugly. His only distinguishing features were the line of tiny crosses etched into the skin of his stomach, one for each kill—and that lethal stare. When he chose to be, he was invisible.

"*Mirë.*"

"Yes. Good." But Hoxha was gone.

Now Gjojak was free to consider Carlos Rivera. What punishment would be suitable for such a blatant failure?

CHAPTER 39

Zach woke abruptly, his heart beating a tattoo against his ribs. Usually, he woke in a sweat from the effects of a nightmare, but he hadn't had another one since his talk about happiness with Christie a week earlier. Rolling toward the middle of the bed, he could see her shadowy figure beside him, and his heart squeezed. *She loves me.* Wanting nothing more than to pull her close and sleep in her arms, he didn't allow himself the luxury. He still had no explanation for his abrupt awakening, and so instead of curling up with his wife, he waited, listening intently to the sounds of the night. There were the distant neighs of the horses, a coyote's howl, and the creak and groan of the ranch house—nothing to explain Zach's sudden shift from asleep to alert. If Gideon had awakened, he would have called out or simply showed up in the bedroom.

In spite of the silence, a flicker of apprehension coursed through him. Then Zach heard it, that squeaky floorboard three steps inside the front door that each of the Marek boys had learned to avoid when sneaking in or out. Not that any of them had ever truly managed to avoid Grace's epic psi powers; she was able to detect even the thoughts of disobedience in her sons. Even now, each brother automatically avoided that step.

Zach slipped out of bed as quietly as possible.

"Where you going?" Christie asked sleepily. "Nightmare?"

He smiled at her even though he knew she couldn't see him. "I'm fine. Truly fine. Go back to sleep," he said, leaning over to kiss her, his mouth connecting with her right ear.

"Sure?" she asked.

"Positive," he replied, and soon she was snoring again.

Pulling on a T-shirt, he retrieved his Sig Sauer from the lockbox he kept it in on top of the dresser. Moving stealthily, he made his way past Bobby's and Gideon's rooms, checking on them, before continuing to the living room. He paused at the doorway, scanning the shadows for a displaced darkness.

"Freeze," he said, his voice quiet but lethal.

"Well, Inspector Marek, it is good to hear your voice," the voice said in a familiar Texan drawl.

Zach clicked on a nearby table lamp, and there before him stood Damaris Quickle, armed with a Glock pointed directly at him. Engaging the safety, she slipped it into her shoulder holster.

"You're looking well," she said, and then, to his surprise, she gave him a slow, sultry up-and-down. "Very well, in fact."

He narrowed his brows, going for irritation rather than the embarrassment he actually felt at being caught in his boxers and a beige bucking bronco T-shirt by the leader of an international task force.

"Why are you here?" he asked, choosing to ignore the blush rising up his neck.

Damaris quirked a brow. "Your brother tells me that you may be willing to help us get Gjojak."

"Gjojak? My life has moved beyond him. My family is my priority now," Zach said. He would never again make the mistake of leaving his little family when they needed him. Not now that he knew that they did need him.

"Zach? Son? Everything okay?" Bud asked, limping into the great room in his faded, threadbare earth-brown dressing gown, the dressing gown Grace had bought for him the Christmas before she'd died. Bud stopped short when he spotted Damaris, pulling his dressing gown closed around his blue cotton pajamas.

"Sorry we disturbed you, Dad." Zach gestured politely toward Damaris. "This is Damaris Quickle. I worked with her on the Albanian task force. She works for CSIS."

"No, I don't," Damaris replied. "Pleased to meet you … uh?" She put out her hand to shake Bud's as she waited for his name.

"Barnard Marek, but most people call me Bud." Shaking her hand first, he reached over to ruffle Zach's hair as though he was still eight years old. "This young man is my son."

Damaris grinned brightly at him. "I believe I've had the pleasure of knowing two of your sons."

Furrowing his brow, Bud replied, "Indeed?"

"Yes. Blake Marek and I have had many occasions to spend time together."

Bud didn't misunderstand her euphemism for counterespionage. In fact, he seemed to see directly to the heart of the message and beyond. "You are the reason that Blake came to hear of Zach's incarceration," Bud said, his assertion made in that matter-of-fact tone he used when he knew he was right. Zach could well remember his mother's annoyance. "Don't you use that tone of voice with me, Bud Marek. You are not as right as you think you are," she would say.

"That would be something that I'm not free to discuss." Damaris turned to Zach and then continued, completely negating her former statement. "I am sorry though that it took so long for word to filter down to me. We got you out as quickly as we could manage."

"Thank you for that," Zach said, truly grateful. He'd felt so alone, abandoned in that prison. And then to discover that the OPP had cast him adrift had really hurt—all because of Carlos. He was surer of that than ever before.

She nodded as though in agreement with his thoughts. "Zach, during that briefing, before the takedown at Gjojak's villa, you said you had some suspicions. What were they?"

"Vera," he replied simply.

"Who's Vera?" Christie asked, appearing at Zach's elbow, slipping her arm around his waist. Lifting his arm over her head, he tucked her against his side.

"*Vera* means wine in Albanian," he explained, kissing her on the side of the head.

"But there must be more to it than linguistics," Bud said vehemently. "What information does my boy have that would be of such value to a scum-sucking drug dealer that the filthy rotter would set him up and throw him into prison?"

"Dad!"

"Bud!"

Christie and Zach exclaimed at Bud's choice of vocabulary.

"What?" he said. "You didn't think I knew those words?"

Damaris laughed heartily for a moment and then grew serious. "Coffee. Mr. Marek, do you think that I could beg the offer of some coffee?"

The Marek equivalent of a palm to the forehead, Bud huffed. "Of course. Please excuse my manners."

"Excellent," Damaris said, following Bud to the large country kitchen and seating herself at the kitchen table. "We need to know what you know, Zach. *All* that you know."

As Christie sat across from Damaris, Zach paced along the bank of windows lining the western wall of the ranch house. Running his fingers through his hair, he tried to organize his thoughts even as he disorganized his follicles. "Shipping labels from an Albanian winery, the Vera Pliny, to a Canadian warehouse, the Horseman's in Fort Erie." He stopped behind Christie, massaging her shoulders. Touching her seemed to order his thoughts. "Moerarty's in Niagara-on-the-Lake is one of the businesses using the Horseman's. And Zander Greave, formerly one of Gjojak's men in Niagara, was carrying a receipt from Moerarty's on his person at the time of his apprehension. In fact, Greave's last word to me was *Vera*. At the time, I thought it was simply a woman's name, but it's neither his mother's nor his girlfriend's name." Zach leaned forward, resting his chin on the top of Christie's head.

Bud nodded thoughtfully. "What happened to Greave?" he asked. "Did you question him?"

Shaking his head, rubbing his chin along the crown of Christie's head, Zach replied, "He was killed by a sniper."

"I remember," Christie said, tilting her head back to look at him. "That's the day you said the EMS was called in because a sniper shot your suspect. Right?"

Leaning down, Zach kissed her upside-down chin. "Yeah. That's the day."

Tapping a rat-a-tat on the table with her fingertips, Damaris ran through the information. "Links from Greave, Gjojak's drug enforcer in Niagara, to Moerarty's winery, which leads to the Horseman's warehouse in Fort Erie, which leads to the Vera Pliny near Memaliaj." She growled low in her throat and then abruptly changed her expression, leaping to a new topic. "Now if we could only discover the source of the leak on the task force, we'd be miles ahead," Damaris said. "I was thinking Raade. He had a very sketchy past."

"No, I don't think so. Raade was many things, but he was a loyal police officer," Zach said. "My brothers and I were discussing this, and, well, I've been thinking that maybe Carlos Rivera was the mole."

"Of course!" Damaris was clearly excited again. "That explains everything. Oh, why, oh, why, didn't I stay behind and watch over that op? Carlos Rivera. Three years as an OPP officer, partnered with a good and honest cop, investigating … essentially … himself. What a cover," Damaris concluded, clearly impressed.

"But who lied to the Albanian police?" Bud asked.

"Or paid them off?" Zach added.

"So you're thinking that the prison term was arranged by Gjojak?" Damaris asked.

"Zach would never do drugs so it had to be a setup all the way around," Christie replied, her voice as soft as her eyes as she gazed at Zach. "Who else would bother to move Zach once he got word out of his presence in Burgu Punës? If he was legally convicted … well, what could anyone do?"

"Indubitably!" Damaris said, her eyes sparkling with excitement. "Is that the proper usage for that word? Never mind. I like the way it sounds."

"Zimmerman didn't need to report anything, did he? Gjojak put some pressure on the local police and a judge. Carlos reported a false statement to Thomason, and, boingo, I'm history," Zach said.

"That makes perfect sense," Damaris said, sounding very reasonable.

"No, it doesn't!" Christie said with her feelings of betrayal layered over her voice. "He was Zach's friend, his partner. How could he do that? Why?"

Zach slipped his fingers across her shoulder to her neck and began lightly caressing the sensitive skin there, trying to provide some comfort. "Everything's going to be okay, sweetheart," he said, burying his nose for a moment in her rose-scented hair.

"Why?" Christie demanded of Damaris.

"Zach was very close to discovering the identity of our traitor, closer than he realized. They needed to be rid of him," Damaris said, explaining simply. "You shared your suspicions regarding the wineries with Rivera, I assume."

"No. But I did record them on my laptop. Any of the men staying with me could have found the information with a little effort," Zach said. "What I don't understand is why they didn't just kill me. They obviously killed Raade because he was too close."

"Please don't," Christie whispered.

"But what is the connection of wine?" Bud asked, clearly frustrated by his confusion.

"Somehow, Gjojak is using the two wineries to transport heroin from Albania into Canada," Zach replied.

Damaris went still. And then she practically exploded into movement. She most resembled Gideon when he was excited, except for the squealing and the arm flapping.

"Of course! Gjojak's using the wineries to transport heroin. We got a completely unrelated report of a wine bottle that smashed at Pearson Airport spilling out its contents of red wine and a teeny tiny bag of heroin. The bottles were for a new wine incorporating elements of Canadian wine and international wines to create a new flavor. They are packaged in opaque black bottles. It's the brand's signature, you could say. The heroin was packed inside in an impermeable bag." She stopped and he could see admiration in her eyes. "Clever. With the black glass, it's almost impossible to see the bag floating in the wine. If that one hadn't smashed, we would never have known."

She wore a beatific smile for a long moment, finally breaking the silence with one word, "Late."

Confounded by her reference—late?—Zach opened his mouth to question her but shut it again as the handle on the front door turned and the door opened. Pulling Christie up and behind him, Zach retrieved his weapon.

"Blake," Zach said with relief, setting his handgun on the table. He met his brother halfway and drew him into a hug.

Bud was at Zach's elbow as soon as he released Blake, engulfing his next-to-youngest son in a strong embrace.

"I'm sorry I'm late," Blake said over his father's shoulder.

"Not a problem, Blake," Damaris said airily.

"Late? What do you mean?" Christie asked as she moved in to get her own hug.

"I made arrangements with Damaris to meet her here this afternoon. But something unexpected came up," Blake said, pulling back to kiss Christie on the cheek.

"Everything okay?" Damaris asked him.

"Yes," he replied simply, supplying no further information.

"Good," Damaris said and then turned to Zach. "What we believe happened," she began and Zach had to scramble mentally to keep up, "is that the prison officials declined to inform your captors that you had been rescued. As a result, Gjojak only recently learned of your escape. Now, he is coming after you."

"What?" Christie grabbed Zach's arm and held on tight.

"It's okay, Christie," Blake said, reassuring her in his soft and gentle voice. "I've come with a plan."

Zach put his arm around Christie and pulled her close, knowing how she hated to discuss the possibilities of his demise. It wasn't exactly his favorite topic either.

"What's your plan?" Zach asked, his gaze shifting between Damaris and Blake.

"A sting operation. We'd like to set you up in a safe house and draw Gjojak in," Damaris said.

"No," Christie said, and Zach felt her stiffen in his arms. "We are not putting his life in danger."

"Christie," Blake said, looking at her with great sympathy in his deep-brown eyes. "He's already in danger. We can either use this to catch Gjojak or …" He gave her the one-shoulder, "do you want your husband to die?" shrug.

"What is that supposed to be?" Christie demanded to know. "Some sort of dramatic pause?"

Damaris grinned at her and then sobered again. "Four days ago, one of Gjojak's lieutenants, Qazim Hoxha, entered the United States, flying into Florida from Puerto Rico after traveling from Portugal. He was spotted in Casper, Wyoming, two days ago. He's an assassin."

"I want my family kept safe," Zach said, speaking quickly to prevent Christie from truly processing what Damaris had just callously told her.

"I think we should put Christie and Gideon in a safe house. Then you'll be able to concentrate," Blake said.

"I don't want to be separated. Not again. Not now that we've found our way back to happy," Christie said, anguish in her face.

"It would put you in danger to keep you together. They're after Zach, Christie. They want to eliminate—" Blake said.

Zach stopped his brother's dire warning with the same gesture he used to make Gideon wait. It worked much better on Blake.

Taking her hand, Zach pulled Christie across the room to lend a semblance of privacy. "I won't put you and Gid in danger. I won't. I love you. But you need to let me do my job," Zach said, cupping her face tenderly.

"Your job is more important than we are?" she asked, her voice barely above a horrified whisper.

"You *are* my job," Zach replied. "If Gjojak is out there, he's a threat to you and Gideon." He dropped his hand to her belly. "And any other Mareks we can make."

"Zach—" Christie began her protest.

"He will use you against me," Zach said and waited for her to compute the implications. She swallowed hard, and he knew that his words had struck home. "I will do anything in my power to keep you and Gideon safe."

After wrapping her arms around his waist, she pulled him close. "Gideon will miss you. He needs you."

"I know. And I need him, too," he said, holding her patiently. "It's only temporary, just until we catch Gjojak or at least this Hoxha fellow."

After a long, sad sigh, she nodded. "I'll miss you, too. Dreadfully."

Zach pulled her close, smiling against her hair. *She's going to miss me.* "You know that I'll miss you, too. I love you."

"I love you, too," she whispered, kissing him.

"Can Zach at least drive us to the safe house, please?" Christie asked Damaris across the room.

Damaris nodded. "That should work. It will take a few hours to organize a place and protection. There's a safe house the US Marshalls use in Sheridan that's free, and I've got Stoner lined up to organize security there and then he can travel on with Zach," Damaris said.

"Stoner?" Bud exclaimed. "I'm supposed to entrust my children to an individual named Stoner?"

Damaris laughed. "Ichabod DeShawn. He's one of the best."

"Blake? Son?" Bud asked, turning to his next to youngest son.

"I've worked with Stone before," Blake said. "He's solid."

"Very well," Bud agreed, as though he trusted anyone his sons trusted.

"Are Dad and Bobby in danger?" Zach asked.

"I don't think so," Blake said. "You know that I would warn you if I thought that was possible," he added.

"I know, son," Bud replied even though Blake had been talking to Zach. He fixed each brother with a stern look as if to remind them to look after each other.

As though they needed reminding, Zach mused.

"I think we should call Luke and Seth to help. I'd feel better if I knew that someone was watching over the ranch," Zach said.

"That's not necessary, son," Bud said.

"I agree with Zach," Blake replied, ending the debate.

"What about Seth's cabin in the Bighorn?" Zach asked. "It's kitted out with a lovely assortment of, shall we say, helpful items."

"I think that would be the perfect place to set a trap for Gjojak," Blake said. "I've already talked to Seth."

"What did he say?" Christie asked.

"What's mine is yours," Blake replied.

CHAPTER 40

And so, ten hours later, Zach drove the rusty green Ford pickup that Blake's organization—whatever it was—had provided, into the driveway of a dingy gray two-story in west-end Sheridan. It looked exactly like all the other houses on the cul-de-sac, small with dilapidated aluminum siding and windows that desperately needed a coat of paint. It was, however, the only house with a rusty swing set in the front yard. The others had torn sofas, an old stove, and at least one rusted-out wreck of a car but no playground equipment—and not a tree in sight.

"You go ahead in, and I'll park the truck around back," Zach said.

"Mommy, swing," Gideon said, gripping his B-52 bear tightly in his fist.

"You park, Zach, and I'll give Giddy a few swings. This transition to a new house is going to be hard enough as it is. If he finds something to like here, it'll be easier," Christie said.

"Okay. Don't stay out too long. The neighborhood seems fairly empty at the moment but the last thing we want is to make a memory for our neighbors," Zach said. "I want to be as cautious as possible until Stoner and his agents arrive tomorrow morning." He added in a mutter, "Maybe I'll get them to help me move the swing to the backyard where it would be less visible."

"Okay, sweetheart," she said, kissing him on the cheek.

"I'll check in with the caretaker, too," Zach said, removing his Sig Sauer from the glove compartment, checking it and tucking it into the back of his trousers. "Don't be long." He kissed Gideon on the top of the head.

"Come on, Gideon," Christie said. "Let's swing."

Christie gave Gideon ten minutes on the swing and then counted down.

"Five-four-three-two-one. Time to go in," she said.

"No go in. Swing me please, Mommy," Gideon said.

"Swing is all done, Giddy. Time to go in," she said, and then she bribed him. "Chocolate milk," she said in her most persuasive voice.

"Chocolate milk," he repeated thoughtfully. "Time to go in."

She laughed softly. "Okay then."

"Gideon likes chocolate milk," he said.

"*I* like chocolate milk," she paraphrased. "Yes, you certainly do," she said as she lifted him off the swing. "Can you walk?"

"No walk, no walk!" Gideon said, protesting as he clung to her like a monkey. His mood was still quite irritable even after the rhythmic swinging.

"Oh for goodness' sakes, I'll carry you then, you big baby," she teased lightheartedly, giving him a little tickle under his arm. She was working very hard to hide her anxiety beneath the facade of fun, using a verbal routine that sometimes calmed him when he was upset.

Gideon squirmed to get away from the tickle, but a small smile broke through and his protest was calmer this time. "No tickling. I'm a big boy not a baby."

Kissing his cheek, she hugged him tightly before flipping him to ride piggyback. "Yes, you are, sweetheart."

They counted the steps to the front door, getting all the way to thirty-six before taking the four stairs to the front door. Gideon kept counting as Christie opened the door and then froze at the sight before her. Her eyes met Zach's stricken face.

"Go back!" Zach yelled at her, stock-still, nothing moving but his eyes.

Christie's eyes darted around the room, taking it all in in an instant: the eat-in kitchen with the large melamine island, the lime-green stove, and canary-yellow refrigerator; the living room filled with mismatched, threadbare pieces of furniture; and the occupants thereof. A short, pudgy, greasy man stood between two ginormous goons, one with an out-of-control afro and one with his head completely shaved, each holding an automatic weapon. The greasy pudge was pointing a silenced handgun at the body of an elderly man lying at his feet, blood pooled around his gray head.

"Zach?" Christie gasped, gripping Gideon's legs more tightly around her waist. The silenced weapon shifted to point directly at Christie.

"Come over here, *fustan*," Greasy said. "Or he's dead."

As he shifted the pistol to indicate her husband, Zach shouted. "Run! Now!"

Spinning about, Christie collided with a massive rock wall of muscle. The enormous man, Jack the Giant, grabbed Gideon, wrenching him from her back.

"Don't touch me!" Gideon screeched, kicking, screaming, and flailing.

"Let go of him!" Christie yelled, punching at the man's solid chest. Vaguely in the background, Christie heard shouting and a tussle, but she had no attention for anything but this giant who was assaulting her son.

Gideon thrust his head back, landing squarely across the man's nose. Blood erupting from his nose, Jack the Giant dropped Gideon to the floor.

"Rotten brat! You'll pay for that," Jack said with the promise of vengeance in his voice and manner.

After jumping up from the floor, Gideon raced across the room and flung himself into Zach's arms, yelling, "Chocolate milk!" Zach ducked with him behind a hideous violet La-Z-Boy chair.

Half a step forward, Jack's meaty paw latched onto Christie's arm, squeezing with such force that her fingers numbed almost immediately. She swung with her other arm, scratching, punching, slapping, anything to make the giant release her. Growling in fury, he shook her, rattling her teeth, and then he slapped her hard. She heard a roar from across the room at the same moment that Jack's hand connected and light exploded behind her eyes.

"Don't you touch her," Zach yelled.

"Too loud. Too loud!" Gideon screamed, clapping his hands over his ears.

Defiantly, the giant wrapped her in a grizzly's embrace. In a blur of motion, Zach dropped Gideon onto an easy chair and launched himself across the room, his impact knocking Christie loose from Jack's grip. She rolled away, gasping for air.

"Run, Christie!" Zach yelled, and Christie realized that she was free. Jack the Giant was slumped in a puddle of blood beside her.

"Mommy-Daddy, Mommy-Daddy!" Gideon yelled jumping up and down on the chair.

Mr. Greasy leaped for him, but Gideon jerked away to run and dive into Zach's arms again. Zach fired his Sig Sauer around the room, and everyone dove for cover.

"Christie. Move!" Zach commanded, his voice finally penetrating the fog of her mind.

Nodding once, she scrambled away from the bloody puddle, half-crouching, half-crawling. *Save us, Father. Please, get us out of here.*

As Christie charged to the farther end of the melamine island, Zach dove behind it from the other side, disengaging Gideon to thrust him into her arms. The terrified child clung, his shrieks rising in pitch and loudness.

"Stay here," Zach ordered, yelling to be heard over Gideon's protests. "When I tell you to, run for the back door. The truck's out back." He slammed the keys into her hand. And then he was gone, and Christie heard more gunshots and screams beyond the shrieks of Gideon.

Abruptly, the shooting stopped. Even Gideon was impressed by the sudden stillness, becoming silent for a moment. Trying to disengage his arms and legs in order to take a look at what was happening, Christie subsided when his shuddering breaths and whimpers increased in volume. Instead, she crawled to the edge of the melamine island. Gideon clung to her in a death-grip, arms around her neck and legs around her waist, his heels digging into her back.

Peeking out, Christie saw blood and matter coating, it seemed, every surface in the living room. Great swaths of crimson stained the rug, the curtains, and the coffee table. There was even a large splash across a fifty-five-inch LED TV. She saw it all in a moment, a snapshot of horror. Retching, trying to control her response, she cradled Gideon's face against her so he couldn't see. *So much blood.*

Collapsing back against the island, she breathed deeply, trying to quell the nausea. When she could finally move again, she crept out a little further and saw Jack the Giant still unmoving by the front door. Another goon had collapsed across the arm of the sofa, and the old man's body still lay on the floor in the middle of the lounge. *Where are you, Zach?*

"Bad man," Gideon whispered, and Christie followed his gaze to see a gunman creeping down the stairs from the upper rooms. *Where are you, Zach?* Suddenly, she spotted him, now on the other side of the La-Z-Boy. If the upstairs-villain came around the corner into the lounge, Zach could get him ... except that Zach was turned the other way. And if Zach didn't see him first, the villain could ... No.

Desperately searching around her for some sort of weapon, she grabbed a cast-iron frying pan. Admonishing Gideon to "hold on" to her, Christie moved stealthily to the edge of the doorway, praying that the villain hadn't seen her yet. Waiting, barely able to breathe past the constriction of Gideon's squeezing arms and legs, Christie held the pan tightly in both her hands, ready to attack and protect. As soon as the "bad man's" head passed into view, Christie swung with all her might. A satisfying clang and thud heralded the end of the villain's plans.

Zach spun, raising his handgun, and Christie backed away, hands upheld in surrender. Glancing down at the victim of her attack, he seemed to quickly calculate her risk and his own. Raising his eyes to her with surprise and pride in his expression, Zach mouthed, "You?"

Quirking a shrug of a grin, she nodded.

A bullet hit the wall just over her head, and Christie dove into the back hallway, landing directly on the unconscious villain's belly, expelling a foul-breathed "Oof." *Ew! Yick!* Gideon bounced his foot off the villain's chin. Scrambling to get away and under cover, Christie rolled toward the back door, keeping Gideon's body tight against hers. *Keys. Pickup truck.*

At the back door, she paused. *Zach.* She couldn't just leave when Zach was still in danger. *But I have to save Gideon.* Indecision tore through her, but a barrage of gunfire helped her decide. She refused to leave Zach to a certain death.

"Too loud!" Gideon screeched, adding to the overall cacophony.

"Christie, go!" She heard Zach call from his position behind the recliner.

I will. I can't. I can't just leave him here. Dear God, please help me. After using her firmest "mommy" voice to insist that Gideon sit and wait, hidden in a deeply shadowed corner beside the back door with B-52 bear still somehow in his arms, Christie crept back to the doorway. Zach was still down behind the chair, but his handgun clicked uselessly. He was clearly out of ammunition.

Looking around her, trying to find something to help, Christie realized the foul-breathed villain must have a gun. Patting around the floor and across his body, she located a handgun and two clips of ammunition.

"Psst," she called, but Zach didn't respond.

"Throw down your weapons, Inspector Marek. You cannot win. If you give yourself up, your woman and child will be unharmed." The greasy man was speaking in a heavily accented voice.

"Not a chance. If you think for one minute that I believe you have any intention of leaving any of us alive, you're as crazy as they say you are," Zach replied, sounding incredibly calm as he frantically searched his pockets for ammunition. His movements became more desperate as pocket after pocket proved empty.

Desperate to help him, Christie loaded the villain's gun, activated the safety, and slid it across the floor, just short of Zachary's foot.

"Zach," she called, whispering tersely while pointing at the gun. His concern quickly morphed into relief, and rising from behind the La-Z-Boy, he fired twice before resuming his crouch.

"Zach. Come," she said, holding the second ammunition clip up as though it was bait.

"Go, Christie," he whispered tersely. "Take the truck. Head toward Wolf. Use the satellite phone and call Seth."

"No, Zach. Come with us. Come now," she said sternly. He shook his head at her, jumping up to fire again. "I'm not leaving without you,

Zachary Clyde Marek," she whispered just as tersely, frowning at him in her best *do-it-now* expression.

Zach seemed locked in indecision for a moment more before he quickly filled the air with bullets and followed Christie through the kitchen and to the back door. A spray of automatic-weapon-fire followed them out, and Zach bumped heavily against her, nearly knocking her down the back stairs.

"Careful," she reprimanded him quietly as she scooped up Gideon. Her nerves were jittering, her grip on her control slipping.

"Sorry," he mumbled in reply as he passed by her, relieving her of the second clip and proceeding through the back door.

After exchanging the clips in the Sig, Zach pressed a finger to his lips and motioned for her to wait. Christie heard two more pops, and then Zach's head appeared back inside the doorway and he motioned for her to follow. Zach fired twice behind them before stepping into the driveway somehow instinctively seeing the man in the bushes and dropping him with two shots.

"You drive," Zach ordered, taking Gideon from her and slipping into the passenger seat. She fired the ignition and locked the doors before reversing out of the driveway. "Turn right onto Big Goose Road," Zach directed her.

Safely away, her control shattered. "What happened in there? Who was that? Zach? Zach!" Christie shouted her questions, her entire body shuddering in reaction to the bloody death they'd left behind.

Gideon shrieked a high-pitched wail in concert with Christie's cries as he swung his fists and rocked his body to escape his father's grip. The emotions careening around the cab were too much for him.

"Quiet," Zach demanded finally capturing Gideon's arms and holding them tightly between them.

Pressing her palm against her mouth to quiet her screams, Christie began to cry, little bubbly sobs escaping past her fingers. Gideon's shrieks morphed into gasping shouts as he continued struggling to get out of Zach's grasp. Zach held on tight, murmuring comfort to his son and then turning to his wife.

"Calm down, sweetheart," Zach told her, keeping his voice even.

Gasping in air, she replied, "Can't."

"Hold it together, Christie. He needs you to calm down." Zach's voice was firm yet somehow she heard the coaxing within it.

"Take a deep breath," Zach said.

A deep breath? Is he crazy? I can't seem to breathe at all. She gasped and felt the burn of tears in her eyes.

Zach placed his hand firmly on her leg. "Deep breaths. Like this." He demonstrated as he reached for her right hand. "Christie, honey, let go," he insisted, and she finally released the death grip she'd had on the steering wheel. He placed the back of her hand over his mouth. "Breathe in through your mouth and out through your nose." She felt the warmth of his breath on her hand and tried to copy him. Then he placed her hand between his chest and Gideon's, holding it there so she could feel the breath of her son and the warmth of her husband at the same time, reminding her that they were all alive.

"Keep breathing," Zach reminded her.

Breathe. Breathe. Gradually, Christie felt her respiration slow, and, as she calmed, Gideon quieted, settling against Zach's chest.

"Thanks," Zach said. His voice was softer now. "I'm sorry for snapping at you."

She nodded, retaking her hand and gripping the steering wheel, just a little bit lighter this time.

"No seat belt," Gideon said, quickly escalating from a little concerned to very upset. "Mommy-Daddy, have to wear a seat belt in the car. Gideon needs his seatbelt!" Very quickly Gideon went from calmly sitting in Zach's arms to screaming and flailing, reaching across to grab his mother's arm, jostling the steering wheel.

Gripping harder to maintain control, Christie tried to reassure him. "It's okay, Gideon." Her voice was shaking so pathetically that she knew she wasn't doing much to calm her son.

Zach took Gideon's arms and trapped them between their bodies again, holding him firmly. His voice was a little breathy but very calm. "Gideon. Usually we wear seat belts in the car, but sometimes it's okay not to wear a seat belt." He repeated himself until Gideon responded.

"Okay not to wear a seat belt?" Gideon inquired. "Okay not to wear a seat belt? Mommy, sometimes it's okay not to wear a seat belt," he murmured, glancing at Christie before settling in his daddy's arms.

"That's right, buddy; sometimes it's okay not to wear a seat belt," Zach confirmed calmly. "I'll pull mine across both of us."

Finally securely belted in, Gideon quieted, but Christie could see the boy's tension in the way he drummed his fingers on Zach's shoulders and the rocking motion of his body, which propelled him repeatedly against the tension of the seat belt. *I wish I could rock, too, Gideon. I can't believe this is happening.*

"Take a few slow, deep breaths, honey. Count with me," Zach instructed. "One, two—"

Gideon quickly took over the counting, and Christie felt the urge to laugh, but she was afraid that it would sound more like a hysterical cackle than a genuine chuckle. *Numbers are far more important than doom and destruction.*

Finally, at number fifty-two, Christie began to feel a modicum of calm. "I'm okay," she said, glancing over to see that Zach was watching her very closely.

"I will protect you, both of you," Zach said, and she heard the determination in his voice. "When I asked if you were all right, I really meant to ask whether you or Gideon were hurt."

"No, I don't think so. What about you?" she asked. Her voice still quivered, but she felt more in control than before.

"Fine. Take Eaton Ranch Road to the left," he said.

Gideon was asleep in Zach's arms, having retreated from the horrors he'd witnessed. He didn't do more than grunt when Zach reached into the glove compartment and pulled the satellite phone out. After dialing Seth's cell phone, he put it on speaker, tucking it into the seat between them.

"Marek."

"It's Zach. We're scuppered," Zach said, quickly, concisely, without pause.

"What happened?" Seth asked. "Never mind. Where are you?"

"Heading to Wolf Gas Co.," Zach replied tersely.

"From there go north to Highway 14 then west to Bighorn Lake.

Cross the lake, and turn immediately right. Rent a boat from Phil at Bob's Marina. I'll call ahead and have Phil ready one for you. Take the river to my cabin. If you hit the boundaries of the Crow Reservation, you've missed it. Park the boat at the marina and then walk up the hill, following the gravel road, to the cabins. Mine has blue shutters," Seth said. "Call me when you get there."

"Call Blake and fill him in," Zach said.

"I can't fill him in, Zach, unless you tell me what happened," Seth replied.

"They were there and waiting for us, Gjojak and five men, Seth. How did they know where to find me?" Zach said.

"I don't know. I'll call Blake," Seth said. "I'll be careful though, there must be a leak."

"Check in with Luke and make sure Bobby and Dad are protected," Zach said.

"Count on it, *cheéte*," Seth said.

Zach disengaged the phone.

"That was Gjojak?" Christie asked.

"Yeah, the greasy comb-over is unquestionably him," Zach replied. "Are you okay to drive?"

"Yes," she said.

"You need to drive faster," he said.

"I will." If she could drive an ambulance through Toronto at rush hour during her internship at Durham College, she could handle this. Sure, she was a little out of practice, but Gideon's and Zach's lives were on the line.

"Go left here and then head west," Zach said.

"West? As in right or left?" she asked.

"Left. That way," he pointed, giving her the support she needed to save their lives.

"Zach, I'm so scared," she said.

"I know."

CHAPTER 41

Christie was cold sitting in the dark on the dock waiting for Zach to sign the papers to rent a boat from Phil at Bob's or Bob at Phil's, whoever it was. She wasn't certain if the cold was from the chilly, damp air or from the fear inside her. It was so much easier to be brave when she was driving away from danger toward a safe haven rather than sitting in the twilight with her son in her arms and bad guys somewhere, anywhere in the dark.

Gideon had been less than impressed when he woke to find that it was dark and there was not only no television but also no chocolate milk to drink. Christie started a counting game with him to distract him.

"A six and a seven," Christie said in a whisper, keeping half her attention on her son and half on her environment. There was one other party still out at this time of night but so far nothing suspicious.

"Sixty-seven," Gideon replied loudly.

"Shh, Gideon. Remember, it only counts if you whisper," she replied, not wanting to attract any attention.

As the couple down the dock unloaded a fishing boat, they seemed overly preoccupied by Gideon and Christie, glancing their way several times. They looked like an older couple, perhaps spending their retirement on the lake, enjoying the beauty of the rugged area. But then why were they so interested in her and Gideon? Oh. They weren't. They were actually waving to the younger couple driving up in a dark sedan. Okay, so now Christie was getting carried away.

The two couples drove away, and then Christie and Gideon were alone on the dock. "Three and two," she said.

"Thirty-two," Gideon said, trying to lower his voice but only managing a slightly less voluble production.

After what seemed like ages, Christie heard an engine in the night as Zach pulled a speedboat up to the dock. Gideon reacted by covering his ears a moment with his hands. Christie held him a little tighter, rocking him to ease his agitation.

Zach held out his hand and gestured for her to pass Gideon to him. "Okay, Gideon. I want you to step over to me," Zach said, his voice gentle and coaxing.

"No," Gideon replied. "Seven and six. Seven and six."

"Come here, Gid. Step over to Daddy," Zach said, trying to coax him across. "Christie, just pass him to me."

"No!" Gideon's voice rose in agitation. "Seven and six. Seven and six." Wiggling in Christie's arms, Gideon's little hands fisted and he punched behind him as though trying to force Zach away.

"Seventy-six. Seventy-six, sweetheart," Christie said. "Nine and two."

"Ninety-two," Gideon replied, shoving his fisted hands down between them, calming a little but continuing to rock. "Five and four."

"Do it, Christie. Now." His voice was sharp enough to make her jump, and then more softly, he added, "Trust me."

"Five and four." Gideon's rocking increased in pace. His voice was high, clearly conveying his anxiety.

She disengaged Gideon's arms and thrust him at his father. "Ask Daddy, Giddy. Hold him, Zach. Hold him tightly." If Gideon became agitated enough, he could fall or hit the controls or cause some other form of damage to himself or Zach or the … Christie trailed off. Okay, she was probably still overreacting.

Zach took Gideon, sitting and holding him on his lap. "Fifty-four, sweetheart. Well done," Zach said, holding him tightly.

Christie sighed in relief, collapsing onto her knees.

"Come over, baby," Zach said, holding out one arm. "Come to me."

Christie nodded and rose. Once she was on board, Zach immediately turned the boat around and headed north toward the river with Gideon in his arms.

Christie had no idea how long they'd been on the water, but she knew that she was very cold. Gideon, snugly buckled into a life jacket and wrapped in a blanket, was completely relaxed, just watching the moonlight sparkling on the opaque waters. Echoing off the smooth canyon walls, the noise of the motor surrounded them, lending the unnerving sense of being pursued, just another reason for Christie to remain off-kilter. She kept a firm grip on Gideon's lifejacket, but for her own sense of security or his, she wasn't certain.

Zach piloted the speedboat up Bighorn Lake, crossing from Wyoming to Montana. The lake soon narrowed to what Christie would have called a river, but what did she know? She never studied geography in college. If she had—and it was daylight not the dark of night—then she would have been able to name the type of rock that formed the canyon walls that bracketed the river. But it wouldn't help her feel any safer. It was terrifying to think that if anything went wrong, they would have no way out, no way to escape up the sheer cliffs.

After a time, the walls gave way to grassy hills and then buildings and the occasional marina, which dotted the waterline.

Finally, Zach broke the silence. "I think this is the spot," he said, slowing the boat and coming up to the dock. "You and Gid wait here while I dock the boat in the visitor's slip."

Gripping the dock, Christie crawled out and then received Gideon from Zach's hands. She unhooked Gideon's lifejacket and her own, tossing them back into the boat. Pointing to a shaded area away from the lights of the marina as a place for Christie and Gideon to wait, Zach pulled out and found a spot to tie up the boat.

By the time Christie carried Gideon to the spot indicated, Zach had jogged over and joined them, gun out and ready.

"Stay close," he said and moved away.

Following the gravel path up a hill, they turned right and continued on and around until the road curved to the left. Three properties in was Seth's cabin, blue shutters and all.

"I'll check it out. Wait here in the dark under these trees. I'll be quick," Zach said.

"Don't forget about Seth's alarms and stuff," Christie reminded him. Squeezing her hand first, he jogged away, his left arm tight to his side.

Zach disappeared through the front door, reappeared at a side door after a long wait, and then disappeared around the outside of the cabin. Christie and Gideon waited in silence until Zach emerged through the lakeside patio doors and onto the deck.

"Come in," he said, gesturing for her to follow him inside.

Christie entered, keeping the lights off not because she was thinking of safety but rather because she felt the prickle of pursuit on the back of her neck and she wanted to feel invisible. The moonlight shining in through the windows illuminated their path up the stairs and to the bedrooms. Christie put Gideon into the last bedroom on the left, stripped him to his underwear and a T-shirt, and tucked him in bed.

When Christie reentered the hallway, Zach was leaning wearily against the wall.

"We should be safe now," he told her, wiping his brow, leaving behind a smear of blood.

"Blood? Gideon. Is he bleeding?" She turned back toward the bedroom, but Zach grasped her arm, his grip quickly slipping away.

"It's not Gideon's," he informed her. Incredulously, she watched as he slowly slid to the floor leaving behind a swath of blood on the cream-colored wall.

"Zach!" Dropping to his side, she passed her hands over his body, stopping on his left side when he flinched. Unbuttoning his shirt and gently peeling it away, she saw the bullet hole. "Oh, Zach, why didn't you tell me? Can you make it to the bathroom so I can clean this? Is there a first-aid kit in the house?"

"Mmm. Seth'll have one. Help me up. Should be one in the bathroom." His words were thick, seeming to cost him heavily.

After slipping her arm beneath his shoulder, she leveraged him up and into the bathroom where she sat him on the commode. Removing his shirt first, she then carefully cleaned the wound with soap and a washcloth before locating the first-aid kit beneath the sink.

"Well, I don't think we have to go hunting," she said as she gently palpated the wound. "I think it passed directly through the fat tissue here."

Breathily, he protested, "Hey, what do you mean 'fat'?"

A small grin quirked the corner of her mouth. "Sorry, mass of muscle tissue, very muscular. It's definitely going to need stitches. There's an exit wound in the front and an entry wound in the back. When did this happen?"

"At the safe house, just as we were leaving."

She paled at the implications of that memory. "It could have struck Gideon after it passed through you. You're sure he's okay?" He nodded, and she forced herself back to the moment, searching through Seth's first-aid kit.

"I found some local anesthetic. It'll help with the pain. Are you sure you don't want me to take you to a hospital?" she asked.

"We can't risk it, baby." Zach looked up to meet her gaze. "I trust you."

She nodded once and then filled the syringe. "This is going to sting."

"Go ahead," he said, gritting his teeth. "Ouch."

She gave him a quelling look. "I haven't started yet." Kissing him on the forehead first, she injected the anesthetic. "The worst is over. We just need to wait a few minutes for it to take effect."

"Come here," he said, drawing her onto his lap, careful of his own injuries. "Are *you* okay?"

"It's best not to ask me right now. I can be a medic, but if I start to be your wife, I'll lose it."

"Okay." He kissed her and held her tightly for long enough that the knot of terror in her belly began to loosen.

"All right, let's get this done," she said. He nodded, and she could see him steel himself. "I'll be careful," she reassured him.

Smiling wryly, he dropped his gaze. "I know. It just seems ... After all the pain I've suffered at the hands of prison guards and interrogators, not to mention Janice and her boyfriends, it doesn't seem like this should bother me, but my stomach's doing a slow waltz of anticipation regardless."

After kissing him on the head, she asked, "Would you like me to find you something to relax you?"

He shook his head. "Maybe just talk to me … to take my mind off it." He was gritting his teeth in an effort to quell the nausea.

"About what?" she asked, loading the needle with surgical thread.

"Teaching. Why did you quit the EMS? You love being a paramedic."

"I needed a job with regular hours and the flexibility to work from home. Gideon couldn't handle the constant change in routine that came with shift work, and I just didn't have enough seniority to ask for a regular shift. This way, I could drop him at the preschool, go to work, and then pick him up for lunch and spend the afternoon with him most days. I lucked out and ended up with the perfect schedule. Most of my classes are in the morning. I write my lectures in the evenings while Gideon is playing. The money's pretty good, and I get benefits and holidays that will almost match those when he's at school." Pausing when she had closed the wound on his front, she stepped back. "Can you sit up on the counter? I think that would give me better access. Besides, my legs are killing me from crouching so long."

"Sure." He perched on the corner of the counter, resting his feet on the toilet lid. She pushed on his back until he was in the optimal position, and then she threaded the needle for another stitch. The tug of the needle must have hurt because he groaned, and she kissed him sympathetically on the shoulder.

She tied the next stitch and then exclaimed, "Wait a minute!" and then bent to her task again.

"Christie?" Zach said, clearly confused. "Hey." He reached back and then must have changed his mind before he touched her arm, probably because she was holding a sharp implement to his side. "You can't just say something like that and then clam up. What's up?"

"Matty Reeves. Do you think he made some kind of report of your incident at the pool hall?"

"Probably," he said.

"Well, if there's a leak in the OPP, like say, Carlos Rivera, your scumbag ex-partner whom I'd like to punch in the gob, then if Matty called the OPP to check out your story, it might have alerted him."

Zach froze. "You are brilliant, sweetheart. I would swing you up in my arms if you weren't holding a needle to my side. That explains how word got back to Gjojak."

"Sure." She tied the last knot. "There. Done. Let me cover this with a bandage, and then I'll wash the blood out of your shirt and jeans."

"Then you should get some sleep. I'll call Blake to fill him in and then join you. Seth's alarm system should warn us if anyone gets near."

"You know, I wish I could see Carlos just one more time," she said.

Zach's brow furrowed, and she saw a glint of green jealousy in his eyes. "Why?"

"So I could beat the snot out of him."

He laughed. "You are fierce when you're crossed, mama bear."

She smiled crookedly at him.

"Come on. The sooner I call Seth, the sooner we can go to bed," he said.

She brandished a loaded syringe. "Antibiotics first. Drop your drawers, Clyde."

"Clyde is my horse," he complained, but he complied.

"Mmm. Nice behind," she murmured, giving him a little pat, and he laughed for just a second and then she shot him full of antibiotics.

"Ouch," he said, but she could tell that he was just trying to make her laugh.

"Well, you shouldn't jiggle just when I'm about to stab you."

"Strange words to hear from your wife." Zach pulled her abruptly against him and kissed her on the mouth. One quick, hard kiss that was not nearly enough.

CHAPTER 42

"Mommy," Gideon said, calling from the bedroom across the hall.

"Gideon," Christie murmured.

Zach hefted himself out of bed. "I'll get him." He couldn't sleep anyway. His side hurt like a drilled tooth.

"Sure?" she mumbled as she pulled the covers up and over her ears.

"Yup." This was a small installment to replace some of the sleep she'd lost while he was in Albania.

Pausing at the door, Zach listened to Gideon as he worked his way through a conversation that didn't seem to need two partners. "What time is it? I don't know. The clock is gone. Where is it?"

Entering the dim room, Zach greeted Gideon.

"Big hug," Gideon said, holding his arms up like a toddler, gripping his B-52 bear in one hand. Lifting him gingerly into his embrace, Zach gave him a firm hug, holding the boy away from his neat new rows of stitches. Gideon shoved his bear down between them and then gripped Zach hard around the neck.

"Yellow," Gideon said.

"I'm sorry, Son. I know what red means and white paper. I even know that your favorite train engine is blue, but I don't know what yellow means," Zach said. "Are you sleepy?"

"Are you sleepy? No," said Gideon. "TV."

"No television. Let's go read a ... well, I don't know if we have any books with us. And maybe if we keep the lights off, you'll feel more like going back to bed." Drawing back the curtain on Gideon's bedroom window, Zach could see the half moon dimly illuminating the yard. "I know. Let's play Pete's a pizza," Zach suggested.

"Pizza okay," Gideon said.

Zach set Gideon down so he could walk downstairs and then had him lie down on the couch so that Zach didn't have to crouch down on the floor. He pulled a stool over so that he was at the right level and then set about rolling Gideon back and forth like a ball of dough and then pressing him flat, providing a good dose of deep pressure.

"What do you want on your pizza, sir?" Zach asked.

"Puppy-roni," Gideon said.

"What is that? Dog meat?"

"No dog, Daddy. Pizza," Gideon said, giggling.

Zach chuckled as he pretended to press pepperoni onto Gideon's arms and legs.

"What else do you want on your pizza?" Zach asked, following the script for the game as Gideon requested mushrooms and tomatoes and lots of foods he would never actually eat in reality, not even on pizza.

"Daddy's turn," Gideon said and then corrected himself. "Your turn."

Zach thought of the bullet wound. "I don't want pizza tonight, Gid. No, thank you."

"Big hug," Gideon said again.

Zach picked him up, and Gideon melted into his body, beginning to relax. Zach paced the room slowly, and soon, he felt the boy's head grow heavy against his shoulder.

"Train," Gideon said, pointing over Zach's shoulder.

"You like trains, don't you, son?" Zach replied.

"Daddy, look. Train," Gideon said, insisting he be heard, pushing Zach's face toward the window.

Complying just in time, Zach glimpsed a single beam of light for a moment before it disappeared. Given the distance to the nearest cabins and the lateness of the hour, it seemed unlikely that one of their neighbors was out exploring with a flashlight. That beam indicated something much more sinister.

"Not a train, sweetheart," Zach said, the warmth of the last few minutes chilling to fear. *Much more dangerous than a train.* "We need to wake Mommy right now."

Sitting on the edge of the bed with Gideon in his arms, Zach shook Christie's shoulder gently. "Christie. Sweetheart. You need to wake up."

"I'm awake," she replied, coming alert without truly being awake yet. "Is Gideon okay?"

"I'm okay, Mommy," he replied, mellow and calm with his head leaning against Zach's shoulder.

Christie's eyes widened at Gideon's sentence. "Did you hear what he said?"

"Yes," Zach replied, acknowledging the triumph even if only briefly. "Gather everything as quickly as you can. Don't turn on any lights." He kept any emotion out of his voice, hoping that would keep her as calm as her son.

"What's going on?" She'd gone from alert to afraid in seconds flat.

"They've found us."

She jumped out of bed and rushed, fumbling, around the room, getting dressed and trying to gather up clothes and toys and toiletries all at the same time.

"I changed my mind. Don't take anything, just grab Gideon and run to the neighbor just west of us." Zach stilled her motion and pointed. "That way." Searching the room, he found a piece of paper and a washable marker that must have been left behind on one of Bobby's visits and drew a map. "Seth says his neighbor always leaves a beat-up Dodge pickup with the keys hidden above the visor. Take it and follow this map." He pointed at the X marking Seth's cabin and then traced the escape route. "Drive out to the left and continue until it T-junctions. Then turn left onto 37 South. Turn right onto 14 West." Zach gave her the instructions she'd need to escape while constantly scanning the environment visible through the windows for clues to the aggressors' progress through the woods. "Follow the signs to Highway 90 into Billings. Find the nearest police station and stay there until I can meet up with you. Or Seth or Blake. Understand?"

She nodded, agreeing, but her eyes were wide with a barely controlled fear.

"Call Seth." He wrote the number down on the page beside his ersatz map and looked up to meet her gaze. "Okay?"

"Yes," she said. He turned to leave, but she snagged his sleeve. "Be safe. I need you."

Taking comfort from her words, he kissed her and then turned to go, pausing to grab something off the couch where he and Gideon had been playing earlier. "Don't forget this," he said, pushing the B-52 bear into Christie's hands.

Christie nodded. Her eyes were wide. "Ho-how do I get to the nei-neighbors?"

"Go out the back door and then directly toward that stand of pine trees across the road. The trees will give you cover until you come in sight of the neighbor's cabin. It's a one story with a sort of faded red wooden siding. Watch carefully before you cross back over. It's very dark tonight with the cloud cover; so as long as you're quiet, you should be nearly invisible. The pickup is usually parked beside the cabin, and the keys will be above the visor. Get in and drive."

"I can't just leave you here."

"Yes, you can. Please. Take Gideon, and go. I'll find my way to you."

Pulling Gideon closer, she nodded, but she didn't look okay. "What will you do?" Her voice was shaking, and she looked terrified.

"Eliminate pursuit," he replied. He didn't want to wait for her to decipher that so he pushed her to the door. "Go now, Christie, and don't stop." *Please protect them, Lord.*

Narrowing his focus to the task at hand, Zach forced Christie and Gideon to the back of his mind where he could—he hoped—keep them safe. Raiding Seth's "closet of toys," Zach pulled out a Glock, a Ka-Bar knife, a mini-flashlight, a length of twine, a permanent marker, and a couple of flash-bang grenades. Slipping stealthily west around the cabin, Zach entered the substantial cover of the juniper forest, using the twine to set a series of snares and booby-traps and using the marker to map his network of warnings on his arm. Judging by the brief flash of light that Gid had seen through the window, the bad guys should be close. *I need to keep them busy long enough to allow Christie and Gideon to get away.*

Backing with great difficulty into the echinated branches of a juniper bush, Zach took the time to text Seth and let him know they were under attack. He soon received a response. "STONER NRBY. B&ME EN RTE."

Pocketing his phone, Zach rechecked his Glock and knife. *What is taking so long?* The stealthy creepers should have reached his first booby-trap by now. Unless ... perhaps they didn't know the location of Seth's cabin. Maybe they were on a search-and-discover. Maybe they would find Christie first.

Fear spiked through him. Zach shot up and out of the grasping arms of a juniper just as Gideon screamed. And then he ran all the faster.

CHAPTER 43

Christie ran. Whenever she tried to set Gideon on his feet, he lifted his legs, and finally, she scooped him up to ride piggyback, gripping his wrists tightly around her neck, and ran as fast as she could manage. She had no idea where Zach was. She merely ran … through the clinging arms of the coniferous trees and straight for the neighbor's just as he'd instructed. Gideon clung silently to her, B-52 bear gripped tightly in his fist.

Through her harsh breathing, Christie heard footsteps behind her. She accelerated, finally tripping onto the road, the prickle of pursuit morphing into a rash.

"Freeze! Or I'll shoot the kid right in the back."

Christie lurched to a halt. *Oh God! Oh God! Oh God! Please help me.*

"Put your hands where I can see them," their pursuer said.

Christie complied, Gideon clinging like a monkey on her back.

"Turn around slowly," the villain said.

Christie turned. A short, wiry man stood before her, dressed all in black from the balaclava he wore to cover his features to the black army boots on his feet. He pointed a nasty-looking assault rifle squarely at her chest.

"What do you want?" she said, struggling to control her gasping breaths.

Ignoring her, he spoke into his radio. "Alpha 2. Come in, Control."

As he awaited a response, he took a half turn away from her, and, refusing to give up without contest, she fled … for one step. A bullet whistled past her head and into a tree with a thunk, bark flying, glancing off her cheek. Gideon's arms squeezed her neck in a spasm of fear.

"I said, freeze," he said but now he sounded just a little annoyed.

Christie did, turning to face the man, putting her body once again between the weapon and Gideon, not that it would make much difference given the power of that rifle.

"Walk," the gunman ordered her, never taking his eyes from her.

Flipping Gideon to her front, she curled her body around him, tucking B-52 bear into his arms. And then she walked, long enough for her feet to hurt and for Gideon's forty pounds to feel like hundreds; she walked until the black-clad villain told her to stop.

"Christie." She froze at the sound of that familiar voice. "I have been waiting for you."

"Carlos?" she said as a light flooded the area around her, revealing what looked like the gatehouse to a waterside community. She'd never been to Seth's cabin before so she didn't know if this was the entrance to his or another. "What are you doing here?"

"Waiting for you," he said, his eyes sparking with irritation. "As I told you."

"Where's Zach?" she asked.

"Soon it will no longer make a difference," Carlos said enigmatically as he held out his hand to her. "Come here. Get in." He gestured toward a black SUV behind him. When Christie hesitated, he repeated the command, enunciating each word as though she were a thick pupil.

When she didn't move, Carlos grasped her elbow in an unbreakable grip, his thumb and fingers digging into her skin. "Now, Christie."

Flinching, she said, struggling to sound in control, "I … I need to wait for Zach."

Extracting a cell phone from his suit jacket pocket, Carlos dialed, waited, and then spoke in a language that Christie didn't understand.

A very tall, very ugly man opened the back door of the SUV, shifting sideways to give his shoulders room to exit the vehicle. He was all muscles and coarse black hair with a thick, crooked nose and massive hands the shape of sledgehammers. His black, beady eyes stared at her over his hooked nose.

"Get in," Carlos said to her again.

"No. I want to see Zach," she said, digging in her heels.

Carlos pulled a handgun from somewhere hidden, Christie never saw from where he'd produced it, and pointed it directly at Gideon. Christie hesitated once more. In retaliation, Hooknose fisted the back of Gideon's shirt and jerked him out of her grip.

"Let go of him," Christie shouted, beating at Hooknose with her fists, kicking at any inch of him she could reach.

Exploding into motion, the little boy swung his arms and legs blindly around him, shrieking at the top of his lungs. "Don't touch me. Don't touch me!"

Hooknose kept his hold on Gideon's shirt and fisted the boy's hair in his other hand for a better grip. Christie went ballistic, punching, scratching, kicking until all at once her elbow connected with Hooknose's nose at the same moment that Gideon's foot connected with his groin, and suddenly, Gideon was free.

"Run, Gideon, run. Run! Find Daddy," Christie screamed, and Gideon ran full tilt, dodging all the groping hands around him, slippery as a soapy bath, and disappearing into the woods, dragging B-52 behind him.

"Find him!" Carlos shouted, cursing and swearing at his henchmen. "Incompetents! You can't control a four-year-old boy?"

Hooknose growled in frustration and slapped her hard. Christie saw stars chased across the canvas of her vision by red flares of pain. He backhanded her before she had fully processed his first assault.

"*Mjaft më.* Enough." Hooknose immediately obeyed Carlos's command. Carlos's furious face replaced his in her line of vision. "Do not force me to do that again, Christie. Call him back."

"No, Carlos," she gasped, her vision still wobbling. "I won't."

Carlos expanded, filled with outrageous anger, and then he abruptly calmed. "Very well. If you do not call him back, I will send my men to capture him with orders to shoot to kill," he said and then paused, his face thoughtful for a moment. "Or you could exchange the boy's life for Zach's. Do you understand my meaning? That boy is nothing to me. But in exchange for his father ..."

Oh, Lord. What now?

"It is Zach that I wa—" Carlos began but then sirens sounded in the distance, a cacophonous riot of sound, and Carlos panicked. "*Le të shkojë!*" Carlos commanded his henchmen, making the "round-'em-up gesture" at the same time.

"Gjojak said—" Hooknose began.

"I cannot be captured. It would destroy my cover," Carlos said, fear in his eyes. "We have Christie. She will help us to take Marek." Carlos growled in frustration. "Come."

Christie never saw Hooknose's fist. Stunned by the punch, she couldn't resist as she was forced into the rear seat of the SUV and squashed between Hooknose and the diminutive balaclava bloke. A woman occupied the driver's seat, and Carlos took the passenger seat. At his word, they departed. Christie looked over her shoulder to see a second identical black SUV following them.

Oh, Father, protect Gideon and Zach. Lord, please bring them together.

CHAPTER 44

Zach smashed his fists onto the rough-hewn spruce table in Seth's cabin and then turned on Blake. "You told me they were after me," Zach said, furious and desperate with need.

"Think it through, Zachary," Seth said in a quiet voice that was meant to say "be calm, my brother."

"What?" Zach said, turning a fulminating glare on his eldest brother. "What, Seth?" he repeated, challenging Seth to give him one good reason not to freak out. "They took my family," Zach said as he paced away, his movements jerky and desperate.

Someone had set off one of Seth's booby traps, alerting Zach with a bellowing siren. It must have been something small like a dog or a fox because when Zach located the spot, there was no evidence that anyone had been there. And then, by the time he'd reached the cabin where he'd sent Christie, his family was nowhere to be found. He might have believed that they'd simply found the keys to the rusty green pickup and driven away except for the screams and the gunshots—and the profusion of tire marks and footprints and shell casings, which all led to the unavoidable conclusion that Zach's family had been abducted.

"We'll find them, Zach. I promise," Blake said, his eyes expressing the pity he obviously felt. "Tell us what happened."

"They took them … shot at them … Gideon was screaming …" Zach growled in frustration. "What is taking Stoner so long?"

They'd searched the area thoroughly finding an abundance of evidence that gunmen had been lying in wait—Why hadn't Zach realized that the attack on Seth's cabin was a ruse to flush them out?—and found absolutely nothing that would help them locate Christie and Gideon. Stoner had volunteered to make a last pass of the marina in case any of the boats had gone missing.

"You're bleeding," Blake said. He stepped forward and grabbed Zach by the arm. "Why are you bleeding?"

"I was shot," Zach said, allowing Blake to lift his shirt and check the bandage.

"Seth?" Blake called his brother. "Can you deal with this?"

Seth stepped over and gently removed the bandage. "You've popped a stitch. Who sewed you up? Christie? It's a very neat job."

"Yeah. Christie." Zach let Blake lead him to a stool.

"I've got a suture kit in my truck," Seth said.

Seth returned, pushing Zach forward over the table so he could see the wound better. He cleaned it with some liquid antiseptic that should have been labelled *liquid fire* it hurt so much.

"You want a shot for the pain?" Seth asked.

"Just fix it," Zach said belligerently.

"Okay," Seth replied, but Zach could hear the doubt in his voice.

"Ow," Zach said at the first prick of the needle. The tissues were inflamed, and the wound was raw—no way did Zach want to go through this again. "I changed my mind," he said through clenched teeth.

"I just need to put in two small stitches. It won't be so bad," Seth said and continued.

Zach felt like vomiting it hurt so much, and it went on forever. He gritted his teeth to hold in his complaints.

"Done," Seth finally said, and Zach unclenched his body.

"You know, you suck," Zach said. "Christie was way better."

Seth snorted.

"But, thanks." Zach resumed his pacing, moving more carefully this time. "Who did this? The leak in the organization must be very high up. They knew exactly where we'd be. Damaris? Stoner? Who else knew where we'd be?"

Zach's tirade was cut off by Blake's cell phone. "Hey, Stone," he said, and his eyes latched onto Zach. "We'll be there in three." He rang off.

"What is it? Is it Christie?" Zach asked.

"Stoner says he found a little boy wandering around the marina who says his father is Zachary Clyde Marek," Blake said.

"Gideon." Zach accelerated, and Blake and Seth followed.

"Did Stoner know where Christie is? She wouldn't have let Gid out of her sight unless …" Zach's voice undulated with his running steps. His belly clutched in fear at the possibilities.

"We'll find her, Zach. Guarantee it," Seth said.

Stoner was waving from the dock. "Little dude's okay, man, just a wee bit bruised and scratched from the looks of it. He won't let me touch him," Stoner said, gesturing him over—as if Zach needed any incentive to move faster.

"Six and two, little dude," Stoner said to Gideon.

"Sixty-two," Gideon said. He stood on the dock, his hands over his ears, rocking on his toes and mumbling a constant refrain of "too loud" interspersed with numbers. "Two and one. Too loud. Too loud." B-52 bear lay at his feet.

"Gideon," Zach called, rushing up to his son. Relief suffused him.

Gideon dropped his hands in wonder and ran with arms outstretched to Zach's waiting embrace. "Daddy!"

Zach held him tightly, kissing him and running his hands over him to ensure he was really there. "Are you okay, son?" Zach asked, trying to pull back enough to get a look at his son's face.

"Nnnnn," Gideon began, squeezing Zach tighter until he relented and just held him.

"I love you, sweetheart. It's okay," Zach reassured him.

"I love you, Daddy," Gideon said, and he squeezed him tighter until Zach felt the blood pool in his head.

"Dude. He okay?" Stoner asked in his surfer-dude drawl.

"I think so. I'll know better after I check him over," Zach said. "Thanks for finding him."

"No problem, man," Stoner said. Picking up B-52 bear, Stoner offered it to Zach and then reached out to ruffle Gideon's hair, but Gideon pushed him off.

"He doesn't like to be touched, particularly not by strangers," Zach said.

"Whatever you say, man," Stoner replied in his lazy drawl. "Autism?"

Surprised, Zach met his eyes. "Yes. How did you know?"

"My sister's kid has autism. He's ga-ga over numbers," Stoner said, giving Zach the click-wink gesture.

Zach carried Gideon back to the cabin.

"Hey, Gid," Blake greeted them. "Are you okay?"

"Nnnnn," Gideon replied.

"No new information," Seth said, pocketing his phone. "Do you think it was Gid who set off the alarm?"

"Maybe," Zach replied, sitting Gideon on the table and removing his shirt and trousers.

"Are you hurt, Gid?" Zach asked, running his hands over the boy's body.

"Ouch. It hurts," he replied.

Seth pointed at the oval welts on Gideon's back. "It looks like someone grabbed him by the back of the shirt—"

"And the hair," Zach said, gently probing Gideon's scalp. He parted the hair at the back. "Look at this scratch. Do you think we could get DNA from that?"

"Definitely. Check out his fingers," Seth instructed.

"There's blood under his nails," Zach said.

Seth met Blake's eyes across Gideon's body. "Get someone here to collect samples ASAP. If the foul piece of filth who dared lay a hand on a Marek survives this, then he is going to prison."

"Agreed," Blake said, and he and Seth were on their phones arranging things.

Zach dressed Gideon again.

"There's someone at the local hospital who can take samples. She'll be here in fifteen minutes," Seth said, ending his call.

"Where's Mommy, buddy?" Zach asked gently.

"Bad man," Gideon whispered, and then he raised his voice, perfectly mimicking Christie. "Run, Gideon, run. Find Daddy." Wrapping his arms around Zach's neck, Gideon took a deep, shuddering breath. "Daddy," he said on a sigh.

"Who took Mommy?" Zach said.

"Smelly," Gideon said, wrinkling his nose.

"Does he not like the smell in here?" confused, Seth asked, holding his hand over the phone's mouthpiece for a moment.

"Smelly. Bad man," Gideon said.

"No. I—" And then all at once, Zach understood. "Carlos Rivera." *Carlos did this.* Fury welled up within Zach. *He'll pay for this.* "Seth, why don't you take Gideon to the ranch? You could return with Luke and then—"

"No can do," Blake replied. "Are you really going to deprive Gid of his mom *and* dad in the same day?" Zach could read the pity in Blake's eyes. "I'm sorry. I know you want to find Christie and make the filthy rotters pay for what they did to your family, but your son needs you. No one else can do that job."

"He needs you," Seth said quietly, supporting Blake's words.

I want Christie. Gideon needs her. Gulping down his anger to maintain control, Zach looked over at Gideon where he was lining up markers to try to put some order into his seriously disordered life. "I know."

Seth clapped Zach on the shoulder. "Look, I've been thinking. I'll hang out here for long enough to meet with the Crow elders and see what help they can provide. You, Blake, and Gideon can return to the ranch, and we'll make that our base of operations."

"But this is where Christie was taken," Zach protested.

"They're long gone, Zach," Blake said. "We can't follow them so we need to find them. And we need to make certain that they pay. From the ranch, we can all participate."

Zach didn't want to lose this last connection with his wife, but he could see his brother's logic. Finally, he agreed.

"Uh, Zach? Why does Gideon think your middle name is Clyde?" Seth asked.

"Christie. She calls me that, has since we were dating," Zach replied, a wistful smile on his face.

"Why?" Seth asked.

"You know that song by Ray Stevens? Ahab the Arab and his stubborn camel Clyde. Well, she, uh, got angry one time and called me stubborn, et cetera, et cetera. It doesn't matter," Zach said.

Seth exchanged an eloquent expression with Blake and gave a short laugh.

Christie was seriously frightened. She had ridden for what felt like hours squashed between two ginormous goons—smelly goons, at that—plotting the downfall of the beady-eyed hook-nosed fiend who dared lay hands on her son. But her anger hadn't outlasted her fear, and now she sat, exhausted and terrified, as she tried to imagine what Carlos had planned for her and what exactly she was going to do to stop him from harming her family.

Eventually, the SUV pulled into a residential area filled with large, luxury homes, many surrounded by high stone walls with wrought-iron gates. The driver took a turn into one such property, stopped briefly at the gate to slide a plastic card through a reader, and then proceeded up the long driveway. They passed rows of planted trees before curving around a marble fountain at the front entrance of a Spanish-style mansion.

Two women met the vehicle, their handguns clearly visible in their shoulder holsters.

"Christie." Carlos turned in his seat to look at her. "You can enter the house under the power of your own steam, or I will tell Thor to knock you unconscious and carry you in."

Christie surveyed her surroundings again: two goons in the back, one gun-toting driver, and two female bodyguards. "I'll walk."

Thor, clearly Hooknose's real name, exited the vehicle at Carlos's instruction and held the door open for her. Christie stepped out of the SUV and then took off at a run around the back of the vehicle and toward the trees on the other side of the driveway. She got about seven steps before being brought up short.

A hand fisted her hair, yanking her back and off-balance. Crying out in pain, she grabbed at the hand she was dangling from.

"You want I should pound her for the boss?" Thor asked.

Evidently furious, Carlos struggled for control. "No. Just ... take her inside." He turned to the women. "Olga. Ivana. Take her to her room and lock her in."

"Yes, boss," Olga said. Or Ivana. Christie wasn't sure. They pretty much looked the same—mouse-brown hair pulled back into a ponytail, slender, tall, and unfriendly.

Thor hefted Christie over his shoulder and then followed Olga into the house and up the stairs.

"Ow. Ow. Ow," Christie complained.

Ivana followed with her gun pointed directly at Christie. But Christie was not ready to go quietly into the night, so she kicked and punched and pulled at Thor's hair, anything in an attempt to escape. But he didn't seem to care. *I have to get away. I cannot let Carlos use me against Zach.*

When she'd irritated him enough, Thor stopped and shook her until her teeth rattled and then settled her back over his shoulder and continued up a main staircase and down a long hallway. He shoved her through the door of a bedroom, and Ivana locked her in.

Christie raced around the room, trying every window and door, but she was securely confined. She took the opportunity to cry.

CHAPTER 45

"We need a plan," Damaris said, repeating Zach's heart's message. "We've searched the entire area around Seth's cabin, including the Crow reservation, with the elders' very gracious permission and assistance. We've collected DNA evidence and learned that a man named Thor, a.k.a. Visar Hida, Albanian drug enforcer, listed on both Interpol's and the FBI's most wanted lists, dared lay hands on the youngest Marek. From this, we can surmise that our Albanian friend, Burim Gjojak, is somehow connected to this situation." Rocking vigorously in Bud's heavy wooden rocking chair, Damaris paused from time to time to stand before returning to the rhythmic movement. "However, we still have no idea where Christie is or why she was taken."

"Then we need to pray," Bud said.

Zach stopped pacing the great room of the ranch house, struggling with himself for a moment. He didn't want to stop. He wanted to plot and scheme and locate his wife.

"Blake?" Bud said. "Boys?"

Blake took his seat at the table, closely followed by Seth and Luke.

"Zach?" Bud said again.

Nodding, Zach took his place and bowed his head, but rather than praying, Bud called across the room. "Join us, Ms. Quickle."

Zach followed his line of sight to see the normally unflappable Damaris looking quite uncomfortable, fidgeting near the doorway, rocking on the creaking floorboard. Was she trying to escape?

"Oh, uh, that's okay," she replied.

"Please. Join us," Bud said. And the brothers murmured their approval, all except Blake, who remained silent, studying the table.

"I, uh, don't really hold with, uh, beliefs … God. Sorry," she said, looking sheepish.

"That's okay. Join us anyway. God doesn't rely on your belief to exist."

She grinned at that and then pulled up a chair beside Blake, who gave her a nod and a small smile.

"Heavenly Father, thank you for your love for us. Please look down on your children here and help us. Rest your hand of protection over Christie and keep her safe. Lead and guide us here as we plan a way to rescue her. If it is your will, please bring us back together. In Jesus's name, Amen."

"Amen," the brothers murmured in response.

"Thanks, Dad," Zach said, squeezing his father's shoulder.

"Very nice," Damaris said in a thoughtful voice. "Now what is our next step?"

All eyes turned to Zach. "Perhaps you could continue to investigate the assassin, Hoxha," he said. "Elsewhere."

Damaris watched him carefully, and Zach knew the instant she realized that he didn't trust her. A mask of neutrality covered her expression. Nodding once, she said, "I'll be in touch," and then exited. Soon, they heard a car drive away.

"I've never had cause to doubt Damaris in the past," Blake said, watching Zach carefully.

"I don't want anyone else involved," Zach said, pacing the great room of the ranch house. "There's a massive great leak, and until I know who it is, I won't trust anyone." Zach stopped and searched the faces around the table. "Except a Marek."

As Zach examined the faces of his brothers, he heard the reassuring sounds of his son and his youngest brother at play.

"You can count on us, son," Bud said, and Seth and Luke echoed his assurance.

"I trust Damaris Quickle," Blake said.

"I did, too, Blake," Zach said. "But she was one of very few people who knew where Christie and I were headed in Sheridan and not many people know about Seth's cabin."

"I'm with you, Zach," Blake said. "I simply wanted to let you know how I feel."

Zach nodded to accept his brother's words. But ... "They knew exactly where we were. I'm sorry, Blake. I trust you, Luke, Seth, and Dad. No one else. I don't trust anyone else with my wife's life," Zach said.

"Then we circle the wagons and get Christie back," Bud said. "I'll speak with Garvin and ask him to organize protection with the ranch hands."

"This becomes our base of operations," Luke said. "I'm going out to buy the software we'll need."

"I'll look after hardware," Seth offered, and Zach knew that he meant guns, not computers.

"Zach, you and I are strategy. We know Gjojak the best," Blake said.

Zach nodded, and the family Marek went about their business, saving one of their own.

CHAPTER 46

"Mommy. Mommy. Mommy." Gideon called for his mother for the third night in a row. He simply couldn't sleep without the security that she provided.

Zach pushed himself off the couch and found Gideon searching for his mother in the bed that she'd shared with Zach here at the Second Chance.

"Come here, Gid," Zach said. Pity clutched at him.

"Daddy, where Mommy?" Gideon asked. He began rocking on his toes, his arms flapping.

"Mommy's not here," Zach said, holding out his hand. "Come here."

Gideon looked around the room once more, rocking up and then settling on his heels. He lifted his arms. "Up."

Zach picked him up and held him tightly, drawing as much comfort from his son as he attempted to give. "Shall we build a fire and make hot cocoa?"

"Make hot cocoa. Marshymellys."

"Yes. Hot cocoa with marshmallows," Zach said.

After carrying Gideon to the kitchen, Zach got out a cast-iron pot, milk, chocolate powder, and, of course, the marshmallows. Together, they built a fire in the fireplace and placed the pot on the cradle over the fire. Once the milk was warm enough, Zach stirred in the chocolate powder. He set Gideon to work counting out the marshmallows for the mugs.

"Five. Six. Seven. Mommy likes seven." Gideon stopped, holding a pink marshmallow between his thumb and forefinger.

"Yeah. Mommy likes seven." Zach waited to see if Gideon would respond, but he kept studying the marshmallow, turning it this way and that.

Gideon had been very withdrawn since Christie's abduction. He spent his days reciting letters and numbers, lining up anything he could get his hands on, and trying out his favorite vowels and consonants, "Eeeee," "Nnnnn," and "oh oh oh." Zach was trying to replicate the routine that Christie had established, trying to pretend that nothing was different, but it wasn't working. They'd taken about five hundred steps back from where they'd progressed to over the past three months. Zach felt like he was fighting a losing battle for his son.

Zach tried something else. "I miss Mommy," he said.

Gideon looked up at him. "Miss Mommy," Gideon said and started to cry. Zach pulled the pot of milk off the fire and then wrapped Gideon in a solid embrace. "Miss Mommy," Gideon repeated, sniffling.

"I miss Mommy's hugs," Zach said.

"Miss Mommy hug. Miss Mommy kiss," Gideon said.

"Yes. Me, too. I miss when Mommy reads stories to us and when she plays games," Zach said.

"Miss Mommy read books. Miss Mommy play trains," Gideon said. His tears slowed, and his voice gradually levelled out.

"Does Mommy like hot cocoa?" Zach asked.

"Mommy like coffee. No marshymellys," Gideon said.

Zach put the pot back on the fire.

"Daddy?"

"Yes, Gid," Zach replied.

"Mommy come home?" he asked, searching his father's face.

"Yes. Uncle Blake, Uncle Luke, Uncle Seth, and me, we are all looking for Mommy. We'll find her," Zach assured his son. *Please, Lord, help us find her and bring her home to Gideon. And to me.*

After finishing their hot cocoa, Zach and Gideon curled up on the couch together. Zach sang every song Gideon requested until, finally, the little boy fell asleep. Zach wrapped Gideon in a blanket and left him on the couch, not wanting to disturb him. Well, actually, he just wanted to keep him close. Zach turned down the lights and sat gazing into the fire.

Gideon's days felt all wrong. Mommy was gone. Playing trains with Bobby helped. But then Uncle Seth came into Bobby's special train room and interrupted them. Gideon tried to ignore him, but Uncle Seth got down low to talk to Gideon.

"Hey, little guy, can we be done trains for a minute? I want to talk to you and Bobby," Uncle Seth said.

Gideon didn't look up. His name wasn't "little guy," and he didn't want to be done trains. Bobby and Gideon played trains together at the Second Chance ranch.

Bobby poked Gideon's shoulder. "Gid, Seff wanna talk t' us."

Gideon looked up at Bobby's face. "First trains, then talk," he said.

"Later, Seff?" Bobby said.

"I'm afraid not, guys. I need to talk to you now," Uncle Seth said.

"Firs' talk then trains, Gid," Bobby said.

Gideon's face felt like it did a frown, but he wasn't sad, so he said, "Okay."

"Come sit over here," Uncle Seth said, and Bobby and Gideon sat on the wooden stools that were in the train room. "I want to teach you a new game, and I want you to practice it while I'm gone, okay?"

"Wha's the game, Seff?" Bobby said.

"Red alert," Uncle Seth said.

"Red alert means unexpected things," Gideon said, telling Uncle Seth and Bobby the words that Mommy had taught him. Where was Mommy? She had been gone a long time.

"Yeah. That's great, Gideon. When something unexpected, like maybe something scary, happens, then you and Bobby play red alert. Okay?" Uncle Seth said. He held out his hand to Gideon, and Gideon took it. Bobby came behind him. "Bobby, do you remember the special room that I built for you and Blake when you were little kids?"

"Yup. A spessoh puh-lace fo' when Llluke and Zach'd bug me," Bobby said. Bobby always said his L words slow and long.

Uncle Seth did a chuckle. C-H-U-C-K-L-E. Seven letters. "If something unexpected happens, I want you and Gideon to go to the special room, stay quiet, and wait for Grandpa, me, Luke, or Zach to come and tell you that everything's okay."

"'Kay," Bobby said.

"Okay. Let's practice. Are you ready?" Uncle Seth said.

"I'm ready," Gideon said.

"Red alert," Uncle Seth said.

Gideon grabbed Bobby by the hand and ran to the special room. It was awesome. That was what Bobby called it. It was a small room and made Gideon feel cozy and good. There was a special blue light and lots of books to read. There were bean bag chairs to sit in and funny hats to wear.

"Okay. Everything's safe. You can come out now," Uncle Seth said.

"Talk all done. Trains," Gideon said as he ran back to the train table.

"Seff?" Bobby said. "Is it a game?" Gideon looked over. Bobby's face looked very serious.

"No, Bob. Some bad people are after …" Uncle Seth's voice got very quiet, so Gideon didn't bother to listen anymore until Uncle Seth said. "Okay?"

"Okay," Gideon said. Maybe then Uncle Seth would play trains or go away and let Bobby play trains.

"'Kay," Bobby said.

Uncle Seth gave Bobby a hug. Gideon bounced over to them. "Big hug," he said.

Uncle Seth smiled. Bobby smiled, and they gave Gideon a two-man hug. One. Two. *Wait.* Three-man hug. One. Two. Three.

CHAPTER 47

"What now, Carlos?" Christie asked, keeping her voice carefully even. "You know you'll never get away with this," she said and then groaned inwardly. What a stupid thing to say! An overused statement that she'd heard on *how many* television shows?

Carlos laughed as though he'd read her mind. "This is just a little hiccup, not even a rib-breaker," he replied, pacing around the room, picking up objects, turning them in his hands and then placing them back in their spots, correcting them until he returned them to their precise location. His vocabulary, his manner, his voice, everything sounded odd to Christie.

"Hiccup? Not a burp or a cough?" she asked, and then she finally had his attention. He narrowed his eyes and strode up to her.

"You are being impertinent?" Carlos asked, his face close enough that Christie could smell the whiskey on his breath.

"Impertinent?" she scoffed. "Don't you think it's rather impertinent of you to kidnap me? To threaten my son? He's not even four years old yet, Carlos. He doesn't need to be exposed to the ugliness of life quite yet," she finished sarcastically.

Carlos went red in the face, and then all the anger seemed to melt out of him, and he looked cool, much too cool. "A new life. And then life will be wonderful," he murmured with a thoughtful expression. "That is what we will have, *pura vida*. Together." Carlos grabbed her by the upper arm and pulled her to the bench at the foot of the neatly made double bed. "You see, I have a small problem. Burim Gjojak ordered me to help his man, Qazim Hoxha, capture Zach, interrogate him to find out just what he knows about the organization, and then eliminate him."

"No," she replied, fighting the horror of Carlos's statement. "There's no need to hurt Zach or Gideon … or me, either," Christie said. What if Zach came after her and was captured? What if he didn't find Gideon? Christie needed a telephone. Or a gun. And a ladder to climb down from the second-story bedroom. Maybe she could climb down the fir tree near the window. She hadn't climbed since she was a girl but—

"But I have got you," Carlos said as he reached for her.

Got me? Christie straight-armed him in the chest, suddenly aware that she needed to be listening very carefully to what Carlos had to say and not plotting her escape at this exact moment.

Carlos continued, "I could give you to Hoxha, the assassin, and he could trade you for Zach but …"

"But what?" she asked, trepidation filling her.

"I want you." Carlos grabbed her hand. His bruising grip made her gasp. "We can be together. I can tell Gjojak that Sheriff Reeves betrayed him by warning Zach, which enabled him to escape, and then you and I can disappear."

"Matty Reeves is a part of this?" Christie asked. *Why that vile piece of rat crap!*

"*Si.* He has been keeping his eyes on Zach. In matter of fact, he is the one who told us about the safe house in Sheridan and your brother-in-law's cabin in Montana," Carlos said.

"All that death, Carlos. Why?" she asked.

"Money. Cover. If I keep my favorite girls properly supplied with drugs, they don't give me any trouble. And I like to gamble. Doesn't everybody? Gjojak understands that," he said.

Favorite girls? "You seriously expect me to consider a relationship with a man who keeps other women?" Christie said flabbergasted to learn the quality of man Carlos truly was. Gideon was right, Carlos was "smelly."

Carlos shrugged, as though entertaining other women was a nonissue to him and should be to her. Then he seemed to reconsider. "Perhaps you are right. What to do with you then?"

Christie patted Carlos's hand. "Let me go," she said and then held her breath.

Shoving her onto the floor in a brusque and callous move, Carlos rose above her, jabbing a finger at her face. "You stupid, ignorant slut! He will kill me for this." Christie flinched away from his anger, scrabbling backward on the floor. Carlos whipped out a knife and took a step toward her.

The door banged open. "*Ndalu!* Stop this!" Hoxha entered the room. In two steps, he'd subdued Carlos and gained possession of the knife. Whining at the pain, Carlos backed away, holding his wrist tightly to his chest.

"*Dal nga skena!*" Hoxha said in a voice that brooked no argument. Carlos complied, leaving the room without another word.

Pointing at her with Carlos's knife, Hoxha commanded, "Stand up."

Christie stood but remained on the opposite side of the room, her back against the wall.

"No trouble," Hoxha said, pointing directly at her face.

"No trouble," she repeated, not entirely certain what he meant. *I won't cause you any trouble? Don't make trouble? What?*

"Where is Zachary Marek?" he asked. Looking at Hoxha was like looking into an iceberg, no warmth, no emotion.

"I d—" She squeaked and then cleared her throat. "I don't know."

He studied her, and she felt like X-rays were passing through her mind. "Where will he go?" Hoxha spoke with a strong accent, but he spoke slowly and precisely so that she could understand him easily if she listened carefully. The menace in his eyes took no skill to detect.

"I don't want you to find him," she replied rather than lying.

He studied her again, and she wondered what he would do. After a long, anxious moment of waiting, he called into the hallway, words that she didn't understand.

Two men entered the room, the two men from the SUV, Thor and the balaclava bloke, a man named Cole. Hoxha gestured toward her and then out the door. Thor and Cole grabbed her by the upper arms in an unbreakable hold and dragged her down the stairs, out the back door, and to a shed. Hoxha unlocked the door, and they threw her in. Christie heard the door click shut before she could protest. And then she was alone in the dark.

CHAPTER 48

"Where is Christie?" Bud asked for the thousandth time amidst the flurry of activity as each brother used his own specific skills to locate Christie.

"I think Hoxha is our best option. If we can discover his whereabouts, I think we'll find Christie," Seth said.

"I disagree," Luke said. "We don't know that Hoxha was on-hand during Christie's abduction, but we do have forensic evidence that this Thor fellow was. I say we track him."

"Rivera is the clearest connection," Blake said.

Zach frowned. "Gideon did confirm that Carlos was there."

"No disrespect, Zach, but Gideon's four years old," Luke said.

"He's got a good memory for things that matter to him, and, frankly, smelly things matter," Zach said. *But what to do with that information?* "If we had a picture of this Hoxha, I could ask Gid if he saw him." *But what would seeing the man who'd kidnapped his mother do to the little boy?*

"Gideon was pretty freaked out at first, but he seems to have settled," Seth said, and Zach could read the optimism in his eyes.

Bud zeroed in on Zach. "You've done well with him."

"Thanks, Dad," Zach replied, feeling a warm glow in spite of the seriousness of the situation.

"I can get a picture," Blake said, sitting down in front of a laptop. "I ran afoul of Hoxha about nine months ago in an operation in Ukraine. Let me see what I can do."

"Let's show him Hoxha and Thor. Seeing them may jog something loose in his memory," Seth suggested.

Blake tapped away for a time as Bud cleaned and oiled a series of handguns and rifles and Luke used the encrypted satellite phone to trawl all of his law enforcement contacts. Seth returned to his wires and pliers that were spread across the kitchen counter.

"Oh, Zach," Blake began. "I forgot to tell you. Thomason's back. He *was* held captive by guerrillas in Bolivia, but his wife managed to scrape together the ransom, all on the sly. Amazing what love will accomplish. You might try him."

"He's the one who fired me," Zach reminded his younger brother.

"I'll ask Damaris to have a word with him," Blake suggested.

"No—"

"All right. All right," Blake interrupted him, raising his hands in a gesture of appeasement. "But if you change your mind, let me know." Blake's hands settled back on the computer keyboard, lightly tapping.

"All set," Seth said, finally finished setting up a series of electronic boxes, wires, antennae, and funny little satellite dishes. "I got my hands on some state-of-the-art surveillance equipment from a buddy of mine. If you have Rivera's cell number, I can try to trace it."

Zach passed him the information.

"I've got the results back from forensics," Luke said, finally putting the sat phone down and joining his brothers. He leaned on the corner of the table.

"How did you manage to do that so quickly?" Seth asked.

Luke shrugged. "People like me," he replied, tongue in cheek.

"What did you learn, Son?" Bud asked, coming to stand beside Luke, reading over his shoulder.

"They found seven distinct sets of footprints. One was definitely from a child, and one could have been a woman's. One I'm pretty sure is Zach's so that leaves at least four individuals, four individuals in the area surrounding the gatehouse. Shell casings from two different AK-47s as well as a Smith and Wesson handgun," Luke said, summarizing the results as he read off copies of the lab reports.

"What about the DNA evidence?" Zach asked.

"Gideon definitely did this Thor dude some damage, and he is a thug known to be associated with Burim Gjojak. So we have proof of connection," Luke said. "The swab from Gid's head revealed nothing new."

"Okay," Seth began. "So we know this is Gjojak and we know that Rivera was present. We highly suspect that Hoxha, Gjojak's pet assassin, is also involved. Where does that leave us?"

Zach ran his fingers through his hair. *Where indeed?*

Christie had no idea how long she'd been held in this garden shed, but it was long enough for her to learn every inch of it, by touch anyway. It was maybe four by four by five and half feet and made with sheet metal walls, the curvy kind, not flat. The walls were coated in what she assumed was a layer of rust from the smell of iron on her fingertips. There was a tall plastic paint bucket, which she'd first upturned for a seat and then used to relieve herself when it became necessary.

Now she stood, the messy top of her head brushing against the ceiling, rubbing her hands briskly up and down her arms to try to maintain some warmth. From time to time, she heard footsteps outside her little black box, but no one disturbed her for what felt like hours.

Without warning, the door to the shed opened and Christie was blinded by the light streaming into her face. Flinching away, she covered her face with her hands, trying to hold back the light until her eyes could adjust. So she'd been in the dark long enough for light to actually hurt. How long did that take?

"Out!" She heard Hoxha's hard command.

Groping to find her way, her labored progress clearly outlasted the assassin's patience. A hard hand closed around her arm and tugged her forward. She tripped on the doorframe, but the bruising grip kept her upright.

Soon, she felt grass beneath her feet and then the crunch of gravel before she was lifted and dropped into the trunk of a car. As she was scrambling to escape, the trunk lid connected with her head when it was slammed shut, knocking her out.

The next thing she knew, she was lying on a hideous floral rug, her cheek pressed against the coarse fibers. There were bookcases lining the wall to her right. When she tried to move her eyes to see more of the room, an ice pick of pain forced her eyes shut again.

"She's awake," Hoxha said. She felt his foot prod her in the ribs. "Get up."

Groaning, she held her head with one hand as she propped herself into a sitting position with the other. The room was clearly a library with floor-to-ceiling bookcases, easy chairs, blue velvet draperies, and a large oversized oak desk. The short, pudgy man with the greasy comb-over whom Christie had first seen at the safe house in Sheridan sat behind the desk. The other men seemed to be taking orders from him. So did that make him Burim Gjojak?

She was clearly taking too long to rise, so Hoxha reached down and hefted her onto her feet.

"Thanks," she muttered, letting him hear her sarcasm. He grunted in response.

"I think it would be best to give Mrs. Marek a chair," the man behind the desk said.

Hoxha reached with one hand for a straight-backed wooden chair and the other to Christie, intending to bring the two into hard contact. Christie pulled back, giving him a fulminating glare as she lowered herself carefully into the chair.

"Are you Burim Gjojak?" she asked as she turned her attention from the unemotional Hoxha to the man behind the desk.

"You may call me, sir," he replied. Yup, that was Gjojak.

"Tell me about your *dashur*, er, your hus-band," Gjojak said.

"He's thirty-three years old, six feet tall, and weighs, I don't know, a hundred and seventy-five pounds? He has hazel eyes and thick honey-gold hair. I love his hair," she said warmly. "And his hands." She could talk about her husband for hours.

"Enough," Gjojak said with a quelling gesture. "I am not writing your romance novel. What I wish to know is what will he now do?"

"How am I meant to know?" she asked.

Gjojak's attention turned to his assassin. "You are right. She is difficult. Where is Rivera?"

"Gone," Hoxha said, the gravel in his voice carrying no emotion.

"But you know where he is?" Gjojak asked.

Hoxha nodded.

"Eliminate him and the sheriff. I do not tolerate errors. They were ordered to bring me the man, not his wife," Gjojak said as he tossed Christie a cell phone. "Call your hus-band." He pronounced the word carefully again, and she couldn't tell whether he enjoyed saying it or despised its meaning.

Thumbing the volume button on the side of the cell phone, Christie then held it at her side, dialing 9-1-1 with her thumb. At least she hoped that she was secretly calling for help. Dropping the phone into her lap, she covered it with her hands. "Why?" Christie asked. "Why do you want me to call my husband? He's safe, and my son is safe. Why would I want to do anything to change that? I love my family, and I can't think of any reason why ..." Christie kept talking as long as she could, in the hope that the 9-1-1 operator would hear her and send help. "I don't appreciate being kidnapped ..."

"She's making a call," one of the goons standing across the room remarked.

Hoxha grabbed her wrist, grinding the bones together, and reached into her lap to retrieve the phone. Fighting him, she slapped at his face, but he subdued her easily, forcing her back into the seat. Her wrist throbbed with pain where he held it.

"Find out who—" Gjojak began just as the heel of Hoxha's boot came down. "*Tarallak!*"

Hoxha obviously didn't like being insulted, so he punched her in the face. And the world went black again as she slumped to the floor.

CHAPTER 49

Zach was rapidly losing patience with Sheriff Matthew Reeves, who'd arrived, knocking on the ranch house door in all his questionable glory.

"So I heard yer kid got roughed up," Matty said, trying to see around Zach's body inside the ranch house. "You didn't report it."

Stepping out of the house and onto the front stoop, Zach took the opportunity to close the door behind him. He didn't want Matty anywhere near Gideon.

"I'm not sure where you're getting your information, Matty," Zach replied.

Matty's jaw clenched. "Sheriff. Call me Sheriff."

Zach returned an implacable gaze.

"You think you're hot snot, Zach-ar-y, but you're nothing. I'm the law officer around here. People listen to me now, not you. I'm the one married to the head cheerleader," Matty said.

"You're a little old for that, aren't you?" Zach asked, purposely baiting the little man.

"Kitty," Matty said, practically spitting the name. "Kitty Langley."

"Oh, yeah. I remember her. She was waitressing at the diner the last I heard," Zach said.

"Well, now she's keeping my house. Mom's very thrilled with her," Matty said.

"How nice," Zach replied, allowing enough sarcasm into his voice to rile Matty.

"I told them," the red-faced Matty said, saliva frothing from his lips. "I told them. Did you know your life was worth only two thousand dollars? You're—"

Before he could even move, the door behind Zach flew open and, as Zach felt himself enveloped in Seth's massive grip, Luke rushed out in a flurry of movement. He hefted Matty off his feet, carrying him down the front steps and slamming him against the passenger door of his vehicle.

"You pissant!" Luke shouted into his face.

Matty pushed at Luke's fists, the toes of his boots scrabbling on the gravel driveway. "Get him off me!" he shrieked.

Luke shook him. "Who contacted you?" He shook him again. "Who?"

"Riv—" Matty lifted himself on Luke's fists, creating room to breathe. "Rivera. Offered me two thousand to keep tabs on Zach."

"How did you know about the house in Sheridan?" Luke asked, shaking Matty again when he responded too slowly.

"It's in the database," he said, his voice tight with strain. "Had a suspect stay there once."

"Seth's cabin?" Luke asked.

"Told them. Seth ... dated ... Kitty's cousin ... for a year," Matty gasped out the words, his face purpling with pooling blood.

"Well, all right, then," Luke said, suddenly calm, abruptly releasing Matty, who crumpled to the ground gasping for breath.

"The US Marshalls will be very interested in this information," Blake said, shaking a digital recorder in his hand. He tossed a pair of handcuffs down to Luke. "You do the honors."

Luke lifted Matty bodily and bent him over the hood of his vehicle, snapping the cuffs in place.

"You have no jurisdiction here," Matty said, his retort followed by a series of other obnoxious protests.

Blake walked down the steps. "I'll look after him." Amidst whines and complaints, Blake loaded Matty into the rear of his vehicle and then took his place in the front, before driving away.

"Christie?" Zach asked, glancing between his older brothers.

"Time's running out. We need to get her now," Seth said from the doorway.

Bobby heard Seth and Luke talking. They said that Rivera and Hoxha were in the same place in Montana on the same day that the bad men took Christie away. All of Bobby's brothers had gone to find Christie. Zach had asked Bobby to please stay and help Dad look after Gideon. Bobby wanted to get his Colt 45 and go with his brothers, but Zach said it was real important to keep Gideon safe. So Bobby stayed and played trains with his nephew.

Dad said he would make popcorn and maybe they could watch a movie together. Bobby wanted to watch a movie about police officers, but Gid would probably want to watch dinosaurs or trains. Sometimes it was a pain to have to share the TV. But Gid missed his Mommy, so Bobby would let him choose. Bobby missed his mom. She had been gone a very long time. She had died. Gid's mom had been kidnapped.

Bobby heard a noise downstairs like someone was sneaking in the window. Bobby peaked around the corner like he saw the spies and policemen do on TV. The man was a stranger. He had black hair, and he was wearing a gray suit that looked like it had been rolled over by an elephant. He was sneaking up on Dad, and Dad didn't see him. Bobby didn't know if he should yell or if he should be quiet. But then Dad turned around.

"Who are you?" Dad asked.

The man showed Dad a police badge. Bobby's brothers Luke and Zach were police officers. Police were supposed to be the good guys.

"Inspector Carlos Rivera," Dad said.

Carlos. Bobby had heard his brothers talking about Carlos Rivera. He had done bad things to Zach.

"Bring me Zach. He has destroyed my plans!" Carlos said and then he took out his gun and pointed it at Dad.

Dad used his "calm down" hands and said, "Now, young man. If you'll just settle down, I can make us a pot of coffee and we can talk about Zach."

This man, Carlos, was a bad man. Seth called him a piece of rat crap. That made this a *red alert*. And Bobby was the only one who could save Gideon.

Bobby tiptoed over to Gid. When he got very close, he put his finger to his lips to say "shh" and then whispered, "Rrred a-lert." He said the words very carefully so that all the sounds came out good.

Gideon stopped and looked at Bobby. He looked really scared, so Bobby whispered, "Don' be scared. Come with me." He reached his hand out to Gideon. Bobby took Gid to the special room just like Seth had told him. Bobby closed the door very quietly and locked it. He took Gideon to the far end of the room, took out a book, and told Gideon a story very, very quietly.

"Bring me ... to Zach," Carlos said, gritting his teeth over the words.

"He's not here, Carlos," Bud said, inching his way toward the kitchen counter where he'd left his cell phone. "The boys have gone to get Christie. I'm surprised you missed them."

"Missed them? *Si*. I missed them. Gjojak put a hit upon my head. His hired weasel is chasing me. But I will not go so easily away, not without Zach," Carlos said.

"Zach is not here," Bud repeated, keeping his voice calm and his movements nonthreatening.

Carlos lost control. "Then get the boy!" he shouted, waving his gun around the room.

Bud stopped his retreat. "If you believe for one moment that I will let you harm my grandson, you are loco," Bud said, standing firm and placing his hand on the knife he always kept in his back pocket.

Carlos screamed and yelled, using his weapon to emphasize his furious desperation. "I will kill the boy. Gideon!" he yelled and then softened his voice. "Gideon, come here, *amigo*. I know where Mommy is."

If Carlos meant to sound persuasive, however, he should have kept the edge of violence out of his voice. "Come here to Mommy."

Bud stepped toward Carlos. "Shut it."

"So he is here," Carlos said, his voice dropping dangerously low. "Bring him, or I will destroy this house."

"Fine. Destroy it," Bud replied, an unearthly calm descending on him. "But you will not harm my family."

Carlos raised his handgun and fired. Bud spun and dropped to his knees, blood dripping down his right arm to his hand.

"Daddy!" Bobby appeared at the top of the stairs to the loft. He loped down as quickly as he could.

"Freeze," Carlos yelled.

"Don't you hurt my dad," Bobby yelled and ran to his father's side, hugging him from the back. "Here, Dad," he whispered as he tucked his Colt 45 in Bud's waistband.

"Thank you, Son," Bud said very quietly, releasing the safety.

"Get away from him," Carlos ordered. "I will kill you. And him. I will kill you all!"

Slowly, Bobby stood, helping Bud to his feet. Bud pushed Bobby behind him, shielding his youngest son with his body.

"What do you have against Zach?" Bud asked.

"What?" Carlos began, spreading his arms wide in preparation to explain. And Bud shot him in the leg. And, yep, he was squealing on the floor like the weasel he was. His handgun was still spinning on the floor ten feet away. Recalling his rusty instincts from twenty years as a US Marshall, Bud retrieved the gun and pocketed it.

"Get the handcuffs, Bobby," Bud said, moving in close, keeping Carlos covered where he lay on the floor. When he was close enough, Bud shoved him over and knelt on his back, pinning him to the floor.

"Bobby," Bud said, and Bobby slid the handcuffs across the floor to him. Expertly, he confined Carlos's wrists in the cuffs, searched him, and rolled him over.

Carlos lay there, gritting his teeth at the pain from the wound that bled sluggishly. "Can you get the first-aid kit, please, Bobby?"

Bobby complied, bringing it over and pulling out the pressure dressing for his father who applied it on Carlos's thigh.

"Greetings, Carlos Rivera."

Bud startled and looked up into arctic eyes, eyes that reminded him of a cold-blooded killer. "Who are you?"

Carlos seemed to panic, swiveling his body to see and then trying to escape by propelling his body along the floor with his heels.

"Hoxha. Stop. Wait! The boy. Marek has his son here. I will find him for you," Carlos begged and pleaded, offering an exchange.

"How old?" Hoxha asked, standing well inside the doorway coolly, his hands at his sides.

"Not quite four years old," Bud replied. "Just a child."

Hoxha nodded thoughtfully before turning back to Carlos. In an instant, he'd removed a silenced pistol and shot Carlos, once in the head and once in the chest, killing him.

Bud pulled Bobby against him to spare him the sight.

"I don't do children," Hoxha said and then walked away and out the front door.

Bud exchanged a word of thanks with his Maker and then checked to see that Bobby was okay.

"Please get Gideon, and be sure that he's safe," Bud said. "I'll call the police."

"The dead guy might scare Gid," Bobby said.

"You're right, Son. I'll cover him," Bud replied.

Bobby soon returned with a frightened and confused Gideon. "Mommy-Daddy home?" he asked.

Bud scooped him up in his good arm and held him close. "Not yet."

"Soon," Gideon replied, gripping Bud around the neck tightly.

CHAPTER 50

Zach waited impatiently in the dark for his brothers to return from their surveillance of Gjojak's current residence, a country retreat just southeast of Hardin, Montana, conveniently placed a few miles from the Fairgrounds Regional Airport. When the elders of the local Crow tribe learned that a drug dealer was moving into their area, they used their own network to track him down and then passed that information on to Seth. Gjojak was staying at the house of local drug lord, Guiliano Borghesi, who was currently serving life. Clearly, drug barons stuck together.

Now that it was clear that Damaris Quickle had been no part of the betrayal, Zach had allowed Blake to contact her. They had a small window of opportunity to go in and get Christie out before the alphabet agencies arrived and took over. Zach did not want his wife caught in the middle of what was sure to be utter chaos.

Finally, Seth, Luke, and Blake returned to Zach's position behind an outbuilding in the juniper forest to the west of Borghesi's villa.

"Six inside. One has been stationary for the past fifteen minutes." Seth showed the others his small monitor. On the screen, Zach could see a small green bean-shaped object, which likely represented a human, lying on the floor.

"Christie?" Blake asked.

"That's what I think. She's clearly alive given the heat signature," Seth switched screens, "but unconscious would be my guess."

"I'm set up to cut communications as soon as you give me the word," Luke said, pulling a minidetonator out of his pack.

"Damaris is on her way with federal backup," Blake added. "She said a nine-one-one call was received from this house earlier today, but when police arrived, they couldn't find a cause."

"Okay," Zach said, pulling out a sketch he'd made of the grounds. "We're here to the west of the house. We have cover to about … here … If we stay within the cover of the trees—bypassing the detached garage—we can come in directly at this point, which looks to me like it matches up fairly closely with Christie."

"If it is Christie," Seth added.

"Yeah," Zach replied without giving the possibility another thought.

"Wait," Luke interrupted. "I have an addendum." Grabbing Zach's sketch, he laid out his plan and the brothers nodded.

"So that's why you paid for collision insurance," Blake said.

"You're sure that there's no way this could hurt Christie?" Zach asked.

Seth shook his head. "Given my last readings, unless they've moved her, unless it *isn't* her, she should be safe."

"All right. Let's go," Zach said. His determination to find his wife trumped all the fear and insecurity he felt.

Luke and Blake moved off to the right, skirting the perimeter of the property, and Zach and Seth moved through the trees until they were directly north of the long windows in the approximate center of the house. They waited.

When Zach heard the enormous roar and crash of Luke's rented H3 bisecting the front of the house, Zach moved in, Seth close on his six. The quiet of the night erupted into chaos. More than once, they slipped silently into a closet or alcove as gunmen scurried past. Orders rang out, filling the air, and the hard rain from the sprinklers soaked them to the skin.

Finally, they reached the room that Seth guessed held Christie. Zach stepped forward, eager to open the door, surprised when Seth pulled him back. A knife sliced through the air where Zach's head had just been.

Seth swung the butt of his rifle up, clipping the guard's chin, but Zach didn't pause to see the outcome of the fight. He burst through the door of Bhorgesi's library, this time alert to the area. It was empty but for a body collapsed on the florid carpet.

Dropping to his knees, Zach gently turned the body. Gasping at the bruises on the face of his beautiful wife, he felt a surge of fury sweep through him. He swallowed it down, sweeping his hands over her body, keeping his touch gentle in spite of his anger.

"Christie?" he called gently. "Sweetheart?"

Zach lightly tapped her cheeks, rubbed her arms, and pushed the hair back from her face. "Christie, baby, wake up."

She groaned.

"That's it, sweetheart. Let me know you're all right," Zach said, beseeching her.

Finally, her eyes flickered open. "Zach?" she said, her voice a bare whisper.

Relief swept through him. He wanted to scoop her into his arms and hug her fiercely to him, but he was afraid to hurt her. "I'm here. I've got you."

Her eyes widened. "Gideon?"

"He's safe. He misses you," Zach said, brushing the hair back from her face so he could see her better.

She smiled as her eyes fluttered closed. "Love you. So glad you're back."

"She's out again?" Seth asked, suddenly at Zach's shoulder. "Let's get her out of here," Seth said. "I'll cover you and then come back to help Blake and Luke."

After gently lifting her into his arms, Zach carried her out through the back door and east toward their vehicle.

"Stop!" A voice cried out of the dim light of the yard.

Zach turned slowly to meet the eyes, once again, of Burim Gjojak, his complexion livid as his hands gripped an AK-47. *No.* No way could he be allowed to win.

Gjojak raised his rifle, cackling hysterically, and Seth shot him dead.

An explosion of gunfire followed, and Seth shoved Zach.

"Keep going," Seth ordered him, and he obeyed, not bothering to look back.

Sirens sounded in the distance. "Damaris is on her way," Seth said.

Soon Zach had Christie in the car and was on his way to the Bighorn County Memorial Hospital. Safe. Finally.

EPILOGUE

"Hi, Daddy," Gideon said. Zach stood abruptly from the hospital bed and wrapped Gideon in a hug, nodding to Bud, who was standing in the doorway.

"This young fellow couldn't wait any longer to see his daddy or his mommy," Bud said.

"Thanks, Dad. I'll keep him with me now," Zach said.

"I thought you might," Bud said, smiling fondly at his son and his grandson. "How is she?" He nodded toward Christie.

"The doctors tell me that she's fine except for the fact that she won't wake up," Zach said.

"And the baby?" Bud asked.

Releasing a small smile, Zach replied, "Fine." Christie was about two months pregnant. Their own decision to expand their family had come a little after the fact, Zach mused happily.

"We'll be waiting for news," Bud said before kissing Gideon on the head and then exited.

"Mommy not feeling well?" Gideon asked, looking up at Zach with concern in his eyes.

"That's right. I think she needs a really big hug." Zach placed Gideon on one side of Christie, and then he slid one arm beneath her and one arm around her and Gideon, wrapping his family in a great big hug.

"I love you, Mommy," Zach said.

"I love you, Mommy," Gideon repeated.

Zach sang with Gideon until he was hoarse, but still Christie slept.

Zach turned on the television and curled up with Gideon on his lap in the easy chair in the room. He kept one of Christie's hands firmly in his.

"Hey, *petit frère*, how goes the battle?" Zach looked over his shoulder to see Luke and Seth enter the hospital room. "How's the mama?" Luke asked.

"Still sleeping," Zach said.

"Hello, Uncle Luke. Hello, Uncle Seth," Gideon said, casting them a brief glance before returning his attention to the television.

Seth reached down and picked Gideon up, setting him on his shoulders. Gideon turned Seth's face toward the television and then patted him on the head when he complied.

Luke walked over to the bed and stroked Christie's hair back from her face. "She looks peaceful. I haven't seen her look this relaxed in a long time."

"It's probably the best sleep she's had in four years," Seth added.

"Yeah," Zach said while quirking an ironic half-grin. "I guess you have to take your comas when you can get them."

Luke laughed loudly enough to be scolded by Gideon and then punched Zach companionably on the shoulder. "Come on, Seth," Luke said, turning away from Zach to Gideon. "Let's get this little man home and to bed."

"Kiss Daddy and Mommy good night," Seth instructed, lowering Gideon to the floor.

"Night, Daddy," Gideon said. He climbed the rails on the hospital bed like a jungle gym, planted his knees beside Christie's hip, and flopped onto her belly, hugging her body. "Night, Mommy."

"Night, baby," Christie murmured.

Gideon snuggled closer, but Zach, Seth, and Luke exchanged shocked glances and then erupted into whoops of joy, hugging each other and slapping backs and shoulders and generally making a whole lot of joyous, raucous confusion. Soon two nurses joined them, admonishing them about their level of noise, questioning what happened.

"Too loud!" Gideon yelled, and the room grew still. "Mommy sleeping," he said and then, curling up in her arms, sighed happily against her. Christie's arms wrapped around him, and she kissed him on the head.

Zach approached the bed. Opening her eyes, Christie looked up at him. "Hello, my love," she said, and his heart expanded, filling his chest with love.

"Hi. How are you feeling?" he asked.

"Happy. How about you?" she asked, reaching a hand out to him.

"More. Better. I love you," he said, lying down on the bed beside his little family and holding them tightly. He didn't bother to respond as Seth and Luke departed, taking the nurses with them.

"Do you think your dad would mind if we moved to the Second Chance?" Christie asked sleepily.

"I ride Clyde," Gideon said, his voice muffled against his mommy's body.

Zach smiled wider. He couldn't seem to stop smiling. "No. I don't think he'd mind at all. I think he'd like it if we took over the ranch. In fact, I think it would be perfect."

"Okay," she replied and then yawned loudly. "Maybe you could be the new sheriff."

Zach laughed. "For now, my only plan is to be a husband and daddy." He tipped her chin up so she could meet his gaze. "And a daddy again," he added meaningfully.

"Again?" she asked, peering sleepily at him. And then she seemed to compute something. "Really?" she exclaimed. "But how?"

Laughing brightly, Zach kissed her noisily on the cheek. "Well, first the mommy bear—"

Christie covered his mouth with her hand. "Very funny," she interrupted, her eyes alight with humor. "Well, baby, here we go again."

"Here we go again, baby," Gideon said.

NOTES

http://www.fco.gov.uk/en/travel-and-living-abroad/travel-advice-by-country/south-america/bolivia#crime (October 19, 2012).

http://www.international.gc.ca/americas-ameriques/priorities_progress-priorites_progres.aspx?view=d (October 19, 2012).

http://www.crivoice.org/perfect.html (September 24, 2012).

http://usefulbible.com/hebrews/meaning-of-perfect.htm (September 24, 2012).

http://visitsiouxfalls.com/visitors/things-to-do/falls-park/ (July 24, 2012).

http://www.accessgenealogy.com/native/tribes/crow/crowhist.htm (July 21, 2012).

http://www.globalpositions.com/terra_absaroka.htm (July 21, 2012).

http://serendip.brynmawr.edu/exchange/node/1898 (June 19, 2012).

http://www1.umn.edu/humanrts/OathBetrayed/SASC-08.pdf (June 19, 2012).

http://www.prisonersfamilies.org.uk/uploadedFiles/Information_and_research/Research%20on%20Prisoners%20Families%20Update.PDF (June 19, 2012).

http://fds.oup.com/www.oup.co.uk/pdf/0-19-922843-4.pdf (June 19, 2012).

http://www.nijacol.com/2011/04/02/customs-and-the-many-tribes-of-nigeria/ (June 8, 2012).

http://www.mapsofworld.com/nigeria/culture/tribes.html (June 8, 2012).

http://www.godrules.net/library/clarke/clarke.htm#commentary (June 1, 2012).

http://www.pc.gc.ca/eng/docs/v-g/oursnoir-blackbear/page3.aspx (May 23, 2012).

http://www.tripadvisor.com/Travel-g60999-c3619/Yellowstone-National-Park:Wyoming:Yellowstone.S.Bechler.Area.html (May 22, 2012).

http://www.nps.gov/yell/planyourvisit/upload/bctrip-planner_2012.pdf (May 22, 2012).

http://gowaterfalling.com/waterfalls/maps/yellowstone.shtml (May 22, 2012).

http://www.attorneygeneral.jus.gov.on.ca/english/glossary/?search=f*

http://www.caselgin.on.ca/services/kinship-care.

http://www.thomasandfriends.com/ca/Thomas.mvc/EngineDetail/Caroline (March 19, 2012).

http://www.yellowsheepriver.com/~qh000001/2007/07eng/jingdian/index.php (March 16, 2012).

http://www.travelchinaguide.com/attraction/qinghai/xining/qinghai_lake.htm (March 16, 2012).

http://www.thinkstockphotos.ca/?countrycode=CAN (January 21, 2013).

http://www.stopvaw.org/albania.html (February 3, 2012).

http://www.usaid.gov/our_work/cross-cutting_programs/wid/pubs/ga_albania_111003.pdf (February 4, 2012).

http://www.autismspeaks.org/about-us/press-releases/first-lady-albania-attends-opening-new-autism-support-center-tirana (February 4, 2012).

http://www.biblegateway.com/versions/New-International-Version-NIV-Bible/ (January 21, 2013).

http://www.biblegateway.com/versions/New-King-James-Version-NKJV-Bible/ (January 21, 2013).

http://child-1st.typepad.com/my_weblog/2010/01/characteristics-of-the-gestalt-learner.html (January 25, 2013).

EXCERPT FROM BOOK 2 OF THE SECOND CHANCE SERIES

THIRTY-THREE YEARS AGO

"You okay, sweetheart?"

Grace Marek glanced over at her husband, Barnard "Bud" Marek. Broad-chested and broad-shouldered, just a hair under six feet, Bud sported a Grizzly Adams beard and a full head of wiry auburn hair. Beneath his grizzled brows, the most piercing blue eyes peered at her now and her heart fluttered. He was so strong and masculine and yet beneath his tough exterior beat the heart of a sweet and sensitive man.

"We've been foster parents for five years. I like to think of our ranch as a haven for troubled adolescents. But we've never taken a small child," she replied, shifting to face him across the console in their Hunter Green Jeep Cherokee. "Why do they think we can help?"

"We're the last resort, at least that's the impression I got. It's us or an institution." Shoulder-checking, Bud took the dogleg at Greybull on US-14.

"He's only three years old, not even four yet. How can things be so dire?" she asked, tucking a stray lock of blonde hair behind her ear.

His eyes tracked the movement and she smiled. They'd been married for nearly a decade but he still looked at her like she was a feast and he was a starving man. "He's been in six foster homes in the past six months, including three placements on the Crow Reservation."

"Why?"

"The little fella put two foster moms in the hospital and took a chunk out of a Rottweiler."

Grace chuckled. "Sorry. I know that should horrify me but, really, at least he can defend himself."

"*He* attacked the *dog*, Grace," Bud said wryly.

"Poor little boy," Grace said, sighing sadly. "And they don't even know his name?"

"No. I guess the mother, Carla Rydel, was a prostitute and she never registered their births."

Grace frowned, asking, "What do you mean *their* births? I thought we were driving from Wyoming to Montana to meet one little boy."

"Didn't I tell you? There were two children in the home. Nobody knows what happened or who killed the mother but her body was discovered in an alley a couple of blocks away from the apartment. She'd been dead about three days they figure. By the time the police found the children, though, the baby girl had died. The boy was underneath the crib, dehydrated, half-dead. He looked Crow so they took him to the Reservation but no one had any idea who he belonged to. They were happy to foster him but..."

"He bit a dog," Grace said drily.

"They've brought in a couple of different psychiatrists and given him about five labels, oppositional defiant disorder, childhood schizophrenia, severe autism," he said, shaking his head and frowning.

She huffed, disgusted. "Hasn't it occurred to anyone that you don't need a diagnosis to explain why a child who witnessed the murder of his mother and then watched his baby sister die bit by bit while locked in a room, that those events alone would explain violent behaviour?"

Nudging the blinker-switch, Bud turned into the parking lot of the Big Horn Department of Public Health and Human Services. "Here we are." Reaching across the console, Bud took her hand, bringing it to his lips, a look of sweet love in his eyes. "Come on."

Watching him as he rounded the hood, she waited to let him help her out of the truck. Not that she needed the assistance, but she recognized that he took pride in being a gentleman. At five-foot-two, a hundred-and-ten pounds, she was small enough that Bud could have slung her over his shoulder and carried her anywhere he wanted to go. But he would never force her away from where she wanted to go. He was her gentle protector.

Slipping her hand in his, she walked beside him into the building to meet what seemed to be a committee of professionals.

"I'm Elizabeth Hardin, Child Psychiatrist." The imposing woman, almost as tall as Bud but not nearly as broad, shook both their hands and then turned to introduce the others. "This is Aislynn Warner who was assigned as a Child Protection Worker to this, uh, child. Bertram Yellowtail representing the Crow Tribal Council, and Harvard Lee, Paediatrician. We have all heard wonderful things about you both." She paused a moment and then frowned severely, the expression emphasizing the tautness of her features. "We are very concerned about this little boy. We believe that you should—"

Grace cut her off. "Before you tell me anything else, I want to meet him. What's his name?"

"He only responds to Kid," Aislynn said, stepping forward.

"Kid? We'll call him Seth, the child who carried on the legacy of Adam." Grace turned aside to Bud. "Shall we?"

Bud nodded, camouflaging a grin. "I think we're ready to see him," he said to the others.

Dr. Hardin looked ready to burst with suggestions but she finally conceded and led them to the large two-way window that overlooked the playroom. Through it, Grace could see a moderately-sized space with little chairs and tables, toys, storybooks, crayons, and colouring books. There were six or seven children in the room playing. A pair of boys was taking turns racing dinky cars down a ramp they'd fashioned from bricks and blocks. A trio of girls was engaged in play with a kitchen set, clearly arguing about who got to be the Mommy. Another girl and boy were colouring at one of the tables.

But there, well away from the others, sitting and rocking in the corner with his back to the wall, was a young boy. Seth. He held two objects clutched in his little hands. He was very thin but tall for his age with raven black hair which was dull and tangled and hanging limply to his shoulders. He had a dusky complexion with obsidian eyes under hooded lids. His face should have been ruddy and round with plump cheeks but instead he looked gaunt and pallid. Grace's heart broke for the poor traumatized lad.

"There's a real geography of space going on in there," Bud observed. And he was right. There was a clear zone around Seth into which the other children never ventured.

"Look," Bud said and Grace followed his point. One of the dinky cars had gotten away from the racing boys, rolling within reach of Seth. Protecting his space, Seth sprang to attention, growling and leaping like a wild beast at the little boy who ventured too close in his quest to retrieve it. Shrieking, the boy abandoned his car, running to the other side of the room. Once the boy had scampered away, Seth settled back to rocking.

"Interesting," Grace murmured. "What's in his hands?"

"He found those on his first day here," Aislynn said. "One of them is an action figure, I think, and the other is a mermaid doll."

"Mhmm." Grace watched the repetitive actions Seth performed with the dolls.

"Repetitive and perseverative behaviour. A clinical sign of autism," Dr. Lee said.

"Hmm," Grace replied. Was he speaking as he bumped those dolls together? If he was, what was he saying? "Does he speak?" Grace looked at the professionals around her.

"No," Dr. Hardin replied.

"Language delays. Another sign," Dr. Lee said and Grace imagined he puffed out his chest in a gesture to match his pompous tone of voice.

"I want to get closer," Grace said. Ignoring the explanations as to why she shouldn't enter the room, she gripped Bud's hand, striding inside. Finding two child-sized chairs, they sat. Grace shifted her chair right to the edge of Seth's zone of protection. Bud followed suit.

"He repeats the same actions," Grace muttered. Bud grunted in agreement. "One action figure. One mermaid. I wish I could hear what he's saying."

When she shifted in her chair, Bud grasped her arm. She turned to look at him, narrowing her gaze. "I am going over there. That poor child has been left alone for far too long. For goodness' sakes, his mother left him locked in a room…" Her speech slowed as realization struck. "That's it. That's what it's all about."

Jumping up, she crossed the room, past the racers, to pull out the bin of action figures from the cubbies along the one wall, rooting around until she found a mailman in a traditional dark blue uniform which she hoped would do the job. She moved slowly toward Seth who had alerted and was tracking her advance. He growled low in his chest, a noise that sounded frighteningly like an irritated Rottweiler. That was far enough, she decided, and sat cross-legged on the floor.

After a few minutes, Seth resumed his pattern of movement. Soon Grace could detect words and then whole phrases. Shifting closer, she listened again from start to finish.

"Grace," Bud said with a note of warning in his voice. She motioned for him to stay back.

Once more through the sequence and she knew she was right. Grace scooted closer, keeping her movements smooth and slow so as not to startle the boy.

"Boss," she said. Other than the narrowing of his eyes, Seth didn't react. "You must not hurt Carla. It is bad to hit mommies."

Grace shifted even closer and then moved her blue-uniformed mailman right up to the male action figure, the one Seth referred to in his mumble as Boss. "You will stop right now." Grace pushed the mailman-cum-policeman against Boss, meeting Seth's resistance with her own. "I am a policeman. I say that you cannot hurt Mommy." Then she turned her attention directly to Seth. "Boss hurt Mommy. Boss is bad. Give him to me. He has to go away." Grace held out her hand.

For the first time, Seth met her gaze directly. "Bad," he said.

Grace heard the gasps of adult voices behind her but she ignored them. Seth's startled gaze flicked up, beyond Grace. She sat up taller to capture his attention again. "It is bad to hurt mommies. I'm sorry you had to see that, Seth," she said while motioning for him to hand over the Boss.

He tilted his head. "Seth."

"Seth," she repeated, keeping her hand out, palm up. "Give me the bad man. He has to go away. He can never hurt you again. He can never scare you again."

Seth looked at the Boss figure in his hands and then held it out to Grace. She took it, placed it behind her out of view. "I'm sorry, Seth," she said, holding out her arms to him.

Seth leaned forward, placing his palm on her cheek. His cavernous eyes bored into her and Grace read despair in his expression. A child should never experience despair.

Slowly drawing him onto her lap, she wrapped Seth in a hug. "Would you like to come home with me?"

"Babygirl?" he whispered, his dark eyes dull with grief and exhaustion.

"I'm sorry, honey. She died," Grace said.

"Mommy dead. Babygirl dead." He looked up at her. "Home?"

"You can come to my home and live with me." Grace gestured for Bud to come closer. "Come live with us." Sitting on the floor beside Grace, Bud reached around, embracing them both. Seth narrowed his eyes at Bud and a low growl erupted in his chest. Grace leaned over slowly and kissed Bud over the fuzziness on his cheek. The wariness subsided and Seth leaned into Grace.

"Are you hungry, Seth?" she asked.

"Baloney sandwich," he said. "An' a apple."

"Bologna sounds fine," Bud said. "And maybe a milkshake."

Seth furrowed his brow at the big man by her side. "Don't know milkshake."

"You'll like it," Bud said.

"Ready to come to our home?" Grace asked.

"Home," Seth repeated.

CPSIA information can be obtained at www.ICGtesting.com
Printed in the USA
LVOW11s1845071214

417629LV00001B/331/P